The Detective Fiction Reviews of
Charles Williams, 1930–1935

The Detective Fiction Reviews of Charles Williams, 1930–1935

edited by
Jared C. Lobdell

McFarland & Company, Inc., Publishers
Jefferson, North Carolina, and London

Library of Congress Cataloguing-in-Publication Data

Williams, Charles, 1886–1945.
    The detective fiction reviews of Charles Williams, 1930–1935 / edited
by Jared C. Lobdell.
       p.   cm.
    Includes index.

    ISBN-13: 978-0-7864-1454-3
    (softcover: 50# alkaline paper)∞

    1. Detective and mystery stories, English — History and criticism.
  2. Detective and mystery stories, American — History and criticism.
  3. American fiction — 20th century — History and criticism.
  4. English fiction — 20th century — History and criticism.
  I. Lobdell, Jared, 1937–   II. Title.
  PR888.D4 W55   2003
  823'.087209 — dc21   2002154745

British Library cataloguing data are available

Cover photograph: ©2002 Photospin

Manufactured in the United States of America

McFarland & Company, Inc., Publishers
  Box 611, Jefferson, North Carolina 28640
    www.mcfarlandpub.com

For my wife,
Jane Starke Lobdell

TABLE OF CONTENTS

INTRODUCTION

This book is made up of this brief introduction, six chapters, an appendix, and an index. The components of what I consider the book's centerpiece (chapters II through V), are popular-press reviews of detective fiction (or mystery literature) in its Golden Age of popularity (1930–1935), by the English editor, literary critic, poet, novelist, theologian, and Inkling, Charles Williams (1886–1945). In the end-pieces, chapters I and VI, I use these reviews as aids in analyzing both the nature of detective fiction and the nature of the fiction written by Charles Williams. The appendix lists the authors reviewed, noting which of their books were reviewed, and on what date, with as much information on each author as I have been able to find. It is a reasonable and productive approach, I believe, to understanding both Williams and Golden Age detective fiction — but a reader might reasonably ask, if I have something worthwhile to say about detective fiction, why do I not say it plainly, and leave Charles Williams out of it? Or, if this is a book recounting something of Charles Williams's insight into the nature of detective fiction, why is one third of it by me? Would it not make more sense for me to "internalize" what Williams said, make it my own, and thus write a single coherent commentary, rather than producing this hybrid?

My answer, such as it is, is that I started out to see whether Williams's detective fiction reviews could be of use in reading his own fiction — they can; decided they ought to be in print, particularly in the United States where they have never been published; and then discovered that they were useful not merely in understanding Williams but in understanding what happened to the Golden Age of Detective Fiction, or, if you prefer, what happened in the Golden Trap. They ought to be in print partly because their cumulative effect is to broaden and deepen our understanding of the phenomenon — of the Golden Age, and partly because they exemplify the proper use of what Colin Watson has called the reviewer's hutch, the few paragraphs set aside in newspapers for detective fiction reviews. Besides, there's a certain pleasure in calling attention to a light-hearted and readable Charles Williams— lightheartedness and readability being neither the demeanors nor the misdemeanors with which Williams is most frequently charged.

Williams was born in 1886 and died in Oxford in May 1945. He was a proofreader and then editor at the Oxford University Press for most of his adult life (in London until evacuated in 1939). He was a poet, critic (Honorary M.A. Oxon., 1942), theologian, and novelist; a friend of C. S. Lewis and his friends, also of Eliot and Auden and Dorothy L. Sayers; an editor of Gerard Manley Hopkins and of Robert Bridges (the collected essays), as well as editor of *Hymns Ancient and Modern*. Like Eliot he wrote a Canterbury play. He was in the Order of the Golden Dawn — and he read thrillers, shilling shockers, detective fiction, for fun and profit. It is my belief that we can profit from his fun.

Chapter I was adapted to appear as a chapter in *The Rhetoric of Vision in Charles Williams*, edited by Charles Huttar and Peter Schackel (Bucknell University Press, 1995). It is reprinted here with the permission of Associated University Presses.

I have assumed in my readers some familiarity with Williams's fiction, particularly the opening of his only detective fiction, *War in Heaven* (1930), which is quoted in Chapter I. I say "only detective fiction" because the other novels, though they are shilling shockers, or thrillers, have not the form of a detective novel. Even *War in Heaven* pushes pretty hard against that form, going from the requisite body in the office and police detective to Prester John and the Holy Grail. Of the others, I should say here that their various *di ex machina* include Tarot cards (*The Greater Trumps*), Platonic forms (*The Place of the Lion*), the Stone of Solomon (*Many Dimensions*), and African magic (*Shadows of Ecstasy*). Rum stuff, all this, for an emulator (as he himself has said) of Sax Rohmer with his insidious Dr. Fu Manchu. These five puzzle-novels, if not detective-novels, were written during the period in which Williams was reviewing detective fiction, while his last two novels, *Descent into Hell* (1938) and *All Hallow's Eve* (1944), are somewhat of a different breed, and less relevant here.

Beyond knowledge of Williams, I have assumed some knowledge of detective fiction, particularly in Chapter VI. Those who are reading this book because most of it is by Charles Williams may be a bit taken aback by this—they are likely to be interested in Williams for quite different reasons—but I think my remarks, if arcane, are not obscure. Still, perhaps it would be well to give a little additional background here, on the idea of a "Golden Age" of Detective Fiction. We may draw a comparison with Science Fiction and its so-called Golden Age: Generations of boys (and some girls) grew up on engineer's fiction, from Jules Verne and Tom Swift to the "scientifiction" of Hugo Gernsback *et al.*, and became the science-fiction "fans" and writers of the 1930s, 1940s, and beyond. Similarly, generations a little earlier had grown up on sensation fiction and Sherlock Holmes and his emulators, and these became the detective fiction readers (indeed, even fanatics) and writers of the 1920s and beyond. The first flowering of the popular literature, as the juvenile "fans" became the adult readers and writers, was a Golden Age, not necessarily for the quality of the fiction but for the range, for the enthusiasm, for the exuberance, and in a way for the youthfulness of the writers. (Compare also the "Golden Age" of Elizabethan drama and poetry, with its inventions and explorations, its voyages, traffiques and discoveries.)

Among the very first fruits of this flowering of detective fiction — which lasted roughly from 1920 to the mid–1930s—were H. C. Bailey, *Meet Mr. Fortune,* and Agatha Christie, *The Mysterious Affair at Styles* (1922), which were part of such an overwhelming flood that already Dorothy L. Sayers, in *Whose Body?* (1922), thought of herself as trying to write something more than the common run-of-the-mill puzzle. These mysteries whose flowering came so suddenly were essentially the same thing the mediaeval "Mysteries" were — that is, morality plays—and their popularity, as the succeeding chapters in this book suggest, was that of redemptive comedy. In times that were out of joint, at least affairs in these stories were put back in joint. They were put back in joint by the deputy stage-manager, the Great Detective. He might be of the odd sort like Agatha Christie's Hércule Poirot (1920), Dorothy L. Sayers's Lord Peter Wimsey (1922), Margery Allingham's Albert Campion (1926), S. S. Van Dine's Philo Vance, or Rex Stout's Nero Wolfe (1934). He might be of the little less odd sort like Philip MacDonald's Anthony Ruthven Gethryn (1926), Miss Christie's Miss Marple (1930), Patricia Wentworth's Miss Silver, H. C. Bailey's Reggie Fortune (1920), Ngaio Marsh's Roderick Alleyne, "Anthony Gilbert's" Arthur Crook. He might even be of the ordinary sort like Freeman Wills Croft's Inspector French or Georgette Heyer's Inspector Hannasyde.

Increasingly, whoever the Great Detective, these were stories about death. There are few enough murders in the Sherlock Holmes short stories, and fewer in most of his serious emulators (though many deaths of villains in the sensation fiction of the 1860s and after). But if it can truly be said that the characters in the Golden Age detective stories have little more personality than marionettes (a frequent charge), it is also true that the dance their strings command is increasingly a dance of death. I suggest that the reason for this has something to do with the purpose of the mediaeval Dance of Death, playing away the horrors of death and the unknown. And that playing away the horrors of the unknown is, I think, connected with the unmasking of the villain and the unmasking of the author's misdirections. We might call Miss Sayers for witness here in her Introduction to the *Omnibus of Crime* (1929, reprinted in Haycraft, *The Art of the Mystery Story* [1946], p. 72), where, observing that the pages of every magazine and newspaper swarm with detective stories, she suggests that in these the reader "finds a sort of catharsis or purging of his fears and self-questionings. These mysteries made only to be solved, these horrors which he knows to be mere figments of the creative brain, comfort him by subtly persuading that life is a mystery which death will solve, and whose horrors will pass away as a tale that is told."

Miss Sayers also suggests (p. 85) that the Great Detective descends in part from Chingachgook in Fenimore Cooper's novels. The hawk-like lineaments of Sherlock Holmes bear witness to the descent, I think. It also seems to me that Cooper is antecessor if not ancestor of Tolkienian fantasy, and this may help explain a linkage between mythopoetic writers and detective fiction writers, remarked upon in Chapter I. We tend to overlook the vast popular reading — and accompanying influence — of Fenimore Cooper for very nearly a century, from *The Last of the Mohicans* (1826) to the Age of Science Fiction (which some date from 1926).

This book is, in fact, however one might think it oddly put together, what I believe to be a needed study in popular literature. Of the two certain things in this world, it has been observed, we have virtually no popular literature on taxes, but one vast and ever-growing on death. In the 1990s, there were innumerable books on near-death experiences and angels, which speak perhaps to the same search for certainty that lies behind both mediaeval mysteries and modern mystery stories, some kind of vicarious guarantee that all will be really right with the world, or really *is* right. I believe that, as the Lord said to the Lady Julian, all will be well, and all *will* be well and all manner of thing shall be well, and I know that was what Williams believed. But though we agree on this as on much else, I do not think it would be all right for me to try to speak with Williams's voice, nor foist mine on him. The book must remain a hybrid and perhaps a trifle odd. Rather like some of the Great Detectives. Or Charles Williams.

— Jared Lobdell

I

CHARLES WILLAMS AS DETECTIVE FICTION REVIEWER

"He always boiled an honest pot," said C. S. Lewis of his friend Charles Walter Stansby Williams (1886–1945; M.A. Hon.). Williams's detective fiction reviews represent one of the longer-simmering pots. They date from the "Ghetto Age" of detective story reviewing (see Mr. Colin Watson's *Snobbery with Violence*), during which time the daily papers devoted an occasional review column to detective fiction, stipulating no more than one paragraph per book. This "Ghetto Age" coincided with the so-called Golden Age of British mystery and was, in fact, its corollary.

The reviews, published in the *Westminster Gazette* and its successors, began in 1930 and ended in 1935. They are reprinted with the permission of the Associated Newspapers. Over those six years, there were some eighty-three columns, which, taken together, provide one of the best critiques of the genre, for all their scrappiness. They also provide an excellent lead-in to Williams's understanding of detective fiction (including "thriller") rhetoric and vision. In this chapter, I use the reviews largely as a key to Williams himself. In Chapter VI, I shall return to the matter of the Golden Age *per se*, and its place in the history of detective fiction. In this, Williams himself becomes less important, but he is not absent, nor could he be.

Charles Williams is best known as a poet, writer of theological thrillers, and friend of C. S. Lewis (1898–1963) and J. R. R. Tolkien

(1892–1973). His meeting with English detective fiction in the Golden Age is, in my view, the sort of thing historians of English literature or popular culture could have hoped for, but not expected. The combination of eccentric genius and original insight that marks all of Williams's work, even the worst, is not customarily applied to the week's or the month's detective fiction. It is as if Umberto Eco, rather than writing *The Name of the Rose*, were serving as "Newgate Callender" for the *New York Times*, or as if Brooks and Warren, in the heyday of the New Criticism, had applied *explication du texte* to the Holmesian canon.

Before turning to what Williams said, I should like to suggest my own view of the genre, formed largely before I read his reviews ... but not immune to his influence. After all, in the essays in his *The Image of the City* there are statements that echo some of the statements in these reviews, and I think as well that I detect some influence of Williams's views in C. S. Lewis's writings on narrative, but on that I will not insist.

In histories of detective fiction, or of mystery fiction, there is usually an unexplained gap between Poe, who is deemed to have invented the genre, and Conan Doyle, who is deemed to have brought it very nearly to perfection. But it has lately been suggested — and in my view very largely demonstrated — that this gap has its origin in improper categorization, and that the genre we should have been looking at all along is what the Victorians called sensation or sensational fiction. This and much more can be found in Mr. R. F. Stewart's wise and diligent study ...*And Always a Detective* (David & Charles, 1980). I shall use it as a starting point for a view of Charles Williams as a critic of such stories, as of "thrillers" that descend, in right line, from the shilling shocker.

At the outset, it would perhaps be wise to define roughly what is meant by the word genre. Perhaps the best way to put it is to say that, in the words of a recent handbook, established genres "carry with them a whole series of prescriptions and restrictions, some codified in the pronouncements of rhetoricians and others less officially but no less forcefully established by previous writers" and that the writer in the genre must always be making a declaration of indebtedness to or a conscious declaration of independence from his or her predecessor (Heather Dubrow, Genre, Methuen, 1982, p. 9ff). Our expectations and thus our understanding of the work are keyed by our knowledge of its stated or intended genre, including its rhetoric.

It is reasonable to call detective stories a kind of mythic comedy, in order to catch at least an echo of Northrop Frye's *mythos* of comedy. Readers may recall Frye's four great *mythoi*— springtime's comedy, summer's romance, autumn's tragedy, winter's irony — with their contrapuntal motion. I wish to suggest here that while science fiction is ironic and hivernal (no credit to me — James Blish said it long ago), detective fiction is comedic and, if you like, vernal. I note that the place of fantasy in this formulation is a matter I have dealt with elsewhere and doubtless will again. For the present, however, our concern is with comedic movement, indeed a particular kind of comedic movement.

This may seem a roundabout way of getting at the work of Charles Williams, but we shall make up on the swings what we lose on the round-abouts, and it is in any case as well to set our groundwork firmly before trying to catch this elusive and mercurial author within our bounds. I am leading up to the point that, as those familiar with Professor Frye's *The Myth of Deliverance* will already have noted, sensation fiction, and partic-ularly detective fiction, fulfills the same function and demands the same responses for and from the reading public in Victorian England that the popular comedic plays fulfilled and demanded in Shakespeare's day. Here is Professor Frye in *The Myth of Deliverance*.

> In a famous chapter of the *Poetics* (xi), Aristotle speaks of reversal and recog-nition (*peripeteia* and *anagnorisis*) as characteristic of what he calls com-plex plots.... Sometimes the effect [of what Frye calls the 'and hence' story, as opposed to the 'and then' story] seems to reverse the direction of the action up to that point, and when it does we are normally very close to the end. Hence a reversal of the action often forms part of an *anagnorisis*, a 'recognition', depending on how much of a surprise it is [p. 4].

Thus, in a detective story, the identification of the murderer is a 'dis-covery' in the sense that we realize he is a murderer for the first time: it is a 'recognition' in the sense that, if the normal conventions of the detec-tive story are being preserved, he is already a well known and established character" (p. 4). This *anagnorisis* is in fact a staple of Victorian popular fiction as well as of Shakespearean comedy: one need only think of the stolen or runaway child *motif* in, for example, G. A. Henty, or the whole matter of *Lady Audley's Secret*, or, in Edwardian times, the double *anag-norisis* of the first of the Father Brown stories. It could even be said that the *anagnorisis* is the sensation of the sensation fiction.

But how does this tie in with Frye's myth of *deliverance*? By the myth of deliverance, Frye means the story-pattern whose essential drive is toward liberation, "whether of the central character, a pair of lovers, or the whole society" (p. 14). The comedy, or the detective fiction, is a ritual enactment of this pattern of deliverance, highly conventionalized. The point is thus not in the guessing "Whodunit?" but in the reader's participation in the *dénouement*, the *anagnorisis*.

But we have been speaking of *detective* fiction, and it may be reason-ably asked, what is the position of the detective in all this? Mr. Stewart has suggested a possible answer in this way: the 'detective' in the phrase 'detective fiction' refers originally not to the character (Dupin or Sergeant Cuff), but to the fact that a process of detection occurs within the story" (pp. 71ff). In other words, early detective fiction had a person or persons engaged in the process of detection, who were therefore called detective(s), but did not center on the person of the detective to the same degree that Chesterton did with Father Brown or Doyle (most of the time) with Sherlock Holmes. (Even Poe pays less attention to the *personalia* of his detective than Doyle to that of his. I recognize the fact that this statement is something of a judgement call.)

The tendency was there, nonetheless, and this raises an interesting point. It cannot be successfully argued that the increasing tendency toward detective omniscience in detective fiction came about as a result of or even as a parallel to an increasing detective omniscience in the "real world." It seems rather than Sherlock Holmes and his successors are, like the disguised Duke in *Measure for Measure* or Prospero in *The Tempest*, stage managers or "deputy dramatists," Frye's term for characters whose function is to make sure "everything comes out all right in the end," to enact the myth of deliverance. As I have observed elsewhere, using T. A. Shippey's term in *The Road to Middle Earth*, Sherlock Holmes may be taken as a "calque" of the White Magician on the Victorian detective. He is a type raised to the dignity of an archetype.

If all this is true, as I believe it is, we can see that Miss Sayers and her colleagues in the Detection Club were acting by a just instinct when they formalized (some would say overformalized) the conventions of their genre. This does not mean that the country house or "Golden Age" English mystery is *per se* a better thing than the American hard-boiled or "Black Mask" mystery. Both, after all, are conventionalized, and both accord with their national myths of deliverance. This, I think, may lie behind the dictum of Henry James that the most mysterious of mysteries—those participating most in the essence of mystery—are those that lie at our own door, so that Lady Audley drives Udolpho from our minds. "What are the Appenines to us or we to the Appenines? Instead of the terrors of Udolpho, we are treated to the terrors of the cheerful country house and the busy London lodgings" (in R. F. Stewart, p. 45).

"Terror" is not, in my view, *le mot juste*, though it points the way to a possible Aristotelian *catharsis* and thence at least toward the communal aspects of the deliverance. But what is involved may better be called *mystery* than *terror;* if it were terror only, no one would reread *The Hound of the Baskervilles*. The first time I read it, I was twelve and terrified (and in a strange house). I read it differently now, but the fact that I know the outcome does not alter my pleasure in the ritual enactment of the myth. But James did have his finger on the importance of tying the story to the world (though I think the mythic world) of the reader.

Let us here consider Charles Williams on the question of pattern, its relation to realism, and perhaps to the self-critical or self-referential mode we referred to above, particularly as it led to the technique of those particular detective story authors that Julian Symons calls the *farceurs*. Although Williams once praised whimsicality (April 15, 1931), he inveighed against signs of "chats and chuckles" in the books of G. D. H. and Margaret Cole (November 4, 1930). But in a way, this is one of the few cases in which he speaks out against any kind of consciousness of the book as a book ... a made thing, an artificial creation.

It is not that he is playing the kind of tongue-in-cheek game that Father Knox played with the rules of detection for the Detection Club. But there is an exaltation of pattern, and not of "chats and chuckles," in his recognition that the status of reality and realism in detective fiction and the "thriller" is a subordinate one. If it were not so, what would we make of a statement like this (December 24, 1930)? "The setting in Africa is pleasantly unusual, the English are pleasantly usual, and the Africans are pleasantly mysterious, so that the whole book is pleasantly satisfying"? This is murder story, remember. Or when he speaks (March 2, 1931) of "a really satisfactorily agonizing death for" a charming murderess?

In reviewing Collin Brooks's *Three Yards of Cord* (June 17, 1931), he says at the end it is "not real, but very good." He divides detection and thrillers (taken as a single category) into four types (October 22, 1931): The whole passage is worth quoting, almost as much for Williams as journalist as for Williams as critic. The quotation with which he begins is, of course, from Rudyard Kipling: "'There are nine-and-sixty ways of constructing tribal lays, and every single one of them is right.' A list would be useful for advanced criticism; in the elementary classes we are confined to four. They are fact, fable, faerie, and fantasy."

It can scarcely avoid notice that three of these four stand against fact. To be sure, fable can be told with realistic detail (as in *Animal Farm*, to take a relatively recent example), and so can fantasy, whatever that may be. In fact, as Tolkien pointed out, if one is to make the rare and beautiful blue moon to shine or put fire in the belly of the cold worm, you had best do it with an accumulation of realistic detail. And if one enters the realm of faerie, be sure that it is strictly an earthbound realm. But, for all that, realism of story inheres not in these three. What inheres is pattern, even myth.

It is this pattern that, if "directly controlled by intense poetic passion," can produce a classic (April 7, 1932). But even a lighthearted or irrational romp can work. As Williams writes of one such author, (July 5, 1932), "His murderers pop in, and his victims pop off, and Mme Storey pops round, and the whole thing is clearly incredible and therefore in its clear insanity fascinating." Or as he writes of J. Jefferson Farjeon's *Ben Sees It Through* (December 21, 1932), it "is a pantomime," and it "has all the knockabout glory of the perfectly irrational ... Mr. Farjeon at his best attracts with perfect nonsense and thrills with fairy tales."

Or of another story he writes (June 5, 1933), "It is quite unconvincing, but it is unconvincing in the right way. There is something very near imagination in it." And of *Murder on the Orient Express* he says (January 17, 1934), "a piece of classic workmanship; almost unbelievable, but exquisite and wholly satisfying." Perhaps the best summary of Williams's view of detective fiction and the "thriller" is given in a (July 26, 1933 review): "The danger and delight of these stories is (1) the immediate awareness of the form and the choice of the author in the form, and (2) the vitality of the characters by whom the form exists."

We have said that genre is conventionalized to permit uses that are either statements of indebtedness or statements of independence. If one looks at the history of the English country house detective novel, one finds in the *farceurs* simultaneous statements of indebtedness and independence, what we might think of as a fuzzy delineation between action within the genre and commentary on it. And this has not only been true of the *farceurs*, though they (and Edmund Crispin in particular) may be the best examples of it. The earliest Gideon Fells are simultaneously within the locked room or puzzle sub-genre and are commentaries on it as well as on G. K. Chesterton.

In fact, if we look at the timing, it is almost as if the genre awaited only the advent of its most conventionalized, most magician-like, most pattern-bound, and therefore most purely mythic detective before its practitioners began their experimentation and independence (or forays into independence) and commentary-within-genre.

The detective I refer to is, of course, Dame Agatha Christie's Hercule Poirot, and the importance of the point for our consideration here is that it establishes the years 1930–1935 as a time (in England particularly) in which the genre was unstable and even shifting. We are accustomed to think of the interwar period as the Golden Age of the English detective story, and in a way it was, but what a vast congeries is encompassed in that Golden Age.

In 1930, the year that Charles Williams began his detective fiction reviews, Conan Doyle had finished with Sherlock Holmes (and at the beginning of the year was, like Holmes, alive in Sussex, though perhaps without the bees), Chesterton had Father Brown stories still to go, *Trent's Own Case* was still in the future, Anthony Ruthven Gethryn was at the height of his career, Lord Peter short of his, and Thorndyke and the Humdrums, as Julian Symons has called them, were going strong. Monsignor Knox, first of the *farceurs*, was publishing stories about the Indescribable, but in that he was distinctly avant-garde.

By 1935, when Williams did the last of his newspaper reviews, we had left-wing detective writers (Day Lewis and Christopher Caudwell), the Humdrums beginning to die off, the year before Chesterton's death, J. I. M. Stewart writing as Michael Innes, Gethryn's creator crossing the Atlantic to Hollywood, two memorable experimental books (one of which Williams reviewed with considerable perspicacity), and Anthony Berkeley as Francis Iles. Of course, Williams did not review only British authors—Ellery Queen, John Dickson Carr, Q. Patrick, S. S. Van Dine, and Dashiell Hammett all make their appearance. And he not only reviewed the experimenters, either—J. S. Fletcher, John Rhode, R. A. J. Walling, G. D. H. and Margaret Cole, Jefferson Farjeon, Gethryn's Philip MacDonald all make their multiple appearances.

In his entertaining *Snobbery with Violence* (London 1971, New York 1988), Mr. Colin Watson remarks that in the so-called Golden Age, "Book reviewers settled into an attitude of good-natured, if slightly supercilious, tolerance. They too had fallen in with the notion of detective stories being in a class quite separate from 'legitimate' literature.... Editors provided a segregated hutch for mystery novels, where they could be dealt with, a whole litter of twenty or thirty at a time, by means of a sentence apiece" (p. 98). Charles Williams's reviews in the *Westminster Chronicle & News-Gazette* and its successors, from 1930 into 1935, may be considered a kind of mini-hutch, as he reviewed three or four books at a time (occasionally five or six), and rather than the sentence apiece suggested by Mr. Watson, it was more often a paragraph, or two, or three a piece.

Mr. Watson goes on to say that there "evolved for this purpose a special style of reviewmanship. It was (and is) slightly facetious in flavour, crisp and insubstantial, like lettuce" (*ibid.*). Charles Williams's reviews are occasionally facetious, as he was occasionally facetious elsewhere, sometimes the facetiousness is akin to Chestertonian paradox. But he is less facetious than many reviewers and far more substantial. In fact, he is the only one of the "hutch" reviewers I can think of who kept firmly in mind the position of the mystery novel *sub specie aeternitatis*. That is one reason for reprinting as well as for analyzing his reviews. The other would be for the light they cast on his own novels, mostly written during this time from 1930 to 1935.

The confines into which detective fiction reviews were squeezed during the "Ghetto" or Golden Age of detection provide us with a Charles Williams we may find it difficult to recognize at first glance. As he said of one of his favorite authors in the genre, we are "never quite sure whether at bottom [he] is a wit, a moralist, or an occultist" (on H. C. Bailey, December 29, 1933). This is the epigrammatic Charles Williams, of relatively simple diction and light and pleasant rhetoric.

Williams's own perception and the need to say something intelligent and arresting about a book in a paragraph (all he was usually given), make it particularly fortunate that he was writing at the time of shifting genre use. It is my contention that, as I read his commentary, not only was he fully cognizant of the sensation fiction origins of detective fiction, but also conscious of the *anagnorisis* involved.

And here I pause to make what may seem to be two digressions, but are really not. First, I want to shift attention back to my earlier remark on the place of "fantasy" in all this and suggest that if we take one highly restrictive definition of fantasy, we can identify the comedic *anagnorisis* with the *eucatastrophe* of faerie. Let me remind you of the relevant passage in Tolkien's essay ("On Fairy Stories" [originally the Andrew Lang Lecture in 1938], collected in *The Monsters and the Critics* [C. Tolkien, ed.], 1984, p. 153):

> But the "consolation" of fairy-tales has another aspect than the imaginative satisfaction of ancient desires. Far more important is the Consolation of the Happy Ending.... I will call it the *Eucatastrophe*.... The consolation of fairy-stories, the joy of the happy ending: or more correctly of the good catastrophe, the sudden joyous "turn" ... this joy, which is one of the things fairy-stories can produce supremely well, is not essentially "escapist" nor "fugitive." In its fairy-tale — or otherworld — setting, it is a sudden and miraculous grace.

Second, I wish to call attention to a curious phenomenon. Many of the detective fiction writers mentioned above had fairly close relationships to the writers thought of as mythopoetic. The relationships range from identity (Chesterton, perhaps Miss Sayers) to familial relationships (Philip MacDonald as George MacDonald's grandson), to friendship and influence (Bentley with Chesterton and — *vide* the mark of the clerihew — Tolkien), to possession of the mythopoetic talent (Doyle), to shared Oxford (Stewart, "Edmund Crispin" — in one of whose books CSL appears as a character — , and of course Day Lewis, who beat out CSL for Professor of Poetry).

It cannot be claimed that the world of the interwar detective story moved far from the world of the mythopoetic. Or, if you like, from the world of the fantastic (but it is not necessarily part of that world). Nor, given what we have said, and given what Tolkien said about the *eucata-strophe*, should we expect to find any great distance between. For, in a way, it might be claimed that the vaunted 'intellectualism' of the detective story novel comes down to this— that the authors are fundamentally concerned, particularly in the time of Williams's reviews, with a set of patterns, a *mythos* if you like, involved in deliverance involving a joyful *anagnorisis*, but (and here we follow James) centered on the familiar rather than the strange. That is, the intellectualism consists in the embodiment of intellectual concerns in a "popular" form. But the concerns are popular as well, as Mr. Watson's book makes clear.

The distinction between the strange and the familiar, which seems simple enough with Burke and Alison in the eighteenth century context and even with James in the nineteenth century, tends to give way as we press on it in the twentieth. But perhaps we might say that the conventions of detective fiction put it into the realm of familiarity as a genre. In such a way, the conventions of the Greek theatre made the action familiar to the playgoers, for all the obvious artificiality of what went on onstage. This is a case parallel to the demand for pattern against realism.

I know of only one case in which Williams specifically considered the question of detection fiction rhetoric. In a review of an utterly forgettable novel by Guy Morton (June 10, 1934), he notes that it "would be a better book if Mr. Morton had not introduced a false rhetoric of action." There is also a passage in which he says that "without exciting words, there is not and cannot be any excitement in crime" (August 23, 1932), though this is capable of more than one interpretation. But his use of allusion should give some clues as to his assumption of the audience's background, and therefore of appropriate rhetoric insofar as rhetoric is not entirely determined by genre.

Our search for these indications of the audience Charles Williams saw for detective fiction and for "thrillers" lies not only in the direct allusions but also in the concealed allusions sprinkled in his reviews. We are not surprised, of course, to find Miss Jane Marple (on her first appearance, in *Murder at the Vicarage*) hailed as Mother Brown, with G. K. Chesterton's Father Brown being her implied counterpart (October 14, 1930). When author J. S. Fletcher is described as standing "to great detection as the other Fletcher stood to Marlowe" (November 17, 1931), the audience is expected to know how the Fletcher of Beaumont and Fletcher stood to Christopher Marlowe in the gallery of Elizabethan and Jacobean dramatists.

When Williams echoes the Horatian ode, "Eheu! fugaces labuntur anni, Posthume! Posthume!" ("Even though, Posthumus, we are all growing old" November 6, 1930) some, at least, of his readers must have been expected to grasp the allusion. When he says of a novel (August 25, 1931), "The story goes into top gear up the Hill Difficulty," the allusion to Bunyan is expected to strike home. (Compare allusions in Buchan, particularly *Mr. Standfast*, and in Dorothy L. Sayers, *Busman's Honeymoon*.) When he says (April 7, 1933), "It is no longer sufficient to look in your heart and write," we may catch the allusion to Philip Sidney ("'Fool!' said my Muse to me, 'Look in thy heart and write!'") and he would expect us to catch it. In the same review, he refers to a "novel whose center is intellectual sensation and only its circumference physical." The concealed allusion is to the definition of God as a circle whose center is everywhere and circumference nowhere. (It was a favorite allusion of his, but whether he expected this to be recognized I do not know, nor would want to guess.

Similarly, when he says (July 26, 1933), "Beauty, fortunately, in this respect, is no longer truth," the reference to Keats is evident to us and I suppose to his original readers. When he says that "'something lingering with melted lead or boiling oil in it' was wanted," we recognize *The Mikado* and assume his original readers would too.

But when he says (March 18, 1931) of *Malice Aforethought* that Dr. Birkleigh "determines and dares and does murder his tyrannical and unpleasant wife," are we, or is anyone, really expected to catch an echo of Kit Smart's *Song of David*, which reads "Seers that stupendous truth believed / And now the matchless deed's achieved / Determined, dared, and done"? I think so.

It is necessary that we carry out three tasks here. First, we should ask, and try to answer the question, whether an examination of Williams's reviews in this area will help us understand him and his views of the appropriate rhetoric for, and the underlying vision in, popular detection fiction and the "thriller." (It will certainly help us understand the canons of Golden Age detective fiction, but that is another story, which we come to later.) The answer to this is quick and easy, and comes (perhaps surprisingly) by way of Sax Rohmer, as we will shortly see.

Second, we should see what it is that Williams looked for in detective fiction. What elements, for him, determined whether a book was good or bad? It is also of interest to see whether his judgments have stood the test of time; so far as I can tell, they have, though some authors he liked — notably H. C. Bailey and R. C. Woodthorpe — are in need of reprinting and critical resuscitation. We have already noted the demand for pattern and the assumptions implied by allusion.

Third, we should look at the classifications and taxonomies Williams used to help reduce the blooming buzzing confusion of the golden ghetto to order. This will lead into the point about "a false rhetoric of action" noted above. These classifications and taxonomies are, in fact, highly revealing for an inquiry into the aesthetic of Williams's own supernatural "shockers" or "theological thrillers," ... besides providing hitherto unused clues on the "Golden Age" aesthetic.

We begin — and virtually end — our first and briefest inquiry with a comment in a review of Sax Rohmer's *The Bride of Fu-Manchu* (December 29, 1933). "There are some few absurd books of my own which exist only because one evening, having finished one of Mr. Rohmer's, I said suddenly to myself, 'I also will write a novel.' It wasn't, when finished, much like any of his, but can one now seethe the mother in the kid's milk?" This passage illustrates three points. The first of these is that Sax Rohmer (Arthur Sarsfield Wade, 1885–1959) was Williams's inspiration as a novelist. He was also Williams's coeval and contemporary in the Order of the Golden Dawn, but his mark as inspiration is more significant here.) It makes clear that Williams was deliberately writing in the tradition of the "shilling shocker," though by now they were seven-and-six. It also suggests, if no more, that characterization will not be Williams's primary interest.

The second point is that the reviewer's *persona* is the traditional self-deprecatory one going back to Chaucer in the *Prologue*— a reference that, had he made it, Williams would have expected his readers to "get" (as he expected them to "get" Bunyan's *Pilgrim's Progress* and even Kit Smart's *Song of David*). And the third point is precisely in this wide frame of reference, and the smile shared with the discerning reader, with which Williams knocks the ball to the boundaries of the frame. Seething the mother in the kid's milk is a humorous turn-about of the Biblical injunction against seething the kid in its mother's milk, and may even refer obliquely to the then-growing popular use of *kid* to mean *child*.

What Williams looked for principally in detective fiction was style. (This from the creator of what I once described as a style "fortunately inimitable," but the contradiction is apparent, not real.) Without multiplying examples needlessly, I note several cases in which he exalts the need for style. Of a novel by Anthony Abbot (Fulton Oursler), for example (March 2, 1931), he writes, "Mr. Abbot's is certainly an ingenious mind; what such a mind needs now is only — O everlasting cry!— style, style, and always style." In a review in June 1931 (June 17, 1931), he speaks of "an ingenuity of style that keeps hinting at dark possibilities." Of Glen Trevor's (James Hilton's) *Murder at School*, "no compliment can be too handsome for style" (January 1, 1932).

Of the forgotten novel, *The End of Mr. Davidson* (April 7, 1932), he writes, "It is a perfectly simple book, with the simplicity of pure style." Of

Ellery Queen's *The Greek Coffin Mystery* (July 28, 1932), "if his verbal style lacks something, his spiritual style is perfect." Of a novel by J. Jefferson Farjeon (December 13, 1932), "This excellent opening demands something finer (stylistically) than Mr. Farjeon gives us." Of a subsequent book by Ellery Queen (June 14, 1933), "Mr. Queen is in danger of denying style by overstating one element of style," and "We demand from him not a solution but a story." The element of style he is overstressing can be seen in Williams's opening line to this paragraph; "A reader does not read to discover the criminal but to discover the book."

Of Philo Vance in *The Dragon Murder Case* (January 17, 1934), "culture does not consist of knowing a lot of unusual facts. It implies a style of intellect to which Mr. Vance is a stranger." And shortly thereafter, of a novel by David Sharp (February 2, 1934), "Mr. Sharp, on the other hand, has a plot that only his persuasive style can carry. The plot is fairy, but the style is real." Five months later, reviewing a book by Ronald Knox, he refers to Father Knox's "keen sense of the sanctity of style" (June 4, 1934). And, in one of his last detective fiction reviews (of *The Bell is Answered*, August 3, 1934), "There is about it a flavour of intelligence: that subtle thing which is style, which is culture, which is irony and common-sense."

Perhaps Williams's strongest statement here is of Martin Porlock (Philip MacDonald): "Mr. Porlock's first novel has style; it has therefore inevitably everything else" (October 7, 1931). The book, is *Murder in Kensington Gore*, but is available in the United States as *Escape*. Williams also observes, "style can only afford to be dramatic about profound spiritual crises, if then" (February 13, 1933), which speaks also to the question of rhetoric. From these comments, I think it evident that style, in the mind of Charles Williams, though connected with verbal felicity, is much more something like an innate sense of the fitness of things. It is connected with culture (a much more difficult word to define); it is connected with rhetoric (which is, after all, that part of writing which is linked to verbal felicity; and also, of course, the fitness of things includes the fitness of rhetoric to pattern or plot).

Pure style would thus be, in detective fiction, a perfect fitness between rhetoric (or technique generally) and pattern or plot. Note that in his praise of Trevor's *Murder at School*, he says not that "no compliment can be too handsome for his style," but "no compliment can be too handsome for style." Like the butterflies and serpents of Williams's own novel *The Place of the Lion*, (1935) style is an absolute, there is a Platonic form of style for detective fiction or sensation fiction, or "thrillers," and for which we can reasonably believe there is a proper rhetoric.

We might now look at the characteristics and taxonomies to which it is linked, and then to the ways in which Williams generally makes sense of the genre whose products he is reviewing. We find that there is, in his reviews, a constant sense of the bounds of the genre and of its nature — in short, of its definition, in both senses of that word. He notes (June 11, 1930) that "every thriller ought to have at least two different kinds of excitements — that of getting to the climax, and that of the climax itself." The excitement thus lies in the story and in its *dénouement* or *eucatastrophe,* in *peripeteia* and *anagnorisis.*

The initial distinction — the climax and getting to the climax is one dichotomy. Williams draws a second, early on in his reviewing, between breathlessness and brain (July 7, 1930), though this will not allow him to accept in full Canon Whitechurch's distinction between thrillers and detective stories (December 13, 1932), while acknowledging that every "clear-minded honest follower of the true path down clues of matches, ciphers, shoe laces, and postcards will enjoy Mr. Whitechurch."

He also remarks (July 30, 1930) that "to be like ourselves is a miracle — in a detective novel." He praises a book for presenting real people in "real surroundings — ladders and tennis courts and so on" (June 4, 1930). He argues for an achievement in which "the mystery is felt to be produced by [the author's] people and not the people by the mystery" (August 26, 1930). He notes that in a particular police procedural "pattern is seen much more clearly as a pattern than when a single mind does all the work" (this of a novel "too extreme for realism but not for pattern" — September 3, 1930). Of a book by M. P. Shiel, he says he responded with "a fascinated irritation. It is unbelievable and it is alive" (October 21, 1930). He acknowledges a "personal passion" for a particular kind of book: "They are circumscribed; they have a pattern; they have unity" (February 9, 1931). Of course, this is not Aristotelian unity, but a unity by pattern.

So at the outset of his reviewing (also the outset of his career as a novelist, marked by *War in Heaven*, which most closely approximates a detective thriller), Williams is seeking a kind of realism of execution, combined with perfection of pattern, in ordinary surroundings (he comes down on the side of Henry James, as against H. G. Wells). Let us look a little further at this matter of rhetoric and vision, most particularly at the question of vision.

In his review of Francis Iles's (Anthony Berkeley Cox) *Malice Aforethought,* Williams calls the story that of a "commonplace crime, but no doubt hell is commonplace" (March 18, 1931). Of a novel of Christopher Bush three months later (June 17, 1931), he remarks that the author "reminds us of the chaos round the corner and writes a thrilling story in doing it." He speculates later (September 16, 1931) that perhaps "we must take a life for a life, but the compensating life must be freely offered." Of one of Philip MacDonald's books (he being the most often reviewed author), Williams says "Mr. MacDonald makes not our flesh, but our souls creep" (November 17, 1931). In January 1932 he issues a dictum (January 7, 1932) that "The more sense of infinity, the better the story."

Of David Sharp's *I, the Criminal*, he says "it introduces us to the spiritual reason of thrills. I feel as if Mr. Sharp had explained the universe by accident in writing an amusing, happy, and restless book" (July 28, 1932). And of another Philip MacDonald book the next year (April 26, 1933), he writes that "before he told me I knew who the madman was, and at that moment a ray of the real sun broke upon his goblin world. But what goblins! What a marvelous capacity for shaking one's soul up." (We will come back to the real sun and the goblin world in our discussion of reality in detective fiction and thrillers.)

I have wondered, in reading a review from June 1933 (June 5, 1933), if Williams was punning: "As the man is dead it might seem not very much to matter but it is always the immaterial that matters so frightfully." (Actually, "frightfully" could be a pun, as well as "immaterial"). But this is by way of a detour on the way to the review in which Williams lets himself go on the spiritual nature of detective fiction. The book, appropriately, is Dorothy L. Sayers's *The Nine Tailors* (January 17, 1934). One contemplates with something akin to envy a reviewer whose column for the week included the new Sayers (*The Nine Tailors*), the new Van Dine (*The Dragon Murder Case*), and the new Christie (*Murder on the Orient Express*) in one morning. Williams writes,

"Laughter and pity and terror, clarity and mystery, inform all these things, and as Miss Sayers's mastery moves on to its climax in the tower of the church where the refugees, admirably ordered by a mortal and immortal ritual, find shelter, the book becomes in itself a kind of judgment. The powers of earth and air denounce and encourage, and below them lies the wide sweep of waters. There is nothing supernatural — unless indeed we and our life and all our art are supernatural, as some have held. But it is the reflection of our dark and passionate life itself which those waters hold and those bells proclaim. It is a great book."

That is the most favorable review of any book in his years of reviewing detective fiction. Next perhaps is his review of Philip MacDonald's *Escape* (Martin Porlock's *Murder at Kensington Gore*), and next to Miss Sayers in *The Nine Tailors*, his favorite author is H. C. Bailey in anything. Here is Williams on H. C. Bailey's *Mr. Fortune Wonders* (December 29, 1933). "He can do a murder, no doubt; but the evils he really hates are pride, hate, cruelty. He seems sometimes almost to imagine spiritual sin, and his cherubic Reginald Fortune thrusts at it like a real cherub. In five of these stories he arranges for death or life at his will. You do not like or dislike them because they are good crime, but because they are good Fortune, and because that means something like good fortune in the world."

These remarks, by the way, show the punning and allusive Williams and the epigrammatic Williams. Because the cherubim of popular art are *putti*, fat, cheerful, and childlike, Mr. Fortune is cherubic, as we speak of a cherubic countenance. Because the cherubim of the Old Testament are fierce and winged lions, he thrusts like them. Without knowledge of the background, there is no pun and little sense to the epigram. The "good Fortune" pun requires less arcane knowledge. But for our present purposes, it is important that all this is testimony to what Williams considers the nature of the detective story vision. (The assumption that the readers of his reviews will understand his allusions speaks, of course, to his rhetoric, as we have noted above, or rather to what he deems the appropriate rhetoric for thrillers and detective stories.)

Here I pause to note something that has occurred to me in reading Williams's reviews. The claim, advanced particularly by C. S. Lewis, that Williams could make goodness interesting is in fact a claim that could be made on behalf of a whole host of Golden Age detective novels, and is implicit in Williams's call simultaneously for character that determines action, and for action that falls within the patterns appropriate for the genre. The interest in character — if there is an interest in character — is directed not toward the villain but toward the detective hero. It is Peter Wimsey or Jane Marple or Gideon Fell that we love, or at least follow avidly, and not their virtually anonymous adversaries. Most of the time. (But his wife wept when a particular murderer was hanged, in one of Inspector French's cases.)

Moreover, Sherlock Holmes may have begun as a cocaine addict, and C. Auguste Dupin was doubtless addicted to some drug or other (his creator certainly was), but for all their silly-assery, Lord Peter Wimsey and Albert Campion and Reggie Fortune (particularly good Fortune, but he is not of quite that ilk) are uncomplicatedly good. Granted that the early Fu Manchu is uncomplicatedly evil, and his opponents uncomplicatedly incompetent, the general rule is that Heaven conquers Hell. As Williams said in another context, "Hell is inaccurate."

It was Williams's peculiar genius to strip this mythic comedy of its pretensions to a purely earthbound existence, to recognize and set forth its essence (I might even say its quintessence), and to set the *visio Caroli* concerning, if not Piers Plowman, then at least ordinary Englishmen (but "we have never met an ordinary mortal") amongst the principalities and powers of comedic redemption. Only the first published of his books retained the form of a detective story, but all derived from that origin, and what he said about rhetoric and vision in that context, is of value in looking at his fiction, no less than that of Miss Sayers, or Mr. Bailey, or Mr. MacDonald. It is in his fiction that the position of the detective story *sub specie aeternitatis* is fully realized.

Williams listed fantasy as one of the four principal, indeed elementary, ways "of constructing tribal lays," for the tribe of the "thriller" or detective fiction reader. I find this of particular interest, for reasons which should become clear, and have a great deal to do with rhetoric and vision. For fantasy, you will remember, as a craft (which is what a tribal poet practices), has rigorous requirements for sub-creation; if the writer is to make the rare and beautiful blue moon to shine, or to put fire in the belly of the cold worm ("On Fairy Stories," p. 122), then he or she had best have managed that elvish craft of enchantment. There, in that word, is the key.

Was Williams wrong in linking fantasy and detection fiction, which includes detective fiction and "thrillers"? Let us see. We know that for the quality of fantasy we must have the craft of enchantment, the power of the strange and other-worldly, and the sudden joyous turn, the *eucatastrophe*. For the genre of detective fiction, we have the conventions of the genre (and the detective process), the power of the familiar and the this-worldly, the magician conventionally on-stage, as it were, and then the sudden turn, the *anagnorisis*. Both promise deliverance, in a way, but in what a different way.

And yet, what of Chesterton? Has he not shown, with Father Brown, that the quality of fantasy can inhere within the conventions of detective fiction? Rather, as his master Dickens showed, that the quality could inhere within the conventions of the English sporting tale? To this I can think of two answers, both of which are in accord, I believe, with Williams's views. First, with the appearance of Sam Weller, the "angel in gaiters," Dickens and *Pickwick* begin to burst the bounds of the genre. The same kind of thing might be said of Father Brown and Chesterton as the stories progressed and still some more of GKC's other detective stories. And second, there is a distinction to be drawn between *Mooreeffoc* fantasy and creative fantasy. Here is Professor Tolkien again (p. 146–147): "*Mooreeffoc* is a fantastic word, but it could be seen written up in every town in this land. It is Coffee-room, viewed from the inside through a glass door ... and it was used by Chesterton to denote the queerness of things that have become trite.... But it has, I think, only a limited power; for the reason that recovery of freshness of vision is its only virtue."

The recovery of freshness of vision is not unlike *anagnorisis*. Creative fantasy, on the other hand, in making something new, promotes delivery not merely from triteness (or from the unexamined life, or should I say, from the mundane?), but out of all our sea of troubles to a new dry land. And this is far more like a full reversal or *peripeteia*, of action, of energy, of reality.

I think the Father Brown stories and particularly *The Man Who Knew Too Much* eventually test the conventions of the genre too severely, and the *Mooreeffoc* comes too automatically at the *dénouement*, as in "The Vanishing of Vaudrey" for example. But in the best of the early stories, the very first, with its double *anagnorisis*, or "The Queer Feet." or even, a little later, that extravaganza in which a corpse is hung on a hatrack and a murderer 'a' babbled o' silver bullets, the detection is real, and the deliverance is real, none the less so (indeed more so) for being salvation. That also is deliverance.

Though creative fantasy may achieve a fuller *peripeteia* than *Mooreeffoc* fantasy, and though detective fiction without fantasy may be stronger on *anagnorisis* than *peripeteia*, we must be careful not to formulate this statement in such a way as to give the impression that fantasy is one genre (stronger in *peripeteia*) and detective fiction another (stronger in *anagnorisis*). Detective fiction is, by our standards, a genre, but fantasy of either kind is not. It is a craft — like poetry, perhaps, or goldsmithing. Or at least it used to be, and still was in the days of which we are speaking here. And it is this that Charles Williams speaks of in his quadripartite division — fact, fable, faerie, and fantasy. (And only "thrillers" or Farjeon's romances can enter even the lands bordering on faerie.)

Chesterton suggests that the quality of fantasy can indeed inhere in detective fiction, as indeed it can in only mythic genres. But there are other kinds of reversal and discovery as well. Because there are other kinds, this discussion may seem another of my roundabouts, but it has a definite purpose here, and a definite connection to Charles Williams.

Because Tolkien wrote what is generally considered fantasy, and C. S. Lewis wrote children's stories (which are thought of as fantasy) and interplanetary novels (which are thought of as science fiction), and because Charles Williams was their war-time friend and also a writer (and a significant influence on Lewis), there is a tendency to think of him as a "fantastic" writer. I dispute the syllogism pretty much *in toto*, but what is important here is that detective fiction, and the sensation fiction from which it comes, be seen as a form of mythic comedy, as presenting the myth of deliverance, but as only possibly (not necessarily) permitting the inherence of the fantastic, and even then more often of *Mooreeffoc* rather than creative fantasy.

For if we fail to realize this, and if we do not seek to find out what Williams thought were the bounds and characteristics of the detection fiction genre, we will not make the proper in-genre response to a detective novel that begins with these words (Charles Williams, *War in Heaven* [1930], p. 7):"The telephone bell was ringing wildly, but without result, since there was no one in the room but the corpse. A few moments later there was. Lionel Rackstraw, strolling back from lunch, heard in the corridor the sound of the bell in his room, and, entering at a run, took up the receiver. He remarked, as he did so, the boots and trousered legs sticking out from the large knee-hole table at which he worked, but the telephone had established the first claim on his attention."

Moreover, unless we are familiar with the genre, its conventions, its origins, and its purposes, we might find it difficult to accept at face value, or even to understand the reasons for, Charles Williams's unequivocal statement that his novels began in emulation of Sax Rohmer. Remembering that Williams's novels, in effect, increasingly move into the realms of powers and principalities, while retaining the rhetoric of detective fiction, we should find this a point of some importance. For, when Williams found the vision of Heaven and Hell in the confines of detective fiction, he was not finding what was not there. He was rather stripping the core of the redemptive comedy for action, as it were, and honing the fineness of the edge for the rhetoric appropriate to Golden Age detective fiction.

After all, it might have been Lord Peter who imagined Shakespeare quiring to the young-eyed cherubim on the underground, and it certainly would have been in Lord Peter's character to have interrupted a disquisition on the proper plural of *rhinoceros* (it is, in fact, *rhinocerotes*) with the lines "The feet of your favorite rhino / Are apt to leave marks on the lino." But in both cases it was Charles Williams, the author himself, *in propria persona*.

Is this important? Yes. The placing of Williams's restless intelligence within the reviewer's ghetto not only confirmed his choice of the theological thriller as the vehicle of his own expression. It also can, and should, go a significant way toward illuminating what was in fact golden about the Golden Age. If we are to believe his reviews, the golden quality inhered in the style, and the style was a function of the rhetoric (almost the "light touch") of the stories, with their fundamental — even archetypal — pitting of the powers of light against the powers of darkness. No, make that the Light touch, and make it the Powers of Light, and the Powers of Darkness. Sun and Goblins. Or perhaps Son and Goblins. In either case, a little capitalization would not be amiss.

Not least on the fortunate meeting of Williams and detective fiction reviewing.

II

THE YEAR 1930

In this, his first year of detective-story reviewing, Williams reviewed seventy-nine novels or short-story collections. Among the authors were John Rhode (twice), Agatha Christie, Jefferson Farjeon (twice), John Dickson Carr, R. Austin Freeman, Philip MacDonald, G. D. H. and Margaret Cole (twice), H. C. Bailey, J. S. Fletcher, R. A. J. Walling, Henry Wade, Freeman Wills Crofts, Ellery Queen, Victor Whitechurch, M. P. Shiel, Gerald Fairlie, Anthony Berkeley, Francis Beeding, E. Phillips Oppenheim, and C. S. Forester.

In *Best Detective Stories of 1929*, he reviews Berkeley's classic "The Avenging Chance"—and recognizes it as a classic. But more impressive to the historian of detective fiction is the series of reviews for October 14 and October 21, 1930, in which he covers Freeman's *Mr. Pottermack's Oversight* and the first of the Jane Marple novels (*Murder at the Vicarage*) on the 14th, followed by M. P. Shiel and Ellery Queen's *The French Powder Mystery* on the 21st—and, incidentally, by a Cole and C. S. Forester's *Plain Murder* on November 4th. It is not merely his perspicacity in reviewing that is of interest—though that is certainly present and interesting—but the sheer opportunity available to the reviewer who had these books pass across his desk. Think of coming fresh and unsuspecting on Carr's *It Walks By Night* or Christie's *Murder at the Vicarage*—not to mention *The Avenging Chance*.

The review of Philip MacDonald's *The Noose* begins his curious love/hate affair with the works of Philip MacDonald (the phrase is as the psychologists would have it—or should I say, thinking of C. Daly King, the obelists?).

Murderers and Their Methods (January 24, 1930)

The Cobra Candlestick, by E. Barker. Hamilton. 7s 6d
Peril at Cranbury Hall, by John Rhode. Bles. 7s 6d
The Mystery of Vincent Dane, by Mrs. Victor Rickard. Stoughton. 7s 6d
The Secret of the Sapphire Ring, by M. V. Woodgate. Hurst and Blackett.
   7s 6d

   The Room-with-locked-doors-and-windows Problem is by now familiar. But Mr. Barker in *The Cobra Candlestick* has altered it by opening all the doors and windows and setting an inmate of the house close by each. No-one can get in or out without being observed, and yet Mr. Marsh-bitter was killed by being struck on the head with the Cobra Candlestick itself: which must have been almost as painful as the fatal attack made with a spanner — all because of his sapphire ring — on a character, reminiscently named Evan Harrington, in Mr. Woodgate's book.

   Perhaps the least painful method was the second one of the five tried on Oliver Gilroy in *Peril at Cranbury Hall.* He was merely gassed after a little gentle drunkenness had been induced. So persistent are the attacks that one half-believes the book to be by Mr. Galsworthy, whose charitable hostility to his unfortunate characters is so persistent. But Mr. Rhode's cypher prevents the mistake. It is a very good cypher, though Dr. Priestley (to whom we are re-introduced) discovered it too late to save Oliver — not that he deserved to be saved — and he died most unpleasantly.

   A similar fate is, perhaps, one of these days, in store for Sir Ulick Lawrence (another old friend), in *The Mystery of Vincent Dane,* though, as he has an Organisation, Mrs. Victor Rickard may have more difficulty. It is the kind of organisation to which the Lord Mayor or a liftman on the Tube may equally belong, and the rush with which it tries to get hold of Janetta Hesketh and her money, is as thrilling as the "subtle, sinuous, slinky, sleek, and underhand ways of the expert detective" (the phrase is Mr. Barker's). Indeed, of these four books, Mr. Barker's *Cobra Candlestick* is the only one which circles round a single murder with critical investigation: all the rest charge on to other murders, robberies, or abductions. (And may I say that the only person I suspected in *The Cobra Candlestick* was the butler — the only one that no one in the book did? Not even, I found at the end, Mr. Barker. But he ought to have been suspected: he was in the room first, for a valuable few seconds, alone.)

   Love, it is gratifying to note, is not allowed to waste any time in any of these books: it is mentioned from time to time, but only as the colour of one or the other of the pieces with which the game is played. Mrs. Victor

Rickard is the most human of these four; Mr. Barker the most intellectual; Mr. Rhode the most murderous; Mr. Woodgate the most romantic.

Murders and Mere Murders (April 10, 1930)

Dynamite Drury Again, by L. Patrick Greenes. Jarrolds. 7s 6d
A Bridport Dagger, by John Milbrook. The Bodley Head. 7s 6d
It Walks By Night, by John Dickson Carr. Harper 7s 6d
Death in the Dark, by Stacey Bishop. Faber and Faber. 7s 6d

Simple straightforward murder is becoming an exile from our fathers' land: daily she is driven more remotely into older times and places. Two of these books follow her. One of them, *Dynamite Drury Again*, goes to South Africa, where Trooper Thomas Drury deals adequately with "rebellious natives, amalgam thieves, murderers, cattle-runners," and Mary — under instructions from Mary in the last case. He was a trooper and she was the C. O.'s daughter — with all that those terms connote. But they connote only enough to vary without disturbing the agreeable adventures with villains, black and white, in which the trooper spends his days.

Detection was a habit with him, whereas it was a rare thing to the hero of Mr. Milbrook's romance, *A Bridport Dagger*, for which he returns to the Dorset of 1835. It is a good clean murder, with a good clean abduction, and a good clean suicide at the end. Emotions were quiter perhaps in 1835, or men ruled them better; at any rate this imagined record of them is (as our magistrates say) "wholesome." But it is wholesome with the excitement of life and death.

Contemporary murder at home — at least, in Paris and New York — is quite a different thing; the thrill she gives is the complex terror-treachery-madness thrill of our sophisticated desire. Witness, in *It Walks By Night*, Mr. Carr's page of chapter headings, which is probably the best thing of its kind in recent days—"How a Man Spoke from a Coffin" and so on — and it is a sufficient compliment to him to say that his book comes as near as living up to that page as any book could. It is really horrible, not so much in its story as in the arrangement of details and in the touch by which the figure of the French "director of police" becomes almost as fantastically terrifying as that of the obscene murderer.

Why was the body of the Duc de Saligny found in that curious kneeling posture in *Death in the Dark*? Obvious, my dear Watson! Because.... But shots from New York recall us to culture. And culture it is. In one superb sentence, Stephen Bayard ("a remarkable man") brings in twenty-two up-to-date cultural names (if indeed they are all real names!). He knows all about "thymocentric" criminals and the effect of pituitaries on crime, even though he (or his friend and author, Mr. Bishop) has the most devastating style. All this is rather a pity, because it blurs an otherwise complex murder-series. But it is a good story, and (as so often in life) neither the science nor the culture really matter a bit.

Crime and Detection (April 17, 1930)

Mr. Fortune Explains, by H. C. Bailey. Ward, Lock. 7s 6d
The Best Detective Stories of the Year 1929. Faber and Faber. 7s 6d
The Fifth Victim, by Dale Collins. Harrap. 3s 6d
Suspect, by Gerard Fairlie. Hodder and Stoughton. 7s 6d

And if one were so unhappy as to have to choose between the first two of these books— between Mr. Fortune, "our own love of other years," and the whole nineteen investigators of the *Best Detective Stories*, how could one choose? Of the nineteen only Roger Sheringham and M. Poirot have anything like a wide reputation: most of the others are new. They deduce and detect with their own minds, whereas with Mr. Fortune one rather feels that it is Providence deducing and detecting through his. This feeling has always been increased by the real mental horror he shows at the more unpleasant crimes; not for him are the thrills of pathology — or if they have to be, they are felt as disgusting.

His publishers do him something less than justice when they say that "his sole concern in life appears to be that he shall not miss his lunch or any other comfort due to him": he has many concerns in life, and one is Justice. But perhaps it must be admitted that the stories are admirable rather in texture than in design; it is the feel of Mr. Fortune rather than his actions— rather than the plots— that his friends look for. And—for one complaint — in this book the Hon. Sidney Lomas, the chief of the C. I. D., is surely a little heavier than before? Mr. Fortune cannot grow old; it is to be hoped that Mr. Bailey does not mean the charming Lomas to age.

The *Best Detective Stories*— which convince us that they probably were — have, on the other hand, rather design than texture, most good, some not so good. Real lovers of detection can no more be satisfied with short stories than real lovers of poetry with lyrics; they yearn for the fuller and richer length of novel or epic. But we cannot have an epic every day, and so must be grateful for lyrics that in so short a space one cannot really mind who murdered whom. Mr. Berkeley's "The Avenging Chance" and Mrs. Christie's "S.O.S." have the best design in them; between them is the torrential colour which is Mr. Chesterton's story of the man who went sane.

Mr. Fairlie and Mr. Collins would be thrilling if only they could be convincing. They tell us about murders and perils and, with a little good-will, we can read them. But they do rather leave the impression that the plaintive tale is flowing about things that don't really matter. Danger by itself is not exciting: Mr. Fortune at his lunch is more interesting than many another hero in his agony.

The Crime Club (May 8, 1930)

The Bowery Murder, by Willard K. Smith. Collins. 7s 6d
Shock, by Virgil Markham. Collins. 7s 6d
The Noose, by Philip MacDonald. Collins 7s 6d

The first three volumes of this new series of detective novels must have been planned for a long day's reading. The intellect is said, probably falsely, to be at its best after breakfast. Whatever intellects grapple with Mr. Smith's *Bowery Murder* will do well to be at their best, partly because of the number of revolvers—no, "gats" or "rods," I should say—and partly also because of the exquisite reproduction of the mannerisms of American newspapers.

The publishers call it "a masterpiece of ballyhoo." Happy world in which "ballyhoo" exists for our delectable horror! Happy England in which it is not naturalised. Mr. Smith has told his story — and how successfully!— in a diction of shrieks and sobs and solemnities, in a style of which one phrase at least should be immortal — the laws given "for the world to for ever obey."

After breakfast then, crime in New York, where financiers and actresses and Manchurian bandits all carry "gats." But after lunch, Mr. Markham, and his sinister and fated family living in an island castle off the coast of Wales, and destroyed one by one — "on horror's head horrors accumulate." It and its climax are quite unbelievable but attractive. There is a poet in it who I had hoped was going to solve the mystery, but he doesn't, or only in another world, to his personal satisfaction. He is, unfortunately, only the kind of poet who occurs in books: he "keeps his mind sterile of all the elements not germane" and shuts himself up for days when he is writing poetry. That kind.

After tea, a little sleep. But after dinner — Mr. MacDonald in *The Noose*, in which our old friend Anthony Gethryn of *The Rasp* and *The White Owl* has six days to find the murderer before an innocent man is hanged. And he does it after the old manner, with very tragical mirth, in a country village, among the people we know, where murders are natural if a little unusual, and style is always style if a little modern. O how pleasant our English tradition of murder can be, and how fine a crown to a good day's reading. But all three books make a good day's reading.

The Police and Outsiders (May 27, 1930)

The Two Ticket Puzzles, by J. J. Conington. Gollancz. 7s 6d
The King Against Anne Bickerton, by Sydney Fowler. Harrap. 7s 6d
The Secret of the Cove, by H. L. Deakin. Methuen. 7s 6d

Of late the fancy of mystery-writers has turned more and more to the official police as satisfactory solvers of their problems. Few Lestrades now provide the private crime specialist with a butt; our hard-worked general practitioners are coming into their own. Even Dr. Thorndyke and Reginald Fortune are semi-official; Mr. Crofts gave us Inspector French, and Mr. Fielding Chief Inspector Poynter, Mr. Conington in his earlier books showed us Chief Constable Sir Clinton Driffield; after whose departure there appeared in *The Eye of the Museum* Inspector Ross, who reappears here to drive an ingenious murderer first to his car and then to his doom.
    Mr. Conington's method is deservedly famous. He generally starts with his simple murder — a body under the seat of a railway compartment, say, as here — and proceeds by pure lucidity of action and thought to a complete and exciting finish. He has little colour and no pyrotechnics, but he has accuracy, coolness, neatness, and speed. His known quantities are always credible, and his unknown never incredible. This book is the Conington method to perfection. But if he shows us the police perfectly achieving the purpose for which they exist, Mr. Fowler, in *The King Against Anne Bickerton* — without propaganda or unfairness — shows us how their own existence may unconsciously become their chief purpose. He presents a difficult poison problem with an innocent and incompetent victim, first in the witness-box before the coroner and then in the dock before a "hanging" judge. With the goodwill of a born writer of thrillers he saves her in the end, but for that he has to supply her with an attractive and lucid friend. Authority does not mean to be unfair, but whoever is accused by Authority thereby becomes guilty. There are no villains all through a

thrilling story except Habit and Duty and Office. And its motto should be "The price of justice is eternal vigilance."

With Mr. Deakin's *The Secret of the Cove* we abandon the police; quite early in the book someone says, "If you're going to them, you can leave me out." He had probably been reading Mr. Fowler. The problem is not one of simple killing: it is of a sinister mad-house and conspiracy and secret service agents and captures and escapes and a quite peculiarly simple and novel method of murder. The secret of the cove is a good secret, though a little international, and it lures the reader to the last paragraph but one.

Crime: The Real Thing and The Romantic (June 4, 1930)

Burglars in Bucks, by G. D. H. and M. Cole. The Crime Club. Collins. 7s 6d

The Hardway Diamonds Mystery, by Miles Burton. Crime Club. Collins. 7s 6d

The Lady of Despair, by Francis D. Grierson. Crime Club. Collins. 7s 6d

Post Mortem, by Gilbert Collins. Geoffrey Bles. 7s 6d

A Clue in Wax, by Fred M. White. Ward, Lock. 7s 6d

There are crimes, and crimes, crimes in which you and I might be involved and crimes in which we never could be. This batch of books shows the difference. Mr. and Mrs. Cole, whose novel, *Burglars in Bucks*, heads the Crime Club series for June, have improved so astonishingly with their last few books that they are now real experts. The present glory is about a theft at a country house, with real people — nice people and profiteers and a poltergeist — in natural surroundings, ladders and tennis lawns and so on. The crime is as natural as the talk or as the detection, the kind of crime which might happen to us if we lived in country houses.

On the other hand, if we lived in the East End or knew an Assistant Commissioner, we might have helped or hindered the recovery of the Hardway Diamonds in Mr. Burton's book. A handcuffed thief trudging through London to his refuge is a good opening, and although the identity of the master-criminal (alas! was he really necessary? And he laughed maniacally too!) is soon obvious, his official discovery contains enough excitement to be pleasing. In Mr. Grierson's *The Lady of Despair* we come to Paris, and leave life for romance. We might manage carbon dioxide, but poisonous flowers and passionate joys are beyond us. The Crime Club Jury will have to keep a severe eye on this kind of thing, or they will let it reach London. And then we shall not believe in them any more.

Post Mortem is an agreeable disappointment. There was a dreadful moment when it seemed about to become a disintegrated tale of the disintegrating atom. But that was merely one set of crooks being clever. There are two sets, one set of private detectives (feminine), a Secret Agent, and Portuguese jewels; there is another master criminal, and two old and cellared houses in Hampshire. Highly complex, highly exciting; a life we like to read of and shall never live. In Mr. White's crime in *A Clue in Wax* we might live — it is a good, unusual, and possible crime — if only we could ever talk in his way, with a mingling of American slang and English sentiment. Or feel that way. Or know so beautiful a girl. Or earn thousands by writing books.

Five Mysteries and Two Kinds of Thrill (June 11, 1930)

The Komani Mystery, by Victor Sampson. Herbert Jenkins. 7s 6d
The Green Complex, by Harold MacGrath. John Long. 7s 6d
The Night Club Mystery, by Elizabeth Jordan. Hutchinson. 7s 6d
Murder from Beyond, by R. Francis Foster. Nash and Grayson. 7s 6d
The League of Discontent, by Francis Beeding. Hodder and Stoughton. 7s
    6d

Every "thriller" ought to have two different excitements — that of getting to the climax and that of the climax itself. In the very best of the kind, these two merge into each other. But there are very few of the very best. In the others we have to be content if one excitement is wholly, and the other only partially, satisfying.

Mr. Sampson's book, *The Komani Mystery,* is rather short but it ought to have been shorter, as it would have been if his policemen had talked like human beings. His climax and solution is good but unfair; there is, so far as I can see, nothing to suggest it to the reader. A man is found shot in a South African house; either his enemy murdered him or he shot himself in order to get his enemy hanged. I wish he had, and succeeded; they were both unpleasant.

The climax of *The Green Complex* again is more exciting than the progress to it. The affection between two American soldiers leads first to their apparent "absence without leave" in Paris after the war, next to the theft of an emerald necklace, and throughout to a great deal of American slang. They are so attached to each other that they nearly succeed, after killing a French criminal, in landing themselves and a "jane" in a French prison. The moral is that even friendship should be frank, and even love lucid. In Miss Jordan's *The Night Club Mystery* (which is deliberately made clear to the reader) the progress is all, and the climax only of importance to the characters. The relationship of these — a young New York banker, a mature gambler, a singer, and supers— is of as much importance as the thrills of the shooting and consequent affrays. Innocence has to hustle and only just wins through.

Spiritualists (it is only fair to warn them) occupy in Mr. Foster's *Murder From Beyond* the place other authors give to Bolsheviks or master-criminals. But it is to be hoped no intelligent spiritualist will mind being put to such use; all creeds and classes nowadays have to suffer in turn. There are three murders (England; a country house), a reporter-detective, and an increasing excitement among the characters which is, before the end, communicated to the reader. But here and there the joins seem a trifle weak.

Mr. Beeding's *League of Discontent* provokes attention throughout. It is pure adventure, in Provence, with English gentlemen on one side, and black enough villains (some of them even Negroes) on the other. And a besieged dovecot. And a captured lady. And documents and motor cars. One can, of course, put it down, but it is a nuisance to have to.

Crime, Breathlessness, and Brains (July 7, 1930)

The Person Called Z, by J. Jefferson Farjeon. Collins. 7s 6d
The Subtle Trail, by Joseph Gollomb. Heinemann. 7s 6d
The Shop Window Murders, by Vernon Loder. Collins. 7s 6d
Murder on the Palisades, by Will Levinrew. Gollancz. 7s 6d
The House in Tuesday Market, by J. S. Fletcher. Herbert Jenkins. 7s 6d
Slane's Long Shots, by E. Phillips Oppenheim. Hodder and Stoughton. 3s 6d

In Heaven we shall perhaps be able to have all our enjoyments at once. Here it is so difficult; while we are attending to one good thing we lose another. Fortunately the other thing is not always there. It is very difficult for the writer of a thriller to be at once subtle and exciting, and even if he succeeds it is difficult for his reader to follow out the subtleties while being shaken by the excitement. Breathlessness interferes with brain. Breathlessness is the rarer thing; ecstasy is always rarer than intellect.

The first two of these books are really exciting. Mr. Farjeon produces the authentic and direct thrill, the simple and sincere reluctance to do anything in the world but find out whether Valerie Thomas and her young friend did or did not escape from the sinister death which crept towards their Cornish cottage. There is a detective (but is he?), a parson (but is he?), and an artist (he was, but he is not — and that is a very nasty thrill). The love is short and bearable; the dangers are many and ominous — especially as the artist comes nearer to the French windows and as his shadow.... Oh, quite good!

The Subtle Trail is equally exciting if the reader does not mind its being much more incredible. Colonel Chandler shot himself and yet was murdered, by psychological means which it took a peculiarly hard-hearted psycho-analyst to detect. The psycho-analyst himself, however, was nearly done for (1) by a gunman, (2) by a neat arrangement of one woman and several chemicals, (3) by an egocentric maniac. He cured Colonel Chandler's daughter of claustrophobia in one evening — fortunately, for otherwise she would later have gone mad. An attractive fellow — ruthless and all that. *The Shop Window Murders* brings us to brain. Two corpses displayed in the fancy dress window of a gigantic stores is an opening of which no writer need be ashamed, especially when one is the proprietor and the other is his "chief buyer in the millinery." There are any amount of clues, all incompatible, and several suspects. The police are pleasant and intelligent; the crisis is quiet but adequate, and excitement is subdued but present throughout.

In Mr. Levinrew's *Murder on the Palisades*, the four accomplished and three unaccomplished murders in the house on the Palisades (a district in New York) are mostly a little medically specialist. But it must be long since so many ingenuities appeared in one criminal career, and all perfectly possible. A new investigator, Dr. Brierly, being himself scientific brain, tracks out their cause through his own subtlety and other people's excitement. He has only one flaw — he objects to a guess if it is called a guess, but admits it if it is called a hypothesis. This is an aged comment, but the fault is aged too.

Mr. Fletcher and Mr. Oppenheim are too well-known to need comment. Mr. Fletcher, in *The House on Tuesday Market*, starts well with an embalmed ten-year-old corpse; the detection is hard-working, successful, but assisted by Providence. Mr. Oppenheim's society criminologist in his new book, *Slane's Long Shots*, is also a little uncertain at his junctions. But then the real excitements of his cases are the drinks, of which there are at least fifty — fourteen cocktails, thirteen whiskies, four ports, three champagnes, two liqueurs, six other differentiated drinks, and six mere wines.

When Scotland Yard begins to live like that, what will happen to the income tax?

Four Holiday Novels (July 30, 1930)

Q.E.D., by Lynn Brock. Collins. 7s 6d
Pinehurst, by John Rhode. Geoffrey Bles. 7s 6d
The Owner Lies Dead, by Tyline Perry. Gollancz. 7s 6d
The Crystal Beads Murder, by Annie Haynes. The Bodley Head. 7s 6d

Colonel Gore must have been much longer at his public school than any of our other celebrated detectives. Nothing else would account for his being "so clean ... and nicely brought up," and also for his silence. In *Q.E.D.*, where one of his best friends, who is also the husband of his dearest, is killed, his brain is at its best, but his habit of asking the police to do strange and sudden things is distressing to them and pleasantly irritating to the reader. But he himself gets so stabbed and knocked about that he has to be forgiven. Mr. Lynn Brock is notable not only for the ingenuity of his main plot, but for the attractive and ingenious details with which he complicates it, and also for the whole-hearted way in which his murderers murder. All these joys are here, and Colonel Gore's reputation (which, I gather, suffered in *The Mendip Mystery*) is entirely re-established. Let us hope that his imminent marriage will no more interfere with his real work than Dr. Watson's did. To avenge the husband and marry the lady — Colonel Gore is too lucky!

There is nothing in *Pinehurst* to show whether Dr. Priestley went to a public school, except his language, which seems too solemn and sonorous to have been learned there. He is called in to help solve the problems of a corpse which has been found instead of a plaster-cast in a car whose driver was drunk, of a house whose owner shoots at anyone entering the grounds, of a burglar who removes all the brass in the same house, but leaves the money, and of a number of stolen lily roots.

There is a sentence on p. 32 which awakens suspicion, but Dr. Priestley did not hear that, and he adequately perseveres until several days' work, and the murderer's career, are done. The last sentence of the book contemplates the incredible but delightful possibility of his turning crook. Cannot Mr. Rhode be persuaded to pervert him? And let him foil the police?

There were 17 dead men and one living in the haunted mine of *The Owner Lies Dead*; the living man was supposed at last to have died from gas, and the mine covered. But when five weeks afterward it was opened, he was found to have been shot. It is a sinister opening to a book with an equally creepy close, and with one other great virtue, that the suspect is quite properly a suspect; he is really a possibility. That he is at the same time the corpse, that one likes him, that there are several other possibilities likeable and unlikeable, all these things go to keep murder awake and crawling among a group of bewildered and distressed people, much like ourselves. And to be like ourselves is a miracle — in a detective novel.

The death of Miss Annie Haynes has removed one of the best writers of the second class of this work. Her books were always industrious and careful; their drawback was that they provoked in the reader himself just that slight sense of conscious industry which a fortunate style prevents. They recorded the Triumph of Good, yet the reader felt a somewhat similar triumph in finishing them. But her plots were well-planned, he details apt, her people — except at melodramatic moments — not inhuman. The *Crystal Beads Murder* is a good example, which may very well be studied by the young and impetuous writer, and may well be read by anyone. She wrote in pain, and kept her head clear; could any genius ask a nobler epitaph.

Murder for the Holidays (August 6, 1930)

The Mark of the Rat, by Arnold Fredericks. Stanley Paul. 7s 6d
The Avenging Ikon, by Charles Barry. Methuen. 7s 6d
The Man with the Squeaky Voice, by R. A. J. Walling. Methuen. 7s 6d
The Bainbridge Murder, by Cortland Fitzsimmons. Eyre and Spottiswoode. 5s

Titles, without doubt, are a trouble: they have a way of being much better than the books, or anyhow promising more than any book could perform. It is unjust to be discontented; in fact, I am not discontented. But against the content that these books in their degree provide, there stirs the desire for a wilder satisfaction. Must not the words *The Mark of the Rat* suggest Mr. H. G. Wells and some supernatural rat harrying mankind from the depth of abominable sewers? Not that Mr. Fredericks has not done very well with merely human characters, and that the murderer, who is finally faced with — the publishers stop there, and so must I.

But it was enough to disconcert any murderer, even though it depended on science. Mr. Fredericks's other variation is to arrange for the several chapters to be written by different persons, so that the style is also a pleasant complication. There is exactly the right amount of love. *The Avenging Ikon* also suggests a supernatural anger, a riot of angelic wrath, which, quite naturally, we do not get. But we have a man killed by apparently falling off a ladder, only the broken rung points the wrong way — up and not down. And the half-dozen points of light which appeared to Hall-Marked Jimmy, though they were not the points of celestial spears, had an even more unexpected and very neat explanation.

Mr. Barry produces Afghans and Uzbegs and Bokhariots operating in London and France, but they are not international, only just criminal. The end has a little final turn on to an unsuspected character which does really "sustain the interest."

The Man with the Squeaky Voice was, I rashly presumed, the villain. He was not; he was the victim — at least, a victim. He was shot in Berkshire, and after all he had gone through it must have been a relief to him. I feel he might almost have developed into something grotesquely horrible and supernatural if it had not been for Mr. Walling's heroine, who is charming, but devastatingly firm and anti-sentimental. With the Squeaky Voice fellow being shot in a car which he afterwards drove three hundred yards, and the hero being not merely suspected, but arrested, and she herself abducted and hidden in a railway arch, rather the hero for her lover than me!

Mr. Fitzsimmons's *Bainbridge Murder* has a straightforward title and is a straightforward tale; that is to say, it has one murder, two unknown women, every kind of contradictory clue, two suicides, an injured wife, and six sets of muddy shoes. All in Long Island. It is a neatly finished curve, with careful work. It is also half-a-crown cheaper than most novels. Cheers!

Mysteries, Murders, and Motorists (August 14, 1930)

The Cauldron Bubbles, by N. A. Temple-Ellis. Methuen. 7s 6d
The Obole of Paradise, by Agnes Miller. Hutchinson. 7s 6d
Dead Men Twice, by Christopher Bush. Heinemann. 7s 6d
Camouflage, by Laurence W. Meynell. Harrap. 7s 6d

This (let us say at once) is a very good batch. All the authors have proved themselves before. Mr. Temple-Ellis's *Inconsistent Villains* was good, and Miss Miller's *Colfax Bookplate* was good and delightful. Mr. Bush and Mr. Meynell I know only by repute and reviews. There are in all these four books moments when one hesitates, when one begins to say, "But.... " But, with a little goodwill, there is nothing that cannot be passed and even enjoyed, with that "willing suspension of disbelief" so desirable in a reader.

Mr. Temple-Ellis's story of a house on the Sussex Downs where the last Victorian great lady is living her last days, of the curious excavations that were made behind a fence by that house, of the horrible farmer who lived near, of a good Jew, of the grotesque threats that pursued the school-master who became involved in the mystery, and finally of the really dread-ful explanation, is much too effective to spoil by any summary. It proceeds by adding inexplicable event to inexplicable event, till the reader begins to lose his own head in the nightmarish succession. I think Mr. Temple-Ellis a little overdoes the adjectival preparation — the words devils and dev-ilish recur rather often; and I hate the short conversations between the aristocrat's niece and the schoolmaster, who had obviously been lectur-ing on Meredith. But otherwise —!

I admit to losing my head entirely in Miss Miller's *Obole of Paradise*. An obole (in case anyone does not know) is a small gold Franco-Saracenic coin, and Paradise is Montlaurier near the Mediterranean. And the exact times at which everyone — the dead gipsy, the living gipsy, the Arab, the various Americans, the Swede, the French widow, and the Rumanian — found themselves in the fortress-church by the Saracen pool, and exactly how they spent their time, and why, a little defeats me. For here also inexplicability mounts on inexplicability, and a mind keener than August provides is needed to follow the exact elucidation. But in its broad lines the book is convincing and attractive; I hope to read it again in December.

Even in these democratic days it is hardly the thing for a butler, as in *Dead Man's Twist*, to be lying poisoned on top of his master's own confession of suicide, the master at the same time lying shot in the room overhead. Servants ought not to get above themselves like that. Michael France was on the point of winning the heavy-weight championship of the world when he was murdered (boxers are in it now), and a black-haired lady had visited him, whereas a few golden hairs were found on the settee — more democracy! But the activity of Scotland Yard and its friends is adept and effective, and the story moves easily to a satisfactory end.

So with Mr. Meynell's *Camouflage* — though this is less detection than thrill: motor-pursuits, an old woman exuding evil, abduction, false-con-fession, and hitting on the head. With the exception of the old lady, all most exciting, and one's car covers the ground in great style. I notice that nov-elists as heroes are on the increase; and a good thing — why should not our class write about itself?

Murder Good and Bad (August 26, 1930)

The Dying Alderman, by Henry Wade. Constable. 7s 6d
The Body on the Bus, by Leonard Hollingworth. Murray. 7s 6d
The Gold and Copper Delamonds, by Agnes Autumn. Methuen. 3s 6d
The Terror of the Torlands, by T. C. H. Jacobs. Stanley Paul. 7s 6d

They all, literally, "got it in the neck"—the Alderman in the Council Chamber, the chemistry lecturer on the bus, and the night watchman at the picture gallery. And none of them really deserved it—not even the Alderman, who was an ungracious fellow. But since Mr. Wade alludes in his account of the matter to an incident which will take place in October 1930, presumably the Alderman is still alive, and may, if he reads the book, mend his ways. He ought to read it, anyhow: it is a good book. From the moment when the meeting of the Corporation of Queensborough is adjourned, up to the moment when two suicides prove two mutually exclusive solutions, Mr. Wade's organisation is excellent. In an earlier book, *The Missing Partners,* he was good, but a little slow. But here he has improved his movement and defined his characters—his three police officers are most attractive—until the mystery is felt to be produced by his people and not the people by his mystery. He has found a last sentence which made me feel a perfect idiot for not being able to see the explanation sooner. All other readers no doubt will.

The Body on the Bus is apparently Mr. Hollingworth's first corpse, and as a result of it I shall have in future to take a taxi home after the theatre. One so easily forgets an old enemy or so, and, once suggested, what better place, towards the end of the journey, to be murdered in than a bus. In this book the ordinary people have souls, and the murderer has a philosophy—even if it is a silly philosophy. This does not prevent the detection being ingenious, the solution bearable if a trifle strained, and the police intelligent. But why—it is the most exciting sentence in the book—does Nonconformity logically lead to agnosticism? English Nonconformity has based itself on individual mystical experience. Now the development of such experience into logical terms must....

But the night watchman calls. In *The Gold and Copper Delamonds,* the (golden) Honourable Rose Delamond (her godfather in the worst crises remembered to call her that to such people as police superintendents and A. A. men —"the number of the Honourable Rose's car") was suspected of killing him and stealing the picture. But there is only a ha'p'orth of crime to a monstrous deal of preparation, and anyhow, she couldn't have done it, for she had a sweet, sympathetic, forgiving nature which was shown by her possessing about a hundred books, "all of them on subjects interesting to the giver." She had apparently bought none of her own, which is carrying sympathy to idiocy. Why not have left her in prison?

The Terror of the Torlands is a "thriller"— or at any rate a decent substitute. Dartmoor and Woolwich, ghostly hands, blackmail, murder in burning houses. But — it is a pity, but one must be honest — there is a poison unknown to medicine. What an age ours would have been for the Borgias!

Sensation and Mystery (September 3, 1930)

Death in a Deckchair, by Milward Kennedy. Gollancz. 7s 6d
Seven Suspects, by Florence Ryerson and Colin Clements. Skeffington. 7s 6d
When No Man Pursueth, by David Sharp. Benn. 7s 6d
Diamonds of Death, by Hilda Willett. Longmans. 7s 6d

On the understanding that the words relate strictly to crime and detection, and not to souls and emotions, I should call Death in a Deckchair a beautiful book. It might, of course, with that title, have been the other kind of beautiful book — autumn and the old man and wistful memories and vistas of the past, rather like a relation of Mr. Galsworthy's Forsytes expiring at half-past four on a Friday afternoon. But it is not; its beauty is that of the well-planned crime. A man has bathed, sits in a deckchair by the sea, and is found as the tide comes in to have been murdered. His clothes are gone, his car is gone, his name is (obviously) gone. Beautiful!

But the detection is equally beautiful. There are lots of police, and each of them does his bit, so that the pattern is seen much more clearly as a pattern than when a single mind does all the work. It is as a design that the book is to be appreciated; the coincidence of the victim having been pursued at the same time by three different enemies — desiring to bring about ridicule, justice, and death — is perhaps too extreme for realism, but not for pattern. The solution enters almost unobserved, and yet is suddenly seen to be completely there in the centre. The means of death is also beautiful. (But I cannot believe that the holiday-seekers at Prince's Bay were so — so much less than beautiful.)

Talking about pattern, however, suggests that the authors of the Seven Suspects (Dead Man's Gulch, California) might as well have provided seven deaths instead of five. The murderer of the Spanish singer was one of those admirable people who, about half way through the book, get into a panic, lose their heads, and begin committing extra crimes for safety's sake. The amateur detective comes to his solution rather pleasantly by regarding the crime as a story to be worked out on the best traditions of the movies; but he almost converts the reader to believing in them. Perhaps he will come to England soon and do a home murder?

The criminal in *When No Man Pursueth* also lost his head, and tried to kill an innocent professor of philology. Also, failing in that, to shut him up in a lunatic asylum, incidentally abducting a doctor and a manservant. The book is one of that newer type which not only contain jokes but rather make a joke of themselves. But a well-written joke may often be more thrilling than a dull history, and this is.

Diamonds of Death has a cipher which, if I have followed it right, is merely our old friend "e is the letter most often used in English." Apart from this disappointment, it goes in for character, humanity, love, Russians, and the White Slave Traffic, with more success—both in character and in thrills—than its name or those words might suggest. But the name of Messrs. Longmans as publishers should have reassured us, though the quotation on the jacket might have been more exciting. We are hardened to forcible drugging by now.

Art and Craft (September 9, 1930)

The Museum Murder, by John T. McIntyre. Geoffrey Bles. 7s 6d
I Like a Good Murder, by Marcus Magill. Knopf. 7s 6d
The Brazen Confession, by Cecil Freeman Gregg. Hutchinson. 7s 6d

Our grandfathers used to hold that art was meant to teach. We have qualified that, at least to the extent of holding that art teaches by showing the desirable instead of telling us what is desirable. It is therefore a compliment to Mr. McIntyre if I say that after reading *The Museum Murder*, I went round the room tidying it up—emptying ash-trays, putting books on the shelves, and collecting papers. Tidiness appeared as a shining virtue, yet I do not remember that the word "tidy" occurs in the book. No, but the book itself is so tidy—almost as tidy as a story could be. pp. 1–62 certainly are a sort of prologue, in which a museum curator is malicious, and an inquirer into cocktails knocks a packet of collars out of a window on the fifteenth floor. But in pp. 63–287 almost all the characters are gathered in the museum; the time occupied is one evening; the solution, not unduly concealed, is a surprise; the solver is one of your cultured amateurs. But he talks as if he really were cultured. The story is intellectually compact, and it is therefore exciting; it is accurate, natural, and delightful. Only I do hate the ways of the American police.

The title of the next book might have been chosen to annoy reviewers. Who can write it down—*I Like a Good Murder*—and not stoop to the personal? It was, however, Miss Molly Sullivan who said so, in the Portcullis Restaurant, and one was provided for her on the—or a very near—spot. In an ardour of detection she disguised herself as a charwoman, and then had to scrub a room out to avoid discovery. Chelsea and Bloomsbury are stirred by the crime; and by another set of criminals who, rather untidily, get mixed up in the catastrophe, and had to be pursued past the Angel out beyond the Lea Bridge-road to the Crown at Loughton. A little more tidiness would have made a better book, but it is attractive and amusing as it stands.

The Brazen Confession is very, very untidy. It begins well with the author asserting that he has committed a murder. I believe Mr. Gregg immediately; he ought to know, and I looked forward to hearing him tell me all about it. But he skipped five years, and shot his man on page 59, and then it was clear he was going mad. Part II took us back eleven years, and worked through an entirely different murder, and it wasn't for a long time that we came to Mr. Gregg's own crime, and by then we had lost interest in that. It is puzzling, and untidily puzzling. There is good fighting, and several nasty villains—one without any hair; and the finger-print complications are unbelievable. A good book, if you like your effects broad and sweeping. But how exquisite the confined space, the confined time, the gathered group, the defined process. Back to tidiness!

The Crime Club Meets Again (September 13, 1930)

Sir John Magill's Last Journey, by Freeman Wills Crofts. Collins. 7s 6d
The Body on the Floor, by Nancy Barr Mavity. Collins. 7s 6d
The Folded Paper Mystery, by Hulbert Footner. Collins. 7s 6d

Who reckoned that "The launch had left Barrow at 9.15 at night and arrived at Portpatrick at 9.40 the next morning, that was 12 hours 25 minutes, (which) into 84 sea miles gave a speed of 6¾ knots"? Only one distinguished Detective-Inspector ever has that kind of work to do, and he always has it. Only Mr. Crofts so continually defies our minds to follow him with proper care, and I feel and expect that he is working up to a climax.

One of these days he will cause Inspector French to make a mistake—he will take the 3.34 Newcastle express from the 6.18 Oxford local and make it the 9.45 to Dover instead of the five minutes stop at Crewe, and the villains will almost get away. But what shall we feel like (I trust I speak for many others) who have so docilely believed in him without working the figures out.

In *Sir John Magill's Last Journey* he is still accurate. But Sir John disappeared near Belfast, and was afterwards found to have been murdered. Every clue that turned up made the crime more complicated. Inspector French does more traveling even than usual, but he is at his most-baffled-brightest. The extraordinary accurate subtlety of his at Mr. Crofts's work is at its best.

But if Sir John died because of money, Mrs. Cole (who was the "body on the floor") died through love — or what she and a faithless and perverse generation call love, an insane and possessive desire. That many of us have been near dying from the same thing, only not so violently, may cause us to sympathise; and in any case she provided in her death a first-rate complication. Miss Mavity ought to make her reporter a trifle more convincing, because she and he are of the greatest promise for a whole series of thoroughly enjoyable murders. It is just arguable that she conceals one small bit of information which would have put us on the track, and could have been mentioned unnoticeably. But the ingenuity of the plot and the variety of the details make it a thoroughly satisfying crime, especially as the murderer's combination of guilt and innocence pleasantly vary the end.

Of Mr. Footner this time I am not so sure. *The Folded Paper Mystery* death is neither love nor money, but a throne, and I confess to having no use for monarchs educated in America; they make fun of royalty instead of mocking at it, which is quite a different thing. The last sentence in the book shocks me. However, there are plenty of dangers and plenty of shadows and shadowers; the underworld of New York is full of gangs of death, and the throne doesn't really come in till the end. But Ruritania was the first and remains the only real kingdom of the sort — except those greater ones we ourselves invented as children.

A Clue, A Corpse, and "Cranford" (October 14, 1930)

Mr. Pottermack's Oversight, by R. Austin Freeman. Hodder and Stoughton. 7s 6d

The Peering One, by Evander Murray. Hodder and Stoughton. 7s 6d

The Murder at the Vicarage, by Agatha Christie. Collins. 7s 6d

Temptation, the saints assure us, can always be resisted. As a general maxim in the workaday world this is no doubt true, but there are rare occasions when it is likely to lead the foolish astray. It is never wise to resist temptation so far as to fly in the face of providence; one must use commonsense even in virtue. When Mr. Pottermack, who was innocent of everything, found himself in the hands of a blackmailer, and found also a deep well in his garden and a sundial to fix over it, would not St. Paul himself, in the course of being all things to all men, have advised him to take advantage of the arrangement? Anyhow he did, and then had to provide an entirely new set of footprints to lead the public past the well. He not only did this but later on provided also an entirely new body.

Only Dr. Thorndike could have discovered the substitution. The original operations and Thorndike's discoveries are described alternately so that both reach their climax at once. The clue is very good; it is one of those ridiculously obvious things which we all ought to notice and none of us do: like how many lumps of sugar our best friends take in their coffee. Mr. Freeman has always had an intense interest in the details of a crime; this book, like his others, is for the connoisseur of criminal methods.

Providence in a rather more supernatural sense is concerned with *The Peering One* in Central Africa, and my only quarrel with a story of several deaths and a lost treasure and a fight with elephants and criminal British Commissioners (and if that is not a thrill, what is?), is that the disembodied spirit is kept too much out of it. "Energy," we are taught, "should be proportionate to the result": yes, but the result should be proportionate to the energy. A ghost represents quite a lot of imaginative energy, and it ought not to be wasted. But, this apart, there is something like horror in the African rain round the haunted bungalow, and the corpse that, having killed itself, pushed up the safety catch of the pistol. Horror and excitement, and a really nice girl.

As for Mrs. Christie, she ought to be a village scandal-monger — she does it so well. But then (on the same grounds), she ought to be a vicar, and a vicar's young wife, and several other things. I rather hoped it was going to be a theological crime — we have too few of them — but the murdered churchwarden was a retired colonel not even interested in prophecy. The police are baffled; so is the vicar, and it takes the intelligence of a kind of worldly Mother Brown (if Mr. Chesterton will excuse me) to solve the mystery. Mrs. Christie is always adequate, and she misleads us here as skillfully as ever, giving us moments of acute anxiety in case the vicar's wife should be guilty. A charming book, only I do want to know all about the other casually mentioned cases of this village life — the changed coughdrops and the butcher's wife's umbrella. Could not Mrs. Christie write a new "Cranford"—a Cranford of crime?

M. P. Shiel's Elaborate Thrillers (October 21, 1930)

Dr. Krasinski's Secret, by M. P. Shiel. Jarrold. 7s 6d
The French Powder Mystery, by Ellery Queen. Gollancz. 7s 6d
The Death of Dr. Whitelaw, by A. Wilson. Longmans. 7s 6d

If George Meredith's brother had married Jules Verne's sister, Mr. Shiel might have had a brother in art. There is in the present book rather too much Meredith to rather too little Jules Verne, and there is a third element which is neither Meredith nor Verne, but more like a minor Elizabethan dramatist. Such a combination of mannerisms and invention and wildness may be hated, but it must be acknowledged. I hate Mr. Shiel's Captain Seymour, who so often "sang" instead of speaking; I am utterly unconvinced by Dr. Krasinski, who hypnotised and made radium jewels and plotted, on the highest principles, to gain much money by taking care "not to strive officiously to keep alive" the immediate heirs; I care no more who lives or who dies than I care who lives and dies in the *Chaste Wanton* (if there is not an Elizabethan play of that name there ought to be).

But from the moment when Dr. Krasinski shut the boy Bobbie up in one room, giving him only wine to drink, up to the moment when an engineer from Stamboul hunted the doctor himself up a deserted tower, through the repelling and attractive style of a repelling and attractive story, I read the book with a fascinated irritation. It is unbelievable, but it is alive.

Thirty pages from the end of *The French Powder Mystery,* Mr. Queen invites us to use our brains and find out the mystery. Let him; why keep a cow when milk is delivered to your doorstep? Admiration is better than labour. But Mr. Queen plays perfectly fairly, and anyone who attends to the title of the book ought to find the important clue. The details of the crime are very well done, from the moment when the corpse falls out of a concealed wall-bed in the window of a great store in New York, and its lipstick is found to differ in colour from its lips. That is the kind of incident that makes the good thriller worth reading.

"Renown," in *The Death of Dr Whitelaw,* "had chosen a resting place on the broad shoulders of a" — what? Professor? Student? No—cricketer. A resting place! But he was accused by the doctor of "behaving in an ungentlemanly manner" towards Mrs. Whitelaw (he had his arm around her waist, because he thought she was about to fall), which brought him an unjust ten years' penal servitude. He then became an enemy of society. But love, in the shape of an English girl, saw his sterling character, and he reformed after he had abducted a judge.

The judge forgave him, but I never will.

Macbeth and Other Murders (November 4, 1930)

Plain Murder, by C. S. Forester. The Bodley Head. 7s 6d
Mystery on the Moor, by J. Jefferson Farjeon. Collins. 7s 6d
Corpse in Canonicals, by G. D. H. and M. Cole. Collins. 7s 6d

It remains true that, as a murder story, *Macbeth* is probably unbeatable. And the reason — or one of the reasons— is that, in proportion as the acts of murder accumulate, so the speeches of the criminal seem to come from deeper places in his nature. They are not merely records of his progress, they are symbols of it: It is at first the hesitating mind that speaks; in the end it is the estranged soul. Macbeth's consciousness falls into a spiritual somnambulism, but it is a somnambulism that is possible only in the very depths of his being, and it is this which echoes through all the style of those last great scenes.

To compare Mr. Forester to Shakespeare would be unfair. But *Plain Murder* is like *Macbeth* in so far as it is a tale of a man — a clerk in an advertising office — who begins with one murder and is driven to follow that up by others, until he too moves, lonely and lunatic, among his fellows. Could Mr. Forester have deepened and intensified his style so as to express that terrible separation, the book might have been profoundly moving. As it is, it is a statement, not a revelation. But the office life is well done, and the multiplication of crimes is credible, if not convincing. And of all murders surely one committed to save one's job is most pardonable. There ought to be a new "unwritten law" on the subject.

Mr. Farjeon's books are always simple in aim; they are concerned simply to thrill. There is often a lonely house and death creeping about it, and for myself, I fall to it, and into it. I read gaping and (almost) gasping; if it were not that two young lovers cannot be parted, I should quite gasp. Here is an old man, and death coming towards him across half the world, through the white mist where the good but guileful girl sprained her ankle. I should, on the whole, have liked it a little bloodier, but anyone who likes good honest excitement can have it here. At the same time, I hope Mr. Farjeon will vary the formula.

Mr. and Mrs. Cole have played with crime before, but they are beginning to play with us. *Corpse in Canonicals* approaches farce, even to the number of clergymen in it. But a clerical corpse at the bottom of a Chief Constable's garden is a pretty thought, and Superintendent Wilson has a good cause for his perplexity. At one point it looks as if he was about to be thoroughly vamped, and it would have served the efficient creature right. Woman, after all, has her own efficiency. Jewel thieves, blackmail, undergraduates— it is not so thrilling as *Macbeth*, but more amusing. I look forward to the next book, as usual, with delight, but with a certain apprehension. Mr. and Mrs. Cole entered the Promised Land of murder after early wanderings; they must not go out into the desert of chats and chuckles.

Three Kinds of Murder (November 6, 1930)

Crime at Keeper's, by Thomas Cobb. Benn. 7s 6d
The Hymn Tune Mystery, by George Birmingham. Methuen. 7s 6d
Murder Backstairs, by Anne Austin. Skeffington. 7s 6d

There is room for a book on poets as murderers, a series of descriptive studies of the way in which Shakespeare removed (say) the rival poet of the "Sonnets," Milton an offensive Episcopalian neighbour, Shelley the Anglican chaplain at Pisa, and Tennyson — but Tennyson would never have murdered anyone; he was not quite a good enough poet for that. The rule that holds in other things holds in this. The more efficient a poet is as a business man the better he is as a poet; the better the poet the better the murderer. Shelley would probably have been caught, but never Shakespeare. The "Sonnets" may hold a darker secret than has been supposed; what about the sinister suggestion in "That you were once unkind befriends me now"? Does not the very sound of the line hint at the tipping of the poison into the malmsey? Listen to the drop of that concluding "now."

However, Mr. Cobb's poet, who did not commit the crime at Keeper's, I regret to say, is more like Shelley than Shakespeare. He was a vegetarian and avoided stepping on worms. The Vicar's nephew, the colonel's son, a vintage scallywag, and the corpse's father, are also in the running; the corpse being a pretty girl who was strangled in the poet's cottage. The plot is complex, the detection industrious, if only Mr. Cobb could make his characters interesting. But the stolidity of his style drives me to admit that I rather hoped all the suspects would be hanged together — with the colonel and the vicar thrown in.

George Birmingham (what happy memories the name recalls!) has brought Trollope's Barchester up to date with a *Hymn Tune Mystery*. The dean is scholarly; the archdeacon is antipathetic. (Why are archdeacons so rarely charming?) The organist is murdered, rather unnecessarily, in the organ loft, and the precentor and the police search for the villains. The precentor is young and bright and quite unlike Trollope. The police and stolid and intelligent. The plot, in the end, is negligible. But George Birmingham is still George Birmingham, even though, Posthumus, we are all growing old and all lived in Arcadia some considerable time ago.

In Arcadia — unlike America (they are not yet the same) — there were no perfume addicts. Yes, really — perfume addicts. They drink scents which contain alcohol. A protest should be made against the title *Murder Backstairs*; in England as well say *Murder Front Door* — it means nothing. Also against the habit of using up charming girts as corpses; it is a lady's maid this time, who is hit on the head with a bottle of perfume costing 40 dollars the ounce and then drowned. The apostle might well have remarked: "To what purpose is this waste?" The young detective has a whole house party to suspect and a parrot to confide in. It is not a bad story, and the ingenuity of detail is good. But all the characters are, in a literary sense, corpses.

More Deaths in Fiction (December 1, 1930)

Horror Comes to Thripplands, by Gilbert Collins. Geoffrey Bles. 7s 6d
Murder at the Pageant, by Victor L. Whitechurch. Collins. 7s 6d
The Mysterious Mademoiselle, by Francis D. Grierson. Collins. 7s 6d

A thousand titles and a million placards have not yet defeated "terror" and "horror"— nor even "tragedy," though that is in a far more critical position. Those words will go beyond almost any examples we can think of: "terror" is itself more terrifying than the terrible.

Not that when Miss Alicia Brooke saw "a huge unearthly shape" radiating sinuous tentacles she didn't quite naturally shriek and swoon. The horror that came to Thripplands was as bad as that, and yet not (I am sorry to say) quite so bad as that. It was just wickedness and not planetary invasions, which it looked as if it might be: good sound wickedness, with an ugly and misunderstood hero, a very good fighting: in fact, there are moments when one has to stop and remember that the book is simply bound to end well. One of the villains has "the eyes of a caged fiend," and so he very well ought.

If you are a lady's maid and you get a letter asking you to meet the writer under the clock at Charing Cross, and when you go a woman offers you £50 to leave your place, don't take it; even if you are in debt, don't take it. Indirectly, that was the cause of the *Murder at the Pageant*. I think a trifle of goodwill is needed for this book, though I hoped against hope that the other pretty girl in the pageant, not the suspected one who was Edward VI, but the Early Victorian, was going to be the criminal. No one was suspecting her; the murdered man had taken the part of a Puritan; and for an Early Victorian to kill a Puritan seemed so suitable —"Time's Revenges," as it were. Apart from this personal disappointment, the book is enjoyable but rather disconnected; the characters insist on being suspected. Which is well-meaning of them but should not be necessary.

The Mysterious Mademoiselle (there were two of them really) is about a master-criminal in Paris who has a house with a steel-lined wardrobe and darkly arranges for his captives to be removed to Siberia. But two English and two French sleuths defeat him easily, so no French crooks will now be able to write to him, Cher Maitre....

Thrills Round the World (December 24, 1930)

The Tragedy of the Chinese Mine, by Ian Greig. Benn. 7s 6d
The Ticker-Tape Murder, by Milton M. Propper. Faber and Faber. 7s 6d
Crowner's Quest, by Adam Broome. Benn. 7s 6d

This, they tell us, is a machine age. We are no longer men; we are becoming mechanisms. I suspect Mr. Propper of being our first mechanism's innocent ancestor. His descendant, if he writes detective novels, may write a longer one than *The Ticker-Tape Murder*, but never one more unmoved or neater. The corpse — on a railway in Philadelphia — winds itself up in a cocoon of clues and suspects, up to page 170. With an almost audible click, it then reverses, unwinds suspects and clues, and on page 340 deposits the corpse of the murderer. A suspected murderer, certainly, because he was so obviously not part of the cocoon that the only place left for him was inside, and as he couldn't be killed he had to be the killer. There is even a brown overcoat that unwinds as a grey, and a 9.55 train that unwinds as a 7.45. This is the kind of book that every writer of murders should read, admire, study, and abandon.

The Tragedy of the Chinese Mine divides also into two halves, but much more easily. In fact, it rather drops apart. The first half wanders all round the world, killing a Chinaman and almost killing an Englishman in

Malaya; arrives in England on page 130, and kills the murderer a little later. As he was a very unpleasant murderer who had orgies (not, alas, described: will no one ever do us a really convincing orgy?), the only anxiety is whether the avenger will be hanged in his turn. The solution —consisting of two thieves— is invented for the purpose, but the suspense is exciting, more exciting than it ought to be. Providence has assisted Mr. Greig more than his casual manner deserves.

Crowner's Quest kills an Acting-Governor. Personally, I like books that kill high officials (*The Four Just Men*, it will be remembered, destroyed a Foreign Secretary), and I had some hopes that the actual Governor had stolen back in disguise to murder his substitute, who was poisoned by a glass of water after playing tennis. The D. P. W. was suspected; you want to be alert on initials or you may easily get mixed with the departments. Mr. Broome unfairly conceals a clue or two and rather strains the solution, but the setting in West Africa is pleasantly unusual, the English are pleasantly usual, and the Africans are pleasantly mysterious, so that the whole book is pleasantly satisfying.

But some of his chattering women! Are they like that? And if so, what are the crocodiles of West Africa doing?

III

THE YEAR 1931

In this second year of Williams's detective fiction reviewing, he covers seventy-four books, including a review of S. C. Roberts, *Dr Watson*, by itself — no accompaniment. There are two by John Rhode, two by J. S. Fletcher, one Christie, one Freeman Wills Crofts, two by John Stephen Strange (Dorothy Stockbridge), two by Anthony Abbot (Fulton Oursler), two by G. D. H. and Margaret Cole, one Eden Phillpotts, one Arthur W. Upfield, one Mignon G. Eberhart, two by Bruce Graeme (better known for "Little Willie in best of sashes / Fell in the fire and was burned to ashes / By and by the room grew chilly / No one likes to poke up Willie"), and four by Philip MacDonald, one under the name Martin Porlock.

The classics are *Murder at Friar's Pardon* (Porlock, better known as Philip MacDonald), and Francis Iles (Anthony Berkeley Cox), *Malice Aforethought*. Once again, Williams recognizes the classic at first sight. His views on John Stephen Strange represent an eccentric viewing an eccentric, but the view itself centers on all the right things (in my view). There is no day in this year with a yield to equal some of those earlier and later, but April 6, 1931, with a MacDonald and a Crofts (and a Graeme), September 7, 1931, with a Christie and a MacDonald, and November 17, 1931, with a MacDonald and a Fletcher (and a Graeme), were all good days. On the whole, however, it is not a distinguished year. Between April and September he reviews twenty-nine books, and the bright spots are the Upfield, the Eberhart, and one John Rhode. It was not a good summer.

First Crimes of the New Year (January 5, 1931)

The Strangler Fig, by John Stephen Strange. Collins. 7s 6d
The Other Bullet, by Nancy Barr Mavity. Collins. 7s 6d
Tragedy on the Line, by John Rhode. Collins. 7s 6d

The last hour or two of 1930 has been almost bearable, and I owe Mr. Strange my profoundest thanks. By the neatest of psychological tricks, he sent my mind off the track of his cold-blooded villain and went on strangling the inmates of his Floridian house till a soft collar seemed a grotesquely inadequate protection for my own neck.

The Strangler Fig is a vine which wraps itself round other trees and kills them, and then in its pretty, perverse way strangles itself. And not, in this case of a human counterpart, before it was time. Mr. Strange is never quite gruesome, but he throws in agreeable hints of gruesomeness — vulture, financiers bribing an inspector to clear an unseaworthy vessel, a seven-year-old skeleton, and he has a turn with a cigarette case which is really thrilling. His people never live, but he makes his readers feel much more alive than they normally can feel, and the reflection that he has apparently written two other books which I haven't read makes the prospect of 1931 almost pleasant. A very horrible New Year to him!

Miss Mavity's reporter in *The Other Bullet* is a trifle tiresome in his devotion to his paper; but that is no doubt our fault. All outsiders are bored by religious fanaticism and nowadays fanaticism hides in such strange places. No doubt all married journalists feel they could not love thee, dear, so much loved they not the — whatever it may be — more. But the corpse of the ranch-hand was dead when the murderess (murderess according to the New Testament, not the law) shot him, and the journalist having got her off (according to the law, not the New Testament) got time off also and searched for the real slayer. The discovery is lengthy in every sense, and the end is not quite pleasing; the unities ought to be considered, even in murder, and the villain should be on stage when, or shortly after, the curtain rises. In this case he is drawn in from a far time and a distant place.

Mr. Rhode is always adequate, and if only he could excite his prose style a little, he would seem as adequate as he is. He lulls us in spite of himself; in *Tragedy on the Line*, the trains are harmonious and the shots soothing. This is a pity, because he has arranged a very good crime — probably his best. His corpse by the line created two wills, neither of which can be found, thus causing two nieces, three nephews and an outsider or so to be all suspected. Even Dr. Priestley is, I gather, half baffled, and Mr.

Rhode himself is driven to make the murderer confess. Like Miss Mavity, however, he goes rather far back for his explanation. Let us all make a New Year's resolution—corpse and capturer, motive and murderer shall all be present in the first 50 pages. That ought to make 1931 the acid test year of crime.

A New Problem for "Thriller" Readers (January 21, 1931)

Who Cut the Colonel's Throat?, by Laing Hay. Longmans. 7s 6d
The Box Hill Murder, by J. S. Fletcher. Herbert Jenkins. 7s 6d
Murder in the Mirror, by W. W. Masters. Longmans. 7s 6d

As to *Who Cut the Colonel's Throat?* the answer is (I say with modest pride) what I thought it might be, though it wasn't more than guessing. But the real problem (which would be too long for a title) is: "Where and when could one conveniently hide a body which had to be discovered at the end of thirty-six hours?" The answer is: On Saturday evening, in the waiting-room of a country station where no trains stop on Sunday. So simple when Mr. Hay has told us!

The refreshing novelty of this opening is followed by an adequate search among the proper people and an exciting climax. But no amount of novelty excuses the catastrophic chat of Mr. Hay's young people. Or their superiority. "'The murderer … cuts his victim's throat.' 'How perfectly ghastly,' Tony shrugged, echoing the other's feelings." Well, after all, who was Tony to be disgusted? If he had been the corpse, now….

There is always a touch of a quiet Sunday afternoon about the minds of Mr. Fletcher's detectives; their intellectual church clock moves slowly from ten to three. But their bodies and their surprise are energetic, and one reads his new novel, *The Box Hill Murder,* to find out what did happen rather than what is happening. Simple hard-working sleuths like Mr. Fletcher's young man, who in the course of an early stroll found a woman's body with the neck broken, would stand no chance without people who remember and recognise and repeat and reveal.

Murder in the Mirror is a catch, and nearly a good catch. The actual method of the mystery ought, I think, to have been explained a little more; it is hardly intelligible as it stands. We begin — very well — with a man playing in a cricket match who has completely lost his memory; and go on to a wandering Babylonian with theories about personality and control which he is able to put into practice. There was a dreadful moment when I thought love (you know the kind) was going to save everybody; but it required apparent death instead. The book, I want to make clear, is a good idea, which just fails to get across; but the publishers are entirely right in begging readers not to look at the end first. The appeal, however, is a dreadful comment on our culture; what decently civilised reader *would* ever look at the end first in any book?

Puzzles for Detectives (February 9, 1931)

The Bell Street Murders, by Sydney Fowler. Harrap. 7s 6d
The Moment After, by Virginia Tracey. Matthews and Marot. 7s 6d
The Tragedy of Draythorpe, by Leo Grex. Hutchinson. 7s 6d

In fiction, normally, the more inventiveness the fewer inventions. Destructive rays are out of it by now; and whatever the disintegration of the atom holds for us in fact it is not likely to hold much in art. The reason is obvious—it is that few writers, though they invent the invention, can also invent the inventor. The mind which discovers is apt to seem to the reader as ordinary as the minds of poets in fiction, or as the Colonel, the Rector, or the Butler; and the discovery is merely tied on to it by string instead of rising from it like a star. There is no heaven, no background, no intellectual space to appreciate. Both Mr. Fowler and Miss Tracey have avoided the dilemma by the dexterity of leaving their inventions unstressed. Mr. Fowler is the more startling; it is a method of preparation of surfaces by which two people can see different things on a cinema screen at the same time, and his inventor (very properly) wanted a million pounds for it, instead of which he was murdered. On the police here, as in *The King Against Anne Bickerton*, Mr. Fowler keeps a stern eye, watchful to point out their tendency to encroach on the rights of the private citizen. The book has the self-possession of the expert writer, and there is a small amount of love which is (very happily) all that it did not promise to be.

For books like *The Moment After*, I have a personal passion. They are circumscribed; they have a pattern; they invoke unity. The whole action takes place in one evening, mostly during a dinner-party at which a District-Attorney has been invited; the death has just taken place in the next suite — in front of one of the guests — and foretold to the police by three telephone messages. The invention here is also chemical — a perfect anesthetic and apparently a perfect poison. But that is a minor matter; Miss Tracey's real praise is that her people are so much more living than her corpse, with not much more room to move about in. And she, like all the best criminologists, keeps her last interest for her last chapter, her last bit of the pattern for her last sentence.

Sir Jasper ... but that gives the game away. Jasper is a name which, since Dickens's Edwin Drood replaced the Revelation of St. John, has become one of the 12 foundations of hell rather than heaven. *The Tragedy at Draythorpe* confines itself strictly to such foundations — to real good people and real bad people. There is a sad owl hooting right at the end, when the revolver shots have died away, and the burning houses have collapsed. But it isn't a bad puzzle, on strictly "straight" lines.

Discreet Crime in Fiction (February 18, 1931)

Inspector Bedison and the Sunderland Case, by Thomas Cobb. Benn. 7s 6d
Proof Counter Proof, by E. R. Punshon. Benn. 7s 6d
Murder by Latitude, by Rufus King. Heinemann. 7s 6d

The First Principles of Discreet Crime, by Professor Moriarity (published posthumously by the University of Chicago, with notes and an appendix on motor oil clues by Sherlock Holmes) lays down as a definite rule: "Never correct a fault in one crime by another of the same sort. Improve a murder by forgery or arson but never by murder. Repetition is self-stultification — probably in every sense." All improvements in criminal methods since those old days, when Moriarity was our only super-criminal, leave the wisdom of his advice — gathered from long experience — unimpaired. My own brochure, *Macbeth to Moriarity*, — now in preparation — will confirm this by many instances.

It is true the temptation is sometimes overpowering. Mr. Cobb's *Inspector Bedison and the Sunderland Case* is hardly a fair example, because his criminal was a homicidal maniac. Now in the great world of imaginative crime homicidal maniacs simply do not exist. They may on earth — that cannot be helped; nature has not yet crept up. The connection between the chloroformed corpse in Hampstead and the battered corpse in Southwood is worthy a better cause. The third death in St. John's Wood saves that third corpse from the suspicions of Inspector Bedison, who is a persevering detective. The book itself has a touch of the same virtue — or, at least, quality.

The title *Proof Counter Proof* correctly describes its book. Few suspects have such good cases made out against them as the many suspects here. The neatness with which Mr. Punshon gets away on a new trail every time is always incredible, and each time only at the last minute when the handcuffs are out. I do not much blame the murderer for the breach of the rule against a second murder; he was working against time. The scene is London and the corpse detestable. Serjeant Bell is a real pleasure.

Murder by Latitude takes place on a ship — a dangerous risk, both for the author and the murderer, but Mr. King justifies himself. The wireless operator is strangled, and the ship cut off from communication. The second death here is a murder for gain — and yet obscurely justified by the acts of human beings, by their egoism and their perversities. There is in his book a hint of that loneliness within and without which so often strikes with an interior terror the reader of Conrad; nor does it seem out of place that the captain, suddenly discovering that the ship is at odds with the constellations, should cry out: "There is something the matter with the stars." Even more like greatness is the other moment when the same captain, overwhelmed, gazing lethargically at the body of the young passenger, says only, thinking of its sea burial, "Our stock of spare canvas is getting low."

Murder and Pure Reason (March 2, 1931)

Quest, by N. Temple-Ellis. Methuen. 7s 6d
The Great Southern Mystery, by G. D. H. and M. Cole. Collins. 7s 6d
The Three Crimes, by Miles Burton. Collins. 7s 6d
The Murder of Geraldine Foster, by Anthony Abbot. Collins. 7s 6d

Mr. Temple Ellis opens *Quest* with a conundrum in Pure Reason. If a single-engine aeroplane is likely to fail once in every thousand times, how often would a twin-engined one, incapable of flying on a single engine, be likely to fail? The answer (so Pure Reason and Mr. Ellis say) is once in every five hundred. I suppose it is, but if it had not been for the necessity of finding out why the young man had disappeared, what kind of murder was being constructed in Dorset, what creature danced in the burning furze — and so on! — I would have disputed it.

Mr. Ellis has an admirable habit of causing every one of his books to grow more exciting and more horrid as it progresses. Pure Reason retired, giving way to a charming murderess who is saved alive at the end — for the usual reason, I very much hope. And while Mr. Ellis is writing his next three or four books about her, will he please also think out a really satisfactorily agonising death for her? He is one of the few writers who may be trusted to do it.

Mr. and Mrs. Cole improve continually on their own standard. This strangled corpse in the Hotel in *The Great Southern Mystery* gives rise to problems almost in Pure Reason. Is it the detective or the drug merchant? And was it dead in the hotel or alive at Victoria? And anyhow, why had it fifty sovereigns in its mouth? (What a divine death, as somebody said of Clarence and the butt of wine!) The fifty sovereigns are the weakest point. Apart from them, the book is a dance of identification, spiralling upward to a murderous conclusion. Mr. and Mrs. Cole are never horrid, but they are lucid, careful, and entertaining.

The other two Crime Club books this month are not, I think, quite up to the usual standard. I was unable, with the utmost goodwill, to avoid guessing the perpetrators of Mr. Burton's *Three Crimes*, and their neat service of God and Mammon. Mr. Abbot's *Murder of Geraldine Foster* is remarkable for two words and two incidents. The words are "lalla-paloosa"— which is apparently not a South Sea island or a town in Spain, but an American quarrel — and "pneumo-cardio-sphygo-meter"— which is a scientific instrument to detect lies. This, even if it doesn't work, is no theme for books which should be devotees of Pure Reason. The incidents are the murder — which is one of the messiest I ever encountered — and a "third degree" mental torture, which is one of the most horrible methods of detecting lies possible to man. But Mr. Abbot's is certainly an ingenious mind; what such a mind needs now is only — O everlasting cry!— style, style, and always style.

Sherlock Holmes's Dr. Watson, a Startling Theory (March 9, 1931)

Dr. Watson, by S. C. Roberts. Faber and Faber. 1s

We have waited long for this brochure (as Sherlock Holmes would have called it), *Prolegomena to the Study of a Biographical Problem,* it is named; but it is much more than that. It gathers together simply and convincingly for the first time in a separate form the facts of Dr. Watson's life, from his birth c. 1852 to the last we hear of him in 1914. Much that has been obscure is now clear; his gambling propensities, his attitude towards women, even his Christian name. Mr. Roberts's suggestion that his mother was a devout Tractarian and named him after Newman is brilliant — as is the demonstration of the second marriage. The pamphlet is exegesis of genius.

At one point I find myself in disagreement with Mr. Roberts. He asserts that after the Return Holmes "displayed an affection for Watson" very different from anything he showed before. I allow the force of the examples given, but these are all of the nature of set pieces, "displays" indeed, but (I claim) dramatic displays. Holmes's general treatment of Watson was much brusquer after the Return than before; just as many of his cases were less important and his treatment of them much less satisfactory.

What is the cause of this? There is a quite simple reason, which has not, I think, been publicly put forward till now. The explanation is that Sherlock Holmes never returned; he lay just as Watson thought, at the foot of the Reichenbach Falls. But his opponent, with an extreme yet justified daring, having avoided the police by precisely the trick he recounts, did return, to gain the loyalty of Watson and the ear of the police. It was Moriarty who came back from London in the disguise of Holmes. Who was after three years' wanderings there to disbelieve him?

There is no space here to produce the evidence for what is, I fear, a revolutionary and may be thought a fanciful theory. But I would beg scholars to give it their attention. Holmes and Moriarty were both tall thin men; there had been a three years' absence. It is true that Moriarty, on this thesis, signaled his return by destroying his second-in-command, Colonel Sebastian Moran; but has no ruler ever mistrusted his vizier? No wonder that, in general, Holmes-Moriarty confined himself to missing footballers or Oxford examination papers: it was not for him to strike at his own side. No wonder he fumbled other cases; his genius and his wish was the construction, not the detection, of crime. I appeal to Mr. Roberts, who has done so much for Watson, to give this theory also his best consideration. It explains why the apparent Holmes, arranging set scenes of affection, grew harsher at ordinary times. I am not at all sure that it has not something to do with Watson's second marriage, and with the more deadly risks which (after the Return) Watson was continually encouraged to take.

Three Crimes in Fiction (March 18, 1931)

Malice Aforethought, by Francis Iles. Mundanus. 3s
Tell No Tales, by George Limnelius. Bles. 7s 6d
Found Drowned, by Eden Phillpotts. Hutchinson. 7s 6d

The title of *Malice Aforethought* is in every way justified. With malicious forethought Mr. Iles has collected one of the most disagreeable groups of characters in criminal fiction; with malice and forethought the sensual and unpleasant Dr. Birkleigh determines to, and dares, and does, murder his tyrannical and unpleasant wife. "A commonplace crime," but no doubt Hell is commonplace.

It is one of the few murder stories which might be called dangerous, for it is one of the few in which the desires and dislikes of such commonplace people as ourselves are the causes and motives of crime and of evil. The horror, that is to say, is in our own souls; Mr. Iles provides us with the thrill with which we recognize horror in action. It is true that the murderer, being a doctor, has advantages denied to most of us; but Mr. Iles (the jacket tells us) has planned a series. I await with terrified ardour the volume in which he describes a publisher's clerk or a poet committing murder.

The people in *Tell No Tales* are "county." Perhaps it is this that sets them a little further off than Mr. Iles's group; one sees rather than touches the unpleasant wriggling mass. But one of them, all just risen from breakfast on the morning of the meet, puts a bullet into the young officer cantering over to join them. They move through the rooms and the grounds, sensuous, well-to-do, repulsive; the Chief Constable, however, who is as repulsive as any, is also uncommonly attractive. The end is extremely sudden — and not quite fair; there should have been a hint or two. But a good book — criminally horrid, if not spiritually.

Mr. Eden Phillpotts needs no praise — it is real respect which prevents the reader from adding here "fortunately." For he breaks one of the oldest rules— he makes the murderer confess. On the other hand, he has set his medical sleuth the hardest possible task — to discover the identity of an unknown body, dressed in the clothes of a living man, and declared, as that living man, to have been "found drowned." Mr. Phillpotts, with his own pleasant literary accent, simply compels Providence to hand out a coincidence or two; and his police inspector sets private faith above public policy. Pluck, I call it!

The Rigour of the Game (April 6, 1931)

The Avenging Parrot, by Anne Austin. Skeffington. 7s 6d
Mystery in the Channel, by F. Wills Crofts. Collins. 7s 6d
The Choice, by Philip Macdonald. Collins. 7s 6d
A Murder of Some Importance, by Bruce Graeme. Hutchinson. 7s 6d

As Bonnie Dundee (not Claverhouse, whose detections and executions were both of a cruder sort, but James Dundee — the hero of *The*

Avenging Parrot) said, "I certainly appreciate your co-operation." All writers nowadays, except the poets, who remain awfully independent, have to say that to their readers, but some more than others. Miss Austin does not need it much; hers is a straight murder — American boarding house, old woman strangled, young woman strangled, bank robbery, suspicion, seizure. "A clear crime, a clean detective, and the rigour of the game" — all very maintained, with increasing speed, to a close finish.

Mystery in the Channel is a yacht with two dead men — company directors. It is also one of the best mysteries that Inspector French has ever solved, and one of the best books that Mr. Crofts has ever written. Remembering all the past, I dare not say the best, but there are fewer calculations and more speed. The other company directors, the chief accountant, the confidential clerk, are all splendidly suspected, and the curve of the story closes beautifully in its source. Even the Inspector himself seems more agile; he has occasionally been a little too stolid. I always expect Mr. Crofts's books with reverence, but I await the next with excitement. Good will is here captured, not persuaded.

Mr. MacDonald's *The Choice* is a curious mixture of success and failure. There are murders and dangers galore. It is impossible to put it down and impossible to believe it. It makes one feel that heaven provided the problem and left Mr. MacDonald to provide the answer, and that by some mistake he put the answer to his next novel here instead. It thrillingly refuses anything so weak as our good will, which yet it badly needs. Mr. Anthony Gethryn is quite unbearable, but he has to be borne with because one must finish the book, and the end is not disappointing but wrong. "A Murder of Some Importance" (it was the French Ambassador) presents a picture — on the authority of Sir Basil Thompson — of Scotland Yard at work. Also of Paris and Berlin at work. This rather than the crime is the centre of the interest; it takes all three to catch the criminal. I have co-operated with pleasure, but I should like Mr. Graeme to say, "I certainly appreciate your co-operation."

Three Crimes in Fiction (April 7, 1931)

Murder in Earl's Court, by Neil Gordon. The Bodley Head. 7s 6d
Murder Out of Tune, by Marcus Magill. Hutchinson. 7s 6d
The Four Answers, by John Cobnor. Cape. 7s 6d

Murder will not come full circle until in some admirable story yet to be written a new Jekyll-and-Hyde is himself at once the corpse, the murderer, the detector. The answer looks like suicide, but in the book of which I dream it would only look like suicide. Psycho-analysis must, I fear, come in; the sub-conscious to murder the conscious and the sublimated to detect the crime. After all, most people hate themselves enough to do it.

Such a reflection is provoked by the variations which these three attractive stories provide. Mr. Gordon, in *The Murder in Earl's Court*, has got hold of a perfectly simple fact which may be put in the form of a question: Why should a criminal buy hundreds and hundreds of packets of cigarettes, in order to help stock a tobacco shop? The mind, however, has not a fair chance, because it is distracted by the serious risks run by a none-too-legal adventurer (he is the variation), and the answer eluded me till the end. The feet and the fists, the pistols and the problem, all go speeding on to a grand climax of one against five, and a glorious shindy.

Through Mr. Magill's *Murder Out of Tune* sounds every now and then the suspicion of a chuckle. Here we are, in a sense, playing at murders, but it is a very good game, with the most unexpected body. The young society girl, mocking herself at the lower middle class Ramblers, is an effective and rather dreadful opening; Lady Wassell-Jowett's detective energies are delightfully effective in the wrong direction. And when Mr. Magill is tired of his game he clears everything up by means of the police. It is a great tune of murder, and the other remote tune of mockery throughout gave one reader additional pleasure.

The Four Answers is concerned with four gentlemen playing a game of detection, and having it turn to a painful truth. It is all very good sleuthing, but the first part is pure art and therefore perfect; the second is applied art, and merely necessary. Besides, I hoped the Vicar was the murderer. Vicars so rarely murder since the Middle Ages, and yet when one thinks of the average congregation...!

Nothing much pointed to the Vicar, but (it is the only fault of the book) nothing at all pointed to the real criminal. And at least one dead finger always should.

Need It Be Murder (April 15, 1931)

The Fleet Hall Inheritance, by Richard Keverne. Constable. 7s 6d
The House with No Address, by E. M. Channon. Benn. 7s 6d
My Particular Murder, by David Sharp. Benn. 7s 6d
The Horror of the Juvenal Manse, by Kenneth Perkins. Hutchinson. 7s 6d

Mr. Keverne, his publishers say, "does not need a murder to make a mystery exciting." I am prepared to debate publicly with Mr. Keverne — the proceeds to go to the fund for the Support of Murderers' Widows — whether murder is not necessary to the highest art. Life is the only possession that is common to everybody, that can always and everywhere be taken, that has no accessories, that cannot be restored, that demands in complete compensation either pardon or death. Murder therefore introduces at the beginning of the book an artistic finality; it is up to the author to maintain this by his invention and conclude it by his climax.

But excitement, if not classic perfection, is certainly possible without murder; Mr. Keverne proves his case, if there were any need. His *Fleet Hall Inheritance* has a freshness as pleasant as the air of his Suffolk village, where a young writer of plays found (like Robert Browning) "a subject made to his hand" in the blind owner of Fleet Hall, the tired secretary, and the girl who is painting the church. He had, however, no time to get on with a play because he was hiding and tracking and loving and fighting, as was his manager. Perhaps that is what is wrong with our theatre; if the managers and dramatists are spending their time crawling through bracken by night, much is explained. Mr. Keverne maintains his thrills and his freshness to the end, and even there does not fail.

Mrs. Channon's publishers say "she never exceeds the bounds of reasonable probability." I should like to debate with Sir Ernest Benn the meaning of "reasonable" — proceeds to go to the Society of Philosophical Studies. The abduction of Rhoda in *The House with No Address* is reasonable in a book — if that is what is meant. But otherwise, otherwise. The story is, however, well worth reading for one particularly magnificent moment — extremely improbable — when a terrifying old woman cries out wildly, "These fig leaves have slime upon them," and the shadows of Egypt and Shakespeare darken the page. Apart from that instant of genius, Mrs. Channon tells her story with quietness, firmness, and no murders, but a complete disposal of a whole family at the end. She has one other likeness to Shakespeare — her young man is intolerable.

With *My Particular Murder* we come to death and whimsicality — a horrid word, but an amusing thing. Mr. Sharp does not ask us to believe his story; his way of telling it shows it to be an invention. But the philological Professor Fielding, who finds a corpse in Thavies Inn and is suspected of causing it, is a most delightful person. If anything he keeps his head almost too well, when abducted by villains or imprisoned by police. And to be saved by a book on Constitutional History is a salvation worth having and reading. It is a charming, witty, and exciting tale, and if Mr. Sharp will only believe in his own murders, he will be among our most comfortable writers.

The Horror at the Juvenal Manse, in New Orleans, starts unpromisingly with glands, improves into voodoo, and finishes beyond expectation with just plain crime. The glands have a purpose, but are very risky, for they promise only nerve-storms instead of intelligence, and the title and the publisher's chat promise them too. But Mr. Perkins is much better than this, even though he multiplies really bloody murders in a way which would shock Mr. Keverne, and is far too reckless for high art. Even so, there is something about murder ... it is so final.

I must apologise to all the publishers.

The Ethics of Murder (May 5, 1931)

Killing No Murder, by M. G. Kiddy. Hutchinson. 7s 6d
The Jungle Crime, by Luke Allan. Arrowsmith. 7s 6d
The Mystery of Hunting's End, by M. G. Eberhart. Heinemann. 7s 6d
Whereabouts Unknown, by Mrs. Baillie Reynolds. Hutchinson. 7s 6d

Mr. Kiddy can settle it with Penzance. "The only attractive thing that the station bookstall had to offer" his hero-murderer was a history book. What a bookstall! Alternatively, what a hero! But the situation made him acquainted with Major Sexby's pamphlet against Cromwell which bore the original title of *Killing No Murder.* Times, however, change; Sexby wrote: "It cannot be but absurd to think it unlawful to kill him that oppresses a whole nation."

Mr. Kiddy's hero, in the full rush of our present return to matriarchy, substitutes romance for politics, and says: "When it came to attempting the life of a girl, and that girl my wife.... " So he turned to an Organisation which was pursuing him and her with knives, petrol, poisoned chocolates, and revolvers. and broke the neck of a British General who was (unusually) a leading figure. There are any number of thrills, though they are a trifle unthrilling.

The Jungle Crime is American, not African. In a night club, amid lizards and snakes (in tanks), a vamp of the worst kind is stabbed and dies saying, "Someone — loves me." Such a proof of it provokes the police and others to look for the lover, who is therefore compelled to kill people whom he doesn't love — or not so much. He joins his beloved in the end, rather against his will; if he could have taken everyone else in the book with him it would have been satisfactory. This is merely definition — they are all the sort of people whose only excuse for existing is violent death.

In *Hunting's End,* on the other hand, it is imperative to know which of the guests in a snow-bound hunting lodge is guilty. The owner had been shot there five years before; the same party reassembles, and another dies in the same room and in the same way. Rising hysteria, mysterious attacks, snow-storms, a drunken cook, a deceitful senility, a knitting needle, rat poison, general death and darkness— all produce a series of thoroughly satisfactory and inexplicable thrills, explicated at last by a new trick. The nurse who tells the story acts sensibly and writes lucidly.

The slight stateliness that sounds in the title, *Whereabouts Unknown*, accompanies the book throughout. Mrs. Baillie Reynolds never permitted herself to become excited over the disappearance of the English girl in France, or over the search and the discovery. The single death is, as it were, a by-product, and offered with a certain bored politeness to the reader. The most thrilling moment is when a young actress jumps on the villain from the top of a chest of drawers. It is a compliment to Mrs. Reynolds to say I have rarely felt so sorry for any villain. Major Sexby, by the way, began his *Killing No Murder*, "It is not my Ambition to be in Print"— but then, he died demented in the Tower. How few of us moderns have the sort of mind that dies demented in the Tower.

The Week's Crime in Fiction (May 19, 1931)

Crime in the Arcade, by Walter Proudfoot. Hutchinson. 7s 6d
Cat and Feather, by Don Basil. Philip Earle. 7s 6d
The Monkshood Murder, by A. C. and Carmen Eddington. Collins. 7s 6d

Unless I can find a method as ingenious as Mr. Proudfoot's, *Crime in the Arcade* ought to have succeeded. It was connected with the fall of a part of the glass roof and was simple in conception and neat in execution. I was sorry not to have been allowed to admire its originator, but he not only wanted money (which is natural) and was willing to kill for it (which is normal), but he was tall, thin, white and a credit to his tailor (which is abnormal). The curve of suspicion is beautifully rounded, with a continual vibration of new interests and discoveries. Mr. Proudfoot ought to be a great gain to us of the steady old murder school.

Cat and Feather has a murder in a boarding house. The chief suspects— emotionally — are a blind man, a doctor, and a student of Torquemada and the Inquisition in general. Blindness, medicine and a power complex run level for some time. The book has only one fault: it leaves me with an intense desire to see by experience if a blind man would be conscious of a sudden gesture near his face. Mr. Basil is also, I believe, new and very welcome.

The Monkshood Murders recall not Torquemada but the Medici — at least Dumas's Medici, and Charles IX, turning the pages of his book on hunting. But this is not to deplore a likeness, but to enjoy a double memory. A newspaper editor dies in his office in New York: his son, the news editor, an evangelist, a police-court reporter, are all suspected. And then it is someone else. A rushing, driving, jumping, thrilling book: with one sudden pause — "It takes more courage, or as much, to kill another as oneself." Does it? The nuisance is that no one can ever find out.

Three Murders in Fiction (June 10, 1931)

The Upfold Farm Mystery, by A. Fielding. Collins. 7s 6d
The Hanging Woman, by John Rhode. Collins. 7s 6d
The Great London Mystery, by Charles Kingston. John Lane. 7s 6d

The Upfold Farm Mystery is a good crime book. Not merely are the characters artistically convincing. They are convincing artists. His painters talk as if they really were painters and not amateur actors taking the part. They do not chat about Leonardo and Cezanne; they are merely enthusiastic about their art. It is extraordinary how rarely that precisely right degree of enthusiasm is conveyed in fiction, and what enthusiasm it creates for the fiction.

By another neat piece of work Mr. Fielding arouses in his readers the precisely right degree of desirable irritation. There is a small brass box, with a winged lion of St. Mark upon it, which is mysteriously connected with the murder (1) of a painter, (2) of a blind girl, and this recurs until I felt I should literally scream if I heard of it once more without knowing the explanation. Infection by the fever of thrills is, even now, too rare: here it is produced and healed to a nicety.

I am not so certain of Mr. Rhode's scientists as I am of Mr. Fielding's artists, but then it is much easier to imagine a picture than an experiment. The unjustly mocked "I don't know much about it, but I know what I like" is still true about pictures, but one can't say even that about experiments, unless, of course, they pop or fizz or change colour or something. "The Hanging Woman" (who involved also a dead aviator and a hail of newspapers) is perhaps more a successful scientific demonstration than a picture. Mr. Rhode has all the talents necessary for his book, and the book is a happy demonstration of his talents.

The Great London Mystery opens with its heroine determining to be a work of art herself by — well, deceitfully — answering an advertisement for "a woman who has been tried for murder and acquitted." She was engaged under this pretence by a man with kindly eyes, who then turned cold and hard to hear. This presents a problem as difficult for the reader to solve as the nominal one of who stabbed the devil at the Albert Hall, and almost more worrying. Being suspected, she is offered money by a journalist for a series of articles on "Dope Kings I have met," and takes it. In spite of this desertion of decency (as too many people call it; but it wasn't as if she had met a single one) she wins through in the end. This book thus provides the amusement proper to murders with an additional amusement of its own.

A Triptych of Detection (June 17, 1931)

Three Yards of Cord, by Collin Brooks. Hutchinson. 7s 6d
Dancing Death, by Christopher Bush. Heinemann. 7s 6d
And Then Silence, by Milton M. Propper. Faber and Faber. 7s 6d

In the triptych of these three books, Death has three separate presentations. In the centre is Mr. Propper's painting — a severe simplicity — Death with suspects arranged as in a pattern. On the left is Mr. Bush, Death holding a bunch of toy balloons, surrounded by several suspects dancing in the snow. On the right is Mr. Brooks, in whose work Death itself is dancing with a number of crazy souls round the only unsuspected figure, that of the detective.

It is no use pretending that in the rather horrible dance of *Three Yards of Cord* I have kept my head. After the discovery of the woman hanging from the gallows outside an inn, Mr. Brooks produces an ingenuity of style that keeps hinting at dark possibilities of guilt. He has taken me in before; he does it again. Lord Tweed is a criminological peer, but he throws the shadow of a criminal. And lengths of cord are sent about by post, and the Dance of Death grows wilder with sadistic aristocrats— oh, all like that; not real, but very good.

Mr. Bush's *Dancing Death* is rather terrible than horrible, for it suggests in its explanation how fragile human happiness is. A business advertisement in the *Times* destroyed three lives as by accident. A woman stabbed, one strangled, and a man lying contorted in the midst of a lot of exploded toy balloons (perhaps symbolical, but anyhow fantastic). The search takes place amid a snow-bound house party, and only at the end is it clear how one murderer slew another, and two women died and one lived. Things might happen thus: Mr. Bush reminds us of the chaos round the corner, and writes a thrilling story in doing it.

Mr. Propper has a more sedate but not less interesting mind. He opens with his strangled women — strangulation is overdone — and then marches up three roads of suspicion at once, tidy, adequate, ingenious. He is especially enjoyable after those other wildnesses, but he is always capable, and the ramifying plot grows naturally under his nourishing care. Philadelphia is a fortunate place to have Mr. Propper looking after its crime.

Three Kinds of Death (July 15, 1931)

Live Wire, by Austen Allen. Geoffrey Bles. 7s 6d
The Night of Fear, by Moray Dalton. Sampson, Low. 7s 6d
Murder at Monk's Barn, by Cecil Waye. Hodder and Stoughton. 7s 6d

Intellectually, Mr. Allen doesn't play fair. He runs through *Live Wire* one of the real live wires of intelligent discussion today: Will men decide to go on living or will they gradually quench their desires until mankind dies out through sheer collapse? And he makes his villain, who supports this "dying out" notion, so intelligent that one quite hates having to like the romantic young American who comes from a quiet life in Chicago to drugs, detectives, and deaths in London.

The argument is so good that I was sorry to get back to the more ordinary excitement of murder. It is, of course, the romantic who means to murder — your romantics always have good reasons for doing what they want — and Mr. Allen ought to have let him do it instead of saving him for marriage. But only an exceptionally abstract intellect (like mine) will object to the book for this reason. It is certainly Mr. Allen's best; it has a vivid background; the story works up to the murder through the criminal concerns of interesting people, and after a narrow escape from hanging, the young American returns to Chicago for peace.

The Night of Fear has invented an almost attractive form of blackmail, which depends on reading up the details of old criminal trials. The blackmailer is stabbed while the house party are playing hide and seek; and Mr. Dalton is one of those delightful writers who go on introducing fresh thrills throughout. At the trial the detective behaves so suspiciously that I began to have serious doubts even of him; and then, on the last page but one, there was a new twist. The actual solution comes rather camel-like, but I have swallowed so many gnats that it gave me no undue strain to gulp it.

The *Murder at Monk's Barn* takes place while the victim is shaving, which is indecent. There should be privacies in fiction, and the detestable necessity of shaving, which nature and fashion imposes on us, is one of them. But the murder itself is ingenious, and uninventive readers will be stimulated to madness by wondering why the flower-pot was marked by luminous paint. The feminine detective was a little put off her stride either by loving the suspect or by not caring for chocolates; I think that if anybody had died at my feet just after eating chocolates I might have wondered if there was anything wrong with them. After all, nowadays, poison flows beside the path we tread — the gorges of the Chilterns and the gutters of Fleet Street run with it, and "grace after meat" has a new and heartfelt meaning.

Perfect Crimes and Imperfect Novelists (July 30, 1931)

The Crime Without a Flaw, by Leslie Despard. Nash and Grayson. 7s 6d
The Sands of Windee, by Arthur W. Upfield. Hutchinson. 7s 6d
The Stolen Cellini, by Alan Thomas. Benn. 7s 6d

The title of Mr. Leslie Despard's book slightly prejudiced me at once — after all, crimes can't be perfect in this world any more than men, and it's no use promising perfection by such a phrase as *The Crime Without a Flaw.* But on page 14 the young Detective Sergeant began to read a poem by Mr. Lascelles Abercrombie, and then it was certain that though the book might fail, it would fail beautifully. It would not be stupid or vulgar or horrid. However, the book does not fail; it is one of the best I have read for some time. There are agreeable details— the victim is made to lie down on a rubbish heap; there is a superfluous but charming grease-mark; Cesar Franck's music provides a (misleading) clue; and the murder takes place in a market-garden. A novelist is suspected. There are alibis which are and which aren't. The style (both of the murder and the book) is uncertain here and there, but I long to read more books about Sergeant Shelter, until he becomes chief of the C.I.D.

As against this, *The Sands of Windee* has no style. But it has a pleasant variation in a half-caste detective who has been called (as a joke — which it wasn't to him and isn't to us) Napoleon Bonaparte. That, however — except for a spiritual wrestle he has to endure at the end — is the worst. The scene is in New South Wales, and the body of the victim doesn't exist; so that the detective has to start from as near to nothing as makes no difference. Through a sheep-station, a township, a camp of aborigines, a bush fire, and a touch of hypnotism, he discovers as well as follows his clues. This is also said to be "the perfect murder." It isn't, but the story is good, and only the detective's name and soul are tiresome.

Mr. Thomas's private detectives in *The Stolen Cellini* are called Maurice Arbuthnot and Cyril Fortescue, and please, if Mr. Thomas is laughing at me I don't like it, and if he isn't, he ought to be. Because they are rather like that—Louis Seize and Handel and Watteau. They disguise themselves and go into the battle, which they win. It is a thief, not a murderer, whom they foil, with a brilliance which is a trifle shoddy. It is just not, but its notness is bearable.

Novels of Crime and Detection (August 25, 1931)

Blood Money, by John Goodwin. Putnam. 7s 6d
The Swan Island Murders, by Victoria Lincoln. Cassell. 7s 6d
Jaws of Circumstance, by Carl Clausen. The Bodley Head. 7s 6d

This business of marrying for money is not so easy as it has, for a century, sounded. The Victorians carried their objection almost to lunacy: it seems that then, if you were engaged to a girl and she had a fortune left her, you went through agonies. Every extra thousand brought an extra throb. It would mean a throb today, but of how different a kind! Then a man wouldn't live on his wife's earnings; now (as Miss Helen Hope pointed out the other Saturday) he is only too willing to do so. Lord Trent, in *Blood Money*, suggested that his son should marry an American girl who had eight hundred thousand pounds. The son fell in love with her companion, and all of them were hunted through Hertfordshire in and by a car, till the pursuers crashed over a quarry. The next morning a discharged footman was found shot, and after that the story goes into top gear up the Hill Difficulty. It is a straight road — in the dark, over the apparent corpse of the heroine to the fortune and the wedding.

My own naturally decadent taste demanded rather more cold fright from *The Swan Island Murders* than it got. When we reached the wood box where the wood in its dark confinement was sprouting in "white, sluggish leaves," and the room where the shadows faced the light, and the secretary kicking a dog, and the woman who was too beautiful to be loved, and the playwright who was full of a mad vitality, I thought we were in for a jolly tale of all the unhealthy things we oughtn't to enjoy and yet do. Miss Lincoln, I feel, was terrified by her own preparations, and balked at the necessary lunacy. But it is a good grotesque, and worthy of being read again when the conclusion is known. Can one say more? (Messrs. Cassell, on the jacket, ask "Why was Nahum afraid of Life?" I don't understand. Aren't Messrs. Cassell?)

Jaws of Circumstance is told by a report of the trial of a young man and young woman for the murder of an old woman — an admirable method: It confines, it presents, it details and persuades. The story is hardly up to the method but the method is very well done. The prisoners were so obviously innocent that I hoped they were guilty. The male prisoner was accused also of trying to get money and the prosecuting attorney was shocked. Couldn't two questions be added to the next census paper (1) What exactly wouldn't you do for money? (2) Why not? This would throw more light on our actual beliefs than any number of statements of our ecclesiastical loyalties.

The Crime Club Meets Again (September 7, 1931)

The Sittaford Mystery, by Agatha Christie. Collins. 7s 6d
The Wraith, by Philip MacDonald. Collins. 7s 6d
Hue and Cry, by Bruce Hamilton. Collins. 7s 6d

The fact that I guessed the murderer in Mrs. Christie's book only shows how easy it is to miss a cog, through dropping one of the threads. Having forgotten the right explanation of a small incident, I smelt a rat that wasn't there, and found a mare's nest which ought to have held a cuckoo's egg. By pure luck it was not; it was the real right one. With this handsome assortment of metaphors as an apology, I warn less excitable readers that they will not guess.

For *The Sittaford Mystery* opens with table-turning and the announcement, by the table, of a corpse, six miles away and a snowstorm off. It proceeds to involve itself in newspaper competitions and correspondents, missing boots, an unscrupulous (emotionally, not morally) but charming girl, and oddments. It ends with one of the neatest devices in modern detective fiction. It is, in fact, one of Mrs. Christie's best books— remembering the past, one can't say more.

It is a tribute to Mr. MacDonald that I loathe Anthony Gethryn almost humanly. His marriage has spoiled him; in *The Rasp* and *The White Owl* he was tolerable. Could the next book deal with his abolition, preferably by his friend Toller, to whom in *The Wraith* he tells the story of his first case? It is a creepy, ghoulish, fascinating case, and suits Gethryn, who is an intellectual public-school sadist if ever there was one. The owner of the manor house is found shot and a deformed keeper of cats confesses to killing him. There is a bog; there is a crashing crisis. There is a little argument about Reason and Experience, which proves that Reason is the better. My Reason tells me Mr. MacDonald may write a poor story. My Experience refuses to believe it.

Hue and Cry is not detection; it is an account of the flight of an unintentional murderer, and of his final escape. The opening chapters are very nearly good humanity — a goalkeeper who makes mistakes on the field and loses his girl. The rest is a steady succession of near-things. I am delighted to find that more people are willing to help him than Mr. Galsworthy, in his famous play about an escaped convict, was inclined to admit. On the whole, for those of us who are rather anxious about our past or immediate future, an encouraging book.

Crime as Escape (September 16, 1931)

The Winning Trick, by Neville Brand. The Bodley Head. 7s 6d
The Hanging of Constance Hillier, by Sydney Fowler. Jarrold. 7s 6d
The Hangman's Guests, by Stuart Martin. Hutchinson. 7s 6d
The Riddle of the Winged Death, by Hazell Phillips Hanshew. John Long. 7s 6d

If art, as some critics have held, is an escape from real life, art ought to be extraordinarily popular just at present. But then novels should be labeled E (escape) or L (life), so that the innocent reader may not find himself unwillingly brought back by a slow or sudden turn into life, with its ethics and its banking accounts and its morals. Two of these novels are E and two are (more or less) L. Mr. Brand's *Winning Trick* is frank E, aeroplane — secret service — death or victory E. It lacks a little of Mr. Brand's usual distinction; he is one of our few adventurous novelists who has a sense of style, and can be enjoyed by the whole mind at once. The publishers compare this book to Bulldog Drummond, and alarm me. Bulldog Drummond is good in his way, but his way is not Mr. Brand's; and either as a good joke, a satire, or from mere boredom, Mr. Brand flings the whole usual gang at our heads. "The gang in a novel are always very much the same.... Standing in that room was the gang absolutely complete." I admire Mr. Brand and I admire his cheek. But I look forward to his speaking with his own successful tongue next time.

Against the better of the E's or the better of the L's, Mr. Fowler (or Fowler Wright) presents us with a very pretty ethical problem in justice and the public good about the answer to which I have no doubt at all — if you hang an innocent person ought you to hang the real murderer? He involves this (which is the main part of the book) with a pretty mystery of the murder of an unpleasant old woman, and accompanies them both with occasional sardonic comments on law, life, liberty, and the pursuit of happiness. Mr. Fowler is always a little hard on our world; he reminds us how stupid we are, how callous. He chastens us, but we take no notice; he sneers at our souls, and we say: "I guessed the right answer." But it is his own fault. His invention is delightful; it was almost impossible to see how this book was to end without disappointment, but it doesn't. It ends impossibly but splendidly.

The Hangman's Guests consists of eight murder stories tied up by a problem, argued by and presented in a Chaplain and a hangman. Ought we "to pity or punish?" to kill or to cure? The answer perhaps is that we must take a life for a life, but that the compensating life must be freely offered. There may yet be a lay order of men and women willing to offer themselves to be executed in the convicted criminal's place: thus we could unite mercy and judgment. It is a profound problem, but it is not a good book.

The Winged Death is arrows—and accidents. It is also manly emotion, a devoted Cockney servant, the bawling *Press*, sinister explorers, Italian circus-performers, and suspicions galore. It provides an escape from the tax on tobacco, but not from the income tax. Only good art can do that.

A New Plot for "Thrillers" (October 7, 1931)

The Crime in the Dutch Garden, by Herbert Adams. Methuen. 7s 6d
Mystery at Friar's Pardon, by Martin Porlock. Collins. 7s 6d
The Crime of the Century, by Anthony Abbot. Collins. 7s 6d

Why do coroners never murder? Are they so used to corpses that they get no thrill out of the idea? Or is it *lèse majesté* or libel or larceny to present them as breaking the law. They would have unequalled opportunities for diverting suspicion, especially if they examined the medical attendant of the deceased. This general reflection is prompted by Mr. Adams's coroner in *The Crime in the Dutch Garden*, whom (in the absence of anyone else) I began to suspect, and then remembered that coroners simply do not do it. Life will have to furnish an example before literature dare, and life will do it; life always does. Watch the coroners! Actually it was a statue of a satyr that fell on Miss Querdling. She objected to people getting married, and as two nieces and several servants objected to her objection, there was every reason for the satyr to be encouraged to topple. And five minutes in a garden in the evening — it took another death to give the intelligent barrister his certainty. I am not too sure about that second death; how does one know when people are going to drink beer in their own rooms, especially the poisoned bottle?

Mr. Porlock's first novel has style; it has therefore inevitably everything else. Style can excite, style can puzzle, style can delight, for style is interest, and without style there is dullness. Friar's Pardon was an old home with a legend of death, and Mrs. Enid Lester Greene (author of *Paradise for Two*, *Oasis Love*, *Sir Galahad Comes Home*; only a novelist of style would have dared to invent that title!) was found drowned in a waterless room on the first floor. It is not gas, but something similar. There are also rumours of supernatural things, and a seance. A delightful, thrilling book, which, if Mr. Porlock retains his simplicity of inventive and communicative style, promises great things.

The Crime of the Century (1931— these superlative titles!) is a great advance on Mr. Abbot's first book. There are no machines and not so much blood. There are two bodies in a boat, and the New York police. The story becomes steadily more thrilling; and the end is quite unexpected; it arrived with a shock of delight. The tabloid phrase "the widow of snow and sneers" is a joy. But "inconceivably cruel, malevolent, and competent"? The word "inconceivably" actually has a meaning, little though it seems so nowadays; it means *inconceivably*.

Four Kinds of Thriller (October 22, 1931)

The Rembrandt Murder, by Henry James Forman. Stanley Paul. 7s 6d
The Secret of the Swamp, by George Bettany. Skeffington. 7s 6d
The Double Solution, by Cecil Freeman Gregg. Hutchinson. 7s 6d
Murder! Murder! by Laurence Vail. Peter Davies. 7s 6d

"There are nine-and-sixty ways of constructing tribal lays, and every single one of them is right." A list of the sixty-nine, which Mr. Kipling's poem did not contain, would be useful for advanced criticism; in the elementary classes we are confined to four. They are fact, fable, faerie, and fantasy. Mr. Forman's *The Rembrandt Murder* is fact — at least, it has the actual manner. The inspired amateur is Professor of Criminology at King's College — not the one in the Strand, unfortunately, but in New York. He was giving a course in Criminal Anthropology, which sounds a mere technical term for the history of the human race, and when a millionaire was shot in his own picture gallery, the professor and two of his students got down to the history of the criminal anthropos. The Rembrandt was stolen at the same time, but that came about through the historic fact of Rasputin. There is a medical fact or two to explain it, and a Siberian religious fact to complicate it. In the absence of better, this is very good.

Fable is represented by *The Secret of the Swamp*—which is entirely unexciting, in spite of the liquor smugglers and mountain police, but surprisingly pleasant. Its men and women all stock the regular fabulous virtues and vices—nobility, meanness, jealousy, passion, greed, and so on. But either Mr. Bettany's real feeling for these feelings, or the unusual country—the border land between Canada and America—and his feeling for that, makes what might have been a dull book a fresh and very nearly moving story. When the half-breed girl threw down her rifle and took to being trained in a Maternity Home because she loved children—but the book survives, and that is the measure of its kind of success.

With Mr. Gregg we come to faerie, though the scene is in the City and Scotland Yard. Another millionaire has a wonderful flat at the top of a City building, with a private and secret lift, a Chinese attendant, and a mysterious and semi-criminal beauty in detention there. He gets a series of letters: "You have three months (weeks, days, hours) to live," and … well, he had. And there is climbing and banging and running and chasing and shooting, and it's all in the best tradition of the active thriller: faerie— that is, non-human, but as jolly as Puck playing tricks on the villagers.

As for *Murder! Murder!*— now it is done it was clearly bound to be done. It is a fantastic dream of living bodies and dead bodies and kaleidoscopic mental pursuits and somnambulistic domestic quarrels and mocking parodies of official investigations. It is about an intoxicated young American who means to kill and then to detect, in a kind of world and a state of mind that Bulldog Drummond would simply hate. The publisher's chat calls it Rabelaisian, which I doubt, since it contains no joy and no nobility. But occasionally, in its macabre and sensual dance, it whirls to a philosophic music, and its deliberate hysteria does undoubtedly send an echoing screech through the reader's mind. Mr. Vail must have simply loved writing it.

More Murders in Fiction (November 17, 1931)

Harbour, by Philip MacDonald. Collins. 7s 6d
Unsolved, by Bruce Graeme. Hutchinson. 7s 6d
Red Stain, by Vernon Loder. Collins. 7s 6d
Murder in Four Degrees, by J. S. Fletcher. Harrap. 7s 6d

Since for all practical purposes we left off believing in the devil, villainy has become very difficult. The wicked capitalist, the wicked Bolshevik, are our pathetic modern efforts to provide a substitute. Crime may have three kinds of villains: (1) the good, (2) the legal, (3) the sinful. Mr. MacDonald's villains are generally sinful: he has a touch of something irrationally evil.

Mr. MacDonald makes, not our skin, but our souls creep. *Harbour* finds a horrid old woman killed and protects her niece with the aid of a pedlar in a lonely cottage, defeats four policemen, falls in love twice and out of love once. But I should like to know what the clergyman had really done; that it was something commonplace and hideous I feel sure.

The Claverings (in Mr. Graeme's *Unsolved*) never lied. The sons also habitually married their wives before introducing them to the family. Maurice Clavering, however, took his future wife home before the marriage, and his mother told her a long story of which the point was that Maurice might be the son, or nephew, of a murderer. One of the Claverings had apparently poisoned his father; unfortunately this involved him in something like a lie also. It upset the family dreadfully; not so much the murder, as the interest the outer world felt in the murder. The criminal here is a good man; the real villain is one of your satyrs. Only I wish there was more of him.

Red Stain succeeds in having human beings, or at least diagrams of them. The book opens with a doctor pouring something out of a bottle on the carpet near a corpse. Mr. Loder is so sedate in his style that I was quite afraid the doctor was going to prove guilty. But I trusted both of them, and the meat skewers justified me. The skewers are very enjoyable, especially those with flags on. Can I do more for Mr. Loder than offer that alluring fact?

Mr. Fletcher is properly Fletcherian. He has made the adjective worth while, though I feel he stands to great detection as the other Fletcher stood to Marlowe. But a grill consisting of an editor, a strange woman, a landlady, and an Indian, is mixed enough for anyone. It is Mr. Fletcher's exclamation marks that worry me; I cannot think we talk like that. His style is louder than his story, his thrills typographical. But his public is large enough to spare one restless heart.

Different Kinds of Death (December 9, 1931)

Dead Man's Watch, by G. D. H. and M. Cole. Collins. 7s 6d
Murder Game, by John Stephen Strange. Collins. 7s 6d
Death Rides in the Forest, by Rupert Grayson. Nash and Grayson. 7s 6d

Mr. and Mrs. Cole are merely heartless. They send a fellow and his girl off on a holiday, arrange a picnic by a creek, and then allow the creek to deposit the body of the fellow's uncle just then and there. There's an economical universe for you!

There are actually two uncles, and the corpse is recognized by its wife as her brother-in-law, but by its nephew as itself. Only as it died of cancer six months before it was drowned, was it really itself? Apart from the heartless opening, it is a friendly story; I lost my heart to Mr. and Mrs. Cole when they introduced a couple of that name — "She's got a bellow like one of those sea-lion things," "he just looks like an old comic." Would any of our more distinguished authors risk a joke of that kind? The plot is ingenious (but the murderer is not left in doubt), and the Cockney girl is a dear. Perhaps we may have her again some time?

Mr. Strange kills the football coach (American football — in which the coach prefers signals to "the huddle," "forty-seven, thirty-nine, seventeen, twenty-five," I know not what they mean) in the middle of a great game. It now remains for somebody to shoot the umpire in the Centre Court at Wimbledon during a final. The rest of the action takes place in the college town, and the professors of psychology and of archaeology and the instructor in physics are all suspect. Professors of literature never murder; it would need a psycho-analyst to explain why — sublimation, I suppose. There is a good rapid ending, with certainty uncertain and forethought frustrated.

Titles like *Murder at Lintercombe* ought to be dropped; they are neither exciting nor elucidatory nor attractive. Now, if Mr. Greig had called the book *Three Murders at Lintercombe* it would have sounded better; it would have sounded, I fear, better than the book. The opening is very encouraging, but there are so many episodes that take us nowhere, and Mr. Greig's style is so … let us call it sedate, that it is quite impossible to mind whether "the maniac who, with one side of his face completely obliterated by blood" — "completely obliterated" — shoots or is shot. I was mildly sorry that he was suffering "unbearable anguish," but he had accidentally fallen on a sharp stump. Sharp stumps simply must not be left about in crime books.

Death Rides in the Forest is about a forest and a hunting lodge, and a moated castle and an imprisoned prince, and an impostor resembling him, and a beautiful princess and an English hero, and a duel in which the victim's own weapon kills him. It made me feel very old, because Mr. Grayson has obviously never, never read *The Prisoner of Zenda*, which has a forest and a hunting lodge, etc. And got on and got off with it much better, or so it seems to me. But, then, I was Ruritanian born.

IV

January 1, 1932–
April 26, 1933

As Williams's pace in reviewing slows down, I have extended the time period covered by this chapter from a year to sixteen months, ending at the end of April 1933. In this period, he reviewed sixty-three books, generally of better quality than the books in the year 1931. His first review of Glen Trevor (James Hilton) sets the pace: he recognizes Trevor's quality while not knowing the name of the author behind the name.

In his second installment of reviews, I experienced a sudden shock. Anthony Gilbert is, after all, my contemporary: I grew up on her books about the egregious Arthur Crook, and shared new Anthony Gilberts with my father almost to his death in 1974: what is Williams doing reviewing her in 1932? Or David Frome and Q. Patrick, for that matter? But there are the true Golden Age writers too— John Dickson Carr, Crofts (twice), J. S. Fletcher (twice), Francis Beeding, Anthony Berkeley, Anthony Abbot (Fulton Oursler), Ellery Queen, Sydney Horler (twice, not a favorite of mine or of his), E. Phillips Oppenheim, Bruce Graeme, the Coles, Jefferson Farjeon (twice), S. S. Van Dine, Val Gielgud, Canon Whitechurch (his last, I think: he died in 1933), R. Austin Freeman, and, of course, Philip MacDonald. There are three MacDonalds—*Rope to Spare*, *Death on My Left*, and *R. I. P.*—and a fourth, as Martin Porlock, *Murder at Kensington Gore*, now known, in this country, as *Escape*, by Philip MacDonald. The best morning, I suppose, was perhaps the last included in this chapter (April 26, 1933), when *R. I. P.* and *The Kennel Murder Case* came across the reviewer's desk, though the reviews for April 7, 1933, included Crofts, Beeding, and Val Gielgud. Not a bad month.

Style and the Detective (January 1, 1932)

Murder at School, by Glen Trevor. Benn. 7s 6d
Stop Press, by Erle Spencer. Hodder and Stoughton. 7s 6d

Mr. Glen Trevor is "an author who has never before turned his hand to detective story writing." He has written "a number of novels distinguished for their penetrating observation of character." In spite of that, if I knew who he was and what they were, I would read them at once. A more handsome compliment can rarely have been paid, but no compliment can be too handsome for Style. Mr. Glen Trevor's book is an almost perfect exhibition of style. There is one point where the polish is a little rubbed by a superfluous red herring; there is a trifle too easy a suggestion that what has, as a matter of fact, happened in life could not happen in the story. But the book as a whole is a delight with sub-acid, sub-sexual, sub-intellectual thrills and amusements. The central clue consists of one word: I beg Mr. Trevor to congratulate me on feeling that something was wrong when I read it, without being so grim a partner as to stop and work it out.

If it had not been for the chance of Mr. Trevor, Mr. Erle Spencer would have had a clear field for his excitement. *Stop Press* does everything that a murder can do, short of Style. A dramatic critic is stabbed in a telephone-box; not, unfortunately, on account of his criticism. If he had been, if Mr. Spencer could have persuaded us to believe in the intensity of art and criticism, if we could have lived a little in the vital imagination, this would have been a great murder. As it is, it is a fine success of the second class. There is a magnificent crowd in Piccadilly, a mounting complication of suspects, and a shock of surprise at the end. I don't for a moment believe in the surprise, but it is permissible because of the necessary final instant which it gratifies. An apparent threat made by an innocent man in another place is more debatable.

The Literary Detective Again (January 7, 1932)

The Body on the Beam, by Anthony Gilbert. Collins. 7s 6d
Sudden Death, by Freeman Wills Crofts. Collins. 7s 6d
Dead Man's Music, by Christopher Bush. Heinemann. 7s 6d

The more sense of infinity the better the story. I don't suggest that Mr. Gilbert spends his days in contemplating "the unpersuadable justice," like Dante, but *The Body on the Beam* is very nearly an abstract study in justice. An unknown woman is found hanging in a house of bad reputation; the book tells of the discovery and steady tracking down of her murderer by a Liberal (cheers!) M. P. whom we have met before — Scott Egerton, and the more often I, for one, meet him again, the better I shall be pleased. It is ingenious and delicate, but the general effect is that of a silhouette portrait of Nemesis. That, however, needn't put anyone off for fear of lack of excitement; a good silhouette of Nemesis is one of the most thrilling things in existence.

Mr. Crofts has varied the steady perseverance of Inspector French by chapters describing the emotions of the housekeeper where *Sudden Death* takes place. She was the daughter of a clergyman, and "though she had acted as secretary to her father in his research for a critical work on the Pentateuch, she had not the necessary training for a business career." If she had come under suspicion, as she nearly did, the training might have been more useful; few things can be such good preparation for any kind of sudden death, official or unofficial, as an intensive study of *Genesis* or *Exodus*. Chapter 28 in *Deuteronomy* is calculated to prepare one for anything. But this is a digression. The lady is killed by an escape of gas in a room locked on the inside; later on, her husband is similarly shot. The second murder is risky, but we all "have a shot at it" in the double sense: the first is nearly safe, but only possible to Mr. Croft's untiring ingenuity. It is clear that murder is becoming as highly-specialised a business as income tax returns. Admirers of Inspector French will add this to their collection with gratitude perhaps rather than with delight.

Dead Man's Music, after the opening corpse, has a most attractive interlude with a man who collects dud china, writes incomprehensible music, and asks questions frankly like crossword clues. We proceed then in a jolly pursuit, careering round in cars, and peering through glass tops of doors, and sitting in Italian hotels, and even talking to disguises. Mr. Bush writes of as thoroughly enjoyable murders as any I know. The academic Dryasdust of detection may prefer the serener abstraction of Mr. Gilbert; the rest of us may be thankful for a catholic taste which can enjoy both the subtle hands and the rushing feet of crime. There is brain in all three books.

"Thrillers" of High Society (January 25, 1932)

Climax at the Falls, by Gregory Baxter. Benn. 7s 6d
The Polo Ground Mystery, by Robin Forsythe. The Bodley Head. 7s 6d
Murder in the Squire's Pew, by J. S. Fletcher. Harrap. 7s 6d

The Duke de Fulano y Querido is unfortunately only a name at the other end of the telephone in the climax of *Climax at the Falls*. The hero is an Earl; the bad woman is the daughter of a Marquis; the heroine is the daughter of an army officer (now a prison governor). The Marquis's daughter intrigues to part the lovers, assisted by a blackmailer, but she fails owing to great and good hearts who do not wear coronets, and has to fall back on the Duke. The blackmailer is thrown over a cliff; whether he is less or more fortunate than she is depends on the Duke. The heroine becomes a chatelaine, and serve her right — she refused to smoke cigarettes in public.

Mr. Forsythe also moves in society, but not quite like that. He has a horrid trick of referring to nicknames—"Fruity" is the worst; and a much more agreeable trick of referring to culture — Byron, permutations, Narcisse Diaz, Corot's letters, and Baudelaire. (Anyone interested might try to decide for which play of Dekker *She Knew Her Business* would have been a good alternative title.) But the cultured should not also talk of "the time-honoured bob" and "pre-marital troubles"; we intellectuals have our proper pride.

That apart, The *Polo Ground Mystery* is a good story of one bullet, two wounds, two shots, and one dead man and three pistols before the end. The method is guessable, but not the murderer. It is really a maze, and the characters are not merely automata. Mr. Forsythe tells us one very important fact — modern smokeless powder doesn't blacken the skin, and leaves no sign of scorching. We shan't be able so easily to judge distances in future.

Mr. Fletcher's *Murder in the Squire's Pew* also has a maze, with the entrance not so much in the squire's pew as in the canon's house. It is one of Mr. Fletcher's best. I still feel that seven volunteered statements are rather excessive, but they do not by themselves take us to the centre. The nearest Mr. Fletcher comes to society is an archdeacon, and he only looms.

Novelist Springs a Surprise (March 7, 1932)

Mystery in Kensington Gore, by Martin Porlock. Collins. 7s 6d
Murder of the Night Club Lady, by Anthony Abbot. Collins. 7s 6d
Mad-Doctor Merciful, by Collin Brooks. Hutchinson. 7s 6d
Moran Chambers Smiled, by E. Phillips Oppenheim. Hodder and Stoughton. 7s 6d

"Jump" is perhaps too strong a word. The fellow whom Mr. Porlock so nicely describes as "a bad reviewer of worse novels" might have used it, but let us be more accurate and say "jerk." At page 53, then, of his *Kensington*

Gore I jerked — O quite definitely! the kind of jerk which I never expected to experience any more. My jaw fell. My hand shook. My eyes started. In short, I was surprised. I hadn't — no, I certainly hadn't expected it. And I hadn't not expected it: it wasn't merely what's left when you remove the expected.

It was just a sudden dramatic bang; and I simply will not give it away. Two other even more expert opinions coincide with mine. From then on Mr. Porlock conducts a wild motor-car flight, till he brings his two fugitives into touch with a stranger who may be hostile or friendly. He keeps us on the jolliest tenterhooks about it. The stranger had something which was "either a sarcastic glance or a sympathetic smile." The hero didn't know which, nor will you. But you will know Page 53 all right.

Mr. Abbot scatters extra murders generously after killing his *Night Club Lady*. She was anything but nice; but the book solves one serious difficulty — what to do with your corpse if you are on the twenty-third floor and need to hide it. It wouldn't work on the third. The whole place had been thoroughly examined by the police, when suddenly one lady went down dead and from nowhere there turned up the corpse of another. This is an admirable example of what I call the "not-expected." It maintains that state of being to the end.

Mad-Doctor Merciful is souls and substitution and diabolic possession. Mr. Brooks delays perhaps a little too long over atmospheres and descriptions and arguments (very good arguments; a really intelligent discussion). Personally, I like a short, clear hypothesis, and then plenty of devils. But the hypothesis here is well maintained. Dr. Merciful is experimenting in order to recover a soul exiled from its body, and the risks he runs are considerable. But I could have done with being a little more frightened.

Mr. Oppenheim's thrills are always stately; he, like Milton, sees "gorgeous Tragedy come sweeping by." Moran Chambers— a man; not, as I thought at first, a block of flats— smiled in the dock at his enemy. But afterwards he took his revenge —financially; stocks whizz up and shares crash down. However, no one is really bad at heart, and Moran hands over a hundred thousand in the end to make everything square. Mr. Oppenheim always seems as if he really knew what it was like to have a hundred thousand. Pounds, not dollars.

The Case of the Misleading Cover (March 22, 1932)

Murder in the Dentist's Chair, by Molly Thynne. Hutchinson. 7s 6d
The Death Film, by P. R. Shore. Methuen. 7s 6d
The Bird Cage, by Eimar O'Duffy. Geoffrey Bles. 7s 6d

It is probably the result of those dreadful sex novels against which we have had many warnings lately that the dust-cover of Miss Thynne's book is misleading. It contains an agreeable young lady poised high and help-less; her right hand is concealed, and as I couldn't bear the thought that she would be murdered I hoped it held a kris or a yataghan, and that she would stab the dentist when he was bending over her, because he had black-mailed her grandmother while in the same chair, with a nurse as accom-plice. The grandmother would occupy the nurse in the next room, and the girl, being a member of the C. I. D., would arrange for the nurse to be hanged.

Miss Thynne, however, went back on her cover, and killed a "fat, old, dyed, painted and powdered" woman in the chair, and then killed a Rus-sian dancer on a doorstep. She has a chess-playing amateur detective, who deserves to be known with the Frenches and the Fortunes, an old Greek, Dr. Constantine, whom once before I met and instantly suspected. The advantage of age is that it rules out love. Miss Thynne admits the Soviet, but she is so good that it can be forgiven.

Just as dope can be forgiven to Mr. Shore, the cover of whose *Death Film* has a much less attractive young lady — but already dead, which makes a difference — and a perfectly horrible man. It consists of detection, and more detection, and then some, and it was all needed. Straight inves-tigation of crooked involution can hardly be better done. The attendants at the cinema are a joy, and the victim and the murderer are alike better dead. But I am not quite sure that the detective ought not to have sat down.

Mr. Turner's cover is just Death laughing — a disagreeable idea. Death ought to go about his work with a respectful, apologetic air; after all, he will have to come to us one day. "Death must have laughed" (a) because the boxer had just toppled over and died in the midst of triumph, (b) because he had been poisoned yet he'd eaten nothing and his clothing was harmless, (c) because everyone who had good reason didn't. This also is detection — a pattern of palpitations.

The Bird Cage is not bad, but the best thing in it is Mr. O'Duffy's explanations that counterfeiters, bankers, and governments all do the same thing, which is called respectively counterfeiting, extension of credit, and inflation. This, and a sardonic execution, reconciled me to the "sense of some embodied evil" when otherwise.... The wretched creature only wanted his own way.

More Fatality in Fiction (April 27, 1932)

Murder in the Zoo, by Babette Hughes. Benn. 7s 6d
Bullets Bite Deep, by David Hume. Putnam. 7s 6d
The End of Mr. Davidson, by Oliver Stonor. Heinemann. 7s 6d

The Zoo is "the animal laboratory maintained by the psychology department" in Earl College. It might almost as well be the philosophical laboratory maintained by the culture department. For the professor who solves the murder of a brother-professor has a scope of reference to which I hardly remember a rival; in one lyrical sentence he includes Seneca, Pliny, Plato, St. Gregory, St. Augustine, Erasmus, Darius, Vincentius Opsopoeus, Villon, and Li Po. He agrees with Li Po against Chuang-Tzu. He quotes Corneille, Oscar Wilde and Arno Holz; also Groucho Marx. I understand that in life Groucho Marx is real. But in this book he is the last straw of unreality that breaks the back of the camel of credulity.

Miss Hughes's error is in giving all this culture to a single mind. The other characters don't recognise Li Po when they hear him. If she would condescend to make culture seem natural to the mind and a little more necessary to the plot, her next book really would be delightful. For the five minutes of the murder here are admirably concealed, and the invention of the story is as charming as the realism of American university life is— entrancing. But Groucho and Li Po....

Bullets Bite Deep is very jolly. In a Warwickshire wood an American gangster is found dead; then another. There are a retired colonel and two retired maiden and Victorian ladies and a retired rum-runner, and an inspector who will not, I hope, retire until Mr. David Hume has written a dozen more books about him, avoiding in those a slight tendency to stress the characteristics of his company, which is quite unnecessary. His balance and swiftness and humour will do the work quite well. It is a pleasant fact that his first chapter is doubly interesting when the last has been read.

The End of Mr. Davidson is neither murder nor detection. But its climax is death, and it is the first sketch for a classic. If its pattern were directly controlled by an intense poetic passion it would be a classic. Mr. Davidson lives through his last twenty-four hours, dies, and is buried; about him in separate interspersed incidents his family and acquaintances live their own lives and reflect his. His climax is the moment of death, yet his climax rather is every moment, for in every moment he is lonely, active, and mortal. It is a perfectly simple book, with the simplicity of pure style.

Crime and Detection in Fiction (June 2, 1932)

Murder in the Basement, by Anthony Berkeley. Hodder and Stoughton. 7s 6d

Gigins Court, by Bruce Graeme. Hutchinson. 7s 6d

Which of Them? by Peter Black. Benn. 7s 6d

Mr. Berkeley has one virtue at least which makes his books unique among murder stories; he has invented an investigator who is sometimes wrong. Not wrong during the pursuit and accidentally, but wrong at the end and completely. Roger Sheringham's deductions and truth are often contrapuntal; they play games with each other, and these games give to his and Mr. Berkeley's work a beautiful freshness. In the end the pea of the criminal is sometimes under a completely different thimble. How rare this is! I would not have the others— Hanaud, Poirot, French, Lord Peter, and the rest — different, but Roger Sheringham is different indeed.

It is always disturbing to find a corpse under the cellar floor, especially one of your unidentifiable corpses. Of late years the process of identifying a corpse has been brought to a high pitch of perfection. There is still room for a novel which should deal successfully with a completely unidentified corpse: one could, I suppose, catch a criminal without catching the corpse? Alternatively, one might catch the criminal red-handed and yet never find out whose the hands were: could an unidentified murderer be hanged? But these are dreams. The victim and the murderer are both characters in the novel ... and the book ends with Sheringham one up on the police. Mr. Berkeley's ingenuity will put that right in another book as ingenious, subtle and entertaining as this.

Mr. Graeme raises the possibility of man being urged to crime just that he might experience the repressed satisfaction of suffering arrest. Without (I hope) being over-Puritan, it seems to me that to kill a man merely that one might enjoy being arrested for it would be almost immoral. But here again there are obvious opportunities which Mr. Graeme has only partly explored. His criminal assists the police to catch himself. It should be done with a lighter touch; a thing which is possible has to be made convincing.

The people in Gigins Court are arranged round a problem, the definition of which is the main theme of the book. What, we are to ask, was the crime? The criminal answers. The book is, perhaps, more amusing than it was meant to be, but (granted the main theme) it is a coherent piece of work, and it has a nice non-moral girl in it. The nice moral girl is less attractive. *Which of Them?* abandons humanity: that is to say, it abandons style. Otherwise it is ingenious and unexpected. If the characters could be called A, B, C, etc., and not allowed to speak it would be a good book. But what can one think of a lady who says: "I was beside myself. Usually I'm not like that in the least."

What Makes a Good "Thriller"? (July 5, 1932)

The Division Bell Mystery, by Ellen Wilkinson. Harrap. 7s 6d
The Theatre Crime, by Fred Andreas. Bles. 7s 6d
Murder at the Moorings, by Miles Burton. Collins. 7s 6d
The Casual Murderer, by Hulbert Footner. Collins. 7s 6d

Background in a story is always a distinction, often an accident, but not necessarily a merit. Miss Wilkinson's background is the House of Commons, but it would not noticeably be a background except for one thing — the doubt which she delicately renews in us whether the House is a reality or a shadow-show.

When the Division Bell rang an American millionaire was shot. He had been dining with the Home Secretary and the Home Secretary's Parliamentary Private Secretary, the chief Permanent official, the Prime Minister, an English financial aristocrat, and other odds and ends of politics and police. The marionettes of government and murder mingle in a dance punctuated by Big Ben. But the real mystery of the division bell is why does it ring? Has it anything to do with actuality, or is it merely a shrill noise in the void. Miss Wilkinson suggests rather faintly that the bell does mean something. But it's a bothering background.

The Theatre Crime is German and earnest. An unknown intruder is hiding in the mazes of a great theatre and a watchman is killed. But the love affairs of the producer — and of the producer's first love, the leading lady — occupy some space. A mad professor stamps in and out at intervals; he also is in love with the leading lady. Her husband, however, leads her way from them both. A curious pathos lumbers through the book. Love of a woman breaks a heart and it is mended; love of the theatre breaks another, and it isn't. And that kind of sentence echoes through the background of the dark theatrical maze.

There is no background, but an efficient foreground, to Mr. Burton's *Murder at the Moorings.* Its chief fault is an obscure poison; its chief virtue is that it cancels nearly all one's guesses as quickly as it raises them. Mr. Burton is on the edge of being very good indeed. His characters begin to move; they promise humanity soon. But his working is a little obvious — one sees the click coming.

With Mr. Footner this is impossible, because (so far as I can see) any click may happen at any moment. His murderers pop in and his victims pop off, and Mme. Storey pops round, and the whole thing is clearly incredible and therefore in its clear insanity fascinating. All three stories in *The Casual Murderer* are extravaganzas of crime; they are not for serious students unless those students are out on a bank holiday rag. And a New York rag at that.

Thrills for the Holidays (July 18, 1932)

Tiger Standish, by Sydney Horler. John Long. 7s 6d
The Mystery of the Monkey-Gland Cocktail, by Roger East. Putnam. 7s 6d
The Cast to Death, by Nigel Orde-Powlett. Benn. 7s 6d
Chinese Red, by Gilbert Collins. Bles. 7s 6d

With the greatest respect I wish to "dare" Mr. Horler. Tiger Standish was aristocratic (the son of a peer), athletic (a champion footballer), attractively ugly, with an endearing grin (three women loved him — a housemaid, an actress, and the heroine), chivalrous (he strangled two villains), tender-hearted (he had a pet cat), full of laughter (he teased his enemies with jokes— and was humorously affectionate to his personal servant), and of course true and pure and gallant and the rest.

Will Mr. Horler, for the sake of making Mr. Standish human, give him just one nasty, mean little failing? Not a brave, bright folly, but a stupid, spasmodic sin? Couldn't he steal from blind beggars or over-eat himself? His dare-devil grin said, "If you don't like me, to hell with you." Now if he could only be made to feel that seriously, how much more thrilling he would become!

Mr. East's country Superintendent, on the other hand, without any particular virtues, is the exciting centre of a real story. *The Mystery of the Monkey-Gland Cocktail* maintains a surprisingly high level of interest throughout, with the right little twist at the end. Mr. East has a new trick to introduce his murderer; he is familiar to us throughout, yet at the end that familiarity is strange. If the gods are kind, Mr. East may be a great gain to us all one day. *The Cast to Death*, Mr. Orde-Powlett's first detective novel, also promises even better things than itself presently. The business man who does a perfectly silly thing in pushing papers under a locked door, in order to bring another business man under suspicion, is exactly the kind of cockeyed imbecile whom we all know. Mr. Orde-Powlett keeps the murderer a little too clear of the trouble; the attentive eye discerns him or her in the clear distance and watches suspiciously. But the exact point at which she or he should be placed is always a difficult problem; it requires a practiced judgment of temperature.

Mr. Orde-Powlett's was too low; I felt the chill and guessed. The ingenuity of the crime is very high. The detective is named Anthony: why are so many sleuths and makers of sleuths named Anthony? Can St. Anthony, who finds our lost things for us, be the patron saint of detectives?

Chinese Red is Chinese red. A little more torture would have made it a more thrilling book; it misses excitement. But it has local colour, and perplexing events, and a nasty half-breed. Only Mr. Collins ought not just to have shot him; "something lingering with melted lead or boiling oil in it" was wanted. Humanitarian feelings are misplaced in the China of fiction.

Sensation for Holiday Readers (July 28, 1932)

The Greek Coffin Mystery, by Ellery Queen. Gollancz. 7s 6d
I, the Criminal, by David Sharp. Benn. 7s 6d
Murder in the Cellar, by Louise Eppley and Rebecca Gayton. Grayson and
    Grayson. 7s 6d

The year has five months to go, but it can't do better than *The Greek Coffin Mystery*. It may do as well; the goodness of Providence is infinite. But there can't be a better opening than one body in a coffin, and there can't be a more unexpected ending than — than this one. An austerer taste than my own — pure classic is your best wear, and I admit to a dreadful romantic streak — confirms this judgment. Mr. Queen has managed to be not merely satisfactory, but surprising; to have an unexpected criminal, too, after 230 pages, is "a bloomin' miracle." The pages are full pages, too, with four separate solutions. There is too much culture ("La Fontaine, Terence, Coleridge ... Temple of Apollo ... Chilo of Thales " ... all in two sentences. You know.) and too heavy humour and a girl whom Mr. Queen may horribly imagine to be a lady. But if his verbal style lacks something occasionally, his spiritual style is perfect. This is as nearly the perfect detective novel as has hitherto been achieved by man.

Mr. Sharp is one of those delicate minds who find pleasure in mocking what they enjoy. Professor Fielding, the philologist, has been involved in several murders; this time it is a burglary, which leads on to darker things, and a burglary of a rare edition of Ben Jonson. On the whole, English detective-writers do their culture better than American, because they have less, or because they don't feel that it matters so much. The professor would never get La Fontaine and Chilo into the same paragraph. But he achieves the exquisite seriousness with which culture can enjoy its dilemmas; he achieves reality by becoming unreal.

I, the Criminal does not "thrill" us, but its very lack of pretence makes us free of something better than thrills; it introduces us to the spiritual reason of thrills. I feel as if Mr. Sharp has explained the universe by accident in writing an amusing, happy, and reckless book. *Murder in the Cellar* is exactly the opposite. It is told by an imaginary woman, who is a very womanly woman, so much so that I am not clear whether the detective was actually unpleasant or only unpleasant in her eyes. He suspected her husband, who had been shooting with the corpse in the cellar and had then vanished. There are a number of false clues, notes, pistols, faces at windows, but the chief interest is the curious vibration, as of an untrained feminine mind, which informs it with realism as the trained mind of Mr. Sharp's philologist informs his. The confusion of clues is jolly; the innocent confusion of the heart is very nearly moving. But that may be the guile of the two feminine authors.

Three Holiday "Thrillers" (August 23, 1932)

Spectral Evidence, by Robert Hare. Hurst and Blackett. 7s 6d
Murder Could Not Kill, by Gregory Baxter. Benn. 7s 6d
Six Lines, by N. A. Temple-Ellis. Hodder and Stoughton. 7s 6d

Both Mr. Baxter and Mr. Hare have a perfectly good idea of thrills, only they lose their thrills because they must tell us so much. Mr. Hare in *Spectral Evidence* has hit on a good idea; an artist thinks he sees the ghost of his nephew, and follows this up, when the nephew is known to be dead, by crystal-gazing; he is himself in process of being poisoned by the "somewhat unpleasant sister" (thus the blurb) of a rather unpleasant young man who fades into suicide "off." And about half way through the book Mr. Hare pulls himself together and gets on with the job, only losing ground here and there when the detecting doctor wanted "to take her in his arms."

Mr. Baxter also has his right sequences of thrills. The murderer's clawing hand with its length of white arm, sticking out of a rushing car, on page two, raises high hopes of a similar rush throughout. The material is all there — a curious will, a lost suspect, dozens of attempted murders, and a grand act of vengeance in a theatre. But the hero is himself so often amazed that it is impossible for us to be so; he is there to be amazed, and we could so easily take it for granted that he was.

Mr. Temple Ellis has thrown us *Six Lines* to amuse us for the time being. He retains his usual quickness of movement and invention of detail. But he has this time picked up a casual lot of words which, though they do not delay his action, do not themselves excite us. And without exciting words, there is not and cannot be any excitement in crime.

"Thrillers" and Horrors (October 7, 1932)

Rope to Spare, by Philip MacDonald. Collins. 7s 6d
Lobelia Grove, by Anthony Rolls. Geoffrey Bles. 7s 6d
Cottage Sinister, by Q. Patrick. Longmans. 7s 6d
The Eternal Moment, by G. B. H. Logan. Stanley Paul. 7s 6d

If Mr. MacDonald had been a poet, what a poet he would have been! The Nineties and Swinburne wouldn't have been in it for sheer gusto of horror and invention of creeps! He sits, like the Borgia (the traditional Borgia; no doubt the real man was a healthy Eton-and-Oxford fellow, but let us keep one of our myths) on an exalted throne and distils the venomous macabre. And in *Rope to Spare* he jolly well does. Even Mr. Gethryn is subdued to likeableness. The anonymous letters, the curious behaviour of the man without legs, the body without a face falling into the hall, the moving rope and the stretched rope, claustrophobia (a perfectly unnecessary extra touch), and one final item of delicately imagined invention — that Mr. MacDonald was once was an intimate friend of Caligula's. But fortunately he survived to give us another example of that extreme and creepy crime which he — almost alone —creates today.

Against Mr. MacDonald, Mr. Rolls (who is another disguised writer "in a different field of literature": what Bacon-Shakespeare-de Vere problems we are leaving to posterity!) is a gay pierrot. He is rather a pierrot, for it is not so much the quite attractive corpse as the garden city suburb which makes his book more delightful than Lobelia Grove itself. There we all are — all of us who do not live in Bloomsbury — posturing and prancing and pushing. It is true Mr. Rolls falls back on a confession, but even that can be excused in view of the paper which Mr. Chickworth read to the Literary Society on "The Beauties of Shakespeare, IV: Beauties of Differentiation." Many and many a distinguished critic has said, in effect, no more than Mr. Chickworth, and much less delightfully.

Cottage Sinister is a good try. It opens well with the death of two ladies' maids on a visit to their mother's country cottage. Ladies' maids are so rarely murdered, especially at tea. It has a neat, though unconvincing, explanation. But it gets rather bothered about love — mother and other — and it appears to treat seriously the notion that a girl about to make a good marriage might poison off her family one by one in order not to hamper her husband's career. It seems, somehow, such an extreme method; is moving to London really so useless?

The Eternal Moment is altogether too human and red-ripe. The hero — yes, really, hero — is badly jilted, and seems to think he has been badly treated. He kills his substitute — for that and other reasons. The killing is excusable, but his sense of his own injury is not. And someone said his love was like "charity." It was — the wrong kind of charity.

Thrillers and Detective Stories (December 13, 1932)

Murder at the College, by Victor L. Whitechurch. Collins. 7s 6d
The By-Pass Murder, by David Frome. Longmans. 7s 6d
Trunk Call, by J. Jefferson Farjeon. Collins. 7s 6d
A Hundred Mysteries for Armchair Detectives, by J. C. Cannell. John Long.
   2s 6d

Mr. Whitechurch, in a very proper preface, points out the distinction between the "thriller" and the detective story. The one, as he says, thrills: the other detects. His own reader is invited to join with his policeman in the game of hunting out the criminal. The difficulty is that the reader, not being confronted with the nuisance of having to make an arrest, can afford to suspect with a lighter heart and a freer mind.

As there are only two people to suspect he will suspect right. No writer ever makes enough allowance for the way he does his work. Mr. Whitechurch stabs a member of a Consultative Diocesan Committee in Exbridge. He casts suspicions on the porter, but the careful way he does it is fatal. And so throughout. Every clear-minded honest follower of the true path down clues of matches, ciphers, shoe laces, and postcards will enjoy Mr. Whitechurch.

Mr. Frome is an engaging writer who in *The By-Pass Murder* is well worth reading either way. Inspector Bull and his civilian friend Pinkerton should be among the most famous of our detectives. His simple maxim, "If it isn't one thing it must be something else," delights the philosophic reader because it is native to Bull, us, and the universe. Such things are what your philosophic reader desires, as the arrest in the shadow of St.

Andrews by the Wardrobe at the end of a swift and complex tale are what your straight reader desires.

Mr. Farjeon is thrills—straight thrills. An author (who makes two thousand a year) shuts up his flat and goes to Torquay. He there hears someone in a telephone box, ask for his own number, and begin a conversation. This excellent opening demands something finer (stylistically) than Mr. Farjeon gives us. He is a little coy — about love — and conscious— about fights. He has a trapdoor and much rushing about, but I cannot feel that he is bloody-minded, not at heart. The straight thrill is the most difficult thing in literature (outside Milton).

The *Hundred Mysteries* vary. Some are so easy as to be almost silly; some are too vague in their facts; some have too wild solutions. But there are some good ones, and the book might be a useful thing for a party which can't play bridge and doesn't like talk. It should be given to the prize-winner.

"Thrillers" Tragic and Comic (December 21, 1932)

Murder by Formula, by J. H. Wallis. Jarrold. 7s 6d
When Rogues Fall Out, by R. Austin Freeman. Hodder and Stoughton. &s 6d
Death of a Star, by G. D. H. and M. Cole. Collins. 7s 6d
Ben Sees It Through, by J. Jefferson Farjeon. Collins. 7s 6d

In *Murder by Formula*— the formula refers to the pattern of the proper detective story, not to the method of killing — the American Inspector asks every one of his suspects "What is your attitude towards death?" This suggested that we were beginning the yet unwritten philosophical detection by which a man's guilt is conclusively proved by his beliefs and disbeliefs. It could be done: Mr. Chesterton has played with it; Miss Sayers has feinted at it; Father Knox subtly suggests that Anglicans are slightly more liable to murder than ... others, let me say. Mr. Wallis abandoned this unconquerable shade for ordinary clues. His formula (which consists of the usual rules) needs one more item — no incident without its logical bearing on the crime. Orphic mysteries in an apartment building are delightful, though I could have done with more Orphism, but they have no necessity. And the creation of necessity is a sign of greatness in art. Things must happen so. But Mr. Wallis's charming little poem at the end is justified. He gets busy; he keeps busy; he scatters suspicion — there is a sculptor with green eyes and a widow who burns her late husband's belongings, and a district attorney who takes the widow up a high, high tower. The widow seems meant for illegal or legal death, but she escapes. The book shapes well, but Mr. Wallis will do much better.

Dr. Thorndyke — who wouldn't read Dr. Thorndyke? *When Rogues Fall Out* has the science and inventions to which we are used: the good old "Hyd cum Creta" as Thorndyke incomprehensibly remarks. This is the good old "Hyd cum Creta," and if Hyd is the villain, he isn't; we know him from the beginning. But the stately ingenuity pursues its way, with a scuffle at the end rather less dignified than usual. There is a charming arrangement by which one takes photographs through the keyhole of the other end of locked rooms, also a fraud which is no fraud. Also, of course, a body, only Mr. Freeman regards a body as subservient to cameras, chemicals, and calculations.

Mr. and Mrs. Cole have hit on the wrong criminal; there ought to be another chapter proving it was the sculptor, after all. On their account of the discovery of the head in the taxi, I don't see how it could have been, but that is where better brains than one's own come in. The *Death of a Star* cries for another stellar twist. We were all — for, of course, one guesses — so right that we ought to have been wrong. The head, the body in the empty house, the plant on the burglar, the neurotic taximan, should have had one final jeer. But the book has all the virtues, logic, complexity, lucidity, and economy: it is unfair to want ironic bitterness as well. Irony, like necessity and philosophy, belongs to genius.

Mr. Farjeon is as economical as a pantomime; in fact *Ben Sees It Through* is a pantomime. It has all the knockabout glory of the perfectly irrational: death, a nasty old man, a sinister Spaniard, Columbine as a true English girl, Harlequin (Ben the tramp) climbing up through chimneys, a chase through London, and so on. Mr. Farjeon at his best attracts with perfect nonsense and thrills with fairy tales. He does it here.

Crime and Detection in Fiction (January 3, 1933)

Poison in Jest, by J. D. Carr. Hamish Hamilton. 7s 6d
The Secret of the Dark Room, by Robert J. Casey. Mathews and Marrot. 7s 6d
The Body Behind the Bar, by C. F. Gregg. Methuen. 7s 6d
The Water Witch, by Russell Thorndike. Thornton Butterworth. 7s 6d

After Christmas, the night "in which no evil thing may walk abroad," we can let loose our fancies with renewed zest after such evil things as still walk abroad. It was Mr. Carr who wrote *It Walks by Night*, and he therefore has some right to come first after Christmas, for this was one of the finest books of this kind ever done. It appears that he has written three more, of which *Poison in Jest* is the third. Why are we not told these things? As soon as the evil things of the financial month are over I shall buy the other two; a nuisance, but inevitable. For Mr. Carr has that rare, curious, and beautiful talent that touches a book with real horror; the infrequent exquisite thrill moves one's heart, and one is near to having bad dreams.

Poison in Jest does not depend on its murders— it has enough of them —but on the kind of murder; it does not even depend on the white marble hand that runs across the sill or the fading beauty drunk by the fire or the fall of the arsenic-tin; no, it depends on Mr. Carr's imagination of murder. He knows more about its soul than almost any other writer, and (to do him justice) as much about its ingenuities and complexities as any. His new detective leaves me a little doubtful: I had rather have the French Bencolin who followed the thing that walked by night.

The secret of *The Secret of the Dark Room* runs a risk of being neglected for the sheer joy of its language. Never has American been more enjoyable. "If (so and so), I'm Abraham Lincoln's horse," "he was just another dumb cluck." Dumb cluck! This natural material Mr. Casey has worked up with a pretty humour of his own into a pretty and ingenious mystery of the developer who was shot while alone in the dark room of the Atlantic News Reel Co., and the politician alone in his hotel room. It is as jolly as Mr. Carr is horrid, busy, ingenious, and exciting. And, in its own phrase, "until I know the answer, I wouldn't give a hoot in a whirlwind for all the coconuts in Tahiti."

But the answer to *The Body Behind the Bar* one ought, by a process of exhaustion, to have guessed. It reminds me of that fine (but unwritten) tale in which the detective finds all the clues and deductions leading to himself, has to arrest himself, and give evidence against himself. And probably hang himself. (But it needn't remind you of that because you have not dreamed of it.) Inspector Higgins finds himself in as many difficult positions— physical and mental — as ever. Mr. Gregg even gets away with a secret passage and a criminal Boss. It is a good healthy crime.

Mr. Thorndike's *The Water Witch* has in its activity a sense of Dickens and wholesome love and redemption. The mystery — of raps on panels and strange efforts at killing on the Medway — is revealed fairly early; much of the book is taken up with a noble and militant clergyman. (Incidentally, a priest surely is only forbidden to reveal what he hears in confession, and not any secret.) The evil things here are — most of them — good at heart; those that are not are shot. This also satisfies an unappeased longing.

Crime in Fiction (January 31, 1933)

The Murder of Caroline Bundy, by Alice Campbell. Collins. 7s 6d
Death on my Left, by Philip MacDonald. Collins. 7s 6d
The Thousandth Case, by George Dilnot. Bles 7s 6d
The Channel Million, by Gilbert Collins. Bles. 7s 6d

Certainly our sensations remain unspoiled by literary murders. The multiplication of death does not harden us to it; if it did there would be a moral case against this kind of novel, for our natural selfishness does not risk any such hardening. As it is, we may read in peace, becoming, it seems, more tender to the hapless life of man. That peace is even enlarged by the goodness of the book and broken by its badness. None of these books break it.

The Murder of Caroline Bundy goes to Somerset, Glastonbury, and the tradition of the burial of the Grail, but that sacred relic does but add a colour; it is not primarily concerned, except as a pleasant variation on hidden treasure. The old woman who held seances with the unpleasant Cockney couple was found dead in a ditch, and her Russian niece is accused. There is no doubt of the murderer, but every kind of doubt whether Miss Campbell will convincingly save her heroine and destroy her villains. She does so with neat twists at all the critical moments. I do not quite believe her, but the timely ingenuity of her movement compels admiration. The Russian niece handicaps her too much; one can believe in the Grail but not in these fierce and splendid barbarians.

There is no doubt of Mr. MacDonald's murderer either, but he is betrayed by his psychology. *Death on my Left*— it is the boxing term, and a great title — produces a number of suspects and knocks them down without much troubling Mr. Gethryn. He, by unparalleled neatness, hits on the only man left, who was the favourite suspect all the time. I suspect Mr. MacDonald of being a little tired of murders and wanting to write another book like his superb "Patrol," only full of more rxtreme spiritual pain. In fact, I suspect Mr. MacDonald of wanting to write a terrifying and intolerable and perhaps great book; and I hope he will. Meanwhile this, if not one of his best, is full of the MacDonald quality. Can one say more?

The Thousandth Case is one of those few books which really convey the ordinary working-day toil of Scotland Yard. It is a sound story — a dead blackmailer, an old criminal in flight, a detective-sergeant in a flooding cellar, a mass attack on a dangerous house, and again an un-particularly-concealed murderer. But the staid and perilous home life of the Yard is the great thing; the thrills are quiet yet as convincing as those of any business house. Think of those, and admire Mr. Dilnot.

The Channel Million is without a murder, but it is a most extraordinarily complicated pattern. The million was sunk by a submarine during the war, and it is a question of salvage by — yes, that is the question. There is a yacht and divers and German and English investigators; and two nice girls; and a wireless operator who is an Englishman who pretends to be an Englishman who was compelled to be a German who.... It works out, and it has a really attractive rich and Jewish yacht-owner, as innocent as the heroine, only in a different way. But why was his wife so stern with him?

Murder and Mystery (February 13, 1933)

The Wailing Rock Murders, by Clifford Orr. Cassell. 7s 6d
Murder of an Initiate, by Milton M. Propper. Faber and Faber. 7s 6d
Dead Man's Alibi, by Leonard Hollingworth. John Murray. 7s 6d
Who Killed Alfred Snowe? by J. S. Fletcher. Harrap. 7s 6d

Too good a book may undo a writer as well as too bad a one; and what Mr. Orr is going to do for his next climax I cannot think. *The Wailing Rock Murders* is all about the murder of a young woman in a fantastic house on the Maine coast, and the runnings to-and-fro of the old detective who tells the story. Personally, I hate young women being murdered; murderers they may be, but not victims. There is something positive, original, and violent about young women which prevents them from being credible victims. It outrages nature. And it is quite impossible to believe (even in a literary sense) in Mr. Orr's plot. But his plot is only a prelude to his climax, and if his style could be a little more sinister he would have got even his plot over. It is a little too palpably dramatic. Style can only afford to be dramatic about profound spiritual crises, if then; about physical thrills it has to be nonchalant.

Mr. Propper is a little deceitful — not by his fault but by modern America's. *Murder of an Initiate,* with its jacket and its opening, raises the dreams of high occult schools and the secret counsels of the restored Way of Union with supernatural things. Blue robes, and yellow, and white; the bound postulants; the altar, the candles, the sacred wine — disappointment can have no sharper edge than the discovery that the postulants are called "pledges," and the purpose of ritual is an initiation into a college fraternity. It is, of course, an admirable variant on locked libraries, with its dying pledgee, and Mr. Propper works the whole thing through in what it is his own fault if we call "slickness." He has a fine capacity for raising suspect on suspect's head; he never falters or delays, he turns the final key in the last page as swiftly and surely as that on the first. But really, an altar! an altar!

Dead Man's Alibi is good and delightful. Mr. Hollingworth approaches murder, as he approaches life, with an exquisite mingling of scepticism, sympathy, and belief. The man who has lost his memory and may have committed a murder, the three possible corpses, the actual women, the medical psychologist and his hypnotism, the final triumphant defeat of everyone by a being who does not exist — all go to make a novel whose centre is intellectual sensation and only its circumference physical. Mr. Hollingworth is in the running for the really great murder novel. Mr. Fletcher — is Mr. Fletcher. His admirers will admire him, and others have no need to interfere.

Murder and Mystery (April 7, 1933)

The Hog's Back Mystery, by F. W. Crofts. Hodder and Stoughton. 7s 6d
The Two Undertakers, by Francis Beeding. Hodder and Stoughton. 7s 6d
Death in the Forest, by Neville Brand. The Bodley Head. 7s 6d
Under London, by Val Gielgud and Holt Marvell. Rich and Cowan. 7s 6d

Day by day it becomes more difficult to know what any adjective in a review exactly means. It is no longer sufficient to look in your heart and write; it is necessary to be sure that your heart's vocabulary has the same definitions as those of your fellows, that when you say "tolerable" you ought not to be saying "terrific," and when you say "good" you ought not to say "gigantic." What then is the use of remarking that Mr. Crofts has a neatness of pattern, an economy of means, an ordered development, a final resolution, pleasing to the instructed reader? None. Very well; let us sin strongly.

The Hog's Back Mystery is in the highest flight of detective aeroplanes (comparison with birds must be left for poetry); its engines are unnoticeable; the Surrey Landscape in which the doctor, the nurse, and the unfortunate visitor are destroyed reveals the highest genius for murder-gardening. The delight it will give in the crudest reader is miraculous; to the sensitive it is catastrophic. In fact, it is a very good book, one of Mr. Crofts's best, and that is to say one of our best. And that is true enough.

Ridiculously enough, one could use superlatives much more easily about Mr. Beeding and Mr. Brand, because their books are of a different kind. Mr. Beeding, proceeding numerically and internationally from the *Seven Sleepers* to the *Two Undertakers*, and leaving himself only the "One Little Indian Boy" to finish with, still defeats international villains by car and revolver and beautiful women. I quite adore Mr. Beeding, as I adore chocolates; nobody else soothes us so well with sensation, in so pleasant and direct a style of both plot and diction. But after the One Little Indian, perhaps he will go back to direct murder; Death walks in Eastrepps again by this time, surely? and not in sinister cigarette factories in Germany.

Death in the Forest is rather loveable than adorable. The forest is Central American, where bands of Indians and revolutionaries fight, and a half-mad priest leads a war to end war (there, anyhow), and English visitors fall now into one captivity and now into another. Mr. Brand possesses distinction of style; there is a bartender and a girl whose adventures are more than merely adventurous, and the ruined city with the serpent image does more than provide a setting — it lifts what might so easily be nothing into a sense of something, a climax and a conclusion.

Under London appeases and oppresses one a little with a sense of the heart of good hearts there are in the world. There is a barmaid and a mate and a baronet and an ex-officer and even a bright young thing who all have good hearts at bottom — some nearer the bottom than others. A sea captain and a Chinaman have either no heart or no goodness, but as the captain is stabbed rather early and the Chinaman is detained, the good hearts are left to run about and avoid the police, with whom their less good behaviour has involved them. They manage this, but they lack both climax and conclusion.

Murder, Mystery, and Madmen (April 26, 1933)

R. I. P., by Philip MacDonald. Collins. 7s 6d
The Kennel Murder Case, by S. S. Van Dine. Cassell. 7s 6d
The Man Who Shook the Earth, by Sydney Horler. Hutchinson. 7s 6d
Slade Scores Again, by Richard Essex. Herbert Jenkins. 7s 6d

R. I. P. — as if Mr. MacDonald would ever let anyone r.i.p. — is about a group of people in a lonely house, circled and hunted by a madman who holds three of that group responsible for the killing of seven hundred men in the war and id determined to kill them in judgment. But who is the madman? Is he one of that group, dressed and polished, or is he not? And they go about, and death goes among them through the night.

Mr. MacDonald never seems to like any of his people. Most authors have a tenderness, a lonely tenderness, for at least one character; their voices soften over him, their touch becomes gentle. If they kill their beloved, they do it with tears; her or his "balmy breath almost persuades justice to break her sword." But Mr. MacDonald is an inhuman angel of death. He slays as if it were dreadfully pleasant. His murders in themselves are no more horrible than any others, but in his books he seems to torment creation; it is why his living people are unbearable and yet it is intolerable to feel them being slain. Still, 40 pages before he told me I knew who the madman was, and at that moment a ray of the real sun broke upon his goblin world. But what goblins! What a marvellous capacity for shaking one's soul up!

The Kennel Murder Case begins with a corpse in a dressing-gown and outdoor shoes, holding a revolver, seated in a chair in a bedroom, locked and with the key gone, a bullet in its head and a death-wound from a dagger inflicted hours earlier. The dagger is found under the chair-cushion on which the corpse is sitting. Mr. Van Dine's plot, as is only right in a book of such culture, approaches its solution through the Austrian Imperial house, just as Miss Sayers in Have His Carcase involved the Tsardom. "Superfluous Kings" are now but the messengers of crime. Mr. Van Dine is Mr. Ellery Queen's only rival; no lesser mind can choose between those kings of New York. It is intellectual detection of the first rank.

Mr. Horler works in broader sweeps; his success is as well known as his name. The Man Who Shook the Earth contains three long stories, and the first startled me by ending just when I thought it had begun to indulge itself with destruction through a Ray. I suspect Mr. Horler of being, like myself, incapable of cruelty, and of liking his fellows. The last story has a pretty turn, though in the highest social circles I hear that African drugs are no longer served; if they were, this is what ought to happen. But, by Mr. Horler's leave, priests must not speculate whether murder is justified; if they do, they go on to become unsound on the Creed and then presently "they don't believe in Adam and Eve," and it leads to letters in the Church Times. Slade Scores Again is a self-contained part of an immense serial. Its chief use is that it provides seven wicked financiers to dislike, but also it makes one very uneasy about Scotland Yard, so that one sleeps no better than before. Mr. Essex might, perhaps, check a tendency to dilate on emotions and incidents. It was, I think, Bacon who said of the science of crime, "Facts, facts, and again facts."

V

June 5, 1933–
February 15, 1935

This chapter covers the period from June 1933 (there were no reviews in May 1933) to the end of Williams's reviewing for the daily paper. There are seventy-four books reviewed, but in most cases four or five (rather than three or four) per column, so that the reviews in general are shorter than in previous years. Among the anomalies are a review of Dashiell Hammett, *The Thin Man*, a column containing reviews of *Redhead* by John Creasey, who is modern, and of Maurice Leblanc (Arsène Lupin), a voice from before World War I. Williams reviews J. C. Masterman (*An Oxford Tragedy*), Rhode, Crofts, Sax Rohmer, Ellery Queen, H. C. Bailey, Leonard Gribble, E. Phillips Oppenheim (twice), Christopher St. John Sprigg, Taffrail, Carroll John Daly, Sydney Horler, Dorothy Sayers, S. S. Van Dine, R. C. Woodthorpe (twice), Talbot Mundy, Val Gielgud, C. Daly King, R. A. J. Walling, Henry Wade, Ronald Knox, Agatha Christie, Harry Stephen Keeler, the Coles, and Creasey.

Aside from the juxtaposition of Creasey and Leblanc (with C. St. John Sprigg), H. C. Bailey and Fu-Manchu, Harry Stephen Keeler and R. A. J. Walling, there were two days for which one envies the reviewer, in particular. On January 17, 1934, Williams reviewed Dorothy L. Sayers, *The Nine Tailors*, S. S. Van Dine, *The Dragon Murder Case*, and Agatha Christie, *Murder on the Orient Express*— not to mention R. C. Woodthorpe, *A Dagger in Fleet Street*. On March 15, 1934, he reviewed Val Gielgud, *Murder at Broadcasting House*, Freeman Wills Crofts, *The 12:30 from Croydon*, and C. Daly King, *Obelists En Route*. His very last review covered Agatha Christie, *Three Act Tragedy*, and Woodthorpe's *Death in a Little Town*.

Woodthorpe is the one author in particular that Williams's reviews suggest should be revived.

Tales of Mystery (June 5, 1933)

An Oxford Tragedy, by J. C. Masterman. Gollancz. 7s 6d
There Sits Death, by Paul McGuire. Skeffington. 7s 6d
Traitor's Rock, by G. E. Rochester. Eldon Press. 7s 6d
Murder at Pringlehurst, by James Corbett. Herbert Jenkins. 7s 6d

The first, third, and fourth of these books are not, strictly speaking, tales of murder. But the statement has a different reason in each case. *An Oxford Tragedy* is not murder because the clues and the killing are of less interest than the dons and the dinners. The perplexity of the Vice-President and Senior Tutor of St. Thomas's, who tells the story, is a development of a moment which we all know. That is the moment in which we all, habituated to our jobs, find ourselves confronted with something quite other than our jobs, and in which we are acutely bothered by some quite disproportionate minor question.

When the classical tutor is found shot in the Dean's rooms, the Vice-President at the telephone is in an agony of indecision whether he ought to ring up the police or the doctor first. As the man is dead it might seem not very much to matter, but it is always the immaterial that matters so frightfully. This pathetic and universal figure moves through the book; he is the book; and at the end, in a small epilogue, he is still wondering and worrying about life. There are a few phrases which seem a little to crude for him, but that is a small matter. Against him the Austrian professor who solves the problem — largely psychologically — is a mass of efficient thought. But Mr. Masterman offers us not so much the problem of how to explain a death as of how to explain a life.

There Sits Death is surprisingly good; it has a new invention of method in it. The place is an hotel; the first corpse is financial; and the story twists upon itself in a very intelligent and gratifying manner. There is an attractive hag and an unattractive beauty, an attractive inspector and an unattractive inquiry agent; and the balance between the suspects and the truth is delicately maintained. *Traitor's Rock* is about a man and a girl and a boy on an island of the Hebrides, who fuel German submarines during the war — until they are stopped. It is quite unconvincing, but it is unconvincing in the right way. There is something very near imagination in it.

I had high hopes of a peculiar pleasure at the opening of *Murder at*

Pringlehurst: "Major Pritchard … glanced over the hedge and saw the dead body in the field. Now he was not used to dead bodies, so…." But it doesn't keep to the standard of that sublime truthfulness; it becomes merely impossible to follow, in diction and detection.

Murder and Mystery (June 14, 1933)

The American Gun Mystery, by Ellery Queen. Gollancz. 7s 6d
The Claverton Mystery, by John Rhode. Collins. 7s 6d
Harlequin of Death, by Sydney Horler. John Long. 7s 6d
Gun Justice, by Jackson Cole. Cassell. 3s 6d
Many Mysteries, by E. P. Oppenheim. Rich and Cowan. 7s 6d

Detection is not as simple as Mr. Queen in his *American Gun Mystery* pretends. He challenges his reader — some 20 pages from the end — to name the criminal, asserting that he has provided all the clues. A reader, however, does not read to discover the criminal, but to discover the book, the peculiar and particular satisfaction which that one book, and no other in the world, may be able to afford him.

He desires a complete pleasure of which accurate deduction is but a part. I do not deny that the more exactly he follows the deduction the more he may enjoy. But I deny flatly Mr. Queen's "You don't know? Ah, but really you should!" One "should" nothing of the sort. On behalf of all the poor, ignorant, illogical readers, I assert that Mr. Queen is in danger of denying style by overstressing one element in style. We have a right to leave the explanation to him, though he has no right (as he agrees) to keep the clues from us; for we demand from him not a solution but a story, not facts but fiction. Certainly, hardly anyone else comes so near uniting both. Mr. Queen is not merely one of the best; he is all but the best of detective authors. The setting, the fullness, and the complexity of his problems are beyond praise. To kill a horseman in a rodeo show before 20,000 people, and then to repeat the murder, to lose the revolver so madly and find it so simply (though I did guess that), to discover always some trick at the end — these are the marks of virtue.

The Claverton Mystery is Mr. Rhode's best story to date, in spite of the fact that the lost capsule obviously had something to do with it; otherwise, why — in a book — was it lost? In life, for a hundred reasons; but in a book only because it helps the book, and is therefore a true or false clue. Mr. Rhode has modulated his people much nearer to humanity than he usually cares to do.

Mr. Horler's *Harlequin of Death* is certainly the best — I dare not say of all his books but of the dozen or so I have read — but I admit that his world is normally as remote from me as the world of Mr. Cole's *Gun Justice*. The sons of peers and the sheriffs of Rio Grande are united by the thrills of revolvers, by bad men, and by fair women. The Wild West and the Wild West End alike execute judgment, and the villains in each case are of Latin extraction.

In *Many Mysteries* Mr. Oppenheim has collected stories by 28 distinguished writers. They are not all mysteries, or all of equal value. But there are over nine hundred pages, with a surprising proportion of interest and excellence, and enough different kinds of thrills to amuse every kind of reader.

Red Herrings in Detective Stories (July 26, 1933)

The Fate of Jane McKenzie, by N. B. Mavity. Collins. 7s 6d
Death Comes at Night, by Kenneth Ingram. Philip Allen. 7s 6d
Dover-Ostend, by Taffrail. Hodder and Stoughton. 7s 6d
Dr. Greenfingers, by Edward Woodward. John Long. 7s 6d

Red herrings have not received the attention they need and deserve. In the book which I plan there will be a chapter on them as fish, followed by one on their place as fable. The second part will be on the R. H. in experience: psychological R.H.s which distract us from the trials of our predestined fish, and in fiction, the R. H. voluntary and involuntary. Many a good novel has gone off after an involuntary R. H., and lost itself for ever, sometimes by the author's fault, sometimes by the reader's. Of the last the Satan in *Paradise Lost* is the greatest example; we have turned the fishiness into a superb Red Herring that has led us far from the centre of the poem.

In murders at least, the Red Herring must be voluntary. The danger and delight of such stories is (1) the immediate awareness of the form, and the choice of the author in the form; (2) the vitality of the characters by whom the form exists. The Red Herring is the concreteness of the abstract quality of all suspects. Miss Mavity's suspects have fishiness, but hardly vitality. When her Red Herring pipes we follow, but we do not dance. In *The Fate of Jane McKenzie,* Jane disappeared during an eclipse of the sun, and, besides the police, Peter Piper, the journalist, searched both places and persons.

Jane's family are unattractive enough to make one wish for more of them, even the heroine. Nowadays to be a beautiful girl is no proof of innocence. Beauty, fortunately, in this respect is no longer truth. There is an admirable young garage assistant who has taken a correspondence course in detection, and of whom we shall, I hope, see much more. But the end is a trifle disappointing, largely because Miss Mavity leans heavily on a humanity which her style has not, up to then, aroused in us. She demands that we shall feel a model as a man. This, however, is measuring her book by the high standards it undoubtedly deserves.

Death Comes at Night has its red herrings partly orientalised; and when the Orient enters, one is inclined to accuse the author of laziness. Professor Bursan dies, and a rationalist and an intuitionalist work on the mystery. Besides the third sex, so to speak, meaning the police, Humanity again closes the book. It is not quite as good as Mr. Ingram's *The Steep Steps*, but that was very good indeed; and so is all the rationalism here. Intelligence can work on the trail and the non-Orient herrings are credible, though unlikely.

Taffrail and Mr. Woodward have little room for herrings, not even in the *Dover-Ostend* route. The pirate leader in that book, who was once a gentleman, is still sufficiently so to use a Red Herring when he wants the abducted hero to think the abducted heroine is being thrashed in the next room. But this is unfair to the reader: herrings were never meant to save us from our few informal pleasures. *Dr. Greenfingers* is the old, old trail of the fomenter of revolutions from Ireland to Chile with dark prisons and incredible resources. I will believe anything on a publisher's jacket except that this theme will "cause me to think deeply." One cannot think about a herring whose very smell has long disappeared.

Mysteries (September 8, 1933)

The Second Case of Mr. Paul Savoy, by Jackson Gregory. Hodder and
　　Stoughton. 7s 6d
The Bank Vault Mystery, by Louis F. Booth. Hutchinson. 7s 6d
The Lonely Inn Mystery, by Leo Grex. Hutchinson. 7s 6d
The Amateur Murderer, by Carroll J. Daly. Hutchinson. 7s 6d
The Menace, by Sydney Horler. Collins. 7s 6d

Mr. Gregory's *The Second Case of Mr. Paul Savoy* is a brilliant business. He begins with a naked, undistinguished body in a taxi (San Francisco), and he then allows Mr. Savoy to conjecture about it. Conjectures, plus luck, lead to the identity. There are one or two doubtful points—the corpse may have been concealed in a cloak, but how were its legs and feet covered? But that Mr. Gregory should here have tackled the fundamental problem of murder — the corpse of the utterly unknown — so persuasively and successfully rouses high hopes for Mr. Savoy, whose only fault is a tendency to gaze mystically into a sapphire ring and get into withdrawn states. He doesn't need them.

Both *The Bank Vault Mystery* and *The Lonely Inn Mystery* are good solid pieces of work. Mr. Booth, in the *Bank Vault*, suffers from the unreasonableness of the human mind. When one, of six people, in a vault must have stolen the money, why is the reader disappointed that one of them has? The longing for excitement, no doubt, which is so characteristic of our day. Excitement Mr. Booth does not supply; but he has one exquisite surprise and a pattern in which every piece is both adequately formed and prettily coloured.

Mr. Grex hides his murderer till the end. But as he was one of the many million people outside the Lonely Inn who might have stabbed one of the five within, this is reasonable. Given his plot, the murderer is very good; he was near, he was possible, but he was unnoticeable. As a choice of criminals he was exactly right, except that he could not, I think, be reasonably guessed. But for myself I can spare that virtue.

Mr. Daly is guns, pure and impure. His Race Williams pops in and out of windows and rooms and trains and cars, and shoots and knocks out his opponents, all to the music of a chatty style which makes *The Amateur Murderer* one of the most pleasant books of its kind. It has a puzzle, but its fusillades drown thought.

Mr. Horler is a little hard on his readers. I cannot believe that more details about the "bizarre abominations of the flesh" to which he attractively alludes would not send his sales rocketing still higher. It is the "bizarre" that attracts; abominations in themselves are so dull. "The Menace" is a blackmailer who menaces London society; in the end he is, rather immorally, given the best of both worlds, on a medical plea which we shall, I hope, all put forward on Judgment Day. And I hope, more fervently, that the heavenly courts will allow it.

Murder and Mystery (December 23, 1933)

Redhead, by John Creasey. Hurst and Blackett. 7s 6d
The Double Smile, by Maurice Leblanc. Skeffington. 7s 6d
Death Comes to Fanshawe, by James Corbett. Jenkins. 7s 6d

The Wrong Murder Mystery, by Charles Barry. Hurst and Blackett. 7s 6d
Fatality in Fleet Street, by C. St. John Sprigg. Eldon Press. 7s 6d

There are, I understand, tests for the tipsy, but few could be as strin-
gent as a sentence in Mr. Creasey's *Redhead*: "He pushed the dead still
body of the bloodless-faced post-mistress behind the counter." It is a curious fact that those sibilants and explosives seem to intoxicate the mind. I
was sober when I reached them; when I went farther I frankly reeled. I went
back to look at the post-mistress to make sure she was there. She was. But
she was not credible to that part of the brain that takes in sounds; nothing quite like those sounds, surely, could happen!

The other part, the purely intellectual, which is out for simple meaning, had been violently shaken by a preceding sentence: "Redhead, the
man who made the crime-steeped blood of American gangsterdom freeze
in the veins of the racketeers." This is not mere jesting at Mr. Creasey; it
is a serious business. Both those sentences distract the attention; it becomes
giddy as with the fumes of alcohol. The exaggeration, physical in "the
bloodless-faced post-mistress," mental in "the crime-steeped blood,"
destroys excitement.

M. Arsène Lupin, who returns in *The Double Smile*, pervades one in
something the same manner. But the cheery topsy-turvydom of Lupin,
with his quite impossible capacities and resources, produces the effect of
a half-tipsy jocundity; if I decline to share it I feel M. Leblanc will only
say: "Well, you're not the man I took you for," and then how ashamed I
should be! So with him I have to pretend to be tipsy!

In Mr. Corbett's *Death Comes to Fanshawe* I must pause to say, without betraying a secret, that it is a sober fact that *Fanshawe* has nothing to
do with the book — not in the remotest way. The explanation on the last
page says so. It therefore corresponds with the statement on the first: "She
was not the outstanding type that attracts attention. Her loveliness was
flawless.... The outline of form was matchless...." Yet in her day even the
lesser beauty of Helen of Troy attracted some note. Between the first and
last pages is a whirl of excitement that stupefies without exhilarating.

Mr. Barry and Mr. Sprigg remain sober, and so do I. They can therefore excite and please, and they do. Mr. Barry mingles with *The Wrong
Murder Mystery* an intellectual problem: ought doctors to be legally allowed
to put to painless death those suffering from incurable disease? and then
pursues his well-concealed murderer through bacilli and burglaries. Perhaps he hardly gives the pro-murder people sufficient emotional show,
and he converts their champion to anti-murder in the end; this is not so
much from unfairness as from a slight woodenness in the talk. But if the

characters are marionettes the show is agreeable, and the heads of the audience remain clear.

Fatality in Fleet Street is very good indeed. It is full of very pleasant writing and a steadily maintained ingenuity, until — literally — the last page. The corpse is a great newspaper proprietor; the suspects are the staff. Anyone who, by accident, sees Russians on a few pages, need not worry; they are only part of the general unity of exhilaration. It is, after all, living unity we demand in a book. Mr. Sprigg never outrages his book with impossibilities of thought or diction.

Murder and Mystery (December 29, 1933)

Mr. Fortune Wonders, by H. C. Bailey. Ward Lock. 7s 6d
The Bride of Fu-Manchu, by Sax Rohmer. Cassell. 7s 6d
The Clue of the Dead Goldfish, by Victor MacClure. Harrap. 7s 6d
The Secret of Tangles, by L. R. Gribble. Harrap. 7s 6d
The Judson Murder Case, by E. A. Aldrich. Butterworth. 7s 6d

I am never quite sure whether at bottom Mr. Bailey is a wit, a moralist, or an occultist. He is a wit, obviously; a moralist, less obviously, in a certain recurrence of demand for absolute justice. *Mr. Fortune Wonders*— about his eight cases, certainly, but also at times whether his unfortunate companions of the police are achieving their full duty, which is not only the discovery but the full prevention of crime. He would have them as terrible and innocent as the bright-harnessed angels— and there his occultism comes in. He can do a murder, no doubt; but the evils he really hates are pride, hate, cruelty. He seems sometimes almost to imagine spiritual sin, and his cherubic Reginald Fortune thrusts at it like a real cherub. In five of these stories he arranges for death or life at his will. You do not like or dislike them because they are good crime, but because they are good Fortune, and because that means something like good fortune in the world. I have loved Mr. Bailey ever since, thousands of years ago, I read a short story about Jacobites and a sheriff who ate a letter; I read every book of his as soon as I can, and I hope there will be many, many more to read.

As for Mr. Sax Rohmer, there again my piety, but this time a more dutiful and less exhilarating piety, comes in. There are some few absurd books of my own which exist only because one evening, having finished one of Mr. Rohmer's, I said suddenly to myself: "I also will write a novel." It wasn't, when finished, much like any of his, but can one now seethe the mother in the kid's milk? The Mandarin Fu-Manchu doesn't seem quite as good as he used to be, for all his poisonous insects and hairless men and orchids of life and schemes of world empire, but that is because he is accompanied neither by real people nor real ideas, one of which is necessary to the successful ingenuity of the grotesque. Peace be to him! He was once a pleasure.

The other three books are more regular crime. Mr. MacClure is perhaps the most deductive; the pages of the *Dead Goldfish* are full of barred shoes and pointed shoes, garden soil and pulverised limestone. It is a pattern of circumspection; the end is with us fairly soon, but the way to the end remains complex and ingenious. Mr. Gribble's *The Secret of Tangles* is more thrilling, and gives less away before the end is reached. There is a pretty piece of personification in it, almost too good to be credible. Mr. Gribble's workmanship is always of a high standard, and the threatened love-affair here is fortunately finished — in marriage — before the book begins. *The Judson Murder Case* is American; it begins with a family quarrel, which suggests patricide. But the equable style prevents one from really hoping for that, and, therefore, the real criminal is bound to be recognised. Its complexity, however, adequately postpones its admission of this, and there is a pleasant hunting on the way.

Murder and Mystery (January 17, 1934)

The Nine Tailors, by Dorothy L. Sayers. Gollancz. 7s 6d
The Dragon Murder Case, by S. S. Van Dine. Cassell. 7s 6d
Murder on the Orient Express, by Agatha Christie. Collins. 7s 6d
A Dagger in Fleet Street, by R. C. Woodthorpe. Nicholson and Watson. 7s 6d
By Misadventure, by Alan Brock. Nicholson and Watson. 7s 6d

"The new Sayers" is not merely admirable; it is adorable. There were, in Miss Sayers's more recent books, signs that a strange element was struggling to be free. In one this element seemed like philosophy; in one like fantasy. It has now become perfectly freed itself, and become perfectly united with her other capacities. *The Nine Tailors* is consequently not a tale of murder, but an experience of life. There is a murder, and there is detection; there is Lord Peter Wimsey. The surroundings are the Fen country; church bells, with all the art of their ringing; a vicar and villagers; dykes, and the breaking of dykes, and a flood.

Laughter and pity and terror, clarity and mystery, inform all these things, and as Miss Sayers's perfect mastery moves on to its climax in the tower of the church where the refugees, admirably ordered by a mortal and immortal ritual, find shelter, the book becomes in itself a kind of judgment. The powers of earth and air denounce and encourage, and below them lies the wide sweep of waters. There is nothing supernatural — unless indeed we and our life and all our art are supernatural, as some have held. But it is the reflection of our dark and passionate life itself which those waters hold and those bells proclaim. It is a great book.

Mr. Van Dine hints at the more ordinary supernatural; the atmosphere of *The Dragon Murder Case* is full of flying dragons carrying murdered men from their lake-lairs to stranger hiding-places. Enjoyable as this is, and admirably as it is done, it has the slight disadvantage that the reader knows not merely that it cannot be true, which wouldn't matter, but that it isn't going to be true, which does. By (I do not say "on") Page 133 one should have guessed at least half the method. Mr. Van Dine, however, puts his dragons over with such sincerity that it is quite possible to miss the murder mechanism in the mythological. Philo Vance is as barbarous in the midst of culture as ever; culture does not consist of knowing a lot of unusual facts. It implies a style of intellect to which Mr. Vance is a stranger. But he is sufficiently distressed and worried here to be forgiven. It is quite one of the best Van Dine thrillers— perhaps the best.

And so of Mrs. Christie; only all different. Her *Murder on the Orient Express* takes place when that train is snowed up in Jugo-Slavia. M. Poirot has the case to himself, and has to solve it by pure mind. There are three parts: "I. The Facts, II. The Evidence, III. Poirot Thinks." This austere method, combined with the method of the crime, makes the book a piece of classic workmanship; almost unbelievable, but exquisite and wholly satisfying. The ice cracks here and there; there is one very dangerous moment connected with Oxford-street, but it just holds.

Mr. Woodthorpe's *A Dagger in Fleet Street* is great fun. He persuades us of his Fleet-street, of his murdered editor, of his horrid proprietor, and of his own kind heart. He lets off the obviously proper murderer, through sheer sympathy, and has to hale and push a substitute through the entire book, including the end. It was nice and human of him. But it was cowardly of him to do it and of me to like it. In a book so enjoyable, however, only a churl would insist on being artistically brave.

By Misadventure is a little idyll of murder. The crime does not take place till towards the end, when a badgered husband destroys his intolerable wife. She has no redeeming points, so his safety is justified. An immoral idyll, but so many idylls are. And a pleasant future to him, and to his maker!

Murder in Fairyland (February 2, 1934)

The Gallows of Chance, by E. Phillips Oppenheim. Hodder and Stoughton.
7s 6d
Marriage and Murder, by David Sharp. Benn. 7s 6d
The Orange Ray, by Maurice G. Kiddy. Hutchinson. 7s 6d
Murder at Grasmere Abbey, by Maurice B. Dix. Ward Lock. 7s 6d
The Campden Ruby Murder, by Adam Bliss. Rich and Cowan. 7s 6d

Mr. Oppenheim's *Gallows of Chance* has a plot which, of its kind, is credible and even realistic. But his language is too lofty for his story. His characters sometimes descend to dinner-jackets; his words always wear white ties. The Home Secretary, abducted and threatened with hanging unless he stops an execution, still, for all his natural agitation, "pronounces," "observes," and "declares." Even the pleasant little middle-class detective mingles his many drinks with majestic diction. The small pubs are dignified. But, subject to the drag of his diction, Mr. Oppenheim has generally had a good story to tell, and this is one of his best — ingenious, dovetailed, adequately prolonged until on the very last page the noble-hearted and noble-mouthed Englishwoman says: "I had to go to the show at Buckingham Palace, but I only stayed an hour." Could anyone but Mr. Oppenheim treat Buckingham Palace like that?

Mr. Sharp, on the other hand, has a plot that only his persuasive style can carry. Professor Fielding's incredible adventures multiply themselves. There is no professor for whom I more willingly suspend disbelief. In *Marriage and Murder* he is married by force, and he carries on, with his own engaging, learned and intelligent simplicity, a war with police and criminals at once. The book begins with that moment of universal helplessness we know so well, with the professor in a strange barber's chair, threatened with throat-cutting. The plot is fairy, but the style is real. Mr. Oppenheim's plot is real, but his style is entirely fairy.

The Orange Ray is betrayed by its title, but if the ray can be forgiven it is a straightforward thriller on the old lines—a young and innocent inventor imprisoned for a murder, malevolently released, subjected to pure and impure passion. Pure passion in art is always so much more attractive than impure that I wonder why the same thing (judging by rumour) is not true of life. But this impurity is Russian, which doubles her difficulty nowadays.

And as with rays so with drugs and detectives. Mr. Dix's *Murder at Grasmere Abbey* has an inspector who is correct only in his detection and hopelessly wrong everywhere else. He makes deadful jokes, he falls dreadfully in love — with the daughter of an Earl — and is dreadfully nervous about the Earl. An intolerable fellow! Yet Mr. Dix has the possibilities of a very pretty horrible imagination, and if he will submit to vigil and fast he could write a really nasty book. But he must not — ever — read Mr. Oppenheim, who manages the Earls of Fairyland so well.

The Campden Ruby Murder is American. It has throughout slightly staccato psychological sentences which jar the mind into sudden unbelief. But its invention is good, and the instrument of death agreeably unexpected. Mr. Bliss has perplexed his readers and justified himself.

Detective Novels (February 20, 1934)

Gallows Alley, by Anthony Skene. Stanley Paul. 7s 6d
The Mysterious Mr. Badman, by W. F. Harvey. Powling and Ness. 3s 6d
Murder in Trinidad, by John W. Vandercook. Heinemann. 7s 6d
The Red Flame of Erinpura, by Talbot Mundy. Hutchinson. 7s 6d
They Came by Night, by Seldon Truss. Jarrolds. 7s 6d

Mr. Skene's first fifty pages are (if you like) crude and violent and unbelievable. But they cause a shock of surprise; they possess imagination. The doorkeeper, who says huskily, "I got a mermaid's kiss," seems, for a moment, outside the book he exists in, and when he is killed, the book goes to pieces. It is a perfectly good thriller even so, with shootings and pursuings round drug distribution, and spasms of return towards its beginnings, as when the London killer defines Life: "When you're in it, you're in it for keeps.... That's what it is, Gallows Alley."

A natural process picked on *The Mysterious Mr. Badman* next. Could it be Bunyan? or was it only Chicago? It was Bunyan; at least it began its mystery with a secondhand copy of his *Life and Death of Mr. Badman*, which is a very terrifying book, and therefore not so popular as the *Pilgrim's Progress*. This happy thought of Mr. Harvey's illuminated his book, and the fact (which ought to be mentioned) that it is published at 3s. 6d. also lit it up. Certainly *Mr. Badman* is but a hiding place, but it is an attractive story. A little more evil would help — a little more of Bunyan.

By *Murder in Trinidad* one approaches the other hemisphere of thoroughly competent murder. Its centre is in a marsh — one of the best marshes I ever crossed, with snakes to frighten and an unusual detective to save. It gets its tropical effect without tiresome descriptions and it crosses its mysteries as neatly as its marshes, making altogether a very good book, with a very good jacket.

Chullunder Grose of *The Red Flame of Erinpura* ought to be better known than he is; so ought his author. Knowing nothing of India, I should have thought that Mr. Mundy's thrillers provided more of India than many more solemn volumes. In them, India is fascinating, strange, and alive — alive quite apart from the adventures. In Mr. Mundy's books we *are* somewhere else: we are not merely hearing of somewhere else through a loud-speaker.

They Came by Night is, of its kind, first rate. It is about a jolly little Caucasian State whose rulers germinate in England a disease that causes blindness. The English, therefore, are going blind at the rate of several hundreds a day. The Caucasians are thwarted at last by the heroism of the Secret Service. The worst villain has "eyes that spoke unuttered and unutterable things." The darling!

Many Mysteries (March 15, 1934)

12:30 from Croydon, by Freeman Wills Crofts. Hodder and Stoughton. 7s 6d
Obelists En Route, by C. Daly King. Collins. 7s 6d
Death at Broadcasting House, by Val Gielgud and Holt Marvell. Rich and Cowan. 7s 6d
The Murder of a Midget, by M. J. Freeman. Eldon. 7s 6d

A reader of Mr. Crofts's *12:30 from Croydon*, found weeping late at night, explained that she couldn't bear the nice murderer to be hanged. Even without this broad hint, I should have guessed he would be, because he is shown committing two murders, and Mr. Crofts would never let anyone off. He kills his uncle by means of a poisoned pill, and then a butler by violence, and my own tears were nearly provoked by discovering the enormous difficulty of providing a poisoned pill. He wanted money and a woman, and no woman is worth it. Mr. Crofts shows us the whole tedious business without letting it become tedious. He maintains the steady interest to the very end. In the end it becomes a question of identification: can an ordinary man, having seen another ordinary man on and off for four minutes, recognise him after ten weeks? Could you, now, identify a man whom you had spent four minutes buying chemicals from a week before Christmas?

The same feminine mind was lost in, but not defeated by, *Obelists En Route*. "Golly! what a book!" It is perhaps not quite so good as Mr. King's *Obelists at Sea*, but that was (yes!) a masterpiece; this comes close. It contains, besides a most ingenious murder on a train, intelligent satire on psychologists, a brief exposition of the Douglas credit scheme, a bearable love affair, and a complete list of the necessary clues at the end. It is one of those delightful books which manage to be completely amusing by being completely serious and vice versa. Mr. King is an American scientist: with profound admiration I can only say I wish he lectured in London.

Death at Broadcasting House and *Murder of a Midget* float at the high water mark of more direct killings. Every radio fan should read the first; every frequenter of American circuses the second. Mr. Gielgud and his partner have improved out of all knowledge. They make the surroundings of the B.B.C. an integral part of the murder and of ingenious detection, and they carry those twined threads of pleasure up to the finale over Portland-place. The end is perhaps a touch overdone; it is the only criticism. *The Murder of a Midget* is more, but not too, melodramatic. It is a good story, with living skeletons, Siamese twins, and snake charmers revolving round a nice girl and a nicer old woman. Why are old women so effective when they detect? Because there is nothing so marvelous on this earth as a really intelligent old woman. She is always so terrifyingly right. But she is rare; Mr. Freeman has caught one of her.

Murder and Mystery (May 1, 1934)

Murder at the Eclipse, by John Alexander. Sampson Low. 7s 6d
Murder — Nine and Out, by J. V. Turner. Bles. 7s 6d
Murder to Measure, by Robert Mason. Pawling and Lees. 3s 6d
Fool's Gold, by S. H. Page. Stanley Paul. 7s 6d
Smash and Grab, by Clifton Robbins. Benn. 7s 6d

Why does no peer do it? The trial of a Viscount before the House of Lords would rescue that Chamber for fifty years. The English, Mr. Alexander says in *Murder at the Eclipse*, have a national genius for pageantry. It is true; they will forgive a great deal to any person or institution that plays a part splendidly. Mr. Alexander has staged a full-dress trial of a peer by peers. Miss Sayers did the same thing in *Unnatural Death* — there is but one Miss Sayers, and hers was immortal. Mr. Alexander's is a good effort, but he is a little shy of the splendour. He writes better of an immoral fishmonger. With the fishmonger as the witness and the peer as the corpse, and a stormy eclipse as time and place, he contrives a crime which fails only because he has created the fishmonger to spoil it. This is called coincidence, but its long arm ends here in an effective criminal hand.

Murder—Nine and Out deals with the ceremonial of boxing and night-clubs. Amos Petrie, the fishing enthusiast, was a happy invention of Mr. Turner's, and he is worth a place in our mental Tussaud's of detectives. Mr. Turner lured me into a wrong suspicion; I was almost certain the Home Office pathologist had something to do with the murder of the boxing manager, and I lost touch with the vaguer criminals. But it was a fair catch. Mr. Turner was good before, and he is good again. The scene of examinations in the club after the death is even very good — it has the authentic touch of natural horror.

Murder to Measure is a curious book. It is all right and all wrong. It is a perfectly good scheme, yet so unreal is the writing that the reader feels all the characters are moving askew and looking asquint. They also are peers and millionaires, but without ceremony; an elongated shadow show. One of them begins the book by being amusing at dinner — it was a mistake.

Fool's Gold and *Smash and Grab* are at opposite points of style. Mr. Page is the shaking, shooting, rushing, rampaging style of New York, Mr. Robbins the solemn pedestrian style of London. No murder can be as blatant as the one or as bourgeois as the other. But both, either in noise or length, provide adequate entertainment.

Murder and Mystery (June 4, 1934)

Still Dead, by Ronald A. Knox. Hodder and Stoughton. 7s 6d
Death in the Quarry, by G. D. H. and M. Cole. Collins. 7s 6d
The Portcullis Room, by Valentine Williams. Hodder and Stoughton. 7s 6d
Stark Naked, by Laurence R. Bourne. Frederick Muller. 7s 6d

I want to discuss with Father Knox several statements he makes in *Still Dead*, and I hope that he will believe that I mean casuistical in its strict sense — the science which resolves cases of conscience. But if I do, I shall give away his superb conclusion. And the first decision of all the moralists of literary crime is— never reveal plots. Father Knox keeps all the laws of detection so finely, which such a keen sense of the sanctity of style (and I mean sanctity, whether Father Knox agrees or not, but I hope he agrees) that in this case betrayal would be a solecism as well as a sin. A body which appears by the roadside early on Monday morning, disappears in half an hour, and reappears in the same spot on Wednesday morning at the same time, preludes a book which maintains that steady level of mystery and lucidity throughout. On that level there are started numerous hares of intellect — heretical and orthodox, which vanish all too quickly, but keep the whole level alive, ending in the final large hare of "What is Murder?"

Where Father Knox always leaves an impression of making his novels during his theological working days, Mr. and Mrs. Cole have often appeared to be doing theirs on an economic holiday. *Death in the Quarry* is not so; it is quite their best. It is true their conclusion would be regarded by Father Knox as part of the loose morality of our modern world. But the old man who is exploded in the quarry by means of one forged and one genuine letter is the victim of a highly complex and satisfying plot. Their line-drawing is fainter than Father Knox's, and this causes their crime to appear more "chancy" than his. For his is based on a profound natural (but heretical) instinct — the belief that the laws of the universe are in favour of our own temporal wishes, whereas Mr. and Mrs. Cole leave the universe entirely out of it, and have therefore a much thinner motive. But their result is as subtly attractive and as procrastinatingly delusive; what more can be asked?

The Portcullis Room is not, I think, as good as Mr. Williams usually is. It seems to drag a little, perhaps because his corpse was the gayest person in the party; one casts a longing, lingering look behind as the foreigners, the Americans, and the Scottish, run to and fro in the castle on a remote Highland isle. With tempests. And love. Their going, and the books, is too often descriptively impeded by adverbs and adjectives. But I respect this Mr. Williams (perhaps more than I do another writer of the same name), and it is a respectful piece of work.

Stark Naked is not, or only the corpse (Male). That is completely bare and might therefore as well be clothed. It is the body with only one shoe on that produces the effect of nakedness. The fanatic who, among other oddities, disapproves of bathing-dresses is a sketch of a character which, stark-naked, would be interesting, but is at present muffled. Nevertheless, Mr. Bourne's book suggests a future competence — both in detection and in thrills.

Murder and Mystery (June 18, 1934)

The Cross-Word Mystery, by E. R. Punshon. Gollancz. 7s 6d
The Thin Man, by Dashiell Hammett. Barker. 7s 6d
Plan XVI, by Douglas G. Browne. Methuen. 7s 6d
The 3-7-9 Murder, by Grey Morton. Skeffington. 7s 6d

It has for some time been clear that detective tales must either change or cease. A few good craftsmen may go on exquisitely reproducing the more austere and ancient plots, but murders must become greater or perish. There are signs that they are becoming greater, and that they will enter on a new career of real imagination.

A few of these signs have been noticed here recently. Separately they might be accidents; together they suggest promise. There was Father Knox's *Still Dead*, with its casuistry; there was, superbly alone, Miss Sayers's *Nine Tailors*. And Mr. Punshon's *Cross-Word Puzzle* is now added to them. It holds its place chiefly by the vigour of the last chapter, not so much by the great but horrible last paragraph as by the steady sweep of energy that moves it all, especially in the wild run of the criminal across the fields.

In case this praise deters any reader, it should be said that it also has a complete plot and a definite addition to the police of literature in Inspector Mitchell and his sub-sardonic comments on life and his art. Mr. Punshon is apparently recreating the plots of Shakespeare's tragedies in modern dress. It would not take quite so many of Mr. Punshon to make a Shakespeare as of most of us.

The Thin Man entranced me by the number of its drinks. But the drinks are, at least, part of a real atmosphere; they are not, like most drinks and cigarettes in novels, utterly unrelated detail. The weak author is always traceable, like a criminal (which he is), by the number of his cigarette-ends—a cigarette cannot be smoked in two paragraphs of conversation. Mr. Hammett's murder is among a number of singularly unpleasant people in New York, who make a singularly agreeable book.

If Mr. Browne's other plans are as sheerly thrilling as *Plan XVI*, he ought to write about them. This is the theft of two liners carrying gold to America and the thrills go on to the last paragraph. The super-criminal a little alarmed me at first, but he lives bearably and dies beautifully. Both Mr. Hammett and Mr. Browne, with different capacities, might, if they have the courage of imagination, quicken the forward movement of murder. The *3-7-9 Murder*, on the other hand, would be a better book if Mr. Morton had not introduced a false rhetoric of action which merely thwarts us. Stuff about Science and Fingers and Machines and Man is dull. Up to that point, however, Mr. Morton is enjoyable except for his detective's mannerisms.

Passionate Policemen! (August 3, 1934)

Constable, Guard Thyself!, by Henry Wade. Constable. 7s 6d
Murder on the Cliff, by Clive Ryland. Grayson. 7s 6d
The Bell is Answered, by Roger East. Collins. 7s 6d

An International Affair, by Bruce Graeme. Hutchinson. 7s 6d
Death by the Mistletoe, by Angus MacVicar. Stanley Paul. 7s 6d

The police are unfortunate this time. Mr. Wade and Mr. Ryland both turn suspicious eyes on them. It is a little surprising that this does not happen more often. Have not policemen passions, as other men, and many more advantages than most? A noble terrorist tale might be written by a mad Chief Commissioner who trained Scotland Yard to crime — a tale, coldly considered, not unlike the mere facts of Europe today. But *Constable, Guard Thyself!* does not go so far, and in the end it rather retreats, since one policeman in it is hardly a policeman at all, or only in the sense that the devil, as well as Mr. Wade, can quote Scripture for his purpose.

Mr. Wade's craftsmanship is always fine. His plots are admirable, but his people have hitherto been a little icy. Here, however, is the beginning of warmth. The murdered Chief Constable, the various police suspects, even the London detective, combine to make a picture of what has before only been a diagram. The final pages achieve a remarkable thing — they convey a sense of exact justice. The victim's death and the murderer's arrest are the only spiritual solution possible. Mr. Wade has thus created and solved a double problem — emotional and technical.

The angels should have stopped Mr. Ryland making his first joke in *Murder on the Cliff*. It occurs on the first page. "'If that's not her car, I'm a ham sandwich'... It was her car. He was not a ham sandwich." The rest of the book is far better and so far as the plot is concerned a very good piece of work. I am not quite so happy about the solution; there is the slightest ham sandwich touch about it. "This," Mr. Ryland seems to say, "is going to be a joke," and "This is the way it's going to come out." Judged by the best standards it is here and there forced. But his book deserves to be judged by the best standards: his next will probably satisfy them.

I discovered Mr. East only recently, but how delightful a discovery! *The Bell is Answered*— it was rung by a lady taking a bath when alone in a house and answered by a strange young footman. The close also has, at the very end, a sudden fresh twist. There is about it a flavour of exquisite intelligence: that subtle thing which is style, which is culture, which is irony and common-sense. Mr. East is not yet at his full strength; his touch is here and there uncertain. But he is certain of our increasing attention, and he has great possibilities. He is civilised.

Mr. Graeme's *International Affair* is about Spain and Mr. MacVicar's *Death by the Mistletoe* about Scotland. If Mr. Graeme would only *write*, and if there were not so many people wandering in and out, and if his plot did not wander, his would be a very good book. And, if Mr. MacVicar's were not so solemn about pre-Druidic secret cults and hypnotism and young love and sacrifice, so might his.

Murder and Mystery (January 23, 1935)

As They Rise, by E. Laurie Long. Ward, Lock. 7s 6d
Ten Hours, by Harry Stephen Keeler. Ward, Lock. 7s 6d
The Diamond Ransom Murders, by Nellie Child. Collins. 7s 6d
The Five Suspects, by R. A. J. Walling. Hodder and Stoughton. 7s 6d

"You can buy fish as they rise, which means, 'You're in the Good Lord's hands and must take what he sends you.'" So Mr. Long explains his title; his noble unsophisticated hero of a tugmaster tries, very sensibly, to take things "as they rise." These four novels are of very different kinds. Mr. Long's own is of the simple herring type, caught in our own seas, suitable for a breakfast cooked by a young bride for a clean-stomached husband. It tastes more of the sea and tugs and harbour-life than of crime, though it has a murder and a "sinister plot" and an illegitimate child. The child grows up into the tugmaster, helps to avenge the murder, thwarts his unknown and not wholly agreeable father, and also thwarts the rather vague international plot, by which it is intended that France shall declare war on us when she finds rifles stamped "Fabrique en Angleterre" used against her in Alsace. Even a French Government might think twice over such evidence; it is clear our breakfast herring has an awkward bone.

For lunch, perhaps, Mr. Keeler would be best as a filleted plaice. *Ten Hours* has something of the unendingness of plaice; it is filling, but unsurprising. This is not from lack of the intention to surprise. An American town is threatened with destruction from aeroplanes by a mad Mexican. Three tramps are arrested as spies, and court-martialled. The trial takes all night, for each tells a fantastic tale to account for his presence, which is in turn disproved. The detail is lengthy, and the language even lengthier. When one reads that the three tramps gazed at each other, "wordlessly, speechlessly," one realises how much more than is necessary one is reading in order to find out what happened.

To compare Miss Child's book with sardines sounds "low." But never was sardine-tin fuller of meat than *Diamond Ransom Murders* of facts, complications and murders. Her first book, *Murder Comes Home*, was all but a miracle. This all but overbalances into a maze. Her people are, I think, less interesting here, and her plot less near perfection. It begins with kidnappings, and then it becomes like a diagram composed of printed words. Every now and then Miss Child stops to pop a bit of human nature (or what she means for human nature) on our plates, like the bread and butter with the sardines. I do not believe in her sardines for a moment, but her name on any label means that there are the goods.

And then Mr. Walling's *Five Suspects* for our grilled sole at dinner on the verandah over the river. It is in a river that the corpse of his country lawyer is found, and in a country town that the clear intelligent action goes on. The suspicion is admirably distributed, and the murderer neatly hidden; I had almost forgotten all about him. Mr. Walling serves his fish with the exact distinction of an English parlour-maid. The book is agreeable, we read carefully, and end contentedly.

Murder and Mystery (February 15, 1935)

Three Act Tragedy, by Agatha Christie. Collins. 7s 6d
Death in a Little Town, by R. C. Woodthorpe. Nicholson and Watson. 7s 6d
The Ragged Robin Murders, by Guy Morton. Skeffington. 7s 6d
Frame Up, by Collin Brooks. Hutchinson. 7s 6d
The Crooked Sign, by Ben Bolt. Ward, Lock. 7s 6d
Dames Errant, by George Norsworthy. Sampson Low. 7s 6d

This time Mrs. Christie sets an almost superhuman problem, which she herself only just manages to solve. I am not sure that, even so, her solution does not strain her own tact with the reader. A harmless clergyman dies after drinking one of a number of cocktails; any cocktail might have been drunk by any guest. If the clergyman was meant, how? If he was not meant, why *anyone*? It is a peach of a beginning; the equal peach of the ending is beyond all reach but Mrs. Christie's.

Mr. Woodthorpe is in the same class. His *Death in a Little Town* is a simple killing this time — a man knocked on the head with a spade — but he surrounds the deed with an ingenuity of pleasant small-town life as well as death. He has humanity as well as mortality. He gives one, therefore, a sense of more leisure than Mrs. Christie; he has comedy and murder and something as near sadness as the nature of his book allows. In fact, he can write.

Which Mr. Morton cannot; or does not, in *The Ragged Robin Murders*. "Pegs," says his great detective," are admirable, but only when used in their correct juxtaposition." To talk like that is a failing; it would be a fault if Mr. Morton's idea were less good. But he has had a good idea, and the outcome is tolerable, so long as one eye is shut to the language and the tricks.

Mr. Brooks dedicates *Frame Up* to the people who read shockers for fun. If I may accept a bit of the dedication I shall be pleased. It is about Cabinet Ministers who are got into compromising situations—as a step towards revolution; and it goes ahead with great vivacity and alacrity, and winds up with a body in a bath and then in a refrigerator, and cyanide of potassium and everything jolly. A knock-about thriller, as it were, and a good knock-about too.

Dames Errant is about wicked armament magnates, whom, if I must choose, I prefer to the Nazis of *The Crooked Sign*, for the sake both of honesty and art. The first is Monte Carlo and such places, and love, and solemn honour; the second is London and Germany, and love, and facetious honour, and a formula. The armament maker is killed, and the formula comes to England. So we ought to be all right in the next war.

VI

THE WAYS OF THE GOLDEN AGE AND THE WAYS OUT

In Chapter I, we noted some of the ways in which these reviews suggest what Williams was about in his own writing. In the course of my remarks there, it was impossible to exclude all consideration of what the detective fiction writers were about, but we concentrated on Williams. What the detective fiction writers were about (and how they got there and what happened thereafter) is our topic here in Chapter VI, though it will not be possible, nor would it be right, for us to exclude from this chapter all consideration of Williams's peculiar and idiosyncratic views. Nevertheless, as Chapter I was principally on Williams, this Chapter VI is principally on the Golden Age and golden trap — what brought it about, what it was like, and particularly what happened after. What were (if any) the ways out of the trap, and what implications did they have for the nature of the Golden Age? First, though briefly, how did this Golden Age of detective fiction in the years between the wars come to be?

Histories of detective fiction have tended to pass swiftly from Poe to Conan Doyle to the Golden Age, generally defined as the years from 1920 to 1939, almost exactly the interwar period. Agatha Christie's *The Mysterious Affair at Styles* (1922) would be almost the beginning (or at least one of the beginnings) of the Golden Age. Now, as one of the distinguishing marks of the Golden Age is the country house novel, and as *The Mysterious Affair at Styles* is precisely a country house novel, it would at first glance seem reasonable to credit Dame Agatha with setting the style with *Styles*. And yet, E. C. Bentley's *Trent's Last Case* (1912), a kind of early exercise in intertextuality, where the author is using detective fiction conventions to comment on the genre itself, is also a country house mystery. It would appear therefore that the country house convention was familiar — even accepted — a decade before *Styles*, unless, of course, it was actually introduced by Bentley. In any case, its precise origins, though interesting and important, are not so important here as the fact that it was already on board when the Golden Age novelists began their flood of novels. Nor are they so important as the fact that Dame Agatha is a highly relevant part of our inquiry. Indeed, if we were constructing a table of contents for a book on the subject, we might reasonably summarize the history of detective fiction (in English, at least) as running (these titles are only my suggestions) from *Reason and Altered States: De Quincey and Poe 1820–1850*, through *Confused Paradigms (I): Detectives and Shilling Shockers 1850–1887*, to *The Age of Sherlock Holmes 1887–1917*, to *The Golden Age of the Limited-Access Mystery: Agatha Christie (and Others) 1919–1939*, through *Confused Paradigms (II): Mysticism, Romance, Detective Stories, and Thrillers 1945– 1976* (the date, by the way, of Agatha Christie's death), to whatever name we choose for the past quarter-century. Two of these five periods include, and are in fact marked, even formed, by Agatha Christie. Not perhaps to the overwhelming degree that Conan Doyle marked and formed the period from 1887 to 1914, or Poe in the 1840s (and the genre as a whole), but still considerably, and over a longer period *in propria persona* (from 1922 to 1976). And it may be worth noting that Sir Arthur and Dame Agatha received their honors (whatever the official reason given) as detective story writers. It is hard to think of another example.

On the other hand — this not so relevant to Dame Agatha — one of the conventions most directly traceable to the Golden Age writers was that of the gilded amateur. Sherlock Holmes was a consulting private detective, as was Dupin, and most of the Holmesian competitors in the Victorian and Edwardian years. So was Hércule Poirot (and, in an odd way, Dame Agatha's other series sleuth, Miss Marple). Some of the Golden Age detectives were reporters or newspaper correspondents (Philip MacDonald's Anthony Gethryn), some were investigative agents (insurance in the case of R. A. J. Walling's Philip Tolefree), some were forensic scientists (Dr. Thorndyke), at least one was a medical man attached to Scotland Yard (H. C. Bailey's Reggie Fortune), and quite a number were policemen (including the gilded professional, Ngaio Marsh's Roderick Alleyne), but among the best-known were Lord Peter Wimsey, Albert Campion, and (in New York) Philo Vance, the gilded amateurs. Amateurs or agents or other, all of them — including Dupin and Holmes— had in common that they were a kind of deputy dramatist, or stage-manager, making things come out right. Oddly, the most straightforward and obvious exemplar of this, among the Golden Age writers, is Agatha Christie's apparently supernatural Mr. Harley Quin in *The Mysterious Mr. Quin* (1930), to which we shall return.

The sensation fiction of the 1860s that came between Poe and Doyle gave rise to several classic detective stories, but its truer heirs were in the kind of fiction exemplified in more recent times by Ian Fleming's James Bond stories, in earlier times by Edgar Wallace and William Le Queux and Sapper and Sydney Horler. They fell into Williams's purview in the pages of the *Westminster Gazette & News-Chronicle*, but it was not, mostly, what the Golden Age was about. Colin Watson has argued in his *Snobbery With Violence* that what the Golden Age and its attendant "little world of Mayhem Parva" were about was cozy reassurance that God was in His heaven and all was right — or could be made right — with the world: "The detective did not stray beyond questions of time-tables, poison analyses, shoe prints, and so on ... [he] was far too occupied in serving justice to indulge in the morbid philosophizing that constant encounters with corpses might have induced in less dedicated operators. Most important of all, the inevitable solving of the crime, the identification and rendering harmless of the murderer at the very end of the book, somehow had the effect of canceling out the death or deaths which had gone before" (p. 173). How did the shilling shocker turn into *this*?

The answer lies, of course, in the popularity of Sherlock Holmes. What Conan Doyle did was, essentially, superimpose the figure of Sherlock, the Avenging Angel of Reason, on the shilling shocker, or, as Professor Thomas Shippey might say, to calque the angelic presence, the god, the archetype, onto the world of Victorian London and the shocker pattern. That the angelic presence was an Angel of Reason gives us the key to what happened after. One way to turn that key is to look at a representative selection of Dame Agatha's stories in the fourth age to see their links with Conan Doyle in the third. (I choose her short stories because in this, in particular, she has based her early work on Conan Doyle.) The stories in *Poirot Investigates* (1925) may be taken as representative.

The first story, "The Adventure of the 'Western Star,'" begins with Poirot and his Watson, Captain Hastings, looking out the window of their lodgings— a scene comparable to that at the beginning for example, of Conan Doyle's "The Adventure of the Beryl Coronet" (1892). The third, "The Adventure of the Cheap Flat," is, in a way, "The Red-Headed League" (1890) turned inside out, but still with a criminal conspiracy taking advantage of an ingenuous citizen, and the detective, through superior knowledge and superior reasoning, setting things more or less right though leaving the citizens in question a little up in the air. The second and fourth, "The Tragedy at Marston Manor" and "The Mystery of Hunter's Lodge," suggest that Dame Agatha took Holmes's "Watson, the fair sex is your department" as satirical, if Hastings is indeed based on Watson (as he is). For the rest, the ending to "The Mystery of Hunter's Lodge" is pure "Five Orange Pips," but the ending to "Marston Manor" is more original, and shows a rare instance where Dame Agatha infuses a little of herself into a Poirot story. (She infuses a lot more of herself into Miss Marple, and into the stories of Mr. Harley Quin.)

The fifth story, "The Million Dollar Bond Robbery," and the seventh, "The Jewel Robbery at the Grand Metropolitan," are both exercises in Holmesian logic transferred to Hércule Poirot — and it is unlikely to be accidental that the jewel robbery has merely been transferred from the Cosmopolitan of "The Blue Carbuncle" (1892) to the Metropolitan. The sixth story, "The Adventure of the Egyptian Tomb," is not especially indebted to Holmes (partly because the archaeological *milieu* is very strong and overwhelms any Holmesian similarities — Dame Agatha's husband was the distinguished archaeologist, Sir Max Mallowan). The eighth, "The Kidnapped Prime Minister," has some links to "His Last Bow" (1917) and is Holmesian in its logic, though of course it lacks the elegiac tone of Doyle's story, and David Lloyd George has replaced the Marquess of Salisbury as the model for a Prime Minister. The ninth, "The Disappearance of Mr. Davenheim," is "The Man with the Twisted Lip" (1891) turned inside out, but the logic is still Holmesian.

The tenth, "The Adventure of the Italian Nobleman," is more modern and perhaps somewhat less Holmesian, and — in my view — not very good. There are some resemblances to some of the Holmes stories; we are, as he was, in a world of international intrigue and blackmail (as in "The Second Stain" [1904], or "The Naval Treaty" [1893], or "Charles Augustus Milverton" [1904]), though the Italians (the spurious Count Foscatini and the government emissary Ascanio) are very much stage Italians. But then, Hércule Poirot is very much a stage Belgian. The eleventh story is "The Case of the Missing Will" (upon which Dorothy L. Sayers may have provided a kind of inter-textual commentary in her slightly later — and significantly better — "The Fascinating Problem of Uncle Meleager's Will"). The story is unremarkable, but the aura is, in fact, the aura of Holmes in the countryside, and the problem of the young woman making her own way is a problem with which we are well acquainted in Doyle's pages.

The twelfth story, "The Veiled Lady," would at first glance seem to recall Conan Doyle's "The Adventure of the Veiled Lodger," but Doyle's story, though apparently taking place in 1896, appeared in 1927, two years after *Poirot Investigates*. The focal point of the deduction — a well-dressed lady, claiming to be of noble blood, was wearing cheap shoes— is perhaps more likely to appear in Dame Agatha than in Sir Arthur, but the deduction is similar in kind. The thirteenth story is "The Lost Mine," which uses the *milieu* of "The Man With the Twisted Lip" (1891) under a title suggesting Conan Doyle's interest in far-off lands (as in "The Boscombe Valley Mystery" [1891] or *A Study in Scarlet* [1887] or *The Valley of Fear* [1915]— to name just a few). The fourteenth, Poirot telling the story of his one failure, is, in pattern, a straightforward Christiean version of Doyle's "The Yellow Face" (1893), even to the injunction (*Poirot Investigates*, Bantam new pb ed 1970, p. 198) "... if you think at any time that I am growing conceited .. *Eh bien*, my friend, you shall say to me, 'chocolate box.' Is it agreed?"— which so closely parallels Holmes's "Watson ... if it should ever strike you that I am getting a little over-confident in my powers ... kindly whisper 'Norbury' in my ear, and I shall be infinitely obliged to you." Of course, in Doyle's story this is the last paragraph, but Christie pushes on, and when Hastings almost immediately says 'Chocolate box,' Poirot does not hear him, or affects not to hear him.

Because Dame Agatha is, with Poirot, so clearly representative of the first wave of the Golden Age country house writers, despite her youth, it is sometimes overlooked that she is an innovator (if indeed someone so imitative and derivative can be considered an innovator) in other areas falling within that same Golden Age. First, there is Miss Marple based, I believe, on Dorothy L. Sayers's earlier but subsidiary Miss Climpson. Here is Williams on the first Miss Marple novel (*The Murder at the Vicarage*, 1930, reviewed October 14, 1930): "As for Mrs. Christie, she ought to be a village scandal-monger — she does it so well. But then (on the same grounds), she ought to be a vicar, and a vicar's young wife, and several other things. I rather hoped it was going to be a theological crime — we have too few of them — but the murdered churchwarden was a retired colonel not even interested in prophecy. The police are baffled; so is the vicar, and it takes the intelligence of a kind of worldly Mother Brown (if Mr. Chesterton will excuse me) to solve the mystery."

Indeed, Williams has caught it — Miss Marple, like many detectives, but most particularly like Father Brown (and, in a different context, like the Stage Manager in Wilder's *Our Town*), is the deputy dramatist, setting things right, in a kind of supernatural context. Not so markedly supernatural here as it is sometimes later in Miss Marple's career, but the comparison with Father Brown (for all that the word "worldly" is inserted) hints at a recognition that Miss Marple links this world with the judgments of God. It is unfortunate, perhaps, that Williams was not assigned to review Dame Agatha's *The Mysterious Mr. Quin* (1930). Here is the conclusion to the eleventh Harley Quin story, "The Man from the Sea" (Berkley pb ed, 1984, p. 221):

> "And you have seen ... that there is such a thing as remorse — the desire to make amends — at all costs to make amends."
> "Yes, but death came too soon."
> "Death!" There was contempt in Mr. Quin's voice. "You believe in a life after death, do you not? And who are you to say that the same wishes, the same desires, might not operate in that other life? If the desire is strong enough, a messenger may be found." His voice trailed away.
> Mr. Satterthwaite got up, trembling a little. "I must get back to the hotel," he said. "If you are going that way —"
> But Mr. Quin shook his head. "No," he said, "I shall go back the way I came."
> When Mr. Satterthwaite looked back over his shoulder, he saw his friend walking toward the edge of the cliff.

And, finally, here in the ending of the final Mr. Quin story, "Harlequin's Lane" (pp. 244-45). At a country-house *fête*, Mr. Quin has danced Harlequin to Mrs. Denman's (Madame Kharsanova's) Columbine. After the dance, her old friend Sergei Oranoff tells Mr. Satterthwaite that all her life she danced Columbine so well because, always, "she danced with a dream Harlequin — a man who was not really there. It was Harlequin himself, she said, who came to dance with her" (p. 243). But she has already (p. 242) told Mr. Satterthwaite (the perennial onlooker whose presence draws Mr. Quin — or is it the other way 'round?), "Always one looks for one thing — the lover, the perfect, the eternal lover. It is the music of Harlequin one hears. No lover ever satisfies one, for all lovers are mortal. And Harlequin is only a myth, an invisible presence — unless— ... unless— his name is— Death." So we are not surprised by the ending. Mr. Satterthwaite sees Kharsanova go down Harlequin Lane with Harlequin. The others see her alone. Satterthwaite finds Mr. Quin beside him.

> "It was *you*," he said. "It was *you* who were with her just now?"
> Mr. Quin waited a minute and then said gently, "You can put it that way, if you like."
> "And the maid didn't see you?"
> "The maid didn't see me."
> "But *I* did. Why was that?"
> "Perhaps, as the result of the price you have paid, you see things that other people — do not...."
> "But *I* ... have never passed down your lane."
> "And do you regret?"

"Mr. Satterthwaite quailed. Mr. Quin seemed to have loomed to enormous proportions. Mr. Satterthwaite had a vista of something at once menacing and terrifying. Joy, Sorrow, Despair. And his comfortable little soul shrank back appalled.... Mr. Quin had vanished."

Agatha Christie was far from a great writer, but she provides in these two collections of short stories the clearest possible evidence (1) that she is carrying on (even to the short-story form) from Conan Doyle, and (2) that the business of the detective-story is supernatural. Also, of course, that the "mysteries" (in the ancient sense of that word) in which detective fiction participates are very English mysteries. As an interesting correlative, in Miss Sayers's *Murder Must Advertise* (1931), there is a harlequinade, and Harlequin is played, of course, by Lord Peter *Death* Bredon Wimsey. Chesterton, too, makes use of the harlequinade in one of the Father Brown stories.

Dame Agatha aside (but that is a large aside), what was it like in the Golden Age? We may begin with the view of Mr. Colin Watson (*Snobbery with Violence*, p. 100) that in the Golden Age "Nine out of ten detective stories were as shoddy and derivative as the rows of semi-villas that ribboned out to accommodate their readers." In Raymond Chandler's words, the average detective story was no worse than the average novel, but then, the average novel wasn't published and the average detective story was (quoted by Watson, p. 100). The mass-produced, jerry-built detective fiction-for-the-masses-yearning-to-breathe-free was a by-word in the magazines of the time, as the famous cartoon line indicates: "I like your book on water-beetles; but couldn't you contrive somehow to introduce a detective interest?" (Watson, p. 99.)

But Watson's view is too limiting, I think. We may distinguish seven sets of authors among those that Williams reviewed. (1) The writers of mysteries or thrillers from before the Golden Age who went on writing in the Golden Age: E. Phillips Oppenheim, R. Austin Freeman, for example. (2) The writers from before the Golden Age who turned to writing mysteries then: the best-known case is H. C. Bailey. (3) The Golden Age writers who were successful in the Golden Age and who went on writing and went on being successful, if sometimes less so: Agatha Christie, Henry Wade, Nicholas Blake, Philip MacDonald, even Christopher Bush. (4) The Golden Age writers who wrote also in other fields, but whose output in this was strictly limited to the time of the Golden Age: these range from "Anthony Rolls" (C. E. Vulliamy) to Anthony Skene to Jackson Gregory. (5) The writers whose entire production was in Golden Age mysteries: Ralph Carter Woodthorpe is a good example (unless there are some military writings I have missed). (6) The writers who started then but are more significant in the later history of the genre: Mignon G. Eberhart, John Creasey. (7) Finally, the one-book (or occasionally two-book) writers whose names very well may be pen-names, and who seem to have written nothing else: Evander Murray, Agnes Autumn, John Alexander, Don Basil, George Stacey Bishop, John Cobnor, for examples.

The writers who deserve further study, in my view, are those in the fourth and fifth categories. They are mostly among the hum-drums; their work is solid, and they may have had a strong influence on the fundamental shift from the short story-based detective fiction of Conan Doyle's day to the mostly novel-based detective fiction of the Golden Age. It may be that the short story is the natural vehicle for detective fiction, and that the novel must either include outside adventures (*The Valley of Fear, A Study in Scarlet, The Sign of Four, The Hound of the Baskervilles*) become social commentary, exhibit a world (a *milieu*) for the reader's additional delectation, convert the detective novel into a study of character (novel rather than romance, in Harold Bloom's dichotomy), or, quite simply, become a "Humdrum."

In the history of literary genre in English, it is probably not coincidental that Doyle grew up on novels published in parts and in magazines (*Punch*, of course, in particular); the Golden Age writers grew up on the solid 384-page, four novels-a-year of G. A. Henty and his emulators; and the post-World War II mystery writers grew up on the abbreviated children's fiction of such as G. E. Rochester and E. M. Channon (to take two authors reviewed by Williams), or, in the United States, F. W. Dixon and Carolyn Keene and Laura Lee Hope. When one of the Humdrums, like Christopher Bush, goes on writing into the 1960s, his novels become shorter and more "modern" (and the dust-jackets more garish). One of the unexpected rewards of searching into the writing careers of the authors Williams reviewed has been the discovery of such outliers as Anthony Skene, whose *Zenith the Albino* (1936) has just been republished (2001) as a classic in British pulp fiction and who seems to be identical with the Anthony Skene who wrote episodes *A, B, and C, Many Happy Returns*, and *Dance of the Dead*, in "The Prisoner." After more examination of lesser mystery writers than I ever anticipated, I can say, very strongly, that I disagree with Colin Watson (and Raymond Chandler) on the quality of the average published mystery novel of the 1930s. But then, of course, I grew up on them, R. A. J. Walling, Francis Beeding, Christopher Sprigg, and all the rest.

The corollary of Mr. Watson's view would be that the so-called classics of detective fiction (one thinks particularly of Dorothy L. Sayers) are classics only by comparison, and that Williams's panegyric on *The Nine*

Tailors is misplaced if not merely silly. Mr. Watson is in fact suggesting that the appeal of the detective novel was to the insular prejudices of the British public, by means of glorifying the British way of life (including silly-ass young noblemen, even if forty-year-old young noblemen). This is not unlike the attack launched on detective fiction by Edmund Wilson ("Who Cares Who Killed Roger Ackroyd" [1945], reprinted in Howard Haycraft, ed., *The Art of the Mystery Story* [1946], pp. 390-97). Mr. Wilson thought *The Nine Tailors* "one of the dullest books" he had "ever encountered in any field" (p. 392) and went on to say that Miss Sayers "does not write very well: it is simply that she is more self-consciously literary than most of the other detective-story writers and she thus attracts attention in a field which is mostly on a sub-literary level" (p. 392).

But there's the clue, of course, if Edmund Wilson had only stuck to it, and if we use the word "sub-literary" in no fully pejorative way. The Golden Age detective story functioned — and indeed its practitioners knew it to function — on a basic mythic level of the sort C. S. Lewis suggested that George MacDonald and Rider Haggard functioned on. "Sub-literary" is no bad word for that. The mythic level, where everything works out "all right" and persecuted virtue triumphs, being basic, is in that sense sub-literary. Consider the interesting essay by Joseph Wood Krutch from *The Nation*, November 25, 1944 ("Only a Detective Story," in Haycraft, pp. 178-88).

In that essay, Mr. Krutch noted that Dorothy L. Sayers was indeed a better writer than most of her compeers (read "Agatha Christie"), but that this did not seem to make any difference to the readers of detective fiction. He went on to quote Dr. Johnson: "A play in which the wicked prosper, and the virtuous miscarry, may doubtless be good, because it is a just representation of the common events of human life, but since all reasonable beings naturally love justice, I cannot be easily persuaded that the observation of justice makes a play worse; or that, if other excellences are equal, the audience will not always rise better pleased from the final triumph of persecuted virtue" (Haycraft, pp. 184-85). We may return to this, but for now let us note that if the audience rises pleased from the triumph of persecuted virtue, this "mythic" and "sub-literary" aspect is a strength, not a weakness.

One of the great virtues of Haycraft's volume is that it encapsulates the first set of critical reactions to detective fiction as that fiction became visible beyond the golden ghetto walls, but not entirely beyond the walls. Besides Krutch, it reprints Miss Sayers's introduction to *The Omnibus of Crime* and her essay on *Gaudy Night*, the famous pieces by Chesterton, R. Austin Freeman, Raymond Chandler ("The Simple Art of Murder"), and

S. S. Van Dine (under his real name of Willard Huntington Wright), the introduction by E. M. Wrong to the Oxford Classics *Crime and Detection* (1926), and Edmund Wilson's blast "Who Cares Who Killed Roger Ackroyd?", among some fifty-odd others. Clearly Miss Sayers, Chesterton, Freeman, Van Dine, and Chandler are all *intra muros*. Indeed, the best short critical piece in the book, "The Detective Story — Why?", is likewise written *intra muros*, by C. Day Lewis as Nicholas Blake, as an introduction for the English edition of Mr. Haycraft's book (1942).

Day Lewis's essay ought to be better known, and I will run the risk of immoderate, indeed intemperate, quotation from it here, partly for sheer pleasure in the prose. But also partly because Day Lewis is one of the authors whom Charles Williams reviewed, who began to tear down the walls of the ghetto, even while obeying most of its conventions. He knew very well what he was about, and he is a good person with whom to begin an investigation of what came after.

"The Detective Story — Why?" That is both title and question. And Day Lewis goes on to define the question (Haycraft, pp. 398ff): "I do not mean by this, to ask why the detective story came into existence when it did. That question has been answered successfully, if negatively, by Mr. Haycraft — 'Clearly there could be no detective stories ... until there were detectives. This did not occur until the nineteenth century.' A negative answer, because it merely re-defines the question: after all, there were no railway engines, either, until the nineteenth century, but their creation did not produce any considerable body of literature about engine-drivers."

We noted in the Introduction that the increasing omniscience of the detective in fiction, in the days of Sherlock Holmes, did not mirror an increasing omniscience of the real-world detective — indeed, rather the contrary. I think we must take issue even with Mr. Haycraft's negative answer, at least insofar as it implies that the real-world detectives were the models and Holmes or Dupin the imitators. After all, as C. S. Lewis has reminded us, the great poetic expressions of the Myth of Progress antedated the successive improvements in machines which might have been thought to be the origins of that myth (*De Descriptione Temporum*, p. 12). But, of course, Day Lewis's tone in discussing Haycraft's negative answer is sarcastic, and my objection may merely be making plain what he implied. He goes on to say thereafter:

> Nor do I intend to discuss at length the subsidiary though fascinating problem, 'Why do we write detective stories?' Many solutions, all of them correct, will suggest themselves to the reader. Because we want to make money. Because the drug addict (and nearly every detection-writer is an omnivorous reader of crime fiction) always wants to introduce other people to the

habit. Because artists have a notorious *nostalgie de la boue*, and our own hygienic a-moral age offers very little honest mud to revel in except the pleasures of imaginary murder....

When a religion has lost its hold upon men's hearts, they must have some other outlet for their sense of guilt. This, our anthropologist of the year 2042 may argue, was provided for us by crime-fiction. He will call attention to the pattern of the detective-novel, as highly formalised as that of a religious ritual, with its initial necessary sin (the murder), its victim, its high priest (the criminal) who must in turn be destroyed by a yet higher power (the detective). He will conjecture — and rightly — that the devotee identified himself both with the detective and the murderer, representing the light and dark sides of his own nature. He will note a significant parallel between the formalised dénouement of the detective novel and the Christian concept of the Day of Judgment.

This echoes the quotation from Dr. Johnson. But Day Lewis then goes on to argue a different point, more controversial, but no less valuable for that. "It is the element of fantasy in detective fiction — or rather, the juxtaposition of fantasy with reality — that gives the genre its identity.... The detective novelist ... is left with two alternatives. He can put unreal characters into realistic situations, or he can put realistic characters into fantastic situations."

Day Lewis goes on (p. 403) to identify Freeman Wills Crofts with the first, and John Dickson Carr with the second. (Presumably, for him, Agatha Christie's work fell into the category of "that most insidious and degraded of mental recreations, the cross-word puzzle" [p. 399], rather than the detective novel, since she wrote about unreal people in "fantastic" situations.) He then suggests that the detective novel of manners (of the Ngaio Marsh sort) might be the future course of the beast, but that the element of fantasy would then be lost (pp. 404-05). Day Lewis does not mean by "fantasy" what we meant in the Introduction, neither *Mooreeffoc,* nor pure fantasy, but something more like the "unreal estates" of C. S. Lewis, or even what I have elsewhere called the *fantastical.* That is to say, a deliberate making of what might be real into the unreal, one might say the deliberate making of life into a puzzle, which is pretty much what Edmund Wilson was attacking.

Does this help us to understand what happened after the Golden Age? Day Lewis was right at least in part, given the meaning he attached to the word *fantasy.* However, as he noted (p. 403), murder itself is so fantastic (unreal) to us, the readers, that the element of fantasy (unreality) will not quite be lost. But both characters and situations are indeed becoming more realistic. The characters in the *roman policier* have taken on real (if sketchy) character, as in Ed McBain's 87th Precinct stories. The situations in which, say, Adam Dalgleish finds himself are presented so realistically that there is at least a willing suspension of disbelief, even when (as in the Dalgleish short story, "Great Aunt Allie's Flypapers") the situation is in fact hideously improbable.

I noted parenthetically above that Agatha Christie's books concerned unreal people in unreal situations, and the same (with the substitution of *fantastic* for *unreal*) could be said of the *farceurs* like Edmund Crispin, and, for that matter, of G. K. Chesterton, whose *most* realistic detective is Father Brown. But this does not vitiate Day Lewis's analysis. In Chesterton, after all, the parallel with the Day of Judgment is open and deliberate, and creations that have the outward and visible form of detective stories have the inward and spiritual grace of God; they are in fact morality plays.

That is a way out of the golden trap, but no one else has been able to take it. Raymond Chandler, in "The Simple Art of Murder" (Haycraft, pp. 222-237), praised Hammett (and Raymond Postgate and Kenneth Fearing and might well have praised himself) for taking the realist's way out of the trap. The passage is worth quoting here; it shows well what Chandler was about (p. 237):

> In everything that can be called art, there is a quality of redemption. It may be pure tragedy, if it is high tragedy, and it may be pity and irony, and it may be the raucous laughter of the strong man. But down these mean streets a man must go who is not himself mean, who is neither tarnished nor afraid. The detective in this kind of story must be such a man. He is the hero, he is everything. He must be a complete man and a common man and yet an unusual man. He must be, to use a rather weathered phrase, a man of honor, by instinct, by inevitability, without thought of it, and certainly without saying it. He must be the best man in his world and a good enough man for any world....

But of course, not all detectives are Philip Marlowe, nor can be, and this way out has been infrequently taken because it requires a high degree of art and a moral imagination (in the Burkean sense) not common in a post-Christian, indeed a post-religious, age. For what Chandler was about is very much what Day Lewis's anthropologist would have concluded he was about, and indeed very much what Chesterton was about: "Down these mean streets a man must go who is not himself mean, who is neither tarnished nor afraid ... the best man in his world and a good enough man for any world"—the chevalier *sans peur et sans reproche*, which is indeed the phrase Chandler translates as "neither tarnished nor afraid."

Dorothy Sayers, as Chandler notes (p. 232), did not like finding herself in a ghetto. In fact, in her essay "Gaudy Night" (1937, in Haycraft, pp. 208-221), called, of course, after the book, she says that she was trying from the very first (*Whose Body?*, 1922) to produce something "less like a conventional detective story and more like a novel" (p. 208). In this she was fundamentally unsuccessful, on her own showing, at least in her Lord Peter books, until *Murder Must Advertise* (1933). Of this she makes the following remark: "the idea of symbolically opposing two cardboard worlds — that of the advertiser and the drug-taker — was all right; and it was quite suitable that Peter, who stands for reality, should never appear in either except disguised; but the working-out was a little too melodramatic, and the handling rather uneven" (pp. 209-10).

Peter Wimsey stands for reality. There it is in plain black and white. This is rather like saying that Father Brown stands for reality — though he is indeed Chesterton's most realistic detective, as we noted above. In the drug world in *Murder Must Advertise*, Lord Peter appears as Harlequin (should we note that Mr. Harley Quin appears as the hero of contemporaneous stories by Agatha Christie?), while in the advertising world he appears as Death Bredon. The connection between the harlequinade and death is traditional (for all that Miss Sayers provided Lord Peter with the full name of Peter Death Bredon Wimsey). All this, to echo Charles Williams, suggests that *Murder Must Advertise* is a matter of style, and was so perceived by its author.

In her essay, Miss Sayers goes on to remark that Peter was largely extraneous to the story of *The Nine Tailors* "and untouched by its spiritual conflicts" (p. 210). But in *Gaudy Night*, though the detection is somewhat extraneous to the story of Peter and Harriet (in my view), the spiritual conflicts are Peter's and Harriet's, and the door is opened out of the trap, but at what a cost. The next step is "a love story with detective interruptions" (*Busman's Honeymoon*), then *The Wimsey Papers* (in *The Spectator*), which are unfinished and not detective fiction of any kind, and *Thrones Dominations*, which she did not finish either, and where (in the published version) I am not sure which parts are by her. She walked out of the trap, in fact, by ceasing to write detective fiction. And she knew what she was about, both *intra muros* and *extra muros*: "I admit that when I had completed my monster ["Gaudy Night"], I felt some of the uneasiness of Count Frankenstein under the same circumstances. Some of my friends were dubious: they admitted that they had ... quite properly suspected the celibates and had been surprised by the final anagnorisis" (p. 217). It is not only Northrop Frye who used the word *anagnorisis* in connection with redemptive comedy.

In the end, Miss Sayers turned to translating Dante (not her only medieval translation, she also did the *Chanson de Roland*). That road led very nearly to Rome; it certainly did not lead to producing a new kind of detective novel. Perhaps S. S. Van Dine was right in claiming that the detective novel could not tolerate realism, and Agatha Christie right in her tenacity holding the line against realism — and yet Miss Marple, as her creator grew older, grew into something more like a recognizable human being, which is to say, perhaps, that the golden trap is detective fiction's proper place. Of course there were other practitioners in that restricted area besides the country house detective novelists of manners, and we will look at them shortly. Before we do, let us check to see whether the heirs of this particular line escaped to a wider world.

Various heirs to Miss Sayers and Margery Allingham and Dame Ngaio Marsh have been proposed; Ruth Rendell and P. D. James come to mind in England, and Carolyn Heilbrun (Amanda Cross) in the United States. There are, moreover, practitioners like Catherine Aird and Elizabeth LeMarchand and Patricia Moyes, who are writing almost pure Golden Age novels set more recently, and the Toby Glendower / Penny Spring novels by Margot Arnold (Petronella Cook), which follow Dame Agatha's archaeological lead, but do not have her sheer unrelenting unreality.

I find Ruth Rendell's novels without Inspector Wexford rather unpleasant, and even the Wexford stories have something of a psychological bad taste to most of them. P. D. James is trying, I think, to take the Sayers road of the 1930s, and judging from the critical reactions, she too is likely to wind up writing novels with only "detective interruptions" and then no such interruptions, which will produce novels I, for one, do not particularly want to read. The world of abnormal psychology is not one in which I wish to take my leisure.

What Julian Symons called the *farceurs* show another line of development. I mean Edmund Crispin (Bruce Montgomery), Michael Innes (J.I.M. Stewart), Father Knox, perhaps early Michael Gilbert, and certainly Heron Carvic (whoever that may be). They accept the conventions of the detective fiction genre even while playing against them, in what we might call a kind of intertextual genre analysis. But this is scarcely a way out of the golden trap; its affinities are with John Dickson Carr's famous locked-room lecture delivered by Dr. Gideon Fell (modeled on Chesterton) in *The Three Coffins* (1935), and with Crispin's Gervaise Fen, who, like Gideon Fell, knows that he is a creature in a novel and acts and talks like one.

One curious way out was taken by the late Ellis Peters (Edith Pargeter), in her Brother Cadfael stories. These might be called medieval stories with detective interruptions. Miss Peters's achievement lies in her finding a situation in which a "series sleuth" might reasonably deal with quite a number of murders, in the disturbed west of England in the time when, according to the *Peterborough Chronicle*, "God and his angels slept," that is, the reign of King Stephen. To be sure, the Middle Ages provide an element of the fantastic, however realistically portrayed. But the claim can certainly be made that the road to Cadfael's priory is a road out of the golden ghetto. In this context we might compare the Cadfael books with Umberto Eco's *Name of the Rose*, which resolutely remains in the ghetto, exploring it through intertextual references (a detective named Baskerville, for example) ... in a way not entirely unlike the way of the *farceurs*.

"Readers," Miss Sayers observed, "seem to like books which tell them how other people live — any people, advertisers, bell-ringers, woman dons, butchers, bakers, or candlestick-makers [and she might have added mediaeval monks] — so long as the detail is full and accurate, and the object of the work is not overt propaganda" (Haycraft, p. 218). On recalls Williams's comment (July 5, 1932) that "Background in a story is always a distinction, often an accident, but not necessarily a merit." An interesting example of the use of background *expertise* in finding a (possibly) reasonable venue for the detective story comes in the novels of Dick Francis, formerly Her Majesty's steeple-chase jockey. In fact, these are an interesting combination of the novel-of-character as a way out of the ghetto with the unusual background as an element of fantasy (in the Day Lewis sense). (I wonder if the same could be said for Edward Woodward, whom Williams reviews.)

But the reasonableness of the venue declines as the series lengthens, and the novel of character tends to fall back into the formula fiction from which it emerged. Besides, there is overmuch pain and general nastiness in these books for my taste, and they are closer to shilling shockers (though good ones) than to detective fiction. In some ways this decline happens also with the stories of John D. Macdonald's Travis McGee, and Macdonald's color-coded titles suggest to me a certain consciousness that this was, and is, inevitable. But McGee is on a different road from Dick Francis (all of Francis's heroes seem to bear a suspicious resemblance to Dick Francis, but do not constitute a series detective). McGee is a series detective (which, of course, increases the improbability of the whole affair, or set of affairs). He is a philosophically inclined former professional football player, and he descends in the right line from Chandler's man who is not mean, not tarnished and not afraid. To some extent, doubtless, these are novels of character, but while we are on a road out of the ghetto of the second-rate, it is not clear that the road is really going anywhere much further.

There is *expertise* in background with Emma Lathen (Mary Jane Latsis and Martha Henissart) in their Wall Street mysteries where the detective is John Putnam Thatcher of the Sloan Guaranty Trust, though the long series of business-related murders escapes the bounds of probability shortly after they begin. But the points on which they turn are frequently genuinely illustrative of business problems (I could use *Accounting For Murder* as a supplementary text for a college course), and the books are fun. They are, however, perilously close to the intertextuality of the *farceurs*, though it is true they use the detective story conventions to comment on business rather than on the detective story itself.

We have not much considered what Julian Symons called the Humdrums, the authors like Freeman Wills Crofts with his timetables for ships and railroads, R. A. J. Walling, John Rhode, G. D. H. and Margaret Cole (odd that leaders of the Fabians should be among the humdrums, or is that perhaps in keeping with the boredom of socialism?). Some of the detectives are police (like Inspector French), some are amateurs with relevant connections (Walling's Philip Tolefree has something to do with insurance, as I recall), but excitement is not in them. They plod.

I have seen or heard it said somewhere that the Humdrums replace Sherlock Holmes with Dr. Watson as the detective. There is an element of truth in that, though only if one sees Holmes and Watson as archetypes, and only if one is conscious of the almost silly cleverness of some of Holmes's answers and the corresponding denigration of Watson's considerable intelligence. But once the first interest in a detective "more like us" has worn off, only a mania for detectives in any and every form can explain the success of this particular version of the Golden Age story.

In fact, the detective story of the Golden Age, whether hardboiled American or Mayhem-Parva British (and whether the detective was Holmesian or Watsonian), was not really on the road to anywhere. Day Lewis had it right: it was the substitute for religious ritual. I recall an Episcopal priest of my acquaintance who called the Episcopalians (and Anglicans generally) the people who get together a read to God out of a book. When they ceased doing that, it seems they would, so to speak, read to themselves out of a book, and mysteries replaced Mysteries.

It may be profitable here to consider the only non-survivor of the five major detective story writers of the Golden Age, H. C. Bailey. Apparently Reggie Fortune was not to the taste of the postwar world, though Margery Allingham's Albert Campion, Agatha Christie's Hercule Poirot, Dorothy L. Sayers's Lord Peter Wimsey, Dame Ngaio Marsh's Roderick Alleyne, and John Dickson Carr's Gideon Fell all were. I do not think the matter is one of gender or of genre. It is true that Reggie Fortune was more a short story detective than a novel detective (though I consider *Black Land, White Land* a good detective novel). But, in fact, the eclipse of Reggie Fortune is curious. To be sure, Reggie was very much a Golden Age character, with his love of good food and taking things easy, and his curiously clipped speech with his habit of using the word "However" as a full sentence, but also with his passion for both justice and mercy above law. But, as a surgeon attached to the C.I.D., he had perhaps the only fully legitimate position I know of for an amateur investigator (unless one believes in Sherlock Holmes as the world's only consulting detective). And Wimsey's silly-assery and Albert Campion's silly-vaguery survived their creators, and even that most asinine of all investigators, Philo Vance, (the phrase is Chandler's) has been reprinted. Even Philip MacDonald's Anthony Gethryn. Why then the eclipse of Reggie Fortune?

I do not know the answer, but I have some suggestions, and I think they show us something of progress within and outside the walls. First, it must be agreed that the Reggie Fortune novels are a bit plodding. Second, there is perhaps overmuch of what Williams called "chats and chuckles" as the character of Reggie becomes better known (though the Reggie short stories are particularly interesting for the inclusion of the detective's wife as a real character, and it is this inclusion that leads, at least, to some of the chats). Yet the short stories are not plodding, the chats are brief, and the reason for Reggie's disappearance from favor must be otherwhere (though perhaps in connected areas). I would suggest that it may lie in the over-development of character and the repetition of *milieu*. Or, perhaps, simply in the fact that Bailey (like Edmund Crispin later) stuck so resolutely for so long to the short story.

If the answer is in the repetition of *milieu*, this would in some ways be like what happened to Peter Wimsey, in *The Wimsey Papers* if not in *Busman's Honeymoon*. Miss Sayers was right in observing that "people like books which tell them how other people live," but if the telling has already taken place in previous volumes, the bloom is off the rose. Granted, Sherlock Holmes retained his audience for forty years of publication, but I think the later stories are shadows and simulacra of the earlier, and by *His Last Bow*, half the attraction is nostalgia for the vanished age before the east wind blew over Europe. The world between the wars waxed nostalgic for the lost age before the First World War, but the world after the Second World War had neither time nor inclination to wax nostalgic for the age between the wars (there were exceptions, to be sure, but let the statement stand).

Campion changed over time, and even Roderick Alleyne changed, and Agatha Christie changed detectives. John Dickson Carr's interest in puzzle construction waned and he switched to historical mystery-romances (and as Carter Dickson he ceased writing when his model for Sir Henry Merrivale gained too great fame). Miss Sayers gave up Lord Peter. But H. C. Bailey and Mr. Fortune, like the old soldier of the song, just faded away.

My own opinion is that a revival is due, as there have been revivals of Nicholas Blake (Day Lewis) and Cyril Hare (Alfred Clark), but perhaps Reggie is too much a creature of that lost time, a generation before Blake and Hare. It may be the case that Bailey's work withered because it was not entirely protected by the meshes of the golden trap.

The Detection Club itself has changed since the 1930s, and many of its members are thriller writers. One can see in Philip MacDonald (1899-1981) a kind of microcosm of what happened to the genre between *The Rasp* (1924) and *The List of Adrian Messenger* (1959). Both are, in a sense, limited-access mysteries, though only the first is a country house mystery. But the element of the thriller is much stronger in the second, and it is no accident that MacDonald crossed the Atlantic, became a screen writer, and even wrote on the fringes of the hard boiled (with a California *mise-en-scene*), between the two books (and he himself wrote the screenplay from his own novel). Of course, MacDonald also wrote thrillers in the British style in between. Perhaps this would be a good place to look at him as a case study for what was going on *intra muros*. He deserves more attention than he has had, at any rate.

MacDonald wrote something like twenty-two novels of detection, counting *The Mystery in Kensington Gore*, *The Mystery at Friar's Pardon*, and *X v. Rex*, all as Martin Porlock. *The Mystery in Kensington Gore* (now better known as *Escape*) is a non-series detective thriller, with a substantial "human interest" (or love story) component. The fiction that it was written by a Martin Porlock was not long maintained (not past 1933, in fact), and when Doubleday set about reprinting MacDonald in omnibus volumes in the early 1960s, it was one of the three reprinted under the title *Triple Jeopardy*. The others in the volume are *Warrant for X* and *The Polferry Riddle*, both Anthony Gethryn novels. The other omnibus volume on my shelves, *Three for Midnight*, includes *The Rasp*, *Murder Gone Mad*, and *The Rynox Murder*. The first is the first Anthony Gethryn mystery, the second has Gethryn's professional associate Arnold Pike, but not Gethryn. The third is *sui generis*. It is a *jeu d'ésprit*, a humorous mystery-adventure spoof, in which the murder is actually a suicide to obtain what is, in effect, a loan from the insurance company that insured the suicide's life. The story begins with the repayment of the loan.

The principal characteristic of the other four, which are in a way classics, is that they are not quite believable and not quite unbelievable or fantastical. *The Rasp* threatens to escape into pure pastiche, but it has a story and a good puzzle, and Gethryn is at least a significant *persona* (a highly loathable one, according to several of my friends who read detective novels). *The Polferry Riddle* (1931, also known as *The Choice*) has a good small boating and "human interest" opening in which one gets to like the murderer, who is not, however, the killer of the first part, though his madness (so to speak) is.

Warrant for X (1938, also *The Nursemaid Who Disappeared*) shows some signs of Americanization. There is a lot of racketing about and hair's-breadth escapes; there is also some quite ingenious (almost Chestertonian) misdirection and redirection. *Murder Gone Mad* (1931) has Superintendent Arnold Pike as detective, as noted above, but not his friend Gethryn, it has, however, a highly Gethryn-like ending, or perhaps that is simply a characteristic MacDonald twist in which the waif who causes the murderer's self-betrayal is in fact a West End star, acting a part.

Gethryn's *milieu* is the upper-crust house-party world of *The Rasp*, but his feats of detection, and Pike's in *Murder Gone Mad*, take place in other *milieux* as well. Nevertheless, the tone of his world is not entirely unlike that of Lord Peter or Roger Sheringham or Albert Campion, or even Reggie Fortune. One wonders, from time to time, whether he is writing entirely seriously. Here he is in *The Polferry Riddle*: "A few minutes before he said that Pike said something about a Sambak razor. Now, I know Sambaks, I've used one. They're not English, but they're good" (*Triple Jeopardy*, p. 444). This is written in England in 1930, or thereabouts, and would serve as a wonderful example for Colin Watson's *Snobbery with Violence* if we could be sure it was seriously intended. The question here is twofold.

First, is MacDonald in fact portraying Gethryn as the kind of man who would seriously say things like that? Second, can Gethryn be seriously saying that? Somewhere, one senses, there is caricature. Either MacDonald is caricaturing an attitude, or Gethryn is becoming a kind of self-caricature, which brings us to the outer limits of the *farceurs*. Of course, the action is not as absurd and contrived as with, say, Michael Innes (J. I. M. Stewart), at whom we will look momentarily, for contrast. I have a clutch of Innes novels before me as I write: *Appleby on Ararat* (1941), *The Weight of the Evidence* (1943), *One Man Show* (1951), and *The Crabtree Affair* (1962).

In *Appleby on Ararat*, the detective is marooned on a South Seas island when his ship is torpedoed, only the cocktail bar surviving as a makeshift raft. They land on what they take to be a deserted island, and one of the group, the black anthropologist Sir Ponto Unumunu, is promptly killed, apparently by savages. But there turns out to be a hotel (Heaven's) on the island, and two apparent archaeologists, with the whole thing a cover for an Axis fuel dump. In the end, Appleby hitches a ride behind a submarine and the fuel dump is satisfactorily blown up. The apparent archaeologists were the fuel dump superintendents, and they had murdered Sir Ponto.

In *The Weight of the Evidence*, an academic quarrel is resolved by pushing a meteorite out of a window so it falls on one of the quarrellers. In *One Man Show* a painter is murdered by an old school friend after he buys a canvas which has a painted over Vermeer on it. The friend paints the plans of the British nuclear station at Waterbath on the canvas and is then killed, and an art dealer exhibits *all* the canvasses of the murdered painter, including this one. Appleby is dragged to the showing; and then two gangs of spies, the police, the art dealer, and the gang that stole the Vermeer all play a highly fatal version of ring-around-the-rosy all over the English countryside, winding up with the triumphant restoration of the Vermeer to its noble owner, still with the atomic research station plans overpainted. At this point, I do not think it necessary to rehearse the story of *The Crabtree Affair*, which involves faked antiques and a gentleman masquerading as a vulgarian masquerading as a gentleman. Suffice it to say that these are fairly typical Applebys, and quite obviously no one is expected to believe that any of this happened or indeed could happen, any more than one believes in the likelihood of the events in a Laurel and Hardy film.

But one could, just barely, believe in the events in Buster Keaton's *The General*, and if one cares for a filmic parallel, one could set Philip MacDonald beside Keaton and Michael Innes beside Laurel and Hardy. In fact, it could be said that, just as *The General* portrays humorously, even comically, what was in fact a deadly and ill-omened adventure in the American Civil War, so Philip MacDonald portrays humorously, even comically, the deadly and ill-omened adventures in death. A Dance of Death, if you like, and almost a merry one. But not absurd. Sir Ponto Unumunu is absurd. But neither killer nor killed in MacDonald is absurd, though the detective sometimes is (and sometimes one yearns to kick him, according to my friends who do not like Anthony Gethryn much). I think the detective is very like the Wise Fool of the Elizabethan stage.

And perhaps the Elizabethan stage was also a golden trap. Quite certainly bad plays were acted then, even as bad detective novels were published in the 1930s. We have already suggested that the detective novel is a form of redemptive comedy, a peculiarly Elizabethan thing, I think, in its stage form, but that may be an irrelevant parallel. It is not irrelevant that the Wise Fool is the comedic element even in the great tragedy of *Lear*. It is time, finally, to turn to one of the best of all critiques of the detective story, which by its very existence derides Haycraft's negative answer to the question why the detective story? For "On Murder Considered as One of the Fine Arts" (1827) antedates not only Poe but the *Mémoires* of Vidocq (1828-29), and thus explains the detective story before there was such a thing, and pretty much before there were such things as detectives.

It may be noted also that this is the second of De Quincey's relevant essays, the first being "On the Knocking at the Gate in *Macbeth*" (1823), which antedates the beginnings of Vidocq's *Mémoires* by five years.

In any case, listen to De Quincey in "Murder Considered as One of the Fine Arts" (quoted in David Lehman, *The Perfect Murder* [New York 1989], p. 49): "Therefore let us make the best of a bad matter; and, as it is impossible to hammer anything out of it [murder] for moral purposes, let us treat it aesthetically, and see if it will turn to account in that way. Such is the logic of a sensible man; and what follows? We dry up our tears, and have the satisfaction perhaps, to discover that a transaction which, morally considered, was shocking and without a leg to stand upon, when tried by the principles of Taste, turns out to be a very meritorious performance."

But also, "So far from aiding and abetting him [a murderer], by pointing out his victim's hiding place, as a great moralist of Germany declared it to be every good man's duty to do, I would subscribe one shilling and eightpence to have him apprehended, which is more by eightpence than the most eminent moralists have hitherto subscribed for that purpose" (p. 48). The point, as David Lehman notes, is that De Quincey's ferocious irony has fastened on a real moral dilemma (Lehman, p. 48): "Murder becomes a drastic metaphor for the great 'is' that stands in the way of any 'ought,' the stubborn resistance of human nature to self-government by any prescriptive moral code." Solving a murder thus becomes the drastic metaphor for replacing the *is* by the *ought*, in a process apparently involving logic (*vide* Holmes), though, of course, one cannot reason logically from *is* to *ought*.

Detective stories are thus (for all the logic of their deductions) a way of replacing logic — or, more extensively, philosophy — by poetry. They are, of course, written in prose, not verse, but the good ones are a kind of poetry nonetheless. I know of no single word correctly qualifying the bad ones. If, indeed, the point of redemptive comedy is the attack on order by *carnival*, and then the replacement of *carnival* by redemptive order, then long before Frye's *mythoi* and Bakhtin's dichotomizing — indeed, before there were detective stories as such — De Quincey had begun the analysis of what detective fiction would be. And it is not impossible for us to see in that analysis the rudiments of its boundaries, a century thereafter.

De Quincey's "hero" is, of course, a commonplace butcher, one John Williams. The first irony of the essay is that Williams's murders are far from a fine art, and De Quincey's praise is fiercely satiric. (Note that in our second quotation he is satirizing, or at least attacking, Kant.) Murder is not a fine art, and to consider it as such is to miss the point; it is a moral, not an aesthetic, matter. No matter how clever the murder, no matter how distinguished the detective or the murderer, it remains true: Thou shalt do no murder. Oh yes, to be sure, Holmes and Moriarity may be the two halves of one man, and so also murderers and detectives from Conan Doyle on (if not before), but the good half conquers the bad, else it's no detective story.

Yet De Quincey knew that in the London of his time, "the tendency to a critical or aesthetic valuation of fires and murders" was universal (quoted in Lehman, p. 46). The taste was there in the popular mind before it was gratified in story. Dare we guess that the Romantic Revolution was in the hearts and minds of the crowd, as well as the poets? Poets may be the unacknowledged legislators of mankind, but sometimes their legislation merely codifies existing custom. And one is reminded of C. S. Lewis's suggestion that the great mythic treatment of progress came *before* the advent of the machines and the Industrial Revolution (*De Descriptione Temporum*, p. 8). One recalls that in that same Romantic Revolution, Satan came to be thought the hero of *Paradise Lost*.

One cannot argue, only affirm, the *ought* from the *is*. To affirm morality in the face of the Romantic Revolution (Raffles does not last well and Robin Hood *must* give to the poor), one must always see the triumph of the Good. Sherlock Holmes must be the angel entertained unawares, an archetype in Victorian England. Whatever his habits, the detective must be the best man in his world. The trap is only the traveling Morality stage writ slightly large: if one escapes it, it is only into the slightly larger stage of Elizabethan Comedy (redemptive comedy), or into some modern production where the King's Messenger arrives at the back of the theatre. Otherwise it ceases to be detective fiction.

Secondary achievements— portraying how people live or lived in London, how bells are rung, how wines are tasted, how steeplechases do or do not work, what life was like in Shewsbury in 1141— become a measure of success in the writing of detective fiction. This is not so much because they are important in themselves, as because they serve to distinguish one morality play from another. Doubtless there were nine-and-sixty ways (or more) of constructing detective fiction, but they were all pretty much the same. We care who killed Roger Ackroyd, not because of Agatha Christie's style, but because we care who kills and who detects, because we participate vicariously in both. I must admit my own aversion to the hero who does both (James Bond, for example), but such heroes too have their defenders and their place in the scheme.

Intra muros, God's in His heaven, and all's made well with the world. *Extra muros*, *hic dracones*, and dragons have no part of the fantasy of the Golden Age of detective fiction, Chandler's, or anyone else's. Or is that true? What were the Golden Age writers doing? They were proclaiming the *ought* in the face of the *is,* and carrying their readers with them, by appeal to incidents of daily life, or by appeal to the romance of the unfamiliar. But a real dragon in the midst of Mayhem Parva would show the morality play for what it is — a play.

What were the Golden Age writers doing? They were making us comfortable within *our* walls. Out there, in the worlds of the detective novel, there are goblin thrills, if under a real sun (see the Foreword, p. 29). We are neither facing the goblins, the dragons, ... even the real sun. We read to ourselves out of a book, and we are comforted. Virtue does triumph. And then the curtain is rung down. Or the service is over.

Appendix

AUTHORS AND BOOKS
REVIEWED

So far as I know, there is no complete bibliography of Golden Age detective fiction or any complete list of Golden Age writers. The most comprehensive, though spotty and idiosyncratic, is Jacques Barzun's and Wendell Hertig Taylor's *A Catalogue of Crime* (revised edition, 1989), which I have consulted at length, and in which I found exactly one half of the 204 authors reviewed by Williams. Some of the birth dates (and a few of the dates of death) in the list here are from Barzun and Taylor. More are from the Library of Congress Catalogue, some from the British Library Catalogue. This list is alphabetical by author's name, with cross-references, and with the books reviewed then listed alphabetically by title. If the name on the book is known to be a pen name, the author's real name, if known, is listed in parentheses. The list of each author's books reviewed is followed by brief note on the author.

A few entries in Barzun contain some additional information that may be of interest here. Herbert Adams (1874–1958) has one book reviewed by Williams, thirteen in the British Library, and eighteen in Barzun. Barzun calls George Birmingham (Canon Hannay) "a delight," which seems to echo Williams's approval. The Douglas G. Browne novel Williams reviews is said by Barzun to be Browne's worst. Three entries in the list, as we will see, belong to Major Cecil John Street (1884–1964), who has more than eighty books listed in Barzun (under three pen names), far more than Dame Agatha Christie's fifty. J. J. Connington, with one review here, has twenty-five books listed (mostly favorably) in Barzun. Moray Dalton has five listed, with a comment that he "deserves thorough looking up." On the other hand, Cortland Fitzsimmons's *The Bainbridge Mystery*, is described by Williams as "neatly finished … with careful work," but is called by Barzun "the perfect stimulus to alternating boredom and hilarity." Williams is also more favorable than Barzun to the work of Harry Stephen Keeler (1890–1967), of whom Barzun says that his "plots defy analysis and credibility."

Barzun may be more favorable than Williams toward David Sharp (though Williams has some good things to say of him), and he finds John McIntyre (1871–1951) more interesting than Williams did. This is partly because (speaking with hindsight) he sees McIntyre's fat young gourmet detective, Duddington Pell Chambers, as a forerunner of Nero Wolfe. Williams finds more in some of the less attractive books, especially American books. For example, he writes of Willard K. Smith's *Bowery Murder*, that the author "has told his story — and how successfully! — in a diction of shrieks and sobs and solemnities." Barzun simply calls the novel "unbearable." The point is, I believe, that Williams is an English Romantic (and born in 1886) and Barzun is a French (and American) Realist (and born in 1907). Perhaps we need a less idiosyncratic *Catalogue of Crime*, but that would seem to be a strange recommendation from an idiosyncratic editor of the even more idiosyncratic Charles Williams.

My bibliographic research in the catalogues of the British Library and the Library of Congress has made it clear that the spate of detective novels in the 1920s and 1930s was not primarily from the attraction of neophytes and one-book authors to the field. Much more needs to be done, even on the authors Williams reviewed, but my search has had some unexpected benefits in helping me understand more of the nature of the Golden Age phenomenon, and in making it clear what a wide range of authors was attracted to the detective story in the Interwar years — particularly in the years of Williams's reviews. Some of my understanding of the nature of the Golden Age has gone into Chapter VI. Here I would like to call attention to the range of writers Williams reviewed.

The very first in the alphabetical list, Anthony Abbot, was, as Fulton Oursler, the author of the huge best-seller *The Greatest Story Ever Told*. Sir John Masterman wrote the classic study of World War II deception and espionage, *The Double-Cross System*. James Hilton gave us *Mr. Chips* and Shangri-La. C. S. Forester gave us Captain Horatio Hornblower. J. M. A. Ressich, Canon Hannay, J. S. Fletcher, Canon Whitechurch, and Hulbert Footner were all distinguished regionalists (Scotland, Ireland, Yorkshire, Sussex, Maryland in the United States). E. M. Channon wrote girls' school stories. Florence Ryerson and Colin Clements gave us half a dozen mysteries and "The Littlest Shepherd: A Christmas Interlude." Eric Maschwitz (Val Gielgud's co-author as Holt Marvell) wrote the best-selling 1940 song, "A Nightingale Sang in Berkeley Square." Gertrude M. Robins Reynolds (Mrs. Baillie Reynolds) began her writing career with nearly half a dozen Bentley three-deckers in the 1880s and 1890s.

G. E. Rochester wrote airplane stories for boys and girls—eighteen of them published in the year 1936. A number of writers of Westerns entered the mystery field. Victor Sampson, a retired South African administrator, published two mystery novels with an African *locale*. The American war correspondent Robert Casey (*Torpedo Junction*) and the British financial leader-writer William Collin Brooks were in the field. So were true-crime writers George Dilnot and Charles Kingston O'Mahony and Guy B. H. Logan. There was the American psychologist C. Daly King, the travel-writer Henry James Forman, the Australian journalist Dominic Paul McGuire with his south-sea islands, and the American John Womack Vandercook with his—all were writing Golden Age mysteries. There was the polymath C. E. Vulliamy, who touched many fields, and, in Goldsmith's tradition, touched few that he did not adorn. There was Sydney Fowler Wright, a modern founder of the science-fiction genre. There were the fantasists M. P. Shiel and Talbot Mundy. There was Monsignor Knox and the Rev. Kenneth Ingram. There were the right-wing authors like Gerard Fairlie and Bruce Graeme and some of the secret-service thriller-writers. There was the Marxist literary theoretician Christopher Caudwell, the Fabian Socialists G. D. H. and Margaret (Postgate) Cole, and the Marxist Fabian Ellen Wilkinson, M.P. One thing in particular is important with all of these writers. Either they made their living by writing, or they got to the position where they made their living (teacher, M.P., clergyman) by writing.

Why they all turned to detective fiction is part of the subject of this book. From Mrs. Baillie Reynolds, born in the year the Crimean War started, to John Creasey, whose later books were written after Neil Armstrong had walked on the moon, the Golden Age—even as in Williams's reviews—showed a wide range of authors, with accomplishments in a number of fields. Perhaps the most difficult figures to comprehend are the writers who apparently came from nowhere, published a novel a year (or even averaged two a year) for six or seven or ten or twelve years and then, nothing. They never published anything out of their field. They seem to have had no existence before 1919 or after 1940. They cannot all be pseudonymous. There is work to be done here. But not by me—or at least, not by me as part of putting this book together.

ANTHONY ABBOT (Fulton Oursler, 1893–1952)

The Crime of the Century. Collins. 7s6d [October 7, 1931]
The Murder of Geraldine Foster. Collins. 7s6d [March 2, 1931]
Murder of the Night Club Lady. Collins. 7s6d [March 7, 1932]

Journalist and reporter, best known for his life of Christ, *The Greatest Story Ever Told*, Fulton Oursler published eight detective novels between 1931 and 1940, a ninth, *Deadly Secret*, in 1943, and provided the first English translation of Simenon's Inspector Maigret (in 1940 as *Introducing Inspector Maigret*). In 1940 he also published with Nadir Khan (Achmad abd'Allah al-Idrisi al-Durrani) *The Shadow of the Master*. His collection of short stories, *These Are Strange Tales*, appeared in 1948.

HERBERT ADAMS (1874–1958)

The Crime in the Dutch Garden. Methuen. 7s6d [October 7, 1931]

The British Library lists thirteen books by Herbert Adams, from *By Order of the Five* (1925) and *Comrade Jill* and *The Crooked Lip* (both 1926), to *Crime Wave at Little Cornford* (1948). *The Crime in the Dutch Garden* was printed in an abridged war-time version in Dublin in 1945 (Mellifont Press).

E. A. ALDRICH (or A. B. Leonard)

The Judson Murder Case. Butterworth. 7s6d [December 29, 1933]

This appears to be a one-time effort, which Williams describes in terms that nevertheless lead me to wonder what real name may lie under the pseudonym or pseudonyms. Williams has the author as E. A. Aldrich, the book is catalogued in the British Library as by A. B. Leonard, and in the Library of Congress as by A. B. Leonard (i.e., E. A. Aldrich). But I have found no other book under either name.

JOHN ALEXANDER

Murder at the Eclipse. Sampson Low. 7s6d [May 1, 1934]

This is another apparent one-time effort, which may be pseudony-mous. It deals with a peer's trial for murder in the House of Lords.

LUKE ALLAN (William Lacey Amy, *d.* 1962)

The Jungle Crime. Arrowsmith. 7s6d [May 5, 1931]

He is best known for his Westerns mostly featuring Blue Pete (from *Blue Pete: Half-breed* in 1920 to *Blue Pete in the Badlands* in 1954), but Luke Allan (the Canadian William Lacey Amy) published more than forty nov-els. Of these eight at least are detective fiction (or nine, if one counts *Blue Pete: Detective* in 1928), and one or two others are adventure stories verg-ing on detective fiction. Compare Jackson Cole (Alexander Leslie Scott).

AUSTEN ALLEN (*b.* 1887)

Live Wire. Geoffrey Bles. 7s6d [July 15, 1931]

The British Library Catalogue lists four novels, one each year from 1929 (*Menace to Mrs. Kershaw*) through 1932 (*The Loose Rib*), and a play (1932), *Pleasure Cruise, a Comedy.* The Library of Congress has only *Live Wire.*

FRED ANDREAS (*b.* 1898)

The Theatre Crime. Geoffrey Bles. 7s6d [July 5, 1932]

Williams's review does not show it (though it certainly hints at it), but this is a translation (by Winifred Ray) of *Die Flucht ins Dunkle.* The German playwright and novelist Fred Andreas had four novels (all trans-lated by Ray) published in English in London between 1931 and 1936. The other three are *In Court* (1931), *Alias* (1933), and *Captain Overboard* (1936). Two other novels, *Das Schiff ohne Liebe* (1929) and *Die gelbe Flagge* (1936) have only the German versions in the British Library.

AGNES AUTUMN

The Gold and Copper Delamonds. Methuen. 3s6d [August 26, 1930]

All the (very scanty) evidence suggests that Agnes Autumn is a pen name. *The Gold and Copper Delamonds* later appeared in an abridged edition, by Mellifont: this may help trace the author. (Amusingly, the British Library Catalogue lists the abridged edition as *The Gold and Copper Diamonds*.)

ANNE AUSTIN (*b.* 1885)

Murder Backstairs. Skeffington. 7s6d [November 6, 1930]
The Avenging Parrot. Skeffington. 7s6d [April 6, 1931]

These are the first two of Anne Austin's six novels in the British Library: all are detective fiction and all were published between 1930 and 1934. The possibility of publication under another name cannot be discounted.

H[ENRY] C[HRISTOPHER] BAILEY (1878–1961)

Mr. Fortune Explains. Ward Lock. 7s6d [April 17, 1930]
Mr. Fortune Wonders. Ward Lock. 7s6d [December 29, 1933]

At the height of the Golden Age, H. C. Bailey was one of the "Big Five" of British detective fiction writers. But he was not originally a detective-fiction writer at all. As Charles Williams says of himself in one of his reviews, Bailey could have said of himself, "But I was Ruritanian born." His first novels bore titles like *Karl of Erbach* (1903), *The Master of Gray* (1903), and *Beaujeu* (1905), and when he came originally to detective fiction in 1920, it was with a collection of short stories, *Call Mr. Fortune*. He is an emulator of Conan Doyle, and he wrote during the Golden Age, but in what I think his strongest detective novel, *Black Land, White Land* (1937), he is as much a regionalist as a Golden Age writer. Reggie Fortune is very much the Deputy Dramatist, but the stories of his detection are also character sketches. I have heard an interesting parallel drawn between Bailey's Reggie Fortune and Joshua Clunk on the one hand, and Erle Stanley Gardner's Perry Mason and Lam and Cool on the other — Fortune and Mason being the Bright Avenging Angels, Clunk and Lam and Cool the darker. His last novel, *Honour Among Thieves*, appeared in 1947. There are fifteen or sixteen Reggie Fortune books, most of them collections. There are 83 card entries for Bailey in the British Library.

E[LSA] BARKER (1869–1954)

The Cobra Candlestick. Hamilton. 7s6d [January 24, 1930]

Elsa Barker was a poet (*The Book of Love*, 1912, *Songs of a Vagrom Angel*, 1916) and occasional novelist (*The Son of Mary Bethel*, 1909). She is best known for her *Letters from a Living Dead Man* (1914), *War Letters from the Living Dead Man* (1915), and *Last Letters from the Living Dead Man* (1919). *The Cobra Candlestick* (1928) and *The C.I.D. of Dexter Drake* (1931) are her only detective fiction.

CHARLES BARRY (Charles Bryson, *b.* 1877)

The Avenging Ikon. Methuen. 7s6d [August 6, 1930]
The Wrong Murder Mystery. Hurst and Blackett. 7s6d [December 23, 1933]

Charles Barry (Charles Bryson) published twenty-four detective novels (according to the British Library) in the twenty-six years from 1925 to 1951, beginning with *The Smaller Penny* (1925), *The Detective's Holiday* (1926) and *The Mouls House Mystery* (1926), ending with *Secrecy at Sandhurst* (1951). *Secrecy at Sandhurst* is, however, the only one published after *The Dead Have No Mouths* in 1940.

DON BASIL

Cat and Feather. Philip Earle. 7s6d [May 19, 1931]

This also seems to be a one-time effort, possibly pseudonymous. It deals with the experiences of a blind man in a boarding house.

GREGORY BAXTER (John Sellar Matheson Ressich, *b.* 1877, and Eric de Banzie)

Climax at the Falls. Benn. 7s6d [January 25, 1932]
Murder Could Not Kill. Benn. 7s6d [August 23, 1932]

The Ressich–de Banzie team produced seven books in ten years beginning with *Blue Lightning* (1926) and ending with *Calamity Comes of Age* (1936). Ressich's first book was a set of sketches called *Oddly Enough* (1922), followed by a collection of tales, *Voices in the Wilderness* (1924), *The Triumph of a Fool* (1926), and *Something I Want to Say* (1927), articles reprinted from the *Glasgow Daily Record*. He seems to have been something of a Scottish regionalist. See also his book on Scottish golf, *Thir Braw Days* (1933).

FRANCIS BEEDING (J. L. Palmer, 1885–1944, and Hilary St. George Saunders, 1898–1951)

The League of Discontent. Hodder and Stoughton. 7s6d [June 11, 1930]
The Two Undertakers. Hodder and Stoughton. 7s6d [April 7, 1933]

John Leslie Palmer died during the War, and after the War, Hilary Aidan St. George Saunders published (with Denis Richards), the three volume series, *The Royal Air Force 1939–1945*. The last Francis Beeding novel, *There Are Thirteen*, was published semi-posthumously in 1946. Between 1926 and 1940 "Francis Beeding" published twenty-one books. These included *The One Sane Man* (1934), *The Two Undertakers* (1933), *The Three Fishers* (1931), *The Four Armourers* (1930), *The Five Flamboys* (1929), *The Six Proud Walkers* (1928), *The Seven Sleepers* (1925), *The Eight Crooked Trenches* (1936), *The Nine Waxed Faces* (1938), *The Ten Holy Horrors* (1939), *Eleven Were Brave* (1940), *The Twelve Disguises* (1942). Note that, although the titles contain the numbers from one to twelve, they were published in no particular order.

ANTHONY BERKELEY [Cox] (1893–1971)

Murder in the Basement. Hodder and Stoughton. 7s6d [June 2, 1932]

As Anthony Berkeley, Cox wrote a number of novels and one classic Roger Sheringham short-story, "The Poisoned Chocolates" (which has a different ending from his novel, *The Poisoned Chocolates Case*). None of his novels is quite as good, and they are oddly in the tradition of E. C. Bentley's *Trent's Last Case*, where the detective is wrong, through and through. All of his thirteen Berkeley novels have been reprinted, almost all by Penguin. [See also Francis Iles.]

[BEST DETECTIVE STORIES]

The Best Detective Stories of the Year 1929. Faber and Faber. 7s 6d [April 17, 1930]

Edited by Monsignor Ronald Knox and Henry Harrington. Contains twenty-eight stories (486 pages), with an introduction by Monsignor Knox.

GEORGE [KERNAHAN GWYNNE] BETTANY

The Secret of the Swamp. Skeffington. 7s 6d [October 22 1931]

The British Library has eleven books by George Kernahan Gwynne Bettany, eight in the period from 1931 (*The Secret of the Swamp*) to 1936 (*Villainy*), the last three in 1946 (*Murder at Benfleet*), 1949 (*Dangerous Haven*), and 1951 (*Man-Hunt*). There are also four books by George Bettany (no middle names), *Brushtail the Prairie Wolf* (1949), *Creatures of a Canadian Lake* and *Creatures of the Snows* (both 1950), and *Pinniped People and Other Stories* (1951/2).

GEORGE BIRMINGHAM (Canon James Owen Hannay, 1865–1950)

The Hymn Tune Mystery. Methuen. 7s 6d [November 6, 1930]

Canon Hannay was an Irish regionalist, a non-detective novelist, a travel writer, a Great War padre (*A Padre in France*, 1918), a biblical scholar, and almost incidentally, in this book, a detective novelist — though as Williams observed, this is in a way Barchester revisited. As a travel writer, he is remembered for *From Dublin to Chicago* (1914), *A Wayfarer in Hungary* (1925), *Round Our North Corner* (1951). As a biblical scholar, he was known for *The Wisdom Book* (1925) and *Do You Know Your Bible?* (1928), though he can scarcely said to be remembered for them. As an Irish regionalist, he gave us *Irishmen All* (1913 with illustrations by Jack Yeats), *The Lighter Side of Irish Life* (1916), *The Lost Lawyer* (1921), *Minnie's Bishop* (1915), *The Northern Iron* (1907), *The Red Hand of Ulster* (1912), *Up! the Rebels* (1919), *General John Regan* (1913, made into a play in 1933), and more others than I care to list here. As a regionalist, he is not on a par with Somerville and Ross, but he is not bad, and he was a fixture in British writing for nearly fifty years. In contradistinction to Monsignor Knox and A. K. Ingram and even Canon Whitechurch, he is more notable as a regionalist than as a cleric.

[George] Stacey Bishop

Death in the Dark. Faber and Faber. 7s 6d [April 10 1930]

This appears to be a solo detective effort. The author would appear to be a psychoanalyst, or at least psychologist, of the school of Sandór Radó.

Peter Black (pseudonym)

Which of Them? by Peter Black. Benn. 7s 6d [June 2, 1932]

This also is a solo effort, and I have not been able to determine the author behind the pseudonym. The line Williams quotes does not suggest any great value to the determination.

Adam Bliss (Robert Ferdinard Burkhardt, 1892–1947, and Eve Burkhardt)

The Campden Ruby Murder. Rich and Cowan. 7s 6d [February 2, 1934]

The Burkhardts, German expatriates in England, published three novels under the Adam Bliss pen name, *The Campden Ruby Murder* (1934), *Murder Upstairs* (1935), and *Four Times A Widower* (1938). The only other items in the British Library Catalogue under the name of Robert Burkhardt are two books in German, *Chronik der Insel Usedom* (1909–12) and *Die Jagd nach Vineta* (1935).

Ben Bolt (Ottwell Binns, *b.* 1872)

The Crooked Sign. Ward, Lock. 7s 6d [February 15, 1935]

There are thirty-nine books by Ben Bolt (the Yorkshireman Ottwell Binns) listed in the British Library Catalogue, from *The Diamond-Buckled Shoe, The Impossible Lover,* and *The Pride of the Ring* (all 1921), to *Linked By Peril* (1939). Most of these are not mysteries or detective fiction, though some of the others besides *The Crooked Sign* may come close.

LOUIS F. BOOTH

The Bank Vault Mystery. Hutchinson. 7s 6d [September 8, 1933]

Louis F. Booth is listed as the author of *The Bank Vault Mystery* (1933) and *Broker's End* (1935). The name may have been a pseudonym.

LAURENCE R. BOURNE

Stark Naked. Frederick Muller. 7s 6d [June 4, 1934]

This is the only book I have found in the British Library or the Library of Congress by Laurence R. Bourne. Williams says it suggests a future competence: whether that suggestion was fulfilled under another name I cannot say.

[CHARLES] NEVILLE BRAND (*b.* 1895)

Death in the Forest. The Bodley Head. 7s 6d [April 7, 1933]
The Winning Trick. The Bodley Head. 7s 6d [September 16, 1931]

Charles Neville Brand published two books of poems (*The House of Time*, 1918, and *Perspective*, 1921), and then thirteen novels, from *Narrow Seas* (1923) to *Winter Landscape* (1949) and *The Dark Lady* (1950). Seven were published in the 1920s and four (I think the only mysteries) in the 1930s.

ALAN BROCK (*b.* 1880)

By Misadventure. Nicholson and Watson. 7s 6d [January 17, 1934]

The British Library Catalogue credits *By Misadventure* (1934) to Alan Francis Clutton Brock, also Clutton-Brock. Block is also credited with *Further Evidence* (1934), *Suspicion Was Aroused* (1936), *Earth to Ashes* (1939), *Murder at Liberty Hall* (1941), *Miss Hamblett's Ghost* (1946), and *Inquiries by the Yard* (1949), and should be credited with *After the Fact* (1935, in fact listed under Alan Saint Hill Brock, the historian of fireworks). Our Alan Brock is the same as the art historian, A. F. Clutton-Brock, author of *Italian Painting* (1930), *An Introduction to French Painting* (1932), and *Blake* (1933).

LYNN BROCK (Alister McAllister, 1877–1943)

Q.E.D. Collins. 7s 6d [July 30 1930]

From 1924 (*The Deductions of Colonel Gore*) to 1940 (*The Stoat: Colonel Gore's Queerest Case*), "Lynn Brock" published twelve of Colonel Gore's cases, several under such enlightening titles as *Colonel Gore's Third Case* (1927), *Colonel Gore's Cases, No. 4* (1928), *Colonel Gore's Cases, No. 5* (1929). He is one of the exhibits in Colin Watson's *Snobbery With Violence*.

[WILLIAM] COLLIN BROOKS (1893–1959)

Frame Up. Hutchinson. 7s 6d [February 15, 1935]
Mad-Doctor Merciful. Hutchinson. 7s 6d [March 7, 1932]
Three Yards of Cord. Hutchinson. 7s 6d [June 17, 1931]

(William) Collin Brooks was a poet (*Poems*, 1914, *Echoes and Evasions*, 1934) and economist (*This Tariff Question*, 1931, *The Economics of Human Happiness*, 1933). Particularly, he was an expert in finance (*The Theory and Practice of Finance*, 1929, *How the Stock Market Really Works*, 1930, *A Concise Dictionary of Finance*, 1934, *Profits from Short-Term Investment*, 1935, *Can 1931 Come Again?* 1938, *Company Finance*, 1939). He was a financial leader-writer (*How to Read the Money-Article*, 7th ed. 1936), financial historian (*Woolwich Equitable Building Society*, 1947, *History of Johnson and Phillips*, 1950), and sometime mystery writer. His ten mystery novels were published between 1927 and 1935. T. S. Eliot delivered an address at his memorial service.

ADAM BROOME (Godfrey Warden James, *b.* 1888)

Crowner's Quest. Benn. 7s 6d [December 24 1930]

Most of the mystery novels by "Adam Broome" (at least eight of twelve) have a West African *locale*. His first African book is *Crowner's Quest*

(1930), his last *The Flame of the Forest* (1943). He also wrote *The Oxford Murders* (1929), *The Queen's Hall Murder* (1933), and *The Cambridge Murders* (1936).

DOUGLAS G[ORDON] BROWNE (1884–1963)

Plan XVI. Methuen. 7s 6d [June 18, 1934]

Douglas Gordon Browne wrote a dozen mysteries, including a collection of shorter pieces, *Death in Seven Volumes, etc.* (1958). His first mystery novels were *The Cotfold Conundrums* and *The Dead Don't Bite* (1933). After 1940 *(Death Wears a Mask)*, he turned to history and military journalism, where he had in fact begun with *The Tank in Action* (1920). He wrote *Private Thomas Atkins: A History of the British Soldier* (1940), *The Floating Bulwark: The Story of the Fighting Ship* (1963), *The Rise of Scotland Yard* (1956), *Sir Travers Humphreys* (1960), *Fingerprints: Fifty Years of Scientific Crime Detection*, and (with E. V. Tullett) *Bernard Spilsbury: His Life and Cases* (1955).

MILES BURTON (Maj. Cecil John Street, 1884–1964)

Murder at the Moorings. Collins. 7s 6d [July 5, 1932]
The Hardway Diamonds Mystery. Crime Club. Collins. 7s 6d [June 4, 1930]
The Three Crimes. Collins. 7s 6d [March 2, 1931]

The British Library has something like sixty-six mystery novels listed under the name "Miles Burton"—from *The Secret of High Eldersham* and *The Hardway Diamonds Mystery* (both 1930) to *Death Paints A Picture* (1960). How many of them are entirely by Major Street is not certain, but since Major Street published under his more famous pen name of John Rhode as late as 1961 (*The Vanishing Diary*), it is quite possible that all of them are all his. Major Street has at least 144 mystery or detection novels in the British Library, as John Rhode, Cecil Waye, and Miles Burton (if those are all his). It has been suggested to me that he may also have written under the "company name" of Moray Dalton — "Miles Burton" being also, originally, a "company name." [See also John Rhode, Cecil Waye.]

CHRISTOPHER BUSH (1885–1973)

Dancing Death. Heinemann. 7s 6d [June 17, 1931]
Dead Man's Music. Heinemann. 7s 6d [January 7, 1932]
Dead Men Twice. Heinemann. 7s 6d [August 14, 1930]

Christopher Bush wrote more than sixty mystery/detective novels, most of them featuring Ludovic Travers, between *The Plumley Inheritance* (1926) and *The Case of the Deadly Diamonds* (1967). Twenty were published in the 1930s. I can recall my astonishment that the brightly-colored dust-jackets of such 1960s titles as *The Case of the Jumbo Sandwich* (1965) covered books by the same Christopher Bush who wrote *The Plumley Inheritance* and *The Perfect Murder* (1929). He was the longest-lived of the Humdrums, neither best nor worst, sometimes slightly tepid but almost always acceptable. He took on some of the color of the post–World War II novelists, without taking on much of their excitement.

ALICE CAMPBELL (*b.* 1887)

The Murder of Caroline Bundy. Collins. 7s 6d [January 31 1933]

From *Juggernaut* (1928) to *The Corpse Had Red Hair* (1950), there are nineteen mystery/detection novels by Alice Campbell in the British Library, two from the 1920s, eight from the 1930s, eight from the 1940s, and one from 1950. No biographical information seems to be available.

J[OHN] C[LUCAS] CANNELL

A Hundred Mysteries for Armchair Detectives. John Long. 2s 6d [December 13, 1932]

J. C. Cannell was associated with the B.B.C. He was noted as a true-crime writer (*New Light on the Rouse Case* 1931), and expert on magic and biographer of Houdini (*The Secrets of Houdini*, 1932, *The Hundred Best Tricks*, 1933, *The Master Book of Magic*, 1935, *Modern Conjuring for Amateurs*, 1940). His *When Fleet Street Calls: Being the Experiences of a London Journalist* also appeared in 1932.

JOHN DICKSON CARR (1905–1977)

It Walks By Night. Harper. 7s 6d [April 10 1930]
Poison in Jest. Hamish Hamilton. 7s 6d [January 3, 1933]

American-born, his first detective a Frenchman, John Dickson Carr needs no biography here. But we might note that his detective Dr. Gideon Fell is closely modeled on G. K. Chesterton, his detective Sir Henry Merrivale (in his Carter Dickson stories) closely modeled on Sir Winston Churchill, and this gives his stories a tinge of commentary within the genre. This aspect of commentary-within-the-genre puts Carr at least on the borders of what commentators now call inter-textuality. He has 144 entries in the British Library Catalogue, from *It Walks by Night* (1930) to *The Hungry Goblin* (1972), but most of his best work was done in the 1930s and early 1940s.

ROBERT J[OSEPH] CASEY (1890–1962)

The Secret of the Dark Room. Mathews and Marrot. 7s 6d [January 3, 1933]

An American, Robert J. Casey was a travel writer (*The Land of Haunted* Castles, 1921, *The Lost Kingdom of Burgundy*, 1923, *Baghdad and Points East*, 1928, *The Four Faces of Siva*, 1929, *Cambodian Quest*, 1931, *Easter Island*, 1932). He was also a war correspondent (*I Can't Forget*, 1941, *Torpedo Junction*, 1942 — his best-known book). And he was an occasional mystery/adventure novelist (seven, by my count), and eventually historian, in *The Midwesterner* and *Pioneer Railroad* (both 1948).

E[THEL] M[ARY] CHANNON (*b.* 1875)

The House with No Address. Benn. 7s 6d [April 15, 1931]

Miss Channon came late and not enthusiastically to mystery novels (of which she wrote only two or three). Her early books had titles like *The Authoress* (1909), *A Street Angel* (1910), *The Real Mrs. Holyer* (1911), *Stoneladies* (1912). In the 1920s and 1930s she wrote girls' school novels— *Expelled from St. Madern's* (1928), *A Countess at School* (1931), *Rose Leaves School* (1933), *A Fifth-Form Martyr* (1935). Her most successful book, also a school story, *The Honour of the House*, appeared in 1931, and was reissued in 1941, 1955, and 1961, and a number of times since. She has thirty-odd books in the British Library.

NELLISE CHILD

The Diamond Ransom Murders. Collins. 7s 6d [January 23 1935]

Miss Child has four books in the British Library, *Murder Comes Home* (1933), *The Diamond Ransom Murders* (1934), *Wolf on the Fold* (1943), *If I Come Home* (1944).

[DAME] AGATHA [M. C.] CHRISTIE (1890–1976)

Murder on the Orient Express. Collins. 7s 6d [January 17, 1934]
The Murder at the Vicarage. Collins. 7s 6d [October 14, 1930]
The Sittaford Mystery. Collins. 7s 6d [September 7, 1931]
Three Act Tragedy. Collins. 7s 6d [February 15, 1935]

Dame Agatha needs no biography here. For the record, she wrote also as Mary Westmacott, but even so, she was not so prolific as her long dominion in the field would suggest. One problem was that she had begun *The Mysterious Affair at Styles* (1922) with a detective who had retired in 1904, and *Murder at the Vicarage* (1930) with a detective already a spinster apparently past middle age. By the final Poirot story *(Curtain,* 1976, though written much earlier), and the final Miss Marple story *(Sleeping Murder,* 1976), her sleuths must have been of biblical age. One interesting indication of her popularity: virtually every one of the "Christies" in the British Library is a modern reprint, the originals apparently having worn out.

CARL CLAUSEN (?Carl Christian Clausen, 1868–1934)

Jaws of Circumstance. The Bodley Head. 7s 6d [August 25 1931]

Whether "Carl Clausen. Novelist" is the Dane Carl Christian Clausen (1868–1934) I am not sure. *Jaws of Circumstance* is apparently his only novel. The British Library has three books by Carl Christian Clausen in Danish, *Vor store Maend udgaaede fra smaa Hjem* (1897), *Danmarks Byer og daeres Maend* (1900), and *Under Palmer: Fortaellinger og Skildringer fra Dansk Vestindien* (1916).

THOMAS COBB (*b.* 1854?)

Crime at Keeper's. Benn. 7s 6d [November 6, 1930]
Inspector Bedison and the Sunderland Case. Benn. 7s 6d [February 18, 1931]

The British Library has 82 items listed by "Thomas Cobb. Novelist" running from *Brownie's Plot* (1889) to *Who Closed the Casement?* (1932) and *The Metal Box* (1933). Two of the early novels, *Wedderburn's Will* (1892) and *The Disappearance of Mr. Derwent* (1894) are self-described as detective stories. Cobb's most successful novel was *Mrs. Erricker's Reputation* (1906), also published as *Mrs. Pomeroy's Reputation* (1908).

JOHN COBNOR

The Four Answers. Cape. 7s 6d [April 7, 1931]

Apparently *The Four Answers* is his only book, unless others appeared under other names. Williams's review suggests an experience mystery-writer, though not one playing entirely by Detection Club rules.

G[EORGE] D[OUGLAS] H[OWARD] AND [DAME] MARGARET COLE (1889–1959 and 1893–1980)

Burglars in Bucks. The Crime Club. Collins. 7s 6d [June 4, 1930]
Corpse in Canonicals. Collins. 7s 6d [November 4, 1930]
Dead Man's Watch. Collins. 7s 6d [December 9 1931]
Death in the Quarry. Collins. 7s 6d [June 4, 1934]
Death of a Star. Collins. 7s 6d [December 21 1932]
The Great Southern Mystery. Collins. 7s 6d [March 2, 1931]

Other Golden-Age writers were also from the political Left — notably Christopher St. John Sprigg (Christopher Caudwell) and C. Day Lewis (Nicholas Blake). But Mr. and Mrs. Cole are unique as the only Fabian humdrums, though as Williams observes, their collaboration through some thirty-seven novels showed some danger of descending into "chats and chuckles." Their detective novels were not their only collaborations: most notable is their classic three-volume edition of Cobbett's *Rural Rides* (1930). (The fact that the Left, in the Coles, and the Right, in Chesterton, both looked to Cobbett, may suggest that something else beyond politics was at work here.) In addition, the Coles collaborated on *The Intelligent Man's Guide to Europe Today* (1933) and *A Guide to Modern Politics* (1934). The British Library Catalogue lists more than 350 items under G. D. H. Cole.

JACKSON COLE (Alexander Leslie Scott, 1893–1975)

Gun Justice. Cassell. 3s 6d [June 14, 1933]

It is something of a surprise to find Jackson Cole reviewed by Charles Williams. To be sure, his first two books, *Gun Justice* (1933) and *The Ramblin' Kid* (1934), are within our time-frame, and *Cowboy's Revenge* and *The Outlaws of Caja Basin* (both 1935) may overlap — but Jackson Cole wrote Westerns, not mysteries, just under thirty (in the British Library), up to *Gunslinger's Range* (1967). He was a prolific pulp-writer in the 1920s.

DALE COLLINS (1897–1956)

The Fifth Victim. Harrap. 3s 6d [April 17, 1930]

A traveler and journalist, Dale Collins published a dozen novels between 1924 (*Ordeal*) and *The Mutiny of Madame Yes* (1934). *Race in the Sun* came out in 1936, then *Far-off Strands* and *Bright Vista* (both 1946) and *Winds of Chance* (1947). His first success was *Sea-tracks of the Speejacks 'round the World* (1923). One unusual item in his bibliography is *When God Dropped In* (1928, reprinted 1956).

GILBERT COLLINS (*b.* 1890)

Chinese Red. Geoffrey Bles. 7s 6d [July 18, 1932]
Horror Comes to Thripplands. Geoffrey Bles. 7s 6d [December 1 1930]
Post Mortem. Geoffrey Bles. 7s 6d [June 4, 1930]
The Channel Million. Geoffrey Bles. 7s 6d [January 31 1933]

There are twelve novels in the British Library under the name of Gilbert Collins, from *The Flower of Nihon* (1922) to *Mystery in St. James's Square* (1937). Eight (all from the 1930s) are evidently mystery novels. He is also the author of *The Valley of Eyes Unseen* (1923), *Far Eastern Jaunts* (1924), *Extreme Oriental Mixture* (1925), *The New Magic of Swimming* (1934) and *The Newest Swimming* (1937).

J. J. CONINGTON (Alfred Walter Stewart, D. Sc., 1880–1947)

The Two Ticket Puzzles. Gollancz. 7s 6d [May 27 1930]

As J. J. Connington, Stewart published ten books in the years 1926–29. These are *Almighty Gold* (1926), *Nordenholt's Million* (1926), *The Dangerfield Talisman* (1926), *Death at Swaythling Court* (1926), *Murder in the Maze* (1927), *Tragedy at Ravensthorpe* (1927), *Mystery at Lynden Sands* (1928), *The Case With Nine Solutions* (1928), *The Eye in the Museum* (1929), *Nemesis at Raynham Parva* (1929). In the 1930s he published eleven: *The Two Tickets Puzzle* (1930), *The Sweepstake Murders* (1931), *The Boat House Riddle* (1931), *The Castleford Conundrum* (1932), *Tom Tiddler's Island* (1933),*The Ha-Ha Case* (1934), *The Tau Cross Mystery* (1935), *A Minor Operation* (1937), *For Murder Will Speak* (1938), *Truth Comes Limping* (1938), *The Counsellor* (1939). In the 1940s there were four more: *The Four Defences* (1940), *The Twenty-One Clues* (1941), *No Past Is Dead* (1942), *Jack-in-the-Box* (1944). As Alfred Walter Stewart, D.Sc., he published *Recent Advances in Organic Chemistry* (1908, 1911, 1918, 1920, 1927, 1931, 1936, 1948). Also, *Recent Advances in Physical and Inorganic Chemistry* (1909, 1912, 1919, 1920, 1926, 1930). Also *Stereochemistry* (1907), *A Manual of Practical Chemistry* (1913), *Chemistry and Its Borderland* (1914), *Some Physico-Chemical Themes* (1922). See also *The Omnibus J. J. Connington* (1930) and his essays, *Alias J. J. Connington* (1947).

JAMES CORBETT (*fl.* 1929–1960)

Death Comes to Fanshawe. Herbert Jenkins. 7s 6d [December 23 1933]
Murder at Pringlehurst. Herbert Jenkins. 7s 6d [June 5, 1933]

There are forty-two Corbett "thrillers" and mystery novels in the British Library, from *The Merrivale Mystery* (1929) to *Murder Begets*

Murder (1951). There is also *How to Write and Sell Thrillers* (1960), which at least suggests how he regarded his own work.

JOHN CREASEY (1908–1973)

Redhead. Hurst and Blackett. 7s 6d [December 23 1933]

John Creasey is the most widely published mystery-writer of the twentieth century, with well over five hundred novels under such names as Creasey, J. J. Marric, Jeremy Yorke.

FREEMAN WILLS CROFTS [F. R. S. A.] (1879–1957)

12:30 from Croydon. Hodder and Stoughton. 7s 6d [March 15, 1934]
Mystery in the Channel. Collins. 7s 6d [April 6, 1931]
Sir John Magill's Last Journey. Collins. 7s 6d [September 13, 1930]
Sudden Death. Collins. 7s 6d [January 7, 1932]
The Hog's Back Mystery. Hodder and Stoughton. 7s 6d [April 7, 1933]

Except for *The Four Gospels in One Story as a Modern Biography* (1949), all of the thirty-six books by Crofts in the British Library are mystery novels, from *The Cask* (1920) to *Anything to Declare?* (1957). He is the king of the timetable mystery. Most of his best work has been reprinted in Penguin paperbacks.

MORAY DALTON (no dates given in Barzun; L.C. lists as corporate name)

The Night of Fear. Sampson, Low. 7s 6d [July 15, 1931]

Thirty novels in the British Library, from *The Sword of Love* (1920, not detective fiction) to *The Death of a Spinster* and *The House of Fear* (both 1951). The Library of Congress lists "Moray Dalton" as a corporate name, and it has been suggested to me that at least some of the Moray Dalton novels were written by Major Cecil Street ("Miles Burton").

CARROLL J. DALY (1889–1958)

The Amateur Murderer. Hutchinson. 7s 6d [September 8, 1933]

Carroll John Daly wrote at least seventeen novels, from *The White Circle* (1927) to *Ready to Burn* (1951). Of these, three appeared in the 1920s, ten in the 1930s, two in the 1940s (1940 and 1947), and two in the 1950s.

H[ILDA] L. DEAKIN

The Secret of the Cove. Methuen. 7s 6d [May 27 1930]

Hilda Deakin has three books in the British Library, *The Square Mark* (1929), *The Secret of the Cove* (1930), and *The Shot That Killed Graeme Andrews* (1931).

[JOHN] LESLIE DESPARD [HOWITT]

The Crime Without a Flaw. Nash and Grayson. 7s 6d [July 30 1931]

Besides *In a Cottage, and Other Verses* (1917, by John Leslie Despard Howitt), Despard has three books in the British Library, *The Mystery of the Tower Room* (1925), *The Amazing Adventures of Mr. Henry Button* (1927), and *The Crime Without a Flaw* (1931).

GEORGE DILNOT (1883–1951)

The Thousandth Case. Geoffrey Bles 7s 6d [January 31 1933]

George Dilnot was the General Editor of the Geoffrey Bles Famous Trials Series from 1928 through 1931, to which he contributed *The Trial of the Detectives* (1928), *The Trial of Jim the Penman* (1930) and *The Trial of Professor John White Webster* (1928). He also wrote *Scotland Yard* (1915), *Celebrated Crimes* (1925), *The Story of Scotland Yard* (1926), *Man-Hunters* (1926), *Triumphs of Detection* (1929), *The Real Detective* (1933), *Getting Rich Quick: An Outline of Swindles* (1935), and *New Scotland Yard* (1938). His novels run from *Murder Masquerade* (1924) to *Tiger Lily* (1939), but he was primarily a true-crime writer.

MAURICE B[UXTON] DIX

Murder at Grasmere Abbey. Ward Lock. 7s 6d [February 2, 1934]

The British Library has eighteen of Dix's novels, from *Twisted Evidence* and *Murder at Grasmere Abbey* (both 1933) to *A Lady Richly Left* (1951). Fifteen were published in the 1930s, only two in the 1940s and one in 1951.

ROGER EAST (Roger D'Este Burford, *b.* 1904)

The Bell is Answered. Collins. 7s 6d [August 3, 1934]
The Mystery of the Monkey-Gland Cocktail. Putnam. 7s 6d [July 18, 1932]

Not counting *Twenty-five Sanitary Inspectors: Superintendent Simmons Investigates* (1935), there are eight novels by Roger East in the British Library, five from the 1930s, then *Pearl Choker* (1954), *Kingston Black* (1960), and *The Pin Men* (1963).

MIGNON G. EBERHART (*b.* 1899)

The Mystery of Hunting's End. Heinemann. 7s 6d [May 5, 1931]

Mignon Good Eberhart published more than fifty novels, from *The Patient in Room 18* (1929) through *El Rancho Rio* (1971). She is noted for her female detective, Susan Dare.

A. C. AND CARMEN EDDINGTON

The Monkshood Murder. Collins. 7s 6d [May 19 1931]

No other books by A. C. and Carmen Eddington are in either the British Library or the Library of Congress.

LOUISE EPPLEY AND REBECCA GAYTON

Murder in the Cellar. Grayson and Grayson. 7s 6d [July 28 1932]

This is the only book by either Louise Eppley or Rebecca Gayton in either the British Library or the Library of Congress.

RICHARD ESSEX (Richard Harry Starr, *b.* 1878)

Slade Scores Again. Herbert Jenkins. 7s 6d [April 26 1933]

As Richard Essex, Starr published seven books of mystery and detection, from *Slade of the Yard* (1932) to *Assisted by Lessinger* (1939)—and then *The Girl in Black* was published in 1966. As Richard Starr, he published forty-six novels with titles like *Married to a Spy* (1915) and *Romantic Inheritance* (1941), his earliest and latest—unless, of course, there were two contemporary Richard Starrs, one of whom wrote as Richard Essex. The "Richard Starr" books published under that name are clearly directed at woman readers, and would seem to be by a woman.

GERALD FAIRLIE (1899–1981)

Suspect. Hodder and Stoughton. 7s 6d [April 17, 1930]

Gerard Fairlie was the collaborator and successor of H. C. McNeile ("Sapper") on the Bulldog Drummond stories, beginning with *Bulldog Drummond on Dartmoor* (1938) and ending with *Calling Bulldog Drummond* (1951). In his own right, he published seventeen novels in the ten years 1927–36. These are *Scissors Cut Paper* (1927), *Stone Blunts Scissors* (1928), *The Man Who Laughed* (1928), *The Exquisite Lady* (1929), *The Muster of the Vultures* (1929), *Suspect* (1930), *Unfair Lady* (1931), *The Man With Talent* (1931), *Birds of Prey* (1932), *Mr. Malcolm Presents* (1932), *The Rope Which Hangs* (1932), *Shot in the Dark* (1932), *Men for Counters* (1933), *The Treasure Nets* (1933), *That Man Returns* (1933), *Copper at Sea* (1934), *Moral Holiday* (1936). After (and during) his sojourn with Bulldog Drummond, he published another eight novels, the last *Please Kill My Cousin* (1961). His last book was *The Life of a Genius: George Cayley* (1965), one of several non-fiction works.

J[OSEPH] JEFFERSON FARJEON (1883–1955)

Ben Sees It Through. Collins. 7s 6d [December 21 1932]
Mystery on the Moor. Collins. 7s 6d [November 4, 1930]

The Person Called Z. Collins. 7s 6d [July 7, 1930]
Trunk Call. Collins. 7s 6d [December 13, 1932]

Joseph Jefferson Farjeon was a nephew of the famous actor, Joe Jefferson, and brother of authors Herbert Farjeon and Eleanor Farjeon. He has more than eighty novels in the British Library, from *The Master Criminal* and *Confusing Friendship* (both 1924) to *Caravan Adventure* (1955), a steady stream through three decades. Mostly they are considered adventure stories rather than pure stories of detection.

A. FIELDING (Dorothy Feilding, *b.* 1884)

The Upfold Farm Mystery. Collins. 7s 6d [June 10 1931]

Dorothy Feilding ("A. Fielding") has twenty-five novels in the British Library, from *The Eames-Erskine Case* and *Deep Currents* (both 1924) to *Murder in Suffolk* (1938), with one last novel, *Pointer to a Crime*, appearing in 1944.

CORTLAND FITZSIMMONS (1893–1949)

The Bainbridge Murder. Eyre and Spottiswoode. 5s [August 6, 1930]

Cortland Fitzsimmons produced nine novels listed in the British Library Catalogue, five in the 1930s, beginning with *The Bainbridge Murder* (1930), and four in the War Years (*The Evil Men Do*, 1942, *Death Rings a Bell*, 1943, *Murder Is Swift*, 1944, and *Tied For Murder*, 1945, his last). He also appears as co-author, with Muriel Fitzsimmons, of *Cooking For Absolute Beginners* (1976).

J[OSEPH] S[MITH] FLETCHER (1863–1935)

Murder in Four Degrees. Harrap. 7s 6d [November 17, 1931]
Murder in the Squire's Pew. Harrap. 7s 6d [January 25 1932]
The Box Hill Murder. Herbert Jenkins. 7s 6d [January 21 1931]
The House in Tuesday Market. Herbert Jenkins. 7s 6d [July 7, 1930]
Who Killed Alfred Snowe? Harrap. 7s 6d [February 13, 1933]

Joseph Smith Fletcher was a poet, historian, regionalist, religious writer, historical novelist, and mystery/detection writer. His first prose fiction, *Frank Carisbrooke's Strategem*, was published in 1888, his last, *Todmanhawe Grange*, posthumously in 1937. His 287 items in the British Library Catalogue range from his *Juvenile Poems* (1879) to his *Picturesque History of Yorkshire* (3 vols 1899, 6 vols 1903–4), *Making of Modern Yorkshire 1750–1914* (1918), *Life and Work of St. Wilfrid of Ripon* (1925). His collection, *Paul Campenhaye, Criminologist* (1918) is pre–Golden Age, and he is in fact an emulator of Doyle from an earlier period who writes into the Golden Age, and is in it — but not entirely of it.

[WILLIAM] HULBERT FOOTNER (1879–1944)

The Casual Murderer. Collins. 7s 6d [July 5, 1932]
The Folded Paper Mystery. Collins. 7s 6d [September 13, 1930]

Like many of the Golden Age novelists, Hulbert Footner began his career in a different genre. The earliest of his more than seventy items in the British Library is *Entertaining a Prince, a Story of Western Canada*. This was followed (at an interval) by *Two on the Trail, a Story of the Far Northwest* (1911), *New Rivers of the North: The Yarn of Two Amateur Explorers* (1913), *The Sealed Valley* (1915), *The Fur-Bringers, a Story of Athabasca* (1916) and *Jack Chanty, a Story of Athabasca* (1917). Later in his life he lived in Maryland and wrote *Sailor of Fortune: The Life and Adventures of Commodore Barney* (1940), *Maryland Main and the Eastern Shore* (1942) and *Rivers of the Eastern Shore* (1944). He began his career as a mystery writer with *Thieves' Wit* (1918) and *The Fugitive Sleuth* (1918) and ended it with *Unneutral Murder* (1944) and *Orchids to Murder* (1945), with sixteen detective novels in between.

C[ECIL] S[COTT] FORESTER (1899–1966)

Plain Murder. The Bodley Head. 7s 6d [November 4, 1930]

C. S. Forester has 133 items listed in the British Library Catalogue. Many of them are printings and reprintings of his Hornblower books. He also wrote *Rifleman Dodd, The Gun, The African Queen, The Ship, The Captain From Connecticut, Death to the French, The Commodore, The*

General, The Good Shepherd. Among his nonfiction works are *The Age of Fighting Sail, The Naval War of 1812, The Voyage of the Annie Marble, The Annie Marble in Germany, The Barbary Pirates, Hunting the Bismarck*. He wrote only two mysteries that I have found.

HENRY JAMES FORMAN (1879–1966)

The Rembrandt Murder. Stanley Paul. 7s 6d [October 22 1931]

Henry James Forman was a travel writer, author of *The Story of Prophecy* (1931), and only in *The Rembrandt Murder* a detective-story novelist. His best-known books are *In the Footsteps of Heine* (1910), *The Ideal Italian Tour* (1911), and *Grecian Italy* (1924). He published no new books after 1931.

ROBIN FORSYTHE (*b.* 1879)

The Polo Ground Mystery. The Bodley Head. 7s 6d [January 25 1932]

Robin Forsythe published *Missing or Murdered?* (1929), *The Hounds of Justice* (1930), *The Polo Ground Mystery* (1932), *The Pleasure Cruise Mystery* (1933), *The Ginger Cat Mystery* (1935), and *The Spirit Murder Mystery* (1936).

R. FRANCIS FOSTER (1896–1975)

Murder from Beyond. Nash and Grayson. 7s 6d [June 11 1930]

Reginald Francis Foster was a short-story writer and author of *How to Write and Sell Short Stories* (1926), *Famous Short-Stories Analysed* (1932), and *Modern Punctuation Handbook* (1947). He wrote *The Lift Murder* (1924), *The Missing Gates* (1924), *The Music Gallery Murder* (1927), *The Moat House Mystery* (1928), *Murder from Beyond* (1930), *Something Wrong At Chillery* (1931)—also *Anthony Ravenhill, Crime Merchant* (1926) and *The Dark Night* (1930). Also *The Secret Places, Being a Chronicle of Vagabondage* (1929), and under the pseudonym of Heather White, he and Jess Mary Mardon Foster wrote *The Wayside Book* (1932). His last book was *The*

Perennial Religion (1969), which may indicate what he was doing with his time at least between 1947 and 1969.

SYDNEY FOWLER [WRIGHT] (1874–1967)

The Bell Street Murders. Harrap. 7s 6d [February 9 1931]
The Hanging of Constance Hillier. Jarrold. 7s 6d [September 16, 1931]
The King Against Anne Bickerton. Harrap. 7s 6d [May 27 1930]

As Fowler, Sydney Fowler Wright wrote thirteen novels of mystery and detection, from *The King Against Anne Bickerton* (1930) to *The Adventure of the Blue Room* (1945). As Wright, he was a founder of modern science fiction, beginning with *The Amphibians* (1925). He translated Dante, edited a number of poetry collections, published several collections of his own verse, and was a pioneer also in stories of the supernatural, as in *The Throne of Saturn* (Arkham House 1948). His collected short stories were published in 1996.

ARNOLD FREDERICKS (Frederic Arnold Kummer, 1873–1943)

The Mark of the Rat. Stanley Paul. 7s 6d [August 6, 1930]

Frederic Kummer published six mysteries as Arnold Fredericks 1916–1930 and then four more as Frederic Kummer 1936–38. He wrote science and history for young readers, also two juveniles, also a history of *The Great Road* (1938) and *Courage Over the Andes* (1940). He also published twelve non-mystery novels, including two as co-author with Mary Christian, *Peggy-Elise* (1919) and *The Pipes of Yesterday* (1921).

M[ARTIN] J[OSEPH] FREEMAN (*b.* 1899)

The Murder of a Midget. Eldon. 7s 6d [March 15, 1934]

Martin Joseph Freeman wrote only *The Murder of a Midget* (1934) and *The Case of the Blind Mouse* (1936), unless he was also the Martin Joseph Freeman who was co-author of *Written Communication in Business* (1936) or the Martin Joseph Freeman who selected *The Reader's Shelley* (1942). In any case, he was an American.

R[ICHARD] AUSTIN FREEMAN (1862–1943)

Mr. Pottermack's Oversight. Hodder and Stoughton. 7s 6d [October 14, 1930]
When Rogues Fall Out. Hodder and Stoughton. 7s 6d [December 21 1932]

R. A. Freeman began with *The Red Thumb-Mark* (1907) and *John Thorndyke's Cases* (1909), but that was after his *Travels and Life in Ashanti and Jaman* (1898). His last books were *The Penrose Mystery* (1936) and *Felo de Se?* (1937). He had thirty books to his credit, but, like Doyle and E. C. Bentley and Anthony Berkeley Cox, his true influence was measured not by number of books but by the creation of a pattern and ambience in mystery stories. Also, it should be remembered that Freeman came before the Golden Age and truly fits into the category of the emulators of Doyle in the previous age, though he wrote well into his seventies, and *The Penrose Mystery* exists in a modern paperback reprint.

DAVID FROME (Leslie Ford or
Mrs. Zenith Brown, 1898–1983)

The By-Pass Murder. Longmans. 7s 6d [December 13, 1932]

There are fifteen "David Frome" books in the British Library, from *In at the Death* and *The Murder of an Old Man* (both 1929) to *Mr. Pinkerton and the Old Angel* (1939), with one last gasp, *Mr. Pinkerton Returns*, in 1951. There are thirty-two "Leslie Ford" books in the Library, from *Footsteps on the Stairs* (1931) to *Trial for Ambush* (1962). From 1929 to 1939, Mrs. Brown wrote fourteen "Fromes" and five "Fords" and from 1940 to 1962 she wrote one "Frome" and twenty-seven "Fords." My own taste is for the earlier books, but that may be the result of an over-all preference for the Golden Age against the years after the War.

VAL GIELGUD and HOLT MARVELL (1900–1981 and 1901–1969)

Death at Broadcasting House. Rich and Cowan. 7s 6d [March 15, 1934]
Under London. Rich and Cowan. 7s 6d [April 7, 1933]

Val Gielgud and Holt Marvell (Eric Maschwitz) collaborated on five novels, *Under London* (1933), *Death at Broadcasting House* (1934), *Death as an Extra* (1935), *Death in Budapest* (1937), and *The First Television Murder* (1940). Maschwitz on his own wrote at least four books, *A Taste of Honey* (1924), *Husks in May* (1926), *Angry Dust* (1926) and *The Passionate Clowns* (1927). He wrote book or lyrics or both for such musical comedies as *Balalaika* (1936), *New Faces* (1940 with "A Nightingale Sang in Berkeley Square"), *The Hulbert Follies* (1941), *More New Faces* (1942), *Serenade* (1948), *Belinda Fair* (1949), *Summer Song* (1958). His autobiography, *No Chip on my Shoulder* appeared in 1957. Val Henry Gielgud on his own wrote a number of adventure stories before and during World War II: *Black Gallantry* (1928), *Gathering of Eagles* (1929), *Imperial Treasure* (1931), *The Broken Men* (1932), *Outrage in Manchukuo* (1937), *The Red Account* (1938), *Confident Morning* (1943). His books after the War include *Fall of a Sparrow* (1949), *Special Delivery* (1950), *The High Jump* (1953), *Gallows' Foot* (1958), *To Bed at Noon* (1959), *And Died So?* (1961), *The Goggle-Box Affair* (1963), *Conduct of a Member* (1967), *A Necessary End* (1969), *The Candle-Holders* (1970). He wrote a number of radio plays and produced Dorothy L. Sayers's *The Man Born to be King* for the BBC. Val Gielgud wrote three or four installments on his autobiography, including *My Cats and Myself* (1972).

ANTHONY GILBERT (Lucy Beatrice Malleson, 1899–1973)

The Body on the Beam. Collins. 7s 6d [January 7, 1932]

"Anthony Gilbert" has 119 items listed in the British Library Catalogue, many of them reprint editions of her books before and after her death. Even so, I count 64 separate titles, from *The Tragedy at Freyne* (1927) to *Missing From Her Home* (1969). She is one of the major links between the Golden Age and the 1960s, and a reader who grew up on Golden Age mysteries—as I did—found her continuing production amazing and even disconcerting and oddly asynchronous.

JOSEPH GOLLOMB (b. 1886)

The Subtle Trail. Heinemann. 7s 6d [July 7, 1930]

Joseph Gollomb was a poetry anthologist (*Songs for Courage*, 1917) and primarily a journalist (*The German Constitution*, 1923, *Scotland Yard*,

1926, *Spies*, 1928, *Crimes of the Year*, 1932, *Young Heroes of the War*, 1946, *Albert Schweitzer*, 1951).

JOHN GOODWIN (Sidney Floyd Gowing, *b.* 1878)

Blood Money. Putnam. 7s 6d [August 25 1931]

Under his own name, Sydney Floyd Gowing published *A Daughter in Revolt* (1922), *Held to Ransom* (1924), *Kim Ruff* (1925), *Sea Lavender* (1925), *Heather Bells* (1927), and *Sealed Orders* (1929). As John Goodwin, he published fifteen books, from *Blackmail* (1910) to *In Full Cry* (1941). The first John Goodwin mystery seems to have been *Dead Man's Treasure* (1929), followed by *Blood Money* (1931), *The Shadow Man* (1932), and *The King's Elm Mystery* (1934).

NEIL GORDON (Archibald Gordon Macdonell, 1895–1941)

Murder in Earl's Court. The Bodley Head. 7s 6d [April 7, 1931]

Archibald Gordon Macdonell's best known book was *England, Their England* (1933), followed by *Autobiography of a Cad (A Novel)* (1938). He also wrote *Napoleon and His Marshals* (1934), the introduction for Hilaire Belloc's *Stories, Essays, and Poems* (1938), and *The Crew of the Anaconda* (1940). As Neil Gordon he wrote *The Professor's Poison* and *The Factory on the Cliff* (both 1928), *The Silent Murders* (1929), *The Big Ben Alibi* (1930), *Murder in Earl's Court* (1931), and *The Shakespeare Murders* (1933).

BRUCE GRAEME (Graham Montague Jeffries, *b.* 1900)

An International Affair. Hutchinson. 7s 6d [August 3, 1934]
A Murder of Some Importance. 7s 6d [April 6, 1931]
Gigins Court. Hutchinson. 7s 6d [June 2, 1932]
Unsolved. Hutchinson. 7s 6d [November 17, 1931]

"Bruce Graeme" wrote a number of "Blackshirt" novels, from *Blackshirt* (1925) to *Blackshirt the Adventurer* (1945). His "non–Blackshirt" novels run from *A Murder of Some Importance* (1931) to *The Lady Doth Protest*

(1971) and *The D-Notice* (1974), and then a late series, *The Snatch* (1976), *Double Trouble* (1978), *Mather Again* (1979), *Invitation to Mather* (1980) and *Mather Investigates* (1980). He would have been the last writing survivor of the Golden Age, if he were ever truly *of* the Golden Age.

RUPERT [STANLEY HARRINGTON] GRAYSON (*b.* 1897)

Death Rides in the Forest. Nash and Grayson. 7s 6d [December 9 1931]

Rupert Grayson published *Gun Cotton: A Romance of Secret Service* (1929), *Death Rides the Forest* (1931), *Gun Cotton, Adventurer* (1933), *Escape With Gun Cotton* (1934), *Gun Cotton Goes to Russia* (1936), *Gun Cotton in Hollywood* (1936), *Gun Cotton Outside the Law* (1936), *Gun Cotton in Mexico* (1937), *Gun Cotton, Ace High* (1937), *Gun Cotton, Adventure Nine* (1937), *Gun Cotton at Blind Man's Hood* (1938), and *Gun Cotton, Murder at the Bank* (1939). I take it he may also be the author of *Voyage Not Completed* (1969), by Rupert Grayson, King's Messenger.

L. PATRICK GREENE (*fl.* 1919–1954)

Dynamite Drury Again. Jarrolds. 7s 6d [April 10 1930]

There are three Dynamite Drury books by pulp-writer L. Patrick Greene, *Dynamite Drury* (1929), *Dynamite Drury Again* (1930), and *Dynamite Drury Patrols* (1946). Greene wrote another thirty-three books, from *The Major, Diamond Buyer* (1926) to *Sergeant Lancey Tells the Tale* (1947). Eight at least deal with the Major, and five with Sergeant Lancey.

CECIL FREEMAN GREGG (*b.* 1898)

The Body Behind the Bar. Methuen. 7s 6d [January 3, 1933]
The Brazen Confession. Hutchinson. 7s 6d [September 9 1930]
The Double Solution. Hutchinson. 7s 6d [October 22 1931]

Cecil Freeman Gregg's forty-two books in the British Library run from *The Murdered Manservant* (1928) and *The Three Daggers* (1929) to *Professional Jealousy* (1960). Eighteen were published in the 1930s, eleven in the 1940s, ten in the 1950s.

Jackson Gregory (1882–1943)

The Second Case of Mr. Paul Savoy. Hodder and Stoughton. 7s 6d [September 8, 1933]

Jackson Gregory's fifty-five books in the British Library run from *Under Handicap* (1914) to *The Silver River* (1950). They are mostly "Westerns" but include *A Case for Mr. Paul Savoy* (1933, also as *The First Case of Mr. Paul Savoy,* 1933), *The Second Case of Mr. Paul Savoy* (1933), and *The Emerald Murder Trap: The Third Case of Mr. Paul Savoy* (1934).

Ian Greig (no dates given in Barzun, BL or L.C.)

The Tragedy of the Chinese Mine. Benn. 7s 6d [December 24 1930]

Ian Greig created Inspector Swinton and published a brief spate of detective novels in the early 1930s, *The King's Club Murder* (1930), *The Tragedy of the Chinese Mine* (1930), *Murder at Lintercombe* (1931), *Baxter's Second Death* (1932), and *False Scent* (1933). The first three were reprinted in *The Inspector Swinton Omnibus* (1934)—and then, nothing. It is suggested that Ian Greig may be a pseudonym.

Leo Grex (Leonard Gribble, *b.* 1908)

The Lonely Inn Mystery. Hutchinson. 7s 6d [September 8, 1933]
The Tragedy of Draythorpe. Hutchinson. 7s 6d [February 9 1931]

As Leo Grex, the author published more than thirty novels, from *The Tragedy at Draythorpe* and *Nightborn* (both 1931) to *Hot Ice* (1983). The earlier novels are pretty much Golden Age, though not anywhere near the best. The latter go back to detection's roots in sensation fiction. [See also L. R. Gribble]

L[eonard] R. Gribble (*b.* 1908)

The Secret of Tangles. Harrap. 7s 6d [December 29 1933]

Under his own name, Leonard Gribble published more than a hundred books, many of them non-fiction (quite a number "true crime"). He wrote juveniles, a number of mysteries (from *The Gillespie Suicide Mystery*, 1929, to *You Can't Die Tomorrow*, 1975), "Westerns" as Denver Lee, and also under the name Sterry Browning. His Inspector Slade novels, beginning in the Golden Age, were appearing as late as *Strip-Tease Macabre* (1967). His anthology *The Jesus of the Poets* (SCM Press 1930) is an interesting "odd-book-out" in his *oeuvre*. [See also Leo Grex]

FRANCIS D[URHAM] GRIERSON (1888–1972)

The Lady of Despair. Crime Club. Collins. 7s 6d [June 4, 1930]
The Mysterious Mademoiselle. Collins. 7s 6d [December 1 1930]

After *The A.B.C. of Military Law* (1916) and *Pan's Punishment* (1917), F. D. Grierson published just over fifty books, beginning with *The Limping Man* (1924) and going on to *The Red Cobra* (1960). Only a few of his mysteries went through more than one edition. *The Zoo Murder* (1926) had new editions in 1935 and 1939. *The Smiling Death* (1927) had a new edition in 1936. *The Blue Bucket Mystery* and *The Green Diamond Mystery* (both 1929) had new editions in 1940. *The Mad Hatter Murder* (1941) had a new edition in 1948. His best writing seems to have come before the Second World War.

[ANTHONY DOUGLAS] BRUCE HAMILTON (*b.* 1900)

Hue and Cry. Collins. 7s 6d [September 7, 1931]

[Anthony Douglas] Bruce Hamilton published ten novels over nearly thirty years, from *To Be Hanged* (1930) to *Too Much of Water* (1958), and, finally, *The Light Went Out: The Life of Patrick Hamilton* (1972). Six of his books (*To Be Hanged*, 1930, *Hue and Cry*, 1931, *The Spring Term*, 1933, *Middle Class Murder*, 1936, *The Brighton Murder Trial*, 1937, and *Traitor's Way*, 1938) came out in the 1930s. Two (*Pro, An English Tragedy*, 1946, and *Let Him Have Judgment*, 1948) appeared in the 1940s, and two (*So Sad, So Fresh*, 1952, and *Too Much of Water*, 1958) were published in the 1950s.

DASHIELL HAMMETT (1894–1961)

The Thin Man. Barker. 7s 6d [June 18, 1934]

Dashiell Hammett published five novels, *The Thin Man*, *The Maltese Falcon*, *The Glass Key*, *The Dain Curse*, *Women in the Dark*, and a number of stories, including the "Continental op" stories in the old *Black Mask*, collected as *The Continental Op* and *The Return of the Continental Op*. Two more selections of stories, *The Big Knockover* and *Nightmare Town*, were published after his death. With Robert Colodny he wrote *The Battle of the Aleutians: A Graphic History 1942–43*. He was blacklisted as a Hollywood screenwriter as a result of his Communist affiliations. Despite a relatively meager output, his influence has been tremendous.

HAZEL PHILLIPS HANSHEW

The Riddle of the Winged Death. John Long. 7s 6d [September 16, 1931]

Hazel Phillips Hanshew published only two novels under her own name, *The Riddle of the Winged Death* (1931) and *Murder in the Hotel* (1932). Her father, Thomas W. Hanshew, was the author of *The World's Finger* (1901), *The Mallison Mystery* (1903), *The Great Ruby* (1905), *The Shadow of a Dead Man* (1906), *Fate and the Man* (1910), *Cleek, the Man of the Forty Faces* (1913), *Cleek of Scotland Yard* (1914). His Cleek stories are almost all mysterious-disguises thrillers, but after he died, his wife, Mary E. Hanshew, and daughter, Hazel Phillips Hanshew, produced his best collection of Cleek stories, still published under his name, *Cleek's Greatest Riddles* (1916). They also produced *The Riddle of the Night* (1915/1916), *The Riddle of the Purple Emperor* (1918), *The Frozen Flames* (1920), *The House of Discord* (1922), *The Amber Junk* (1924), and *The House of the Seven Keys* (1925). Some of these were published as by T. W. Hanshew, some as by T. W. and M. E. Hanshew. It is believed that those with both names may have been written entirely by Hazel Phillips Hanshew, the others by Mary E. and Hazel.

ROBERT HARE (?*b*. 1887)

Spectral Evidence. Hurst and Blackett. 7s 6d [August 23 1932]

Robert Hare Hutchinson published four novels, *The Fourth Challenge* (1932), as by Robert Hare Hutchinson, *Spectral Evidence* (1932), *The Doctor's First Murder* (1933), and *The Hand of the Chimpanzee* (1934), as by Robert Hare. His only other book in the British Library is *The "Socialism" of New Zealand* (New York 1916).

W[ILLIAM] F[RYER] HARVEY (1885–1937)

The Mysterious Mr. Badman. Powling and Ness. 3s 6d [February 20 1934]

William Fryer Harvey was a Quaker scholar, author of *Quaker Byways* (1929), *John Rutty of Dublin, Quaker Physician* (1933), and *We Were Seven: Reminiscences* (1936). He wrote *Midnight House, and Other Tales* (1910), *The Misadventures of Athelstan Digby* (1920), *The Beast With Five Fingers, and Other Tales* (1928), *Moods and Tenses, and Other Tales* (1933), *The Mysterious Mr. Badman* (1934), *Caprimulgus* (1936), *Mr. Murray and the Boococks* (1938). Two collections were put together after his death, *Midnight Tales* (1946) and *The Arm of Mrs. Egan, and Other Stories* (1951). With W. F. Halliday he published *A Conversation About God* (1923).

[WILLIAM] LAING HAY (*b.* 1892)

Who Cut the Colonel's Throat? Longmans. 7s 6d [January 21 1931]

This is the only book by (William) Laing Hay I have found in the British Library, nor have I found any others under either William Hay or Laing Hay.

ANNIE HAYNES (*d.* 1929?)

The Crystal Beads Murder. The Bodley Head. 7s 6d [July 30 1930]

Annie Haynes wrote eleven and (perhaps) three-quarters mystery novels in the time from 1923 through 1929. From 1923 through 1926 these were *The Abbey Court Murder* and *The Bungalow Mystery* (1923), *The Secret of Graylands* (1924), *The Blue Diamond* and *The Witness on the Roof* (1925), *The House in Charlton Crescent* (1926). From 1927 through 1929, these were *The Crow's Inn Tragedy* and *The Master of the Priory* (1927), *The Man With the Dark Beard* (1928), *The Crime at Tattenham Corner* and *Who Killed Charmian Karslake* (1929). *The Crystal Beads Murder* was completed by another hand and published in 1930.

JAMES HILTON (1900–1954)

Murder at School. Benn. 7s 6d [January 1 1932]

James Hilton, author of two classics, *Lost Horizon* (1933) and *Good-bye Mr. Chips* (1934), wrote a dozen other novels, including *Murder at School* (1931) and *Was It Murder?* (1933) Like Sir John Masterman's *An Oxford Tragedy*, and C. S. Forester's two mystery novels, this is an unexpected benefit of the craze for detective fiction in the Golden Age.

LEONARD HOLLINGWORTH

Dead Man's Alibi. John Murray. 7s 6d [February 13, 1933]
The Body on the Bus. John Murray. 7s 6d [August 26 1930]

Leonard Hollingworth (novelist) has three novels in the British Library, *The Body on the Bus* (1930), *Death Leaves Us Naked* (1931), and *Dead Man's Alibi* (1933). He may also be the Leonard Hollingworth (English Master) who published *A New Basis for School Grammar and Composition* (1937).

SYDNEY HORLER (1888–1954)

Harlequin of Death. John Long. 7s 6d [June 14, 1933]
The Man Who Shook the Earth. Hutchinson. 7s 6d [April 26 1933]
The Menace. Collins. 7s 6d [September 8, 1933]
Tiger Standish. John Long. 7s 6d [July 18, 1932]

Sydney Horler was primarily a thriller writer — one of his collections (1936) is called *The Sydney Horler Omnibus of Excitement.* The British Library shows 240 items under his name, though many of them are reprints, and some, such as *Goal! A Romance of the English Cup-Ties* (1920) and *McPhee, A Football Story* (1923), seem far apart from most of his work. His earliest book is *Stanley of the Rangeland* (1916), his earliest "thriller" perhaps *The Ball of Fortune* (1925) or *False-Face* (1926) or *The Black Heart* (1927), his last (of more than one hundred) *The Man in the Hood* and *The Man in the Shadows* (both 1955). He was fantastically popular; I do not always find him pleasant.

BABETTE HUGHES (*b.* 1906)

Murder in the Zoo. Benn. 7s 6d [April 27 1932]

Babette Hughes was primarily a playwright (mostly one-act plays) and also a translator from the French. Her mystery novels were *Murder in the Zoo* (1932) and *Murder in Church* (1934), both written before she was thirty. This novel, as Williams notes, shows both her academic background and her tendency to bewilder the reader with cultural references.

DAVID HUME (John Victor Turner)

Bullets Bite Deep. Putnam. 7s 6d [April 27 1932]

The pseudonymous David Hume (John Victor Turner) published thirty-five mystery novels from *Bullets Bite Deep* (1932) to *Heading for a Wreath* (1946), an average of seven books every three years— besides the eight he published as John Victor Turner from 1931 to 1936. In 1935 alone, under the two names, he brought out seven novels. So far as I have been able to find out, he did not publish under other names. [See also John Victor Turner]

FRANCIS ILES (Anthony Berkeley [Cox], 1893–1970)

Malice Aforethought. Mundanus. 3s [March 18, 1931]

Anthony Berkeley (Cox) published three novels as Francis Iles, *Malice Aforethought* (1931), *Before the Fact* (1932), and *As For The Woman* (1939). [See also Anthony Berkeley]

[ARCHIBALD] KENNETH INGRAM (1882–1965)

Death Comes at Night. Philip Allen. 7s 6d [July 26 1933]

Archibald Kenneth Ingram was a clergyman, author of *Fifty Years of the National Peace Council* (1958), *History of the Cold War* (1955), *A Manual for Church of England Scouts* (1913), *Is Divorce Needed?* (1914), *The Anglo-Catholic Case* (1923), a total of some eighty books and pamphlets on Christianity and the modern world, including devotional books. He also wrote *The Steep Steps* (1931) and *Death Comes At Night* (1933).

T[HOMAS] C[URTIS] H[ICKS] JACOBS
(T. C. H. Pendower, 1899–1976)

The Terror of the Torlands. Stanley Paul. 7s 6d [August 26 1930]

Thomas Curtis Hicks Pendower (T. C. H. Jacobs) began with books like *The Terror of the Torlands* (1930), *The Bronkhorst Case* (1931), and *The Kestrel House Mystery* (1932). Fifty books and four decades later, he published *Security Risk* (1972). He published eleven books in the 1930s, seven in the 1940s, sixteen in the 1950s, sixteen in the 1960s, and that one in 1972. He is wrongly listed in Barzun as Jacques Pendover.

ELIZABETH JORDAN (*b.* 1888)

The Night Club Mystery. Hutchinson. 7s 6d June 11 1940

Elizabeth Garver Jordan published *As Cooks Go* (1950, on her experiences as a cook), several plays (including *The Lady From Oklahoma*, 1911), and nearly twenty novels, beginning with *May Iverson Tackles Life* (1912) and *May Iverson's Career* (1914). *The Night Club Mystery* (1930) seems to be her only effort in that genre.

HARRY STEPHEN KEELER (1890–1967)

Ten Hours. Ward, Lock. 7s 6d [January 23 1935]

Harry Stephen Keeler published forty-five books from *The Voice of the Seven Sparrows* (1924), *Find the Clock* (1925) and *The Spectacles of Mr. Cagliostro* (1926) to *The Murder of London Lew* (1952). Three — *The Barking Clock* (1951), *The Case of the Transposed Logs* (1951), and *Stand By! London Calling* (1953) — were published as by Harry Stephen Keeler and Hazel Goodwin Keeler.

MILWARD KENNEDY (Milward R. K. Burge, 1894–1968)

Death in a Deckchair. Gollancz. 7s 6d [September 3, 1930]

Milward [Rodon]Kennedy [Burge] published sixteen novels, from *The Corpse on the Mat* and *Corpse Guard Parade* (both 1929) to *Two's Company* (1952). Nine appeared in the 1930s, when "Kennedy" was selected by the Detection Club to contribute to the jointly written *Ask A Policeman* (1933) — with Anthony Berkeley, Gladys Mitchell, John Rhode, Dorothy L. Sayers, and Helen Simpson. Three came in the 1940s (*Who Was Old Willy?* in 1940), and two on the 1950s.

RICHARD KEVERNE (Clifford James Wheeler Hosken, 1882–1950)

The Fleet Hall Inheritance. Constable. 7s 6d [April 15, 1931]

Richard Keverne (Clifford James Wheeler Hosken) published twenty books, from *Carteret's Cure* (1926) to *The Shadow Syndicate* (1946). His collections, *Crook Stuff* (1935), *More Crook Stuff* (1938), and *Crooks and Vagabonds* (1941) were not reprinted, nor were *Missing From His Home* (1939), *The Black Cripple* (1941), *The Lady in No. 4* (1944), or *The Shadow Syndicate*. But every one of his novels published between 1926 and 1939 went through two or three editions. His *Tales of Old Inns* (1939) was revised and edited by Hammond Innes (1947).

MAURICE G[EORGE] KIDDY (*b.* 1894)

Killing No Murder. Hutchinson. 7s 6d [May 5, 1931]
The Orange Ray. Hutchinson. 7s 6d [February 2, 1934]

Maurice George Kiddy published seven mystery-romances from *The Devil's Dagger* (1928, primarily a romance) to *The Orange Ray* (1934). Only *Stonewall Steevens Investigates* (1933) *sounds* like detective fiction.

C[HARLES] DALY KING (1895–1963)

Obelists En Route. Collins. 7s 6d [March 15, 1934]

C. Daly King published *Obelists at Sea* (1932), *Obelists En Route* (1934), and *Obelists Fly High* (1935), where the detectives are a team of psychoanalysts. His *Psychology of Consciousness* (1932) and (with W. M. and E. H. Marston) *Integrative Psychology* (1931) place him among the American pioneers in the 1920s/1930s revision of Jamesian psychology. *The Curious Mr. Tarrant* (1935), a collection of his stories, was reprinted by Dover. His other mystery novels are *Arrogant Alibi* (1938), *Bermuda Burial* (1940), and *Careless Corpse* (1937).

RUFUS KING (1893–1966)

Murder by Latitude. Heinemann. 7s 6d [February 18, 1931]

The American novelist Rufus King has fifteen mystery novels in the British Library, mostly centering on Lt. Joseph Valcour, from *Murder Deluxe* (1927) to *Duenna to a Murder* (1951). There are twenty-seven in the Library of Congress, from *Murder Deluxe* (1927) to *Malice in Wonderland* (1958), *Steps to Murder* (1960), and *Faces of Danger* (1964). His play "I Want A Policeman" was put on by The Federal Theater in San Diego in 1936 and 1938.

CHARLES KINGSTON [O'Mahony] (*b.* 1884)

The Great London Mystery. John Lane. 7s 6d [June 10 1931]

Charles Kingston [O'Mahony] began as an historian of famous crimes and famous trials—*Remarkable Rogues* (1921), *Dramatic Days at the Old Bailey* (1923), *Famous Judges and Famous Trials* (1923), *Rogues and Adventuresses* (1928)—and of the more difficult side of royalty *Royal Romances and Tragedies* (1921). His eighteen mystery and detection novels (in the British Library) run from *The Highgate Mystery* and *The Guilty House* (both 1928) to *Death Came Back* (1944), nine of them from the 1930s.

[MONSIGNOR] RONALD A[RBUTHNOT] KNOX (1888–1957)

Still Dead. Hodder and Stoughton. 7s 6d [June 4, 1934]

Historian, controversialist, Christian apologist and wit, author of *Let Dons Delight!* (1928, new ed. 1939), Monsignor Knox was scarcely a great detective story writer, and of his 180 items in the British Museum, only a handful can be considered detective fiction. There are *The Viaduct Murder* (1925), *The Three Taps* (1927), *The Footsteps at the Lock* (1928), *The Body in the Silo* (1933), and *Still Dead* (1934). He also edited (with H. Harrington) *The Best Detective Stories of the Year 1928* (1929).

MAURICE LEBLANC (1864–1941)

The Double Smile. Skeffington. 7s 6d [December 23 1933]

Maurice Marie Émile Leblanc appears in Williams's reviews like a *revenant* from past times. *Arsène Lupin, Gentleman–Cambrioleur* appeared in Paris in 1907, *Arsène* Lupin *vs. Herlock Sholmès* in 1908, *L'Aigulle Creuse* in 1911, *Le Bouchon de Cristal* in 1912, *Les Confidences d'Arsène Lupin* in 1913. The first was translated as *The Exploits of Arsène Lupin* (1909) — made into a play by Leblanc and Edgar Jepson, called simply "Arsène Lupin" (1909). The second, third, fourth, and fifth appeared as *Arsène Lupin vs Holmlock Shears* (1909), *The Hollow Needle* (1911), *The Crystal Stopper* (1913), and *The Confessions of Arsene Lupin* (1915). After the Great War, Leblanc published seven more Arsène Lupin novels, ending with *The Return of Arsène Lupin* (1933), in which year he also published *From Midnight to Morning* and *The Double Smile*. His earliest book in the British Library is *Une Femme* (1893), which went through several editions in its first year.

WILL LEVINREW (William Levine, *b.* 1881)

Murder on the Palisades. Gollancz. 7s 6d [July 7, 1930]

William Levine ("Will Levinrew"), an American, published *The Poison Plague* (1929), *Murder on the Palisades* (1930), *Murder from the Grave* (1931), *For Sale — Murder* (1932), *Death Points a Finger* (1933) — and after that, nothing.

GEORGE LIMNELIUS (Lewis George Robertson, *b.* 1886)

Tell No Tales. Bles. 7s 6d [March 18, 1931]

Lewis George Robinson ("George Limnelius") published, as Limnelius, just two books, *The Medbury Fort Murder* (1929) and *Tell No Tales* (1931). As Lewis G. Robinson, he published *The Manuscript Murder* (1933), *The General Goes Too Far* (1935), *No More Ancestors, A Military Divertisement* (1938), and *The Inward Glance* (1940).

VICTORIA LINCOLN (1904–1981)

The Swan Island Murders. Cassell. 7s 6d [August 25 1931]

In later life, Victoria Lincoln published biographies of St. Teresa of Avila and Lizzie Borden. Her novels include *The Swan Island Murders* (1931), *February Hill* (1935), *The Wind at My Back* (1947), *Celia Amberley* (1950), *Out from Eden* (1952), *The Wild Honey* (1954), and *Charles, A Novel* (1962).

VERNON LODER (John George Hazlette Vahey, *b.* 1881)

Red Stain. Collins. 7s 6d [November 17, 1931]
The Shop Window Murders. Collins. 7s 6d [July 7, 1930]

As Vernon Loder, J. G. H. Vahey published twenty-two novels, in addition to sixteen (and a book of poetry) under his own name. The earliest "Loder" was *The Mystery at Stowe* (1928), the last *Kill in the Ring, The Button in the Plate*, and *A Wolf in the Fold* (all 1938)—an average of two a year for eleven years, as "Loder." In 1931–33 he published four as "Walter Proudfoot," and under his own name, sixteen from 1925 to 1935. Total, forty-two books of prose in fourteen years, three a year. [see also Walter Proudfoot]

G[UY] B. H. LOGAN

The Eternal Moment. Stanley Paul. 7s 6d [October 7, 1932]

Guy B. H. Logan was a true-crime writer (with time out for *The Classic Races of the Turf*, 1931). His output includes *Masters of Crime* (1928), *Guilty or Not Guilty?* (1928), *Rope, Knife, and Chair* (1930), *Dramas of the Dock* (1930), *Great Murder Mysteries* (1931), *Verdict and Sentence* (1935),

Wilful Murder (1935), *Studies in Crime* (1937). Also *The Eternal Moment* (1932).

E[RNEST] LAURIE LONG (*b.* 1886)

As They Rise. Ward, Lock. 7s 6d [January 23 1935]

This is [Ernest] Laurie Long's only mystery novel (that I know of), though he wrote more than seventy books dealing with the sea, from *Port of Destination* (1933) to *Loot Curran, R.N.* (1963).

VICTOR MACCLURE (1883–1967)

The Clue of the Dead Goldfish. Harrap. 7s 6d [December 29 1933]

Victor MacClure published some early fantasy novels (*The Ark of the Covenant*, 1924, *The Golden Snail*, 1925), five books on food (*Good Appetite My Companion*, 1955, *Party Fare*, 1957, *Mainly Fish*, 1959), and novels on Esau and Mary Magdalen. He also wrote seven Archie Burford detective stories, from *The "Crying Pig" Murder* (1929) to *Hi! Spy! Kick the Can* (1936) and *The Diva's Emeralds* (1937). Except for his food books, he seems to have published nothing after 1937.

PHILIP MACDONALD (1899–1981)

Death on My Left. Collins. 7s 6d [January 31 1933]
Harbour. Collins. 7s 6d [November 17, 1931]
R. I. P. Collins. 7s 6d [April 26 1933]
Rope to Spare. Collins. 7s 6d [October 7, 1932]
The Choice. Collins. 7s 6d [April 6, 1931]
The Noose. Collins 7s 6d [May 8, 1930]
The Wraith. Collins. 7s 6d [September 7, 1931]

Though he has been collected and (to some degree) reprinted, Philip MacDonald has fallen under the shadow of two other "mystery" Mac-Donalds. The British Library shows more than sixty editions of twenty-four books. These begin with *The Rasp* (1924) and run through *The List of Adrian Messenger* (1959), the most frequently reprinted being *The Rasp*

(1924, 1932, 1937, 1956, 1957, 1977, 1979) and *Patrol* (1927, 1934, 1935, 1956, 1957). This does not count his "Martin Porlock" novels. His collection, *The Man Out of the Rain* (1957), shows a Hollywood (even a hardboiled) influence from his years there as a scriptwriter. He wrote his own script for *The List of Adrian Messenger*. Philip MacDonald was the grandson of the Scottish novelist George MacDonald (1824–1905). [see also Martin Porlock]

HAROLD MACGRATH (1871–1932)

The Green Complex. John Long. 7s 6d [June 11 1934]

The American writer Harold MacGrath began his writing career with *Arms and the Woman* (1899). His last three books (of more than forty) were *The Blue Rajah* and *The Green Complex* (both 1930) and *The Other Passport* (1931). He wrote a popular novelization of F. Lonergan's "photo-play," *The Million Dollar Mystery* (1915).

ANGUS MACVICAR (*b.* 1908)

Death by the Mistletoe. Stanley Paul. 7s 6d [August 3, 1934]

Angus MacVicar was a prolific Scottish writer of essays, romances, science fiction, history, and several mysteries, including *Death by the Mistletoe* (1934), *Flowering Death* (1937), *Death on the Machar* (1947), and *Murder at the Open* (1965). He has more than seventy items in the British Library, with titles like *Bees in My Bonnet, Rocks in My Scotch, Silver in My Sporran.* It has been said that a little of Angus MacVicar goes a long way.

MARCUS MAGILL (Brian Hill, *b.* 1896, and Joanna Giles)

I Like a Good Murder. Knopf. 7s 6d [September 9 1930]
Murder Out of Tune. Hutchinson. 7s 6d [April 7, 1931]

"Marcus Magill" (Brian Hill and Joanna Giles) published six novels: *Who Shall Hang?* and *Death-in-the-Box* (both 1929), *I Like A Good Murder* (1930), *Murder Out of Tune* (1931), *Murder in Full Flight* (1932), and *Hide, and I'll Find You, A Diversion* (1933)—then, nothing.

[DOMINIC] PAUL MCGUIRE (*b.* 1903)

There Sits Death. Skeffington. 7s 6d [June 5, 1933]

Paul MacGuire was perhaps best known for *Australian Journey* (1939), *The Price of Admiralty: The Royal Australian Navy* (1944), *The Australian Theatre* (1948), and *Inns of Australia* (1953), along with his historical study of the British Commonwealth, *Experiment in World Order* (1948). He published eleven mysteries in eight years, from *Murder in Bostall* (1931) to *Burial Service* (1938). His *Funeral in Eden* (1938) is noted by the critic David Lehman for its title, representative of the Golden Age.

JOHN T. MCINTYRE (1871–1951)

The Museum Murder. Geoffrey Bles. 7s 6d [September 9 1930]

John Thomas MacIntyre published several Ashton Kirk books, *Ashton Kirk, Secret Agent* (1916), *Ashton Kirk, Investigator* (1921), *Special Detective Ashton Kirk* (1922), and his Duddington Pell Chambers mystery, *The Museum Murder* (1929/30). He seems to be the John Thomas MacIntyre who wrote *Fighting King George* (1905) and *The Boy Tars of 1812* and *John Paul Jones* (1906). And he seems to be the author of *"Slag"* (1927) and *Drums in the Dawn* (1932).

VIRGIL MARKHAM (*b.* 1899)

Shock. Collins. 7s 6d [May 8, 1930]

Virgil Markham published nine novels, from *The Scamp* (1926) and *Death in the Dusk* (1928) to *The Deadly Jest* (1935) and *Snatch* (1936). So far as I know, none has been reprinted.

STUART MARTIN (*b.* 1882)

The Hangman's Guests. Hutchinson. 7s 6d [September 16, 1931]

Stuart Martin's first novel was *The Return of Christ* (1907), his next *Inheritance* (1912), his next-to-last *Minto of the Movies* (1935), his last *Ghost*

Parade (1947). He may be the Stuart Martin who wrote *The Story of the Thirteenth Battalion 1914–1917* (1918). He was not primarily a mystery novelist, but *The Hangman's Guests* (1931) was his most popular novel (three editions in 1931, another in 1944).

ROBERT MASON (*fl.* 1934–1952)

Murder to Measure. Pawling and Lees. 3s 6d [May 1 1934]

Robert Mason has twelve books in the British Library. From the 1930s there are *Murder to Measure* (1934), *The Slaying Squad* (1934), and *Courage for Sale* (1939). From the 1940s, there are *Three Cheers for Treason!* (1940), *And the Shouting Dies* (1940), *More News from the Middle East* (1943), *Arab Agent* (1944), *Cairo Communique* (1944), *Tandra* (1945), and *There is a Green Hill* (1946). From the 1950s, there are just two—*The Tender Leaves* (1950) and *No Easy Way Out* (1952).

[SIR] J[OHN] C[ECIL] MASTERMAN (1891–1977)

An Oxford Tragedy. Gollancz. 7s 6d [June 5, 1933]

Sir John Masterman wrote two classic books, *An Oxford Tragedy* (1933), which is fiction, and *The Double-Cross System in the War of 1939–1945* (posthumously, 1979), which is not. He also wrote *The Case of the Four Friends* (new ed. 1988).

W. W. MASTERS

Murder in the Mirror. Longmans. 7s 6d [January 21 1931]

W. W. Masters has only three books in the British Library: *Air-Ways: A Story for Boys and Girls* (1927), *Eleven* (1929), and *Murder in the Mirror* (1931).

NANCY BARR MAVITY (*b.* 1890)

The Body on the Floor. Collins. 7s 6d [September 13, 1930]

The Fate of Jane McKenzie. Collins. 7s 6d [July 26 1933]
The Other Bullet. Collins. 7s 6d [January 5, 1931]

Nancy Barr Mavity (b. 1890) has eight books in the Library of Congress, ten in the British Library. In both are *A Dinner of Herbs* (1923), *Hazard* (1924), *The Tule Marsh Murder* (1929/30), *The Other Bullet* (1930), *The Case of the Missing Sandals* (1930/31), *Sister Aimee* [about Aimee Semple McPherson] (1931), *The Fate of Jane McKenzie* (1933), *The State vs Elna Jepson* (1937). In the British Library but not the Library of Congress are British and American editions of *The Body on the Floor* (1929/30) and *The Man Who Didn't Mind Hanging* (1932).

LAURENCE W. MEYNELL (*b.* 1893)

Camouflage. Harrap. 7s 6d [August 14, 1930]

Laurence W. Meynell also wrote as A. Stephen Tring. From *Mockbeggar* (1924) and *Bluefeather* (1928) to his "Hooky Heffernan" stories in the 1980s, he produced nearly 150 books, fiction and nonfiction.

JOHN MILBROOK

A Bridport Dagger. The Bodley Head. 7s 6d [April 10 1930]

This is John Milbrook's only book, unless he wrote under another name. The book is an historical novel, with the mystery set in Devon in 1835.

AGNES MILLER

The Obole of Paradise. Hutchinson. 7s 6d [August 14, 1930]

Agnes Miller wrote *The Colfax Book-Plate* (1926) and *The Obole of Paradise* (1930).

GUY [EUGENE MAINWARING] MORTON (1884–1948)

The 3-7-9 Murder. Skeffington. 7s 6d [June 18, 1934]
The Ragged Robin Murders. Skeffington. 7s 6d [February 15, 1935]

Only one of Guy Morton's seventeen novels in the British Library shows more than one edition, his first, *Rangy Pete* (1922 and 1923). His last were *The Burleigh Murders* and *Mystery at Hardacres* (1936) — unless, of course, there were two authors writing at the same time under the same name.

TALBOT MUNDY (1879–1940)

The Red Flame of Erinpura. Hutchinson. 7s 6d [February 20 1934]

The fantasist and orientalist Talbot Mundy began his writing career with *Rung Ho!* (1914), *The Winds of the World* (1916 — note the echo of Kipling in the title) and then his most famous, *King, of the Khyber Rifles* (1917). His last (of nearly fifty) were *Old Ugly-Face* and *The Valiant View* (both 1939). He is not noted as a mystery writer.

EVANDER MURRAY

The Peering One. Hodder and Stoughton. 7s 6d [October 14, 1930]

This is Evander Murray's only book, unless under another name. It is a slightly supernatural mystery in an African setting.

GEORGE NORSWORTHY

Dames Errant. Sampson Low. 7s 6d [February 15, 1935]

George Norsworthy published seven novels in seven years, six in the first four. These were *Casino* (1934), *A House-Party Mystery* and *Dames Errant* (1935), *Crime at the Villa Gloria* and *The Hartness Millions* (1936), *Murder at Mulberry Cottage* (1937), and *Murder in Sussex* (1940).

EIMAR O'DUFFY (1893–1935)

The Bird Cage. Geoffrey Bles. 7s 6d [March 22 1932]

Eimar Ultan O'Duffy was a poet (*The Lay of the Liffey*, 1918), unorthodox economist (*Life and Money*, 1932, 1933, 1935), Irish observer (*The*

Wasted Island, 1920, 1929), playwright (*Brieriu's Feast*, 1931), novelist, and author of *The Spacious Adventures of the Man in the Street* (1928, 1929).

E[DWARD] PHILLIPS OPPENHEIM (1861–1946)

Many Mysteries. Rich and Cowan. 7s 6d [June 14, 1933]
Moran Chambers Smiled. Hodder and Stoughton. 7s 6d [March 7, 1932]
Slane's Long Shots. Hodder and Stoughton. 3s 6d [July 7, 1934]
The Gallows of Chance. Hodder and Stoughton. 7s 6d [February 2, 1934]

E. Phillips Oppenheim wrote plays, novels, short stories, more than 200 items in the British Library, from *Expiation* (1887) to *Mr. Mirakel* (1943). A biography by "Robert Standish" was published in 1957, *The Prince of Storytellers: The Life of E. Phillips Oppenheim*.

NIGEL ORDE-POWLETT (*b.* 1900)

The Cast to Death. Benn. 7s 6d [July 18, 1932]

Nigel Amyas Orde-Powlett, 6th Baron Bolton, published a book of poems (*Vale*, 1918), two novels (*The Cast to Death*, 1932, and *Driven to Death*, 1933), *How to Combine Sport with Forestry* (n.d.) and *Profitable Forestry* (1956).

CLIFFORD ORR

The Wailing Rock Murders. Cassell. 7s 6d [February 13, 1933]

Clifford Orr published two novels, *The Dartmouth Murders* (1929/31) and *The Wailing Rock Murders* (1932/33). It would appear he was an American.

S[TANLEY] H[ART] PAGE

Fool's Gold. Stanley Paul. 7s 6d [May 1 1934]

Stanley Hart Page published *The Resurrection Murder Case* (1932/3), *Sinister Cargo* (1932/3), and *Fool's Gold* (1934).

Q. PATRICK (Richard Watson Webb, *b.* 1901, and Martha, Mrs. Steven Wilson)

Cottage Sinister. Longmans. 7s 6d [October 7, 1932]

Although "Q. Patrick" is generally the pseudonym for Hugh Calling-ham Wheeler and Richard Wilson Webb, this book is traced to Webb and his cousin-by-marriage, Mrs. Steven Wilson — though not by the British Library). Between 1932 and 1941, "Q. Patrick" published thirteen books, the first eleven in the 1930s. They are *Cottage Sinister* (1932), *Murder at the Women's City Club* (1932), *Murder at the 'Varsity* (1933), *S. S. Murder* (1933), *Death in the Dovecote* (1934), *Darker Grows the Valley* (1935), *Death Goes to School* (1936), *Death for Dear Clara* (1937), *File on Claudia Cragge* (1938), *File on Fenton & Farr* (1938), *Death and the Maiden* (1939). *Death and Bermuda* came in 1941, and *Danger Next Door* semi-posthumously in 1952.

KENNETH PERKINS

The Horror of the Juvenal Manse. Hutchinson. 7s 6d [April 15, 1931]

Kenneth Perkins was an adventure-story writer, mostly Westerns. The original title of *The Juvenal Mansion* was *Voodoo'd*. The twenty-one Ken-neth Perkins novels in the British Library run from *The Beloved Brute* and *Ride Him! Cowboy!* (both 1924) to *Three Were Thoroughbreds* (1940). Only this and *The Mark of the Moccasin* (1929) seem to be mystery novels.

TYLINE PERRY

The Owner Lies Dead. Gollancz. 7s 6d [July 30 1930]

This is apparently a solo effort, but according to Williams a good and believable one, centering on a mine "accident" that turns out to be murder.

EDEN PHILLPOTTS (1862–1960)

Found Drowned. Hutchinson. 7s 6d [March 18, 1931]

Eden Philpotts has at least 367 items in the British Library Catalogue, at best tangentially connected with the Golden Age of Detective Fiction, most of them off in a realm of their own.

MARTIN PORLOCK (Philip MacDonald, 1899–1981)

Mystery at Friar's Pardon. Collins. 7s 6d [October 7, 1931]
Mystery in Kensington Gore. Collins. 7s 6d [March 7, 1932]

The pen-name "Martin Porlock" hid Philip MacDonald for less than two years. Under it he published *Mystery at Friar's Pardon* (1931), *Mystery at Kensington Gore* (1932), *X v. Rex* (1933). [See also Philip MacDonald]

MILTON M. PROPPER (1906–1962)

And Then Silence. Faber and Faber. 7s 6d [June 17, 1931]
Murder of an Initiate. Faber and Faber. 7s 6d [February 13, 1933]
The Ticker-Tape Murder. Faber and Faber. 7s 6d [December 24 1930]

Milton Propper has fourteen novels in the British Library, from *The Strange Disappearance of Mary Young* (1929) to *Murders in Sequence* (1947) and *You Can't Gag the Dead* (1949). Ten were published in the 1930s, *Hide the Body!* in 1940.

WALTER PROUDFOOT (John George Hazlette Vahey)

Crime in the Arcade. Hutchinson. 7s 6d [May 19 1931]

As Walter Proudfoot, Vahey published *Crime in the Arcade* (1931), *The Trail of the Ruby* (1932), *Arrest* and *Conspiracy* (1933). [See also Vernon Loder]

E[RNEST] R[OBERTSON] PUNSHON (1872–1956)

Proof Counter Proof. Benn. 7s 6d [February 18, 1931]
The Cross-Word Mystery. Gollancz. 7s 6d [June 18, 1934]

Ernest Robertson Punshon published fifty-eight novels, from *Earth's Great Lord* (1901) and *Constance West* (1905) to *Six Were Present* (1956). The popularity of his mysteries is attested to by *The Carter and Bell Detective Omnibus* (1933) and *Three Cases of Murder* (1956), both of which include *The Cottage Murder* (1931).

ELLERY QUEEN (Frederic Dannay, 1905–82, and Manfred B[ennington] Lee, 1905–71)

The American Gun Mystery. Gollancz. 7s 6d [June 14, 1933]
The French Powder Mystery. Gollancz. 7s 6d [October 21 1930]
The Greek Coffin Mystery. Gollancz. 7s 6d [July 28 1932]

"Ellery Queen"—private-investigator son of Inspector Richard Queen, anthologist, author with more than 200 items in the British Library Catalogue, founder of *Ellery Queen's Mystery Magazine*—needs no introduction to anyone with knowledge of the twentieth-century mystery novel (and short story). But it may be well to remind ourselves of the pattern of *The Roman Hat Mystery* (1929), *The French Powder Mystery* (1930), *The Dutch Shoe Mystery* (1931), *The Greek Coffin Mystery* (1932), *The Egyptian Cross Mystery* (1932/33), *The American Gun Mystery* (1933), *The Siamese Twin Mystery* (1933), *The Chinese Orange Mystery* (1934), *The Spanish Cape Mystery* (1935). All these had a challenge to the reader after all the clues had been given: all have been called puzzle-books rather than novels.

MRS. BAILLIE REYNOLDS (Gertrude M. [Robins] Reynolds, 1854?–1939)

Whereabouts Unknown. Hutchinson. 7s 6d [May 5, 1931]

Gertrude M. Robins Reynolds (Mrs. Baillie Reynolds) goes back even beyond E. Phillips Oppenheim. The line of more than seventy books begins with two Bentley "three-deckers," *Keep My Secret* (1886) and *A False Position* (1887)—and they were not her last three-deckers. Her last novel was *It Is Not Safe to Know* (1939, the year she died). She came late to detective fiction, with *Accessory After the Fact* (1928).

JOHN RHODE (Maj. Cecil John Street, 1884–1964)

Peril at Cranbury Hall. Geoffrey Bles. 7s 6d [January 24 1930]
Pinehurst. Geoffrey Bles. 7s 6d [July 30 1930]
The Claverton Mystery. Collins. 7s 6d [June 14, 1933]
The Hanging Woman. Collins. 7s 6d [June 10 1931]
Tragedy on the Line. Collins. 7s 6d [January 5, 1931]

"John Rhode" was the name under which most of Major C. J. Street's fiction was published—more than eighty books in the British Library. These run from *A.S.F.* (1924) to *The Vanishing Diary* (1960). His detective, Dr. Priestley, is loosely modeled on R. A. Freeman's Dr. Thorndyke, slightly on H. C. Bailey's Reggie Fortune. He has been called the King of the Hum-Drums. [See also Miles Burton, Cecil Waye.]

MRS. VICTOR RICKARD (Jessie Louisa [Moore] Rickard)

The Mystery of Vincent Dane. Stoughton. 7s 6d [January 24 1930]

Jessie Louisa Rickard published thirty-eight novels, from *Young Mr. Gibbs* (1911) and *Dregs* (1914) to *Shandon Hall* (1950). Also, *The Story of the Munsters at Etreux, Festubert, Rue du Bois and Hulluch* (1918). She is not noted as a mystery novelist.

CLIFTON ROBBINS (*b.* 1890)

Smash and Grab. Benn. 7s 6d [May 1 1934]

Clifton Robbins published nine "Clay Harrison" mysteries: *Dusty Death* (1931), *The Man Without a Face* (1932), *Death on the Highway* (1933), *The Devil's Beacon* (1933), *Smash and Grab* (1934), *Methylated Murder* (1935), *Murder by Twenty-Five* (1936), *Six Sign-Post Murder* (1939), *Death Forms Threes* (1940). The first three were collected into *The Clay Harrison Omnibus* (1933).

[SIR] S[YDNEY] C[ASTLE] ROBERTS (1887–1966)

Dr. Watson. Faber and Faber. 1s [March 9 1931]

Sir Sydney Roberts, long of the Cambridge University Press, wrote *The Story of Dr. Johnson* (1919), *The History of the Cambridge University Press* (1921), and *Introduction to Cambridge* (1948), along with this monograph.

G[EORGE] E[RNEST] ROCHESTER

Traitor's Rock. Eldon Press. 7s 6d [June 5, 1933]

George Ernest Rochester wrote juvenile air-piracy stories, juvenile air-adventure stories, juvenile ghost and horror stories, a few World War II air stories, and a few non-air mystery/adventure stories. His earliest book in the British Library is *Traitor's Rock* (1933), the one Williams reviewed. The last of his more than fifty books seems to have been *The Drums of War* (1957). In 1936 alone he published eighteen books: *The Air Ranger, The Air Trail, The Black Hawk, The Black Mole, Brood of the Vulture, The Bulldog Breed, Dead Man's Gold, The Despot of the World, The Flying Cowboys, The Freak of St. Freda's, Grey Shadow, Jackals of the Clouds, The Mystery of Flying V Ranch, Pirates of the Air, Porson's Flying Service, The Shadow of the Guillotine, The Trail of Death: War Adventures of the Flying Beetle, Wings of Doom.*

SAX ROHMER (Arthur Sarsfield Wade, 1883–1959)

The Bride of Fu-Manchu. Cassell. 7s 6d [December 29 1933]

There are at least fourteen Fu-Manchu books, from 1913 through 1959. These are *The Insidious Dr. Fu Manchu* (1913), *The Mystery of Dr Fu-Manchu* (1913), *The Devil-Doctor* (1916), *Return of Dr. Fu Manchu* (1922), *The Book of Fu Manchu* (1929), *Daughter of Fu Manchu* (1931), *The Bride of Fu Manchu* (1933), *The Mask of Fu Manchu* (1933), *President Fu Manchu* (1936), *The Drums of Fu Manchu* (1939), *Island of Fu Manchu* (1941), *Mask of Fu Manchu* (1953), *Re-Enter Fu Manchu* (1957), *Emperor Fu Manchu* (1959). In addition, Sax Rohmer published, among others: *Romance of Sorcery* (1914), *Yellow Claw* (1915), *The Exploits of Captain O'Hagan* (1916), *Brood of the Witch Queen* (1918), *Golden Scorpion* (1919), *The Green Eyes of Bast* (1920), *The Haunting of Low Fennel* (1920), *The Dream-Detective* (1920), *Bat Wing* (1921), *Fire Tongue* (1921), *Grey Face* (1924), *Yellow Shadows* (1926), *She Who Sleeps* (1928), *Emperor of America* (1929), *Moon of Madness* (1929),

The Day the World Ended (1930), *Yu'an Hee See Laughts* (1932), *White Velvet* (1936), *Seven Sins* (1943), *Bimbashi Baruk of Egypt* (1944).

ANTHONY ROLLS (C[olwyn] E[dward] Vuillamy, 1886–1971)

Lobelia Grove. Geoffrey Bles. 7s 6d [October 7, 1932]

Colwyn Edward Vulliamy ("Anthony Rolls") was something of a polymath. Besides the four "Rolls" novels, *Lobelia Grove* and *The Vicar's Experiments* (1932), *Family Matters* (1933), and *Scarweather* (1934), he published as C. E. Vulliamy, *Don Among the Dead Men: A Satirical Thriller* (1952). He also published *Letters of the Tsar to the Tsaritsa 1914–17* (1929), *The Red Archives* (1929), *Crimea: The Campaign of 1854–56* (1939), *The Archaeology of Middlesex and London* (1930), *Immortal Man: A Study of Funeral Customs, etc.* (1926), *Our Prehistoric Forerunners* (1925), *Man and the Atom* (1947), *Outlanders: Imperial Expansion in South Africa 1877–1902* (1938), *Unknown Cornwall* (1925). He published biographies of *Voltaire* (1930), *John Wesley* (1931), *James Boswell* (1932), *Judas Maccabaeus* (a satire, 1934), *Aspasia* (1935), *Mrs. Thrale* (1936), *Byron* (1948).

FLORENCE RYERSON and COLIN CLEMENTS (*b.* 1894 and 1894–1948)

Seven Suspects. Skeffington. 7s 6d [September 3, 1930]

Florence Ryerson and Colin Campbell Clements wrote plays and monologues together (*The Littlest Shepherd: A Christmas Interlude*, 1932, for example). They also collaborated on *Seven Suspects* (1930), *Fear of Fear* (1931), *Mild Oats* (1933), *Shadows* (1934). Their last collaboration was a musical, *Oh! Susanna!* (1948).

CLIVE RYLAND [PRIESTLEY] (*b.* 1892)

Murder on the Cliff. Grayson. 7s 6d [August 3, 1934]

Clive Ryland [Priestley] published twenty-three murder-mysteries from *The Notting Hill Murder* (1932) to *The Selminster Murders* (1952), eleven in the 1930s, seven in the 1940s, five in the 1950s. The word "journeyman" comes to mind.

VICTOR SAMPSON (?*b.* 1855)

The Komani Mystery. Herbert Jenkins. 7s 6d [June 11 1934]

Victor Sampson was a poet (*Collected Poems*, 1932), student in South Africa of criminal and Roman law, author of *Anti-Commando* (with Sir Ian Hamilton), of *My Reminiscences* (1926) and two novels, *The Murder of Paul Rougier* (1928) and *The Komani Mystery* (1930).

DOROTHY L. SAYERS (1893–1957)

The Nine Tailors. Gollancz. 7s 6d [January 17, 1934]

Dorothy L. Sayers, creator of Lord Peter Wimsey, author of *The Man Born to Be King*, translator of Dante and *The Song of Roland*, needs no note here. This is her most famous Lord Peter Wimsey mystery, and an extreme example of learning a subject (campanology) before incorporating it in a novel.

DAVID SHARP (no dates given in Barzun, *fl.* 1931–34 in L.C.)

I, the Criminal. Benn. 7s 6d [July 28 1932]
Marriage and Murder. Benn. 7s 6d [February 2, 1934]
My Particular Murder. Benn. 7s 6d [April 15, 1931]
When No Man Pursueth. Benn. 7s 6d [September 3, 1930]

David Sharp, novelist, published ten books in the 1930s, though none in 1935–1937. The first five are *When No Man Pursueth* (1930), *None of My Business* (1931), *I, the Criminal* (1932), *The Inconvenient Corpse* (1933), *Marriage and Murder* (1934). The second five are *Disputed Quarry* (1938), *Elderly Gentleman Shot* (1939), *Everybody Suspect* (1939), *The Frightened Sailor* (1939), *Exit Second Murderer* (1940). Thereafter — nothing.

M[ATTHEW] P[HIPPS] SHIEL (1865–1947)

Dr. Krasinski's Secret. Jarrold. 7s 6d [October 21 1930]

Matthew Phipps Shiel, the horror-fantasist, began his publishing career with *Prince Zaleski* (1895), *The Rajah's Sapphire* and *Shapes in the Fire* (both 1896), *The Yellow Danger* (1898), *Contraband of War* and *Cold Steel* (both 1899), *The Man–Stealers* (1900), and *The Purple Cloud* and *The Lord of the Sea* (1901). Ten more books followed before 1914 (*The Dragon*, 1913, being the last). Nothing then until *The Children of the Wind* (1923), *How the Old Woman Got Home* (1927), *Here Comes the Lady* (1928), *Dr. Krasinski's Secret* (1930), *The Black Box* (1931), *The Invisible Voices* (1935), *The Young Men Are Coming* (1937)—and after that, only autobiographical writings and reflections.

P[ETER] R[EDCLIFF] SHORE (*b.* 1892)

The Death Film. Methuen. 7s 6d [March 22 1932]

P. R. Shore published *The Bolt* (1929) and *The Death Film* (1932), both by Methuen, the first in the "Methuen Clue Stories."

ANTHONY SKENE

Gallows Alley. Stanley Paul. 7s 6d [February 20 1934]

Anthony Skene produced *Five Dead Men* (1932), *The Masks* (1933), *Gallows Alley* (1934) and *The Silver Circle* (96 pp., 1934), and *Monsieur Zenith* (1936)—and then *The Ripper Returns* (Manchester 1948). His *Zenith the Albino* (also 1936) has just been reprinted. In the 1960s he was the writer for several episodes of "The Prisoner."

WILLARD K. SMITH (no dates given in Barzun)

The Bowery Murder. Collins. 7s 6d [May 8, 1930]

Willard K. Smith, an American, published *The Bowery Murder* (1929/30) and possibly *The Sultan's Skull* (1933). Nothing more is known of him — at least by me.

ERLE [ROSE] SPENCER (1897–1937)

Stop Press. Hodder and Stoughton. 7s 6d [January 1 1932]

The consumptive Newfoundlander, Erle [Rose] Spencer, a reporter on Lord Beaverbrook's *Daily Express*, published two sea-juveniles, *The Young Sea Rover* (1925) and *Contraband* (1926). *The Piccadilly Ghost* (1929) and *Stop Press!* (1932) are set in the London newspaper world. *The Death of Captain Shand* (1930) is an adventure-story set in Oporto, *The Four Lost Ships* (1931) in St-Pierre, *The King of Spain's Daughter* (1934) in Newfoundland, *Or Give Me Death!* (1936) in Greece. At his death he left an unpublished short mystery, *Death of a Millionaire*.

CHRISTOPHER ST. JOHN SPRIGG (1907–1937)

Fatality in Fleet Street. Eldon Press. 7s 6d [December 23 1933]

Christopher St. John Sprigg—better known by his Marxist *nom de guerre* of Christopher Caudwell—published a number of airplane and piloting books, including *Fly with Me* (1931), *The Airship* (1932), *British Airways* (1934), *Great Flights* (1935), *Let's Learn to Fly* (1937). His novels include *Crime in Kensington* and *Fatality in Fleet Street* (both 1933), *Death of an Airman* and *Perfect Alibi* (1934), *The Corpse with the Sunburnt Face* and *Death of a Queen* (1935), and *The Six Queer Things* (1937). After his early death, were published his *Illusion and Reality: A Study of the Sources of Poetry* (1937) and his more famous *Studies in a Dying Culture* (1938). Long afterwards came *The Concept of Freedom* (1977), *Scenes and Actions* and *Collected Poems* (both 1986).

OLIVER STONOR (*b.* 1903)

The End of Mr. Davidson. Heinemann. 7s 6d [April 27 1932]

Oliver Stonor has four books in the British Library, a translation of Francois Beroalde de Verville, *The Way to Succeed* (1930), *The End of Mr. Davidson* (1932), *The First Book of Synonyms* (1963), and *The Awful Spellers' Dictionary* (1964).

JOHN STEPHEN STRANGE (Mrs. Dorothy [Stockbridge] Tillet, *b.* 1896)

Murder Game. Collins. 7s 6d [December 9 1931]
The Strangler Fig. Collins. 7s 6d [January 5, 1931]

John Stephen Strange (Dorothy Stockbridge Tillett) published twenty-four novels from *The Man Who Killed Fortescue* (1928) through *Eye Witness* (1962). Eight were published in the seven years 1928–34, six more in the years 1935–42, one in 1944, six in 1948–53, and one each in 1955, 1959, and 1962.

TAFFRAIL [HENRY TAPRELL DORLING] (1883–1968)

Dover-Ostend. Hodder and Stoughton. 7s 6d [July 26 1933]

Henry Taprell Dorling ("Taffrail") 1883–1968 was essentially a naval writer, his best-known books being *Carry On!* (1916), *Pincher Martin, O.D.* (1916/1917), *The Sub* (1917), and his classic work on *Ribbons and Medals* (Centenary ed. 1983). Besides *Dover-Ostend*, he published *Michael Bray* (1925), *Chenies* (1943), *The Jade Lizard* (1951), *The New Moon* (1952).

N. A. TEMPLE-ELLIS (Neville Aldridge Holdaway, *b.* 1894)

Quest. Methuen. 7s 6d [March 2, 1931]
Six Lines. Hodder and Stoughton. 7s 6d [August 23 1932]
The Cauldron Bubbles. Methuen. 7s 6d [August 14, 1930]

Neville Aldridge Holdaway ("Temple-Ellis") published nine books in seven years: *The Inconsistent Villains* (1929), *The Cauldron Bubbles* and *The Man Who Was There* (both 1930), *Quest* (1931), *Six Lines* (1932), *A Case in Hand* (1933), *The Hollow Land* and *Three Went In* (both 1934), and *Dead in No Time* (1935). A tenth, *Death of a Decent Fellow*, appeared in 1941.

ALAN THOMAS (Ernest Wentworth, *b.* 1896)

The Stolen Cellini. Benn. 7s 6d [July 30 1931]

It is almost as though Alan Thomas had two writing careers, though both are told in his *A Life Apart [Reminiscences, with special reference to the First World War]*, published in 1968. From the early career comes *The Death of Laurence Vining* (1928), *The Tremayne Case* (1929), *Daggers Drawn* (1930), *The Lonely Years* (1930), *The Stolen Cellini* (1931), *Summer Adventure* (1933), *Death of the Home Secretary* (1933), *That We Might Live* (1935). After a reissue of *The Death of Laurence Vining* in 1951, he wrote *The Mask and the Man* (1951), *The Fugitives* (1953), *The Director* (1958), *The Governor* (1961), *The Judge* (1966), and *The Professor* (1969).

[Arthur] Russell Thorndike (b. 1885)

The Water Witch. Thornton Butterworth. 7s 6d [January 3, 1933]

Arthur Russell Thorndike wrote a biography of his sister, Dame Sybil Thorndike and with her a biography of Lillian Baylis. He is known for his retelling of Dickens for children and his *A Wanderer With Shakespeare.* Also he wrote *Dr. Syn: A Tale of the Romney Marsh* (1915), and its sequels *Dr. Syn Returns* (1935), *Dr. Syn on the High Seas* (1936), *Amazing Quest of Dr. Syn* (1938), *Courageous Exploits of Dr. Syn* (1939), *The Shadow of Dr. Syn* (1944). Note also *The Slype* (1927) and *The Master of the Macabre* (1947).

Molly Thynne

Murder in the Dentist's Chair. Hutchinson. 7s 6d [March 22 1932]

Molly Thynne has seven books in the British Library, *The Uncertain Glory* (1914), *The Red Dwarf* (1928), *The Murder on the "Enriqueta"* (1929), *The Case of Sir Adam Braid* (1930), *The Crime at the "Noah's Ark"* (1931), *Murder in the Dentist's Chair* (1932), *He Dies and Makes No Sign* (1933).

Virginia Tracy

The Moment After. Matthews and Marot. 7s 6d [February 9 1931]

The American actress and writer Virginia Tracy has four books in the British Library, *Merely Players: Stories of Stage Life* (1909), *Persons Unknown* (1914), *The Moment After* (1930/31), and *Personal Appearance of a Lioness*

(1937). The Library of Congress also has her *Starring Dulcy Jayne* (1927). Her early story "The Lotus Eaters" appears in the 1905 Collier collection of *Short Story Classics (American)*.

GLEN TREVOR (James Hilton, 1900–1954)

Murder at School. Benn. 7s 6d [January 1 1932]

As noted in the discussion under his own name, James Hilton ("Glen Trevor"), author of two classics, *Lost Horizon* (1933) and *Good-bye Mr. Chips* (1934) wrote a dozen other novels, including *Murder at School*. Though Williams did not penetrate the pen-name to find out who was behind it, he clearly suggested that some known writer was.

[LESLIE] SELDON TRUSS (b. 1892)

They Came by Night. Jarrolds. 7s 6d [February 20 1934]

Leslie Seldon Truss had both a Pre–World War II career — eighteen books from *Gallows' Bait* (1928) through *The Disappearance of Julie Hintz* (1940) — and a Post–World War II career. In that second career, he published twenty-four books, from *Where's Mr. Chumley* (1949) and *Ladies Always Talk* (1950) to *The Corpse That Got Away* (1969). His later books are hardboiled (*The Doctor Was a Dame*, 1953), his earlier a little more violent than the average for the "Golden Age."

J[OHN] V[ICTOR] TURNER (fl. 1931–1936)

Murder — Nine and Out. Geoffrey Bles. 7s 6d [May 1 1934]

Under his own name, John Victor Turner published eight books in six years: *Dynamite Don* (1931), *Death Must Have Laughed* and *Who Spoke Last* (both 1932), *Amos Petrie's Puzzle* (1933), *Murder — Nine and Out!* (1934), *Death Joins the Party* and *Homicide Haven* (both 1935), and *Below the Clock* (1936). [See also David Hume.]

ARTHUR W. UPFIELD (1888–1964)

The Sands of Windee. Hutchinson. 7s 6d [July 30 1931]

Arthur W. Upfield was the creator of the Australian half–Abo detective, Napoleon Bonaparte, appearing in more than thirty books, most of them after World War II. The earlier ones are the better, in my view (though hum-drum), before the background has become a little slapdash and the detection somewhat formulaic.

LAURENCE VAIL (*b.* 1891)

Murder! Murder! Peter Davies. 7s 6d [October 22 1931]

Laurence Vail edited *365 Days: Tales* (1936), with Kay Boyle and Nina Conarain, translated *The Life of Madame Roland* (1930), *Bubu of Montparnasse* and *On the Make* (both 1932), and published *Murder! Murder!* (1931).

JOHN W[OMACK] VANDERCOOK (1902–1963)

Murder in Trinidad. Heinemann. 7s 6d [February 20 1934]

John Womack Vandercook was a Caribbeanist and student of the Pacific Islands. His *Black Majesty* (1928) is a life of Henri Christophe, King of Haiti. He wrote *"Tom-Tom"* (1926), *Dark Islands* (1937), *Caribbee Cruise* (1938), *Discover Puerto Rico* (1939), *King Cane: The Story of Sugar in Hawaii* (1939) and his four travelogue/mysteries. These are *Murder in Trinidad* (1933), *Murder in Fiji* (1936), *Murder in Haiti* (1956), *Murder in New Guinea* (1960).

S. S. VAN DINE (Willard Huntington Wright, 1888–1939)

The Dragon Murder Case. Cassell. 7s 6d [January 17, 1934]
The Kennel Murder Case. Cassell. 7s 6d [April 26 1933]

Willard Huntington Wright ("S. S. Van Dine") published *The Benson Murder Case* (1926), *The Canary Murder Case* (1927), *The Greene Murder Case* (1928), *The Bishop Murder Case* (1929), *The Scarab Murder Case* (1930), *The Kennel Murder Case* (1933), and *The Dragon Murder Case* (1933). These were followed by *The Casino Murder Case* (1934), *The Garden Murder Case* (1935), *The Kidnap Murder Case* (1936), *The Gracie Allen*

Murder Case (1938), *The Winter Murder Case* (1939). Wright was an art-historian, best known in that field for his *Modern Painting* (1916, new ed. 1928).

HENRY WADE ([Sir] Henry Lancelot Aubrey Fletcher, 1887–1969)

Constable, Guard Thyself! Constable. 7s 6d [August 3, 1934]
The Dying Alderman. Constable. 7s 6d [August 26 1930]

Sir Henry Lancelot Aubrey Fletcher was author of *The History of the Foot Guards to 1856* (1927), and under the name of Henry Wade, of twenty-two mysteries, from *The Verdict of You All* (1926) through *A Dying Fall* (1955) and *The Litmore Snatch* (1957). By and large, his later books are just about as good as his earlier, and both are near the top of the second rank.

R[OBERT] A[LFRED] J[OHN] WALLING (1869–1949)

The Five Suspects. Hodder and Stoughton. 7s 6d [January 23 1935]
The Man with the Squeaky Voice. Methuen. 7s 6d [August 6, 1930]

Robert Alfred John Walling edited *The Diaries of John Bright* (1930), wrote *A Sea-Dog of Devon: The Life of Sir John Hawkins* (1907), *George Borrow* (1908), *The Charm of Brittany* (1933), *The West Country* (1935), *The Green Hills of England* (1937), and *The Story of Plymouth* (1950). He also wrote twenty-eight mysteries centering on Philip Tolefree, from *Murder at the Keyhole* (1929) to *A Corpse Without a Clue* (1944). His earliest book is *Flaunting Moll, and Other Stories* (1896).

J[AMES] H[AROLD] WALLIS (1885–1958)

Murder by Formula. Jarrold. 7s 6d [December 21 1932]

J. H. Wallis wrote *British War Poems, by an American* (London 1916) and *The Testament of William Windune, and Other Poems* (New Haven and London 1916). He also wrote ten novels, from *Murder By Formula* (1932) to *the Synthetic Philanthropist* (1945), none published between 1935 and 1943.

Cecil Waye (Maj. Cecil John Street, 1884–1964)

Murder at Monk's Barn. Hodder and Stoughton. 7s 6d [July 15, 1931]

In addition to his more than 160 books published under the names if John Rhode and Miles Burton, Major Cecil John Street published four under the name of Cecil Waye: *The Figure of Eight* and *Murder at Monk's Barn* (both 1931), *The End of the Chase* (1932), and *The Prime Minister's Pencil* (1933). None is especially distinguished. [See also Miles Burton and John Rhode.]

Fred[erick] M[errick] White (*b.* 1859)

A Clue in Wax. Ward, Lock. 7s 6d [June 4, 1930]

Frederick Merrick White began his publishing with *The Robe of Lucifer* (1896)—unless one counts his attack on Ignatius Donnelly, *The Doubting D- or a Cranky Cryptogram* (1888). More than seventy books later, he published *A Broken Memory*, *A Clue in Wax*, *The Green Bungalow*, and *On the Night Express* in 1930, nothing thereafter.

Victor L[orenzo] Whitechurch (1868–1933)

Murder at the College. Collins. 7s 6d [December 13, 1932]
Murder at the Pageant. Collins. 7s 6d [December 1 1930]

Canon Whitechurch achieved some early success with church novels and to an extent, perhaps, as a Sussex regionalist: his first book (in the British Library) was *The Course of Justice* (1903), followed by *The Canon in Residence* (1904), *The Locum Tenens* (1906), *The Canon's Dilemma* (1909), *Concerning Himself* (1909), *Off the Main Road* (1911), *Left in Charge* (1912), *A Downland Corner* (1912). Some hint of the shape of things to come was given in his *Thrilling Stories of the Railway* (1912, with his odd detective, Thorpe Hazell), but he returned to his last with *Three Summers* (1915), *Downland Echoes* (1924), and *A Bishop out of Residence* (1924). Then came *The Templeton Case* (1924), *The Crime at Diana's Pool* (1927), *Shot on the Downs* (1927), *First and Last* (1929), *Murder at the Pageant* (1930), *Murder at the College* (1932)—before he returned to his work as a regionalist in *Mute Witnesses: Being Certain Annals of a Downland Village* (1933).

[RT. HON.] ELLEN [CICELY] WILKINSON (1891–1947)

The Division Bell Mystery. Harrap. 7s 6d [July 5, 1932]

The Rt. Hon. Ellen Wilkinson, M.P. (Labour), contributed to *A Worker's History of the Great Strike* (1927), wrote *The Town That Was Murdered: The Life-Story of Jarrow* (Left Book Club, 1939), published two novels (*Clash*, 1929, and *The Division Bell Mystery*, 1932), and was one of the authors (with then Communist V. K. Krishna Menon) of *The Condition of India: Being the Report of the Delegation Sent to India by the India League in 1932* (1934). A brief biography is in Terence Lockett, *Three Lives: Samuel Bamford, Alfred Darbyshire, Ellen Wilkinson* (1968).

HILDA WILLETT (*fl.* 1904–1946?)

Diamonds of Death. Longmans. 7s 6d [September 3, 1930]

Hilda Willett's first publication in the British Library is *Two Songs* (1904, words by Percy Shelley and Sir Philip Sidney), followed by *On Denzell Downs* (1922) and *Her Eyes Are Stars* (1923). Her mysteries include *Tragedy in Pewsey Chart* (1929), *Diamonds of Death* (1930), *Murder at the Party* (1931), *Mystery on the Centre Court* (1933), *Found Shot* (1934), *Accident in Piccadilly* (1935). Also, *So It Goes On* (1930), *April, May and June* (1931), *Bucket in Well* (1932), *Peril in Darkness* (1935). Her last book was *It's Quiet in the Country* (1946).

[GEORGE] VALENTINE WILLIAMS (1883–1946)

The Portcullis Room. Hodder and Stoughton. 7s 6d [June 4, 1934]

Valentine Williams was one of the Detection Club contributors to *Double Death* (1939), with Dorothy L. Sayers, Freeman Wills Crofts, F. Tennyson Jesse, "David Hume," and Anthony Armstrong. His best-known series character was "Clubfoot" (The Man with the Clubfoot), in *The Man with the Clubfoot* (1920), *The Return of Clubfoot* (1922), *Clubfoot the Avenger* (1924), *The Crouching Beast* (4th ed., 1928), *The Gold Comfit Box* (1932), *A Clubfoot Omnibus* (1936), *The Spider's Touch* (1936). Among his other books are *The Knife Behind the Curtain* (1930), *Death Answers the Bell* (1931), *The Clock Ticks On* (1933), *The Portcullis Room* (1934), *Masks Off at Midnight*

(1934), *The Clue of the Rising Moon* (1935), *Dead Man Manor* (1936), *Courier to Marrakesh* (1944). His autobiography, *The World of Action: The Autobiography of Valentine Williams*, appeared in 1938. Though more an espionage and thriller writer than a Golden Age detective novelist, he was a member of the detection Club, and he was a major figure during the Golden Age.

A[LEXANDER DOUGLAS] WILSON (*b.* 1893)

The Death of Dr. Whitelaw. Longmans. 7s 6d [October 21 1930]

Like Valentine Williams, Alexander Douglas Wilson was primarily an espionage and thriller writer. His eighteen books from 1928 (*The Mystery of Tunnel 51* and *The Devil's Cocktail*) and 1929 (*Murder Mansion*) to 1940 (*Double Masquerade* and *Chronicles of the Secret Service*) include *Wallace of the Secret Service* (1933), *Get Wallace!* (1934), *His Excellency, Governor Wallace* (1936), *Wallace at Bay* (1938), and *Wallace Intervenes* (1939). From 1933 (the first Wallace book and *The Crimson Dacoit*) through 1939/40 he published fourteen books in seven years.

M[ILDRED] V[IOLET] WOODGATE (*b.* 1904)

The Secret of the Sapphire Ring. Hurst and Blackett. 7s 6d [January 24 1930]

M. V. Woodgate wrote *The Children of Danecourt Park* (1924), *The Secret of the Sapphire Ring* (1930), *Pauline's Lady* (1931), *The Two Houses on the Cliff* (1931), and *The Silver Mirror* (1935). Laurence Housman wrote the preface to her juvenile production, *The World of a Child* (1913). Otherwise, she published short biographies of *Père Lacordaire* (1939), *Louise de Marillac* (1942), *Madame Elizabeth of France* (1943), *Jacqueline Pascal and Her Brother* (1944), *The Abbé Edgeworth* (1945), *Madame Swetchine* (1948), *Charles de Condren* (1949), *Father Benson* (1953), *Father Congreve of Cowley* (1956), *St Vincent de Paul* (1958), *St Francis de Sales* (1961), *Juniperro Serra* (1966), *St Dominic* (1967), *Thomas More* (1969), *St Columba* (1969), *Thomas Becket 1118–1170* (1971).

R[ALPH] C[ARTER] WOODTHORPE (*b.* 1886)

A Dagger in Fleet Street. Nicholson and Watson. 7s 6d [January 17, 1934]
Death in a Little Town. Nicholson and Watson. 7s 6d [February 15, 1935]

Between 1932 (*London is a Fine Town* and *The Public School Murder*) and 1939 (*Rope for a Convict* and *The Necessary Corpse*), R. C. Woodthorpe published eight novels, the other four all in 1934 (*A Dagger in Fleet Street* and *Silence of a Purple Shirt*) and 1935 (*Death in a Little Town* and *The Shadow on the Downs*). Woodthorpe was a military man, but I have not been able to trace him beyond noting that he was a correspondent of B. H. Liddell Hart in the 1930s, and beyond a vague personal recollection of hearing his being referred to as "Brigadier Woodthorpe."

EDWARD [EMBERLIN] WOODWARD

Dr. Greenfingers. John Long. 7s 6d [July 26 1933]

Edward Woodward was a turf and sporting writer (*The Pigeon Wins,* 1924, *"Midas" Monkhouse, M.F.H.,* 1932, *The Race* Gang, 1940, *The Turf Bandits,* 1941, *Bill Marshall, Turf Sleuth,* 1942). Of his nearly forty books in the British Library, perhaps a half dozen (besides *Bill Marshall*) fall into the mystery and detection category, including *Black Sheep* (1926), *Dr. Greenfingers* (1933), *Each Night We Die* (1936), *Death Amidst Satin* (1940), *Dead Man's Plaything* (1950, his last).

INDEX